Fields
of
Joy

ZHOU DAXIN

Translated by
Justin Hebert and **Zhou Dan**

SINOIST

University House
11-13 Lower Grosvenor Place,
London SW1W 0EX, UK
Tel: +44 20 3289 3885
E-mail: info@alaincharlesasia.com
Web: www.alaincharlesasia.com

Beijing Office
Tel: +86(0)10 8472 1250

Author: Zhou Daxin
Translators: Justin Hebert & Zhou Dan

Published by Sinoist Books (an imprint of ACA Publishing Ltd) in association with the China Translation and Publishing House

Original Chinese Text © 安魂 (Ān Hún) 2012, Zhou Daxin

English Translation © 2018, by China Translation and Publishing House, Beijing, China

This translated edition first published in 2020 by ACA Publishing Ltd, London, UK

Hardback ISBN: 978-1-83890-516-3
Paperback ISBN: 978-1-910760-94-9
eBook ISBN: 978-1-910760-95-6

A catalogue record for *Fields of Joy* is available from the National Bibliographic Service of the British Library.

FIELDS OF JOY

ZHOU DAXIN

Translated by
JUSTIN HEBERT & ZHOU DAN

SINOIST BOOK

Dedicated to my son Zhou Ning, who passed in his prime.

Dedicated also to every parent who has lost a child.

PREFACE

Ning, that day, 28 September 2005, is forever seared into my memory. I remember thinking it was one of the finest days we'd seen in Beijing that year. This ancient city always looks its magnificent best during the autumn, and that year the feeling was heightened by the suspension of construction work that had been in full swing ahead of the 2008 Olympic Games. As a result, the ever-present air pollution had diminished, and some rain a few days before had removed most of the dust, leaving the sky clear and bright. Nothing else disturbed the brilliant blueness of the sky except the faint remains of a few vapour trails far away, left by fighter jets on training exercises.

The windless air was still and silent. Birds frolicked all over the barracks, singing and soaring high into the sky before diving like kites with broken lines, then floating to the peaks of the poplar, locust or walnut trees. Along that whole section of Chang'an Avenue, our barracks proudly stood out as having the most trees and the best-manicured gardens. It created an idyllic sanctuary that was home to numerous birds and just as many of their songs.

Aside from the glorious weather, I was also in high spirits that day because before you left for work, you told me you had finished the first important task your boss had assigned to you: a scientific research report that had taken you most of the past two days and nights. It was clear that you were taking your job seriously, and it made me a proud and happy father to see that you had grown into such a capable young man.

It wouldn't be long, I thought to myself, before you and your girlfriend got married, and my role as a parent would come to an end. Then I would finally be able to write my novel and wait for the arrival of grandchildren to dote on and play with in my twilight years.

I was also happy that day because I had asked for some time off from work so that I could take you and your mum to visit your grandparents in Henan. I'd already phoned them to make the arrangements. I'd always been so busy with work during your school years, and it had been years since the three of us had visited my hometown together. Now we could finally return home for a family reunion with your grandparents on the National Day holiday.[1] What could be better? How could I not be filled with joy?

Unfortunately our Creator doesn't always allow our plans to play out how we hope they will. He likes to make clear from time to time that it's He and He alone who writes our life plan and controls our destiny. He also has a habit of revealing His presence at the most unexpected moments. It wasn't until 28 September 2005 that I truly understood this.

That afternoon, you went with a colleague to watch a National Day celebration performance in the barracks auditorium. Your mum was at work, as usual, and I went to the barber's shop to get a haircut before our trip. So there I sat, in the barber's shop, quietly reading the newspaper as I waited my turn. As I sat there, I couldn't possibly have known that destiny would soon unfold to reveal the Creator's cruel hand.

The prelude to any tragedy is rather reminiscent of a battle: it is quiet, with no obvious sign of anything untoward or unusual.

My phone rang. *Unknown Number*. I almost ignored it. There was only one more person ahead of me in the queue for the barber's chair and I didn't want to miss my turn. But since I was in such a good mood I answered it in high spirits.

"Hello?"

"Director Zhou? I'm a colleague of your son Zhou Ning. I'm sorry to have to tell you this, but he passed out during the show. We've just taken him to the outpatients department at the hospital. Please come straight away!"

I was flustered and panicked, unable to believe what I'd just heard. How was this possible? My son was only twenty-six years old, in his prime. He was an athlete, a basketball player! He was fine when he left for work this morning. How could he suddenly have passed out? Could there have been some mistake?

I didn't hang around as these thoughts raced through my mind. I just got up and bolted out of the barber's shop. I needed to find out what had happened to you. It was only about three hundred metres to the hospital. I ran there in what seemed like a single breath and burst into the emergency room. My worst fears were confirmed: it was indeed you, lying there.

A medical team surrounded your bed, giving you emergency treatment. My heart was in my mouth. "He's waking up," said one of the doctors. Thank goodness! I pushed my way through to your bed, looked at your pale face and met your eyes as they slowly opened.

"Son, what happened?" I asked. "Are you in any pain?"

"Dad, I've no idea what happened," you replied weakly. One of your colleagues who had carried you to the hospital explained what had happened.

"We were watching the show in the auditorium. Zhou Ning was sitting next to me. The speakers were loud and the bright lights swirled around. I heard a sudden gasp from Zhou Ning. I turned to him and saw that his eyes were closed. His body was convulsing and sliding down the seat. I had to move quickly to catch him."

Just then your mother rushed into the room. Seeing that you were awake, she grabbed your hands. "Zhou Ning, you scared your poor mother to death!"

I asked the doctor what could have caused you to pass out. He couldn't be sure; it might have been the stress of work, or possibly some problem with your brain. The only way to find out was to go to a larger hospital for further examination.

I quickly convinced myself that it must have been due to your heavy workload. For two days you had stayed up day and night, sat in front of your computer as you completed your science report. You certainly didn't get enough rest, and you barely ate. Your mother agreed with me, so we took you home, made you lie down for some rest, and prepared a meal to help start your recovery.

You slept well that night. Your mum and I were relieved, though we agreed to take you for a thorough check-up the next day, just to be safe. After you fell asleep, your mum and I started to pack our things for our visit to our hometown.

We couldn't have known it at the time, but the curtain had just risen on the first act of a three-year tragedy, and the director was waiting for the leading characters – you, your mum, and me – to take the stage.

1

_____

Ning, how could I have imagined that I would never see you again after 3 August 2008? It was truly the darkest of days for our family.

That day, we were separated forever. Never again would your mum and I see you running up and down the basketball court; sitting in front of your computer in that old sweater you always wore; playing outside in the snow; or lying shirtless on your bed, reading a book.

After that day we no longer inhabited the same world.

The third of August: that was the day our hearts were shattered. After that day we would never hear your voice again. Never again would we hear you call from the kitchen, "Dad, dinner's ready!"; or your teasing in my study, "Dad, you're so terrible with computers!"; or your joke with your mum and me, "Mum, Dad, are you _sure_ you can't spare me a little money?"

The third of August: the day your mum and I were engulfed by despair. After that day, we would never again be able to smell you: your sweat; the fragrance of your facial cleanser; the subtle hint of tea on your breath. Never again could we touch your hair, put an arm around your shoulder, or pat you on the back. No longer could we count on you to help move the couch or a flower pot, to carry a heavy bag of rice or some luggage.

The third of August: after that day, the clear line of death separated us forever.

Why did God so indiscriminately and casually take away a twenty-nine-year old's life? We never did anything to deserve such cruel punishment. Why should we receive this in return?

It was just so senseless, so unfair.

Dad, you need to calm down and face the facts. I have left your world and will never be able to return to you and Mum. It cannot be changed. You need to force yourself to accept this fact and adapt to reality. You both need to control your emotions so you can figure out how you're going to live your lives without me there.

There's no point wallowing in grief, recrimination and self-pity. It's really not good for your health, you know? Scientists have shown that grieving excessively can increase the risk of heart attack. You and Mum should be careful. Everyone's life is a one-way journey; my journey was just a bit shorter than it should have been.

Maybe it was for the best. Imagine if I'd lived for a few dozen more years. I would then have had to taste all the bitter pills that life has to offer: to struggle, striving to support a family and to achieve something for myself. Isn't it perhaps better that I never had to experience those hardships? Think of it this way: they need plenty of young people in the afterlife. So perhaps it's a blessing from God that I was summoned here. I really hope you'll be able to take some comfort from thinking about it like this.

Hardly anyone avoids the agony of losing a loved one. However, very few people seem to think about it rationally. They always blame the Creator, when in fact they have no choice but to accept it. In the end, everyone must accept that the Creator is completely impartial when it comes to life and death. He doesn't take bribes, doesn't bend for personal reasons, or grant anyone special favours. He cannot offer anyone immunity from death. He charts the same destination for everyone, and the only difference is the timing: some arrive sooner, some later. But since we all end up in the same place eventually, why are those who leave later considered luckier than the ones who go before them? Within the same generation, people care deeply about who goes early and who late. But across the generations, no one really cares.

You need to move on, Dad. You told me once that you are not ambitious, neither powerful nor wealthy, but that you're strong. Now is the time, Dad, for you to be strong, for the family's sake. You taught me how to say the word *goodbye* when I was little. So now it's time for you to say goodbye to me.

Goodbye, Dad. Please tell Mum to say goodbye too. Until we meet again.

Son, how can you say 'until we meet again'? Where can I see you? In our hometown in Zhengzhou, Henan? In the schools where you studied, in Nanyang, Xi'an or Zhengzhou? In the military compound where we lived in Jinan, Shandong, or the Wanshou Road in Beijing? No, Son. Your mum and I will never see you again, ever!

Lu Kun from the Ming Dynasty said, *"After the final breath, there is no reincarnation; the soul departs the body, and there is no life eternal."*

So this is farewell forever. We will never meet again.

Dad, don't be so pathetic! Your despair is all in your mind. Of course I can't see you again in this life. Even if I did visit, you and Mum wouldn't feel it. But it's not the only life in which we can meet. Hasn't science determined that there are ten or more dimensions in space? So in addition to time and the three physical dimensions we inhabit, there are at least six others.

I remember some famous physicist once said that if we take a place and make it spin faster than the speed of light, we could travel to the past. Wormholes are real. If we achieve that, couldn't we meet again? Also, heaven *does* exist. Haven't you and Mum heard of the Kingdom of Heaven or the Western concepts of Heaven or Paradise? They're just different names for the same place.

When you and Mum come here one day, you'll be able to see me. You just need to believe that my departure is only temporary. Think of this as a business trip to America or Africa, and I can't come back or call

3

you because I have a complicated task to complete. Thinking about it this way may ease your suffering.

But please have faith that we will see each other again some day.

Son, I often wish that your grandparents hadn't give birth to me. If I hadn't been born, I wouldn't have grown up. I wouldn't exist in this world and I wouldn't have consciousness. I wouldn't know about love, your mum and I would never have got married, and you would never have been born. We wouldn't have lost you, and we wouldn't have ended up in such misery.

Who can truly comprehend the agony of losing a child? It's not just heartbreak; it's an indescribable and unbearable pain that envelopes your entire being. I regret my very existence! If I had known that the price for being born was to endure such pain, I think I would have told our Creator, "Forgive me, but I do not wish to enter this world."

But I had no choice then, and I have no choice now. I must simply endure the pain. But why?

Dad, you're not thinking straight! God doesn't owe us any favours. He brought so much happiness to us. How happy were you when you held me as a toddler on your shoulders and ran around the house? When you and Mum took me to my grandparents' house for the Spring Festival, where we lit firecrackers, ate dumplings and drank wine? When you cheered whenever I scored on the basketball court? The allotment of happiness to each person and to each family must be limited. And we had our fair share of happiness, so we really shouldn't complain.

Someone once said that life is a cycle of laughter, tears and everything in between. We had the laughter and the in-between, so now it's our time for crying. And there's nothing any of us can do about it.

Dad, when I was little, a woman wearing a white veil would often visit me in my dreams. It occurred so many times that I remembered it clearly throughout my life. She would stand silently by my bed, waving at me, though I couldn't see her face. I asked you and Mum what it meant. "People often have strange dreams," you told me. "All sorts of things can happen in dreams, so don't take them too seriously."

When I was older, I turned to the work of Sigmund Freud to try to interpret the woman's regular appearances in my dreams. Maybe subconsciously I wanted a woman in my bed. I certainly didn't expect to see her again after I left you. But sure enough, there she was, standing by my bed in the hospital, waving to me and beckoning me to follow her. On my journey to the afterlife, it was she who led and accompanied me. Only later, as I stood on the banks of the River Styx, did I realise that every departing soul has their own veiled companion.

The veiled woman visited me in my dreams long before I died. So don't you see? My name was circled even when I was young, and God had sent a guide to lead me to Him. So think of it as a blessing that I was able to delay my inevitable death until 2008, when I was twenty-nine. It might have been much earlier.

I hope this makes you feel better, and that you can learn to console yourselves.

Son, for as long as death has shadowed life, God's messenger has taken people away according to the natural order of things. The elders leave first, then the youngsters later on. I never imagined that the first death I experienced would be yours.

I had never witnessed death before. I was too young to remember anything when my grandparents passed away. Before you, I rarely even thought about death. It was far, far away in my mind. Even though it dawned on me from time to time, I was always concerned with my own life. How long would I live? What disease might I succumb to? Where would I be buried? Even then, I knew I had you to count on. When I died, you would take care of everything for me. Suddenly, however, fate thrust me into a situation I had never contemplated. The natural order was reversed and I, who should have gone first, was there to witness your death.

God, Allah, Jesus, Buddha, Heavenly Lord, Creator, King of Heaven: which one of you can give me a reason? Someone, please give me a reason!

Dad, all kinds of things happen for no apparent reason. In the Tangshan earthquake of 1976 and the Wenchuan earthquake of 2008, many people died. Why? Many Indonesians and Japanese died from the resulting tsunamis. Why? So many people died in those disasters, children and babies among them. They had only just come into this world, and hadn't even seen it properly. Why take them away? Did they deserve that? Was there a reason? Or was it just a series of tragic accidents and coincidences?

The only answer that provided any comfort was that those poor souls were needed in another world. If not, who could ever put their faith in religion? Who could respect any Creator? Many deaths occur without any warning or logic. And yet these tragic events instil in us the concept of fate and a fear of uncertainty.

Dad, you're a writer. You know that fear is a vital human instinct. If a person has no fear, gruesome consequences can follow. So Dad, stop seeking an explanation for my departure. No one can provide that for you. Just tell yourself that there are reasons for my departure, and one of them is that I was young and needed in another place.

2

_____

Son, during your illness I remember you read *The Heart of the Prajna Paramita Sutra (The Heart of the Perfection of Wisdom)* for strength and to be closer to Buddha. Your mum and I invited an elderly lady, a convert to Buddhism, to pray for your salvation. She would sit on the sofa next to you, and while looking into the distance she would chant quietly, then hum, the scriptures:

Put away what you had,
Take back what you expect,
Forget your loss,
And cast away your sadness.
Remember your beloved family,
Appreciate your kind neighbours,
Bow to your friends,
And kowtow to your land.
Rest in peace, let go of all attachments,
Rest in peace, let go of all unfulfilled desires,
Rest in peace, let go of all resentment,
Rest in peace, let go of all worry.

Son, do you remember that? If you do, then please take heed of what the elderly sage chanted, and rest in peace.

Ning, you came into the world in hardship and left far too soon. The night you were born, at midnight on 4 November 1979, it was early winter; gloomy, windy and freezing cold.

It was hardly an ideal moment for your mum and I to introduce you to the world, and we were so unprepared. We had no knowledge about giving birth, post-natal care or how to plan ahead for your arrival. To even discuss the details of childbirth was frowned upon at that time.

You came into the world in a small maternity ward in Nanyang Hospital. I'll never forget how your mum's screams punctured that night! It was a very difficult labour, but thankfully, finally, you opened your eyes to see the world. Maybe you were scared of the new world. Your grandma told me you cried a lot, much louder and for longer than other newborns.

Unfortunately, I wasn't there to welcome you. I was sitting, agitated, heading home on the train from Jinan. I'd only been granted two weeks' leave from work, and I didn't dare leave my unit early. The earlier I left, the earlier I would need to return to work. So the plan was for me to arrive home on your due date. Of course, then you arrived early!

When the train finally pulled in at Nanyang station, it was four o'clock in the morning. I hurried home in a pedicab. No one answered my knock at the door, and my thumping heart missed a beat; your mum must have been in the hospital.

It was dark and the cold chill was bracing. None of the other houses had their lights on except for one, whose nanny had just woken up to prepare breakfast. I left my luggage there and rushed to the hospital.

It was just about daylight when I reached the delivery room. I saw your mum on a bed in a room with two other expectant mothers, and your grandma was sitting by her side, feeding her some soup. I realised that you'd already been born. I rushed over, elated. Before I could even say anything, your grandma announced blissfully, "A boy, nine pounds, was born an hour ago."

The hospital rules back then didn't allow newborn babies to stay with their mothers. You were only brought in to nurse. I held your mum's hand, guilt-ridden that I had missed the birth. I found out a few days later that a colleague had taken her to the hospital. She just smiled silently, uncomplaining.

Your mum really suffered through her labour because you had such a large head. It really was a trial for her. Your grandma tried to help her through it by using the traditional method from the countryside, which involved feeding your mum five or six eggs to build up her strength. But Mum couldn't handle that and threw up everything she had in her stomach. The labour had sapped almost all of her energy, which made the situation all the more perilous.

Eventually the doctor had to pull you out with forceps. Perhaps that's how your head got injured in the first place, foreshadowing your disease. The doctors were apparently worried about a potential infection, so they gave you a shot of antibiotics.

How could we have known the consequences of these things? Why couldn't I have come home earlier? If I had, I could have taken your mum to the hospital myself, and then I could have asked for a caesarean section instead of a natural birth that caused all the problems. If I had done that, they wouldn't have needed to drag you into the world with forceps!

I am so full of regret.

That year, 1979, had been very eventful. At the start of the year, the Chinese army had fought the brief Sino-Vietnamese War on the southern border of Vietnam, in response to that country's invasion and occupation of Cambodia the year before. Another war ensued too. Later that year, there was fierce debate in China around economic reforms. The year ended, but the economy hadn't improved. Rationing was in force, and people used their coupons to get hold of essential items: food, cooking oil and eggs mostly, also cloth.

Looking back, we probably shouldn't have planned for you to be born that year. It would have been much better if we'd had you a few years later, in the 1980s. The year, the month and even the hour in which we're born can profoundly affect our fate.

I met you for the first time the next morning, when you were brought in to feed. The nurse carried you over. I saw you, your eyes closed, sound asleep. You were a large baby, with a round face. Mum took you in her arms. You woke up, suckling instinctively. I watched you, thrilled with joy. I had a son! The two other mothers both had sons too. My biggest worry was that the nurses might mix up the three of you, and that you'd be taken home by the wrong family! I specifically talked to a nurse about it, asking if they had ever made that mistake before. The nurse smiled patiently and told me not to worry. She said they attach an ID wristband to every baby and that nothing could go wrong.

After your mum fed you, I held you for the first time. I had no idea how to handle a baby, and I held you carefully in both hands. And as I looked at your delicate and perfect face, I realised how magical is the miracle of life. I was overwhelmed by joy and happiness. I could scarcely believe that I had a son! Meanwhile, I was gripped by a sudden sense of profound responsibility. I resolved to try to make more money and provide you with the best possible life.

From that morning onward, I bought crucian fish in Guandong market. This meant that your grandma could prepare fish soup for Mum so she was better able to feed you. The market economy had only just started around that time, so each morning I went to the market very early since there weren't many fish stalls. I was quite ashamed that I earned so little money then and couldn't afford much. I was really only able to afford enough fish to supply your mum with food for one day at a time. If only I'd been able to afford more fish for your mum. Maybe then we would have been able to feed you better and equip you to fight your disease more effectively later on in your life.

While you and your mum were still in the hospital, in addition to preparing fish soup and sending meals to the hospital, I also gave the house a thorough clean and made up the bed to welcome you back home.

After bringing you both home, there was nowhere for me to sleep but on the floor. I didn't mind at all, though; you were my reward for enduring any hardship. You cried at midnight every night after you came home. At the time, your mum and I had no idea why. Long afterwards we came to understand that there was not enough nutrition in your mum's breast milk. You were fed a lot, but with little substance. It saddens me to say it, but you cried in the night because you were hungry. I didn't realise that we should also have fed you some formula milk, and that left you nutritionally deficient at the most critical time in your life.

Perhaps that's what caused your disease. If we had fed you better, you would have grown up healthier, you would have had a stronger immune system and perhaps been spared your later suffering. Why didn't I ask more questions, or read some books? I just didn't understand the basics of parenting. How could I have been so stupid?

My two weeks' leave flew by, and soon I needed to return to work. Your mum pleaded with me to send a telegram and extend my leave. At that time, though, it was important to be seen to be making personal sacrifices for the greater good. I was young and ambitious and afraid to be seen to be prioritising my personal interests. It would only have upset the powers that be and ensured that I lagged behind my peers in terms of career progress and promotion.

I never did ask to extend my leave. I did take one extra day, though, to comfort your mum and get everything ready for her before I returned to work. I carried home two carts of charcoal in a borrowed tricycle, brought home a bag of flour and some fish, then left for the train station.

I really thought it would be no big deal for me to go back to work a day late, and I was sure my boss would understand. Instead I was suspended and ordered to undergo 'self-reflection' upon my return. Only a few months later did I discover that you became sick after I'd left. Our neighbour Li took you and your mum to the hospital one night on his tricycle.

With hindsight, I should have stayed at home with you until you were at least a month old. I was so stupid not to appreciate the importance of a baby's first month. Perhaps my selfish departure was another reason why you succumbed to this disease.

Dad, yes I did hear them, the incantations of peace from the old lady. But don't worry, I'm quite willing to let everything go and leave this world with no baggage.

But please stop blaming yourself and calm down. And stop crying, you'll ruin your eyes!

Leaving this world isn't as painful as you might think. It's not death itself that's scary, but the sense of impending doom. That was the hardest time: being ravaged by the cancer and knowing I was doomed. Confined to my bed, unable to move my hands and feet, my head in splitting pain, drips inserted into my arm and leg. I was tortured by various monitors for blood pressure, the ECG and especially the one for blood oxygen, which made me restless. The oxygen tubes irritated my nose. The fever made me dizzy. You and Mum fed food and water to me through my nose. I couldn't even use the toilet and you had to clean me up constantly. Every day felt like an eternity.

When God finally decided to take me away, I simply closed my mouth, stopped breathing, and left my body. As I looked back at my body from just a few metres away, I was honestly relieved to leave it behind. I felt relaxed as never before. I needed no more injections or medicine; no more being forced to hear the constant moaning and groaning of the other patients; no more listening to the bickering between the doctors and nurses; no more MRI scans or blood tests; no need to endure the pain of brain surgery or the torment of chemotherapy; no need to rely on your help just to turn myself over in bed; and no need to smell that awful, sterile stench of the hospital.

No Dad, at that point I became free. Are you listening, Dad? I'm free now.

I know my death devastated you and Mum. You're right, it shouldn't have been my time to leave, according to the natural order of things. And yes, I know I should be by your side for you to depend on when you grow old. This is one thing that does concern me. You raised me from a boy into a man, but I left without ever repaying you. It's not right, and all I can do is ask for your forgiveness.

I'm sorry Dad, but I just couldn't endure the pain any longer. It was nobody's fault that God took me away before my time, but I still feel bad for you and Mum. When I think about you growing old and being unwell in the future, I'm overwhelmed by guilt that I won't be around to look after you.

Dad, please stop talking about my birth. I have no memory of it. Even if you had been there, what could you have done? You were only in your early twenties, and couldn't possibly have been expected to know anything about childbirth or babies. At that time there simply weren't any books you could have read. And in any event, how could you have made better decisions than the doctors?

So come on, Dad, stop blaming yourself. It was fate, nothing more, nothing less. So just accept it for what it is and try to stop feeling so guilty. Don't you think it's time to move on?

Ning, the first time you left home was when you were six months old. I wrote to your mum, hoping you could both visit me in Jinan. She wasn't sure, but she agreed to come. That wasn't one of my smartest decisions. Babies really shouldn't travel before they are at least a year old. Your body hadn't developed sufficiently to handle the sudden change of environment. But how could I have known that at the time?

It was late spring, early summer. Your mum carried you in one arm and a bag in the other. We couldn't afford a crib for you on the train, so you were both crammed into one seat and travelled for two days before you reached Jinan. Of course I couldn't see your suffering during the journey, but it was clearly evident in your mum's tired face when you arrived.

In my tiny single-room accommodation in Jinan, I prepared the best food for Mum, to ensure you both ate well. I invited a well-known military photographer, Li Shiwen, to take a photo of you. You weren't yet able to sit upright so I bent down to support you. You can see my fingers in that picture if you look at it carefully. The photographer lived up to his reputation. That picture captured your expression perfectly, a slightly uneasy disdain in your innocent eyes. Your unease was understandable since you were still adapting to the dry and windy conditions of Jinan after travelling from the warmer Nanyang climate. More surprising was the disdain. Was it my decision to bring you on the long journey, or just your reaction to this unfamiliar and bustling city?

Your mum and I took you to Daming Lake and Baotu Spring. I told you stories of one of our local heroes, Tiexuan, who originally came from Zhengzhou and had risen to become the Shandong commissioner and minister of war. He was fiercely loyal and fought bravely to the death during the Jingnan period. I also read you some poetry written by my favourite poet, Li Qingzhao:

Live as a hero in this life
And after death a hero remain.
The memory of Xiang Yu is cherished to this day
For he chose to die, not to cross the river, after his defeat.

I longed to teach you the essence and achievements of these people, but of course you were too young to understand. Only the boats in the lake and the red carp in the spring interested you as you gestured and babbled at them.

Your visit to Jinan didn't go entirely smoothly, though. There was one drama. One morning I was assigned a task from the office: to collect other soldiers' opinions on the new Special Economic Zones in Shenzhen, Zhuhai, and Shantou in Guangdong Province, also Xiamen in Fujian Province. Many conflicting opinions were swirling through the army. Some saw the SEZs as a crucial step on the road to economic reform; others saw them as the start of the erosion of capitalism. I was too young to have a view either way, and afraid to get into trouble with the powers that be. At that time the Party had ways to find out anything and everything.

When I arrived home at noon, I was really stressed about this new assignment. Just then, you dropped a bottle of ink on the floor. The ink splashed everywhere, all over the floor and up the wall. I snapped, and without thinking I raised my hand to smack you. You burst into tears. So did Mum; she was so angry with me.

"He's so little. What does he know? How could you smack him just because he knocked over a stupid ink bottle?" It was the first time I'd laid a finger on you, and I regretted it instantly. What on earth possessed me to lose my temper like that?

After that, you became wary of me, and I could tell you were scared and resentful. For a few days, you even refused to let me hold you, preferring to lie by yourself and suck your thumb. I was distraught. Such a temper from so tiny a person! Whenever I reached out my arms to hold you, you would start to cry. Your mum was entirely unsympathetic. "As you brew, so you must drink," she said.

You were so little, yet I'd lost my temper and smacked you. Is that how a good father behaves? That episode still haunts me to this day.

Dad, why on earth would you still think about that? A little slap never hurt me. Mum and I went to Jinan many times, and I have very few memories of those trips. I remember once running after Mum as we ran through Luoyang station to catch our connecting train. She carried a bag as I ran behind her, but I couldn't catch up. Scared of being left behind, I called out, "Mum, Mum, wait for me! Wait for me!" Mum stopped, turned around, picked me up and carried on running. The heavy bag and I weighed her down. Poor Mum, she was really out of breath. Even today I can still remember her panting.

Children's memories are very reliable. Once they store a memory, they will never forget it. Like the old saying goes, 'People's childhood memories always leave the deepest impressions. Once logged in the memory, they are never forgotten.'

Train journeys were always the worst experiences for me during those years. Whether it was to visit you in Jinan, or travelling to my school in Xi'an or Zhengzhou, the trip always started with the challenge of getting tickets. Then, even if we managed that, the crowded train always reeked of various unpleasant smells.

Yes, those train rides were torture, completely different to today when we can fly everywhere. Having a human body can be a real burden, prone as it is to the cold and heat, aching and soreness; to fatigue, thirst and hunger; to sweetness and bitterness. But without a body, all those sensations fall away, leaving only lightness and comfort.

The human body can bring some gratification to us, but it also constrains the unbridled joy of a free spirit.

Think about this: those who are obsessed with power, wealth and fame during their lives – mustn't that torment their bodies?

———

Son, I often look at the photo we took of you at Qianfo Mountain in Jinan. Photos are the only way I can still see you, and that one is my favourite. Every time I look at it I remember the joyful time we had when we climbed that mountain.

Qianfo Mountain was drenched in sunshine that day. Mum and I took it in turns to carry you and we stopped for a short rest under a tree after a prayer to Buddha. We took that photo under a nearby pomegranate tree. I remember asking the official mountain photographer to take it for us. He used a camera that wasn't common at that time. One roll of film could take twelve pictures and a single photo didn't cost much.

You look perfect in that picture. With one arm wrapped around the tree you stuck your head out, your eyes sparkling with wonder and curiosity. You weren't quite walking then, not even old enough to stand up by yourself for very long. But I always thought you looked like a little soldier in that picture. Later on I always kept it next to my bed.

You were only six months old, but looking back I owe you so much for that trip to Jinan with your mum.

Every morning you would wake up crying at five o'clock and wouldn't go back to sleep until we fed you some biscuits. I never understood why, and I was always grumpy because I was so sleepy. And every time I fed those biscuits to you, I would scold you. You couldn't talk of course, but I could tell you were upset because there would always be tears in your eyes.

It was only much later that your mum and I realised you were waking up because you were hungry. We were so stupid, we had no idea! We just thought you were being irritable. The truth is, I simply wasn't qualified to be a father.

Later, Mum brought you to Jinan when you were four years old. I took you both shopping. You stopped at the toy shop and stared at other children playing with Transformers, the toy craze of that year. Your eyes were glued to those plastic figures, and of course you wanted one. I knew it wouldn't be cheap, but I was shocked when I learned it cost almost thirty *yuan*. That was half my month's salary! I told you we couldn't afford it and tried to take you away. You refused, no matter what Mum and I said to you. You struggled and wriggled away each time I carried you out of the shop. Exasperated, I threatened to leave you there alone if you didn't stop causing such a scene. Mum and I even turned around and walked away, as if to show you that we really would abandon you there. Petrified, you burst out crying. When we didn't look back, you muffled your crying and hurried to catch us up.

I am so full of regret now. Why couldn't I give up twenty or thirty *yuan*? Why was I so mean? How could a Transformer toy bankrupt our family? How could I be proud of threatening my young son like that?

Son, it saddens me to admit that I owe you so much that can never be repaid.

Dad, will you stop it with these meaningless ancient anecdotes? I was an emotional child. If you'd given me everything I wanted, where would it have ended?

I don't have any memory of Qianfo Mountain. The place I remember the best is the zoo in Jinan. I remember you took me there to see the pandas, monkeys and black bears. There were a lot of black bears in that zoo. I remember we stood on a hill to watch them trying to catch the food people threw to them. They were so greedy! No matter what they caught, they would put it into their mouths. I threw a banana down, and one of the bears caught and swallowed it. When I didn't have any more bananas, I threw down a banana peel. The bear just picked it up and put that into his mouth too! I thought it was hilarious, and I remember laughing about it for ages.

I don't have many clear memories from back then, just some blurred impressions. The few clear memories I do have were so precious to me, reminding me of simple happiness. Childhood is an almost carefree time, a time when the Creator shows His mercy. Then, when we reach adolescence, the misery starts to creep in, which then grows exponentially into adulthood and throughout life.

So Dad, stop being so harsh on yourself. You and Mum did everything you could to give me a good childhood. So many other children went without basic necessities or suffered from the fear of wandering from one shelter to another. You and Mum gave me a great childhood, so please don't keep beating yourself up about it.

Dad, I believe that when a man becomes a father, his most important responsibility is to give his children love and a happy home. I received both of these from you. Yes, you did have a short temper occasionally. Perhaps that's something you might want to work on...

I'll admit it, Son: I know I have a temper. But to lay a hand on you when you were so young was unforgiveable.

Do you know that when I lived and worked away from you, my happiest moments were our family reunions in Nanyang? That's the mysterious nature and unbreakable strength of family bonds. Even though you hadn't seen me for such a long time, and even though I had scolded and smacked you, you would always rush into my arms and tell me all the news from home: about the eggs grandma had boiled for you; the sweets Mum had bought for you; a stranger's cat or a visit from the neighbour's dog. And as I held and kissed you, I felt overwhelmed by an unforgettable sense of pure joy.

After your mum left for work, I would take you out for a stroll. I would look out for the bookstores or book stands, while you were focused on finding a tofu pudding vendor. Once you saw one, you would shout, "Look Dad, there it is!" I knew you wanted tofu pudding, and you always begged me to buy you a bowl.

To tease you, I'd pretend not to know what you wanted. "What, Son?" I'd reply. "What are we looking for?" You would roll your eyes in disgust, take my hand and drag me towards the vendor.

"Can we have a bowl, please?"

The vendor would smile and say, "Certainly, young man! One bowl coming right up!"

I would pay one *mao* (10 cents) for the bowl of pudding, and you devoured it all, every time. I couldn't have been happier if I'd eaten it myself. But what I didn't know back then was that that sweetened tofu pudding is bad for your stomach. It causes gastric acid if you eat too much. How could I have known?

Every holiday when I went back home, I would put a child seat on the front of my bicycle. I carried you in it to visit the cottage of Zhuge Liang in Wolonggang, the art galleries of the Han Dynasty, and the statue of Zhang Zhongjing in the shrine. We went to see jade carvings in the jade factory, and the pyrographed pictures of figures, landscapes, and flower-and-bird burnings in the pyrograph factory. I knew you were too young to understand, but I hoped that exposing you to these things would instil in you an appreciation of culture and beauty.

Your mum and I took you to the cinema in the Red Oriental Theatre, but you would only concentrate for a short time before you cried and wanted to leave to buy some sugar cane at the gate. I'd get annoyed if it happened during a film I really liked. I scolded you but you only cried louder, leaving me no choice but to take you outside.

Your favourite pastime was watching television. The most important thing I did on that vacation was to buy a *Shanghai* brand 14-inch black and white television, which cost five hundred *yuan*. It was a huge expense, given my monthly salary was only sixty *yuan*. I'd saved up for that television for a long time, and had asked a technician from the Jinan military culture department to help me pick it up. It was the first real household appliance I'd ever bought for our home. On the train back to Nanyang I held it tightly on my lap, nervous in case it got damaged. I bought a red velvet cover for it, to protect it from dust. I set it up on the table at home, and turned it on. When we saw the pictures on the screen, I was so proud. You cried out with joy, and immediately went out to invite your friends to come and watch. From then on, you loved to spend time watching TV with your grandma.

To be honest, I was glad that you focused on the television, since it gave me time alone with my books. I had no idea that watching too much TV would damage your eyesight, until your eyesight began to deteriorate. After that, Mum and I started to limit your TV time. We may have known more about parenting than previous generations, but we still had so much to learn.

The time flew by whenever I came home for a holiday. In the blink of an eye, it would quickly be time for me to return to work. Sometimes I couldn't help but wonder if the calendar was missing a few pages. Once, your mum took you and a neighbour to see me off at the train station. You were determined to board the train with me, no matter what your mum said to you. You were stubborn, though, trying to break through your mum's arms and come to me, almost choking yourself from sobbing.

It was heart-breaking. To be honest it was the first time that I'd experienced the anguish of being separated from you. Up to that point, you had just been a source a wonderment for me. I'd never felt such a strong emotional bond until that moment, when I felt the pain of those bonds being broken. Eventually, the train started to move and I left you there, crying on the platform, disappearing into the distance. Tears filled my eyes...

Dad, I still remember watching TV with Grandma. After you went back to work, I would always nag her to turn on the TV for me while Mum was at work. Sometimes she refused to turn it on because she wanted to take me out with her to buy groceries. Without fail I would burst into tears. Grandma could do nothing about it except turn on the TV for me. After it was on, I would play around with the remote control and switch to whatever I wanted to watch. Grandma couldn't read the subtitles, but I knew a few words Mum had taught me. Grandma would ask, "Ning, tell Nana what it was about." I would make a guess based on the few words I knew, and told Grandma what I believed it said. I had no idea if I was right, but she was always impressed.

"Ning is so clever!" she would say. "Much cleverer than Nana." I was so happy and proud to receive her praise. It did wonders for my self-esteem, and even then I developed a sense that I might be able to accomplish something great in the future.

Unfortunately, I rarely received any praise from you or Mum. You always seemed to focus on my flaws. "How did you get dirty?" you would ask, or, "Why did you make your friend cry?" or, "Why can't you write better?"

You always seemed to criticise me for doing something wrong or something I needed to improve. You often used sarcasm. You probably thought it would push me to improve myself, but in fact it had the opposite effect. Your criticism discouraged and saddened me. I suppose I resisted it and even rebelled against it.

I always thought that Grandma was more educated than you and

Mum, since she always seemed to know how to talk to me. I realised later that you and Mum loved me every bit as much as Grandma did, and more. But you didn't seem to understand how to give the type of positive encouragement that can make a child happier and more confident. But there was nothing you could have done. After all, you were both young and had only just become new parents. Even parents need time to learn.

3

Son, I know you're right: your mum and I did criticise more than praise you. I was always quick to see your weaknesses and failings, and I compared you unfairly to other children. In our simple way, we thought that being strict would be good for you. We didn't really appreciate the power of praise and encouragement.

You never liked leafy green vegetables, and you refused to eat them, no matter what I said. It maddened me and I scolded you for being spoilt and ignorant. One time I even threw your bowl away. Later on I watched as your grandma fed you. She picked up some green vegetables and said, "Ning is such a good boy, he'll eat anything. Nana wants to feed him some green vegetables today. I'm sure he'll eat them all, won't you, Ning"

I couldn't believe it when you actually did eat all those vegetables! I was amazed and looked incredulously at your grandma. I simply didn't realise that this magic came from positivity and the power of encouragement. It was a lesson I should have learned, but for some reason never had, from your grandma.

I have no doubt that our negative parenting style affected you as you grew up. You were always so risk-averse and you worried about failure in everything you did. The simple truth is that I just didn't know how to be a good father.

Ning, in 1985 I was assigned to conduct interviews on the front line of the battlefield in Yunnan. You were only five years old at the time, and I wrote a letter to you in case I didn't return. On the front line, the two sides were engaged in see-saw battles: we would seize their positions, then they would seize ours. It was complicated by the treacherous landscape of high mountains, dense forest and tall grass fields, all of which provided perfect cover for enemy attacks. From one day to the next, no one knew what would happen. Even as journalists, we expected to be attacked. Our vehicles would often try to pass areas that were blocked by enemy fire. Several vehicles were hit by 85mm shells. That was when I wrote that letter to you, in case I perished on the front line and couldn't see you again.

I remember writing three things in that letter: first, if I died fighting for our country, then you shouldn't bear a grudge against me for leaving you and Mum, nor against those that had sent me to the battlefield.

Second, since I was the eldest son and you the eldest grandson in the family, you should study hard and become the main breadwinner for the family when you grew up. You should renovate the old house, I wrote, and take care of your mother and grandparents.

And third, you should burn some paper money on the annual tomb-sweeping day, so I would always have some money in the next world.

I posted the letter to your mum from Shangdong, then left immediately for the battlefield in Yunnan. Fortunately, I came back alive and you never needed to read it. What I could never have anticipated was that you would be the one giving your final instructions to me!

"No matter what happens to me," you told me, "never leave Mum alone. Always take care of her. And Dad, don't tell Grandma and Grandpa about my death. They're too old to handle this devastating news. Just tell them I went abroad. Dad, I'm sorry I won't be there when you're old, that I won't be able to take care of you in the hospital if you're unwell. So make sure you make plans to find a nurse."

How could it ever have been you saying those words to me? How could God have chosen to do things in that order?

———

Dad, Mum did tell me about the letter you had sent from the battlefield. She didn't explain it in detail, but I remember being shocked with the realisation that death might separate us. Up to that point, I'd always assumed we would be together forever, as a family.

As I grew older, I started to understand what accidents were, as well as sickness and death. But I always felt like death was too far away for us to think about preparing for it. I certainly never expected death to strike us so suddenly, especially not my own. I was supposed to be the strong and healthy one! But God clearly had other ideas, and my fate in this world would deny me a natural death.

I never wrote a letter to you, as you had to me. In fact, I didn't have much to write about, even if I'd wanted to. I'd only ever worked for a few months, so I had no money to leave for your retirement. What's worse, my disease had drained all of your own savings. I never married or had children, there was no other family to worry about. And at work, my research hadn't even really begun. All in all, I had nothing much of value to share with you, so it just didn't make sense to write a letter.

My only concerns in this world were you and Mum. She would even get worried when I came home late sometimes. My death absolutely devastated her. You handled it better than her by throwing yourself into writing your novel. What could Mum do?

Dad, I really think you should remove all of my pictures and things that remind her of me. Burn all of my clothes and possessions. Take Mum out and distract her from thinking about me. Didn't she love *The Heart of Prajna Paramita Sutra*? You should encourage her to read it more often. Maybe she'll draw some strength and solace from it. Maybe you could even think about adopting a child? A girl would be best; maybe a little girl running around at home would help Mum to recover.

I worry most about the nights. Mum always checked on me every night before bed. How does she cope with not seeing me there? Dad, I think you should just keep my bedroom door locked.

In fact, Dad, maybe you should just move. Move to a new home, make a fresh start.

Son, actually we did move to another building in the same complex. Then your mum started worrying that you wouldn't be able find your way home if you came to visit us. So we wrote our new address on a piece of paper and burned it at the door of our old place. She wanted to tell you where our new home was. I hope you received it.

Son, I often think about your primary school, where you went when you were six and a half. Those memories do provide some comfort.

Your mum and I decided to send you to the best primary school in town, which was No. 15 Primary School in Nanyang. Almost everyone wanted to send their children to that school, and your mum and I pulled every string we could to get you in.

After you were accepted, we discovered that there were more than seventy pupils in each class in the first year, due to the very high demand for places. It far exceeded the Ministry of Education regulations. Three or four children would be crammed around a desk made for two. You all had to tilt your bodies simply in order to write properly. As a result, you developed the habit of always tilting your body when writing, and your writing was always slanted.

Only much later did I realise that everyone was guilty of conformist thinking. How could the primary schools in Nanyang be so different from one another? Why were so many children crowded into the same school? Were the teachers there so different from those at the other schools? Surely they weren't *all* excellent? Everyone was just following the herd, I'm certain of it.

You were so happy during your primary school years, which were full of happiness and laughter, and also a few tears. I remember the first time you cried because you spent all your money on treating your friends. You told us that school had asked for five *yuan* from every child. Mum couldn't find any change so she gave you a ten *yuan* note. That was a big one – there weren't any fifty or hundred *yuan* notes back then – and Mum told to you bring back the five *yuan* change. We didn't have a lot of money then, and since I was at home that day, I told you the same thing. You promised to bring back the change.

Your mum and I were surprised when you weren't home by lunchtime, as you usually were. Had your teachers kept you in school for some reason? We waited for about fifteen minutes before we went to ask a neighbour. The neighbour's child told us that school had dismissed you all on time, but that you hadn't come home because you'd invited some classmates to lunch at a nearby restaurant. Your mum and I were shocked that our young son was treating his classmates to lunch! I immediately jumped on my bike and rode to your school. Sure enough, when I arrived at the little restaurant, there you were, you and three of your classmates, sat at the table like in a TV show, each with a bowl of noodles and a drink in front of you, and a plate of fried eggs in the middle!

I flew into a rage. Five *yuan* was a lot of money back then. My salary for the whole month was only seven! And while we were struggling to make ends meet, there you were, wasting money on your friends! Where would it end, if you started to live so extravagantly at such a young age?

I waited at the gate until you'd finished eating, then I stormed over to your table. You stood up nervously and greeted me, as did your friends. I didn't reply to them but spoke only to you. "You're coming home with me. Now!"

You sat obediently on the back seat of my bike as we rode home. You knew I was upset and you tried to distract me with casual conversation. I ignored you. Once we arrived home, I commanded, "Kneel down!"

"Why should I kneel down?" you asked. Then I smacked you with no explanation.

"Kneel down, *now!*" I shouted. You knelt down with tears streaming down your face.

"Tell me why you took your friends out to lunch," I demanded.

"Because they're always sharing their snacks with me," you explained matter-of-factly. "Sometimes they give me an ice lolly or a fried pancake. But I never give them anything in return. Today I had five *yuan*, so I invited them for lunch to pay them back."

"You had the nerve to do that? How dare you use the five *yuan* for lunch without asking me or your mum first? Don't you realise how wasteful that was?"

"But you invite other people to dinner and you never ask me first!" you retorted.

Your reply infuriated me. I slapped you again. "How dare you talk back like that? I never even buy the one *yuan* lunch box on the train. I just nibble on some bread if I'm hungry. I always saved the one *yuan* so I could put it towards your education. What makes you think you can be so extravagant?"

Your mum encouraged you to admit your mistake and promise not to do anything like that again. I could see the defiance as well as the tears in your eyes, but you did as Mum had asked, for fear of being slapped again.

"I was wrong. I'm sorry, I won't do it again."

That was one of the other times that I hit you. Looking back, I regret it so much. It was only five *yuan*! Did I really need to slap you and force you to kneel down? Was that really the best way to deal with the situation? It never even crossed my mind that, even though you were so young, you appreciated the help you'd received from your friends, and you recognised that you should return the favour by treating them to lunch. Wasn't that a good thing, something to be proud of? Why was I so angry and belligerent? It must have been so traumatic for you. Do you remember that happening? I can't tell you how sorry I am.

The second time you cried in primary school was because of your addiction to video games. I can't remember exactly when Nanyang became infested with video arcades, but it didn't take long for many children around your age to become hooked. Those with self-control would only go to the arcades after school. Others, those without such restraint, quickly became addicted and would prioritise the games instead of their schoolwork. You were one of them, I think because we never cultivated a sense of academic discipline in you. You often visited the arcade on the way to school. And sometimes you even forgot to come home after school.

Before long, your teacher issued a warning to your mum and me, informing us that your grades were suffering. We talked to you about it again and again, and you promised not to play any more. But you simply couldn't stop yourself from going to the arcade. I became really concerned. Your mum and I had high hopes that one day you would go to one of the elite universities like Peking or Tsinghua. We just wanted you to have the opportunities that we'd never had. But while I'd pinned my hopes on you one day going to one of the top universities, here you were, allowing video games to destroy your future.

One night, you still weren't home by the time it was dark. I quickly got on my bike and went out looking for you. I had a good idea where to find you, but when I arrived, you were so absorbed in the game that you didn't even notice me until I coughed to get your attention.

I dragged you away from the game and we left the arcade. I was furious, determined to teach you a lesson. I made you sit on the back seat of my bike and off we rode. But instead of going straight home, I took you to the bank of the Bai River, just outside town.

"Dad, where are we going?" you asked timidly. I was ready to explode with rage.

"Mum and I have decided to abandon you. I'm going to leave you here by the river. From now on you can go wherever you want and do whatever you please."

The river bank was unlit and in total darkness. I put you down, and turned away with my bike. You burst out crying, then ran to catch up with me. You grabbed the back of my bike, sobbing.

"I'm sorry, Dad. I'll never play video games again. Please take me home. I promise I won't play again."

As I sit here thinking about it today, how could I have been so stupid that night? What on earth was I thinking? What kind of father was I? Son, you must have been terrified that night.

Dad, only two things left much of an impression on me during my primary school days: one is that day I took my classmates out to lunch. I had no idea about the hardships we faced, nor your constant efforts to support the family.

Yes, I did spend all the money you gave me that day. And I was defiant and upset when you told me to kneel down. It was only when I reached adulthood that I really came to understand what made you tick.

I never did break my habit of overspending. Even at university my living expenses were always higher than those of my friends. Maybe it was because you often sent money from your earnings as a writer. Each payment may have been small, but they came often, which made it very easy for me to spend. I didn't appreciate that the money would only last as long as you were able to continue writing. Please forgive me for that, Dad.

The second thing I remember was my addiction to video games. What can I say? I was entranced by them the first time I saw them, and before long I was hooked. While playing games, I was in a different world. I could forget everything, even dinner, let alone my homework. You're right: video games ruined the education and futures of many children, many of whom dropped out of school completely. Some young people even lost their lives through over-indulging. Video game designers may have had good intentions initially, but some of the longer term effects were devastating.

For every one of mankind's inventions, we should be open-minded to the benefits as well as wary of the dangers. When it came to video games, I guess I was just addicted and couldn't control myself.

I was really angered by your intervention that night. I was consumed by hatred, and I'm ashamed to admit that I even doubted that you were my real father. Was this an example of a generation gap, a chasm between us that caused misunderstanding and conflict? I think so: you saw video games as dreadful and threatening monsters, while I was enchanted by them. But while I was hooked on them, you did everything you could to stop me from playing them.

If I'm honest, Dad, that conflict led to a huge misunderstanding between us. I really thought that you just didn't want me to be happy.

4

Ning, when you were in the fourth grade (around nine or ten), you watched a funeral broadcast on TV.

"Dad, what's that?" you asked me. When I told you they were holding a funeral, you asked why.

"To commemorate and pay respects to the dead," I explained. You asked me when people had a funeral. "When someone passes away," I replied.

"When will you pass away?" you asked. I was taken aback.

"Not for a long time yet," I replied. "But it's hard to say."

You looked at me seriously. "When you pass away," you told me, "I will arrange your funeral." I was surprised to hear you say that, but it was wonderful that you did. I took you in my arms.

"Thank you, Son." Of course, it was quite normal for sons to hold a funeral for their fathers. How could I foresee that it wouldn't work out that way for us. On the contrary, I would be the one to organise your funeral! I ended up choosing your casket, your gravestone, everything.

My heart bled when I did those things. If the Creator cared enough to listen, He would have heard the trickle of blood.

Dad, I know you were torn apart by grief. But I was around you when you did those things. You carefully chose an artistic design for my casket and put great effort into the elaborate design of my tombstone. Before you and Mum decided to put my ashes in the beautiful Tianshou Garden, you visited almost all the cemeteries in and out of town.

How I wished I could comfort you both during the funeral. It must have been very difficult for you to do this yourself, with no one else to count on. My funeral should have been organised by my children, your grandchildren. Unfortunately I didn't stay around long enough to have any.

Let's just forget about it and accept that this was our fate. Only then will our grief, despair and hatred fade away. What else can we do? You yourself told your readers in your novel to find the right frame of reference for life. You now need to follow your own advice. So don't look at those with healthy children as your reference. It will only make you even more miserable.

Think of it this way: God spared you some time to prepare yourself before losing me. You were able to show how much you loved me in the hospital. Many fathers are separated from their sons without any warning at all. They may be together an hour before a car accident takes their sons away. Remember that horrific car accident on the highway that took the lives of several university students? Compared to those parents, didn't the Lord show His mercy to you?

Dad, other than this, I can't think of any other way to comfort you. So try to have some perspective and consider those who are in even deeper misery.

Son, while you were in primary school, we became embroiled in an awful lawsuit. Your mum and I became so obsessed with it that we neglected to take care of you properly or pay attention to your school grades. And at that most critical time for your development!

I've always suspected that your body became weaker during that time. We became so preoccupied with the lawsuit that we asked Aunt Qin and Uncle Zhengjiang to look after you for a while in Beijing. But even though they looked after you well, it was the first time you'd ever been separated from us. I felt your sadness even though you never showed it to us. You were a sensitive boy, and you must have had some inkling of what was going on. But you never shared your concerns or worries with us.

As the lawsuit continued you developed a cough, but no medicine seemed to work. Some of the family suggested you might have contracted tuberculosis. We should have taken you to a large hospital to be thoroughly checked. But Mum and I were so preoccupied with the lawsuit that, instead, we asked some relatives to take you to the local hospital. They were unable to give any clear diagnosis. They only suspected that you had tuberculosis and prescribed some medicine. Unfortunately the medicine had side effects on both your stomach and liver. You lost a lot of weight and I'm sure it must have weakened your immune system.

What's worse, you were also subjected to regular x-rays to monitor your recovery. The doctor was my friend and he was doing this as a special favour for us. But x-rays can be really harmful, too.

By the time we finally won the lawsuit, you had become very weak. How stupid your mum and I had been. What was more important, your health or the lawsuit? I had clearly prioritised my personal honour over your health. And yet, so long as you were healthy, why did it matter if we were wronged? The worst possible outcome would only have been a few years in jail. I just didn't think it through properly and had lost sight of the fact that you were the most precious thing of all. Nothing else mattered, and I've always hated myself for thinking otherwise.

Dad, I do remember the lawsuit. Yes, I was young, but I still understood the gravity of the situation. Children become aware of things at different ages. Some will mature quickly when something bad strikes their family. I clearly remember that night when someone suddenly dropped by, the afternoon when Grandma and Grandpa wept, and the afternoon when you decided to send me to Beijing with Aunt Qin and Uncle Zheng. It was the first time I'd left home and left Mum for such a long time. Although Aunt Qin and Uncle Zheng accompanied me, I understood that I was a refugee rather than a guest.

At night, I missed you and Mum terribly as I curled up under the duvet. Sometimes I wet myself. I was so embarrassed but I didn't want to cause any more trouble for Aunt Qin, so I'd say nothing and just kept my pyjama trousers on until they dried themselves out.

I think my self-esteem did suffer during the time of the lawsuit. I developed an inferiority complex and became much more introverted. An outgoing and confident personality is nurtured in a happy and non-judgmental environment. Unfortunately for me, that environment seemed to disappear from my life during that time in Nanyang. Still a young boy, I began to examine other people's faces, I watched my tongue and became very careful about my behaviour so as not to offend anyone. This made me feel insecure and depressed, which I'm sure couldn't have been good for my long-term health.

Dad, please don't think I'm complaining. I'm not saying you shouldn't have pursued the lawsuit. I just wanted you to know why my personality changed. Anyway, let's not talk about this any more. What's the point of bringing it all up now?

Nothing happens in life without a reason. This is probably just what I was destined to go through.

Ning, when you were young, you and your Mum always complained that I never took you out. I admit that other fathers were much better at this. It's just that I was always so busy, and what little spare time I did have was always spent reading and writing. I didn't think it was a good use of time to take you out. I never considered it my responsibility, nor did I understand that travel would broaden your outlook. I was never really aware of the importance of leisure in life. I always thought there would be plenty of time later on for me to take you both out. How could I have known that we would have so little time together?

Now I'll never be able to take you anywhere again. Only twice did I take you and Mum away on a holiday. The first time was to Xi'an, while I was taking a course at the Academy of Political Science. I invited you and Mum, also your grandpa, for a visit to that ancient city.

We went to the Banpo remains, the Big Wild Goose Pagoda and the Little Wild Goose Pagoda. We visited the Terracotta Warriors and the

Huaqing Pool, where Yang Yuhuan had once bathed. At the edge of the Huaqing Pool, you asked aloud after the guide's explanation, "But where is Yang Yuhuan?" Your mum and I looked at each other and smiled.

"The water in the pool is still clear," the guide explained, "but the plump and beautiful Yang Yuhuan will no longer appear. Time has turned all the beautiful things into historic relics."

On the way up Li Mountain, you led the way as the three of us raced to the top. Our laughter echoed through the mountains, startling the birds away. It may very well have been the same road that Emperor Minghuang and Yang Yuhuan had walked, as well as Jiang Zhongzheng and his guards later on in history. It seemed like a fitting memorial for us to leave our family's footprints there.

The other trip we took was to Mount Tai. We took cars to Zhongtian Gate, and as we drove along the rugged road that threaded around the mountain, you were entranced by the sight of the cliffs, the valleys, the streams and trees. Mount Tai was so novel to you, since you were from the plains. We had planned to take a cable car to the top, but the queue was too long due to the volume of tourists, plus your grandpa was feeling tired. Your mum and I decided not to go to the summit this time.

At the Zhongtian Gate, I pointed to the summit in the distance and gave you an introduction to the South Tianmen, the Tianjie, and the Baizhang Cliff, where you stood and gazed for a while.

"Dad, next time we must go to the summit," you said. I agreed, and promised you that next time we would climb there on foot if we couldn't ride the cable car.

I was never able to fulfil that promise to you. I was always busy, immersed in the creation of a novel or another essay. I didn't satisfy your wish, and I've regretted it ever since.

Dad, one thing sticks in my mind from our trip to Xi'an. You bought two bottles of water before climbing Li Mountain. I was thirsty, so I took both bottles.

"Ning, give one of the bottles to Mum," you told me. I refused, insisting both were mine. Mum said nothing but gave me a smile. You scolded me on the spot.

"Don't be such a selfish brat!"

I was upset and protested. "Why can't you just buy another bottle for Mum?"

Looking back today, I feel so ashamed and sorry that I treated Mum like that. If I couldn't even look after her, who else would I deny my love to?

A child's love for his parents is dwarfed by a parent's love for their children. I would only learn that later on, after I became ill. Mum always deprived herself but spared no expense to find food and medicine that might help my immune system. Mum, when I finally learned about the concept of filial piety, I left you forever, unable to repay your love.[1] I am so sorry.

Son, when you were in elementary school, your mother hurried to my office one day to tell me that some scouts from the local sports school had gone to your school to select some potential talent. Apparently you had caught their eye and you were to be assessed at the long jump in the city stadium. If you did well there was every chance that you'd be invited to attend the sports school. Your mum asked for my opinion. I frowned. "Our son shouldn't do sports," I said. "Athletes are well past their best by the age of thirty. What on earth will he do then? Far better that he becomes a scientist when he grows up." And with that, I got on my bike and hurried to the city stadium.

When I arrived, one of the sports school coaches was assessing several pupils in front of the long jump pit. You were in next in line. After the boy ahead of you had finished, I approached the coach. "My son Zhou Ning doesn't want to go to the sports school," I told him. "Please send him back to his primary school."

The coach gave me a steady gaze. "But this is a wonderful opportunity for your son," he explained. "Very few ever have a chance to go to sports school. We only take the best of the best."

I shook my head. "Thank you," I replied, "but we really don't want this opportunity."

The coach sighed. "Look at your son's legs," he pointed out. "They're long and well developed. If he trains hard at the sports school, then with his natural ability he has every chance of achieving something in the future. That would bring great honour to your family. Please think this through before closing the door."

I shook my head again. "I don't need to think it through," I insisted. "He's not going to be an athlete!"

The coach then turned to you. "Zhou Ning, it's your turn. Take your jump in your own time." You went to the line, swung your arm and kicked a little bit to get ready, then you ran and jumped. I was surprised; I really didn't expect to see you jump so far. The coach turned to me again.

"You see how good your son is? Preventing him from becoming an athlete would be a real waste of his talent." Even then I still didn't ask you for your opinion.

"We don't need to discuss this any more," I said. "My son is not an athlete!" I declared stubbornly. Then I led you out of the stadium, leaving the sports school coach sighing in frustration.

On the way home, you asked me, "Dad, why can't I be a long jumper?"

"Being an athlete is not a long-term career," I replied. "Most people are considered old by the age of sixty, but athletes are past their prime at thirty. By then it will be too difficult for you to start a new career."

"But when I'm thirty," you protested, "I could be a long jump coach." I was stunned by your words and shook my head.

"What's the point of being a long jump coach?" I asked. "Who would respect you if you're a sports coach?" You didn't answer and shuffled along silently behind me.

Looking back, the reason I discouraged you from pursuing athletics is that I'd always looked down on people in sports. I didn't consider the long jump a true skill. I could see no long-term value in it whatsoever. What I cared about wasn't physical or sporting prowess, but the intellectual qualities needed to climb the political ladder.

I had worked in the field of literature my whole life, studying human psychology and interaction. I knew very well that in China, a person's value was measured not by personality nor their contribution to society, but by their rank, by how high they rose in their career. I had always pretended to assume the moral high ground and stay away from politics. But deep in my heart I believed that a man's career should be in the government. To that end I always wanted you to become a party official, to bring honour to our family. In truth, I was still an ordinary person who had been indoctrinated by traditional official values.

If you had pursued your own dream to attend the sports school, and had trained all day long, maybe you would have become stronger and more immune to disease. Why had I stubbornly insisted on getting my own way? Why did I drag you away from that wonderful opportunity?

Without my intervention, your life may well have followed another path. In a very real sense, I changed your destiny by force of will. Did I have that right just because I was your father?

People have all kinds of interests and talents, and I believe they are absolutely intertwined with our physical and mental health. To suppress them risks upsetting the balance of mind and body, leaving people prone to invasion from illness or disease.

Dad, don't regret the life you carved out for me. It was only because of you that I could read books so easily. That's how I was admitted into the Xi'an Institute of Telecommunications, where I would meet so many of my friends and teachers. Then later on I attended the Zhengzhou University of Information Engineering, where I specialised in information security. None of that would have happened without your guidance.

Even if I had gone into sports, is an athlete's life stress-free? Before a competition, how many athletes toss and turn at night, unable to sleep for worrying about their performance? Just one mistake in a competition can impact their whole life. And even if they do achieve good results or win medals, they're always under constant pressure to maintain and improve those standards.

No, Dad, a professional athlete's life is not an easy one at all. Athletes train at an intensity that far exceeds the normal limits of the human body. That alone can easily cause injury and permanent damage. So even if I had become an athlete, would it have been beneficial for my health? Would it have spared me from illness? I'm not so sure.

Dad, everything in life comes at a cost. Nothing is free and nothing is perfect. So don't be so hard on yourself.

As for your claim that you could never imagine me becoming anything other than a government official, I get it. You certainly shouldn't blame yourself. How many people are truly honest with themselves about this? How many people in China *didn't* want to become government officials? You certainly weren't alone in thinking that way. It's just the way things were.

Son, before you moved on from primary school, your mum and I had known for a while where we wanted you to go to next: No. 13 Middle School, one of the two best schools in Nanyang. It had an excellent reputation and teachers to match. It was also close to home.

You were apprehensive, though. "Dad, Mum," you said, "the exam scores to qualify for No. 13 Middle School must be so high. How can I possibly pass?"

Common sense should have dictated that we ask you which school you wanted to attend, but we didn't; I just became frustrated and angry.

"Do you have no ambition whatsoever?" I asked sarcastically. "Nothing in this world is easy. Aiming for No. 13 scares you, plain and simple. With that attitude, what else can you hope to accomplish in the future? Would you rather be a failure and looked down upon? Only by going to No. 13 will you be able to go to a good high school after three years, then to a good university. A young man should set his targets high! If you don't get into No. 13 Middle School, I'll be humiliated, and that doesn't seem to bother you at all!"

"Why would you be humiliated if I don't go to No. 13?" you asked. "There are so many other schools in Nanyang. Are all the parents of pupils at those schools humiliated?"

"Is it an honour to go to an ordinary school?" I asked. "Why can you not be as motivated as your mother and me? Are you really content just to stay in your comfort zone? In fact, I'm beginning to wonder if we took the wrong baby home from the hospital. Maybe you're someone else's son, not ours!"

Your mother scolded me, telling me to stop my nonsense.

38

Meanwhile your whole face was red to the neck because of my sarcastic and harsh words.

My criticism and the pressure of my expectations undoubtedly increased your mental stress. You weren't even able to sleep properly in the nights leading up to your exam. You often stayed up late after Mum and I had gone to bed. In the end your mum had no choice but to give you some sleeping pills. Sleeping pills, even though you were still so young! Of course I was concerned, but I justified it by telling myself that it was all helping to build your future, so I wouldn't allow you to become complacent or lower your own expectations.

Once again, you lost weight due to the stress.

The results of the exam came out, and you got into No. 13 Middle School! Mum and I were so thrilled. I even bragged to her, "See, a little pressure did him no harm. Without that pressure, he never would have got in!" You weren't that bothered about getting in; you just said you wanted to sleep for a few days.

When you were eventually diagnosed with cancer, the doctor told us it was unlikely to have developed suddenly. Even though the precise cause was unclear, he thought it had probably developed over time and may have been brought on by stress. Looking back, one of the reasons may have been that I forced you to apply to No. 13 Middle School against your wishes.

Maybe it was even the *main* reason.

Why on earth did I have to push you so hard towards your death? Yes, I was concerned for your future, but it really just boiled down to my own vanity. I was simply afraid of the embarrassment I thought I would suffer if you didn't go to one of the top schools.

At No. 13 Middle School, you started to develop a problem with your phlegm. It wasn't a big deal at first, but from time to time you would spit up a little, often too suddenly to reach the spittoon, and it would hit the ground. I put it down to a bad habit that you'd developed, so I complained and said you shouldn't spit.

I never considered why you had phlegm, nor did I arrange for a traditional Chinese doctor to examine you. In fact, Nanyang was home to Zhang Zhongjing and many other traditional Chinese doctors. If only I had had someone check your pulse and prescribe some Chinese medicine, there's a good chance the issue would have been resolved. However, I didn't pay much attention to it, and only gave you some Western medicine, leaving the root of the disease unchecked.

Only after you were diagnosed with cancer did I consult a traditional Chinese doctor and begin to understand that phlegm was a symptom of depression and knots in the veins, which eventually caused stasis of the blood in the intracranial mass, the early stage of a tumour. How utterly stupid I was to turn a blind eye to the root cause of your cancer.

And still I regarded myself as a responsible and good father. A good father? What a joke!

Dad, No. 13 Middle School was a real challenge for me. I always thought it was a bad idea to bring all the brightest pupils together in one school, to then be differentiated even further by their test scores. Even the pupils with the lowest scores at this school were so much more advanced than those at other schools. But that did nothing to inhibit their feelings of inferiority, depression and embarrassment. This distorted mentality undoubtedly affected their future development.

When I first entered No. 13 Middle School, I was appointed to be a subject representative. By the end of the academic year, though, I had been overtaken by other pupils. It was bound to take a toll on my mental health.

But there were happy times too, in particular playing basketball with my school friends. I learned to play basketball in the school playground. It was the high point of my day to go to the basketball court with a few friends after school. I was growing quickly at that time, getting taller every week, it seemed. It gave me a clear advantage in the game and I could sense the envy of my shorter classmates.

I quickly fell in love with basketball. My body burst with exhilaration every time I picked up a ball, took a shot or grabbed a rebound. I was full of joy and laughter every time I played. All I wanted from you and Mum at that time was a pair of basketball shoes. You gave me a pair of military grade rubber-soled trainers, comfortable and flexible and perfect for helping me to jump and catch the ball. My friends were envious, telling me that I was only able to jump so high because of my trainers!

Just as had happened before with video games, I grew so obsessed with basketball that I soon became distracted from my school work. At the weekends we went to the basketball court at No. 2 High School of Nanyang until dark. We continued to play even under the dim light of distant street lights, oblivious to our homework and dinner. Eventually you would come and find me, then drag me reluctantly home.

Son, our family moved to Beijing in 1995, after your graduation from middle school. By then you had grown into a tall young man. I remember when I picked you and Mum up at Beijing Railway Station. I stood waiting for you both as the train pulled in, but I couldn't see you even after all the other passengers had left. Finally you appeared at the door of the train and told me anxiously that Mum was suffering from motion sickness and couldn't move. Worried, I followed you to the train.

"I thought you were in the sleeping carriage?" I asked. "So why was Mum travel sick?" You told me that she'd vomited after eating a piece of fruit. Then, afterwards, she felt dizzy and breathless. I went to your bunk and saw your mum lying there, pale as anything. I helped her off the train while you carried all the luggage, and we made our way out of the station. As I watched you with all the luggage, I realised for the first time that you were now a responsible young man I could rely on.

It took a while for Mum and you to adjust to life in Beijing. The first thing was the climate; unlike the heat and humidity of Nanyang, Beijing was very dry. Pimples soon popped up all over your face.

Second was the challenge of building new friendships. Without any of your old friends or classmates, everyone in Beijing was a stranger. At school you had no friends to chat or play basketball with. So you were quite lonely for a while.

Third, the school timetable was quite different from Nanyang, with no self-study period in the morning or evening. You also weren't accustomed to walking such a long way to and from school.

Finally, your Mandarin wasn't very good, so you were quite shy to talk to other people.

People tend to migrate in their quest for happiness, but happiness isn't always so easy to find. It's like a stubborn woman: there's sometimes a high price to pay before you reach fulfilment. In your case, your unfamiliarity with Beijing may have be one of the costs.

Before long, however, you began to integrate yourself into the hordes of young people in Beijing. Within a few months you had made some good friends, you were playing basketball again, staying on top of your new school timetable, and improving your Mandarin.

While you were in high school, I attended several parent-teacher meetings. I soon discovered that the teaching methods in Beijing were quite different from those we were used to in Nanyang. Just take study time and subject scores as two examples. Far less strict than our hometown teachers, the emphasis in Beijing was to teach students *how* to learn, and then to encourage the students to consciously make their own connections and conclusions in their learning. I secretly worried; were you equipped to handle all your various subjects by yourself? I urged you to do your homework and spend more time reading your books. I also began to interfere with your daily schedule as well. In the end, I became more like your academic supervisor than your father.

What's more, you were going through puberty at the time. Your mum and I didn't understand a boy's physical and psychological changes at all. We simply weren't equipped to deal with your transformation, and we often argued with you about trivial things as a result.

You wanted to watch TV on weekdays. Your mum and I said no: the less you watched TV, the better it was for your studies, and they were the most important thing in your life. *You need to focus on preparing for your exams!*

You wanted to play basketball after school to relax. Your mum and I said no: *homework comes before basketball!*

You wanted to read a novel or some other non-academic book for a change of pace. Your mum and I said no: your top priority was to succeed in the college entrance examination. *You can read whatever novels you want after you get to college!*

You never wanted to go to bed early. Your mum and I disagreed: *going to bed early will help you to study better tomorrow!*

You started to complain that you had no freedom. I told you that you didn't understand the importance of the college entrance examination for your success in later life.

Slowly but surely, these frictions led to confrontation.

After school, you ignored my 'homework first' policy and went to the basketball court instead. You turned a deaf ear to my warnings. I was so outraged one time that I punctured your basketball with a needle to let all the air out. You cried when you saw the shrivelled ball.

You treated my 'no TV on weekdays' policy with the same disdain. After your homework, you'd lock yourself in your room and watch TV with the volume turned down low. You even used an umbrella to block out the light from the screen so we wouldn't know! Mum and I thought you were studying in your room, until we realised that your door was locked. I moved a bench outside your window so I could climb up on and see what you were doing. Once I realised, I unlocked your door in a fit of rage and we got into a fight.

I didn't know where or how you had managed to borrow a romance novel! You had camouflaged it with the cover of one of your textbooks to fool your mother and I into thinking that you were studying. We were blissfully unaware until I discovered by chance that it was a novel. Another confrontation ensued.

Those incidents made me angry, and your mum was heartbroken. You hated what you saw as our interference in your adolescence; we believed you were at a critical point in your life and needed our guidance, whether you realised it or not.

You protested indignantly. "If you don't stop this, I'll withdraw from the *Gaokao*."[2]

"And what will you do if you don't take the *Gaokao*?" I demanded angrily. "What kind of career do you think will there be for you? How will you survive?"

"I could sell CDs at the subway," you replied defiantly.

"And how much money could you make doing that?"

"Enough to survive."

"What about marriage? How will you ever have enough money to support a wife and family?"

"Maybe I'll just stay single."

Infuriating though it was, that argument forced us to make some concessions, and after that, we gave you some leeway to make your own decisions.

Being a good father requires an understanding of a child's physical and psychological needs, but I truly didn't understand. I knew only coercion and pressure, which filled your adolescence with frustration and pain. It took me a long time to come to terms with the fact that it was I who had caused your suffering.

Didn't that period in your life also do some physical harm to your body? I'll bet it did.

If only someone had taught me how to be a father to a high school boy.

This is another flaw of mine: to blame society and avoid taking responsibility. It all boils down to my own vanity. I just wanted you to go to the best schools. A friend had suggested that business school would be a good fit for you. I replied dismissively, saying we didn't think that was the right path for you.

Dad, my biggest problem in high school was my acne! Pimples erupted all over my face after we arrived in Beijing. I hoped to be a good-looking young man, but acne had other ideas. I became very self-conscious about my appearance and quite depressed as I tried all kinds of ways to treat it. I spent my pocket money on several different drugs and cosmetics, but nothing worked. At school, I was nervous when talking with my classmates, especially around girls. I was afraid they would focus on my blemishes. I was also worried about my face attracting attention from people during my walks to and from school. I began to walk with my head down, always talked in a low voice, and I avoided places with lots of people. I tried to evade people's attention and worried about becoming a laughing stock.

My personality changed and I became more and more introverted. I was quickly rattled by the laughter of my classmates, worried that they were mocking me. Even random laughter from strangers in the street made me paranoid that it was directed at me.

At that time I was really upset and especially sensitive to your intervention in my life, which threatened the last bit of freedom I had. During those days, your only concern was whether I would be admitted to college; all I cared about was how to cure my acne. Two things, two objectives, a thousand miles apart. How could we possibly not have clashed?

Ning, in high school you wanted to take the liberal arts course, majoring in history later on. You had always enjoyed history books when you were young and would often talk about historical figures and events at dinner. It was so impressive and I should have respected and encouraged your ideas and curiosity. After all, you were the one taking the exams, and being truly interested in a subject is the best motivator of all. At that time, though, I thought history was too interrelated with politics. Historians cannot help but comment on current affairs, and I was worried that you'd be sucked into the political sphere. It would inevitably lead to trouble, so I figured that science would be better for you. Being dedicated to scientific research ensured a lifetime of relative safety.

Although I was young during the Cultural Revolution, I saw many cases of political persecution. As a result I became forever wary of politics and didn't want you to get involved. In any case, there were always more university places for science students, which meant higher admission rates and better job prospects.

Ultimately I made the decision for you: you would enrol in the science course. You weren't keen but didn't oppose my decision. And so you became a science student. It was inevitable that you would feel trapped, being stuck doing something you weren't really interested in. That was another foolish thing I did.

You struggled in your studies after that. It wasn't until I helped you prepare for the *Gaokao* exams that I realised how difficult it was to be a science student. You were better suited to images and emotions, to the arts. To be immersed in a world of science and logic was never going to be easy for you.

But somehow you managed and completed the *Gaokao*. I cannot help but think that if you'd been on the liberal arts course and studied history as you'd always wanted, your life would have been easier, maybe more fulfilled.

How could I have tortured my own son like this? Because I became conceited. I was opinionated, even arrogant. And I didn't respect you; I treated you like a naive child.

Dad, you're doing it again! Stop being so hard on yourself. It's true that I wasn't that interested in science to begin with. But interest can always be cultivated, and I was gradually drawn into it. Science is fundamental for all-round development. Anyone can teach themselves about the liberal arts, but it's very difficult to learn science without proper guidance. If I hadn't been on the science course, I honestly don't think I ever would have got into military school or had any of my later scientific research achievements along with my peers in the military.

Dad, I don't regret the path I took, and neither should you. My illness and studying science weren't connected at all. You only need to look at all the healthy science students to see that. The cause of my illness can't be explained by medical experts even today. Most likely it was simply genetic.

I still remember when you accompanied me to the *Gaokao* exams. You took leave from work for those three days. After making sure I had everything I needed for the exams, you came with me to school on your bike. At the gate you gave me some warm water, then watched as I entered the school. You sat outside on the street, waiting for me until I'd finished the exam, then rode home with me for lunch. It was hot, around thirty degrees. You were dripping with sweat, yet for three days in a row you were there for me. On the way home from school, you ensured I took the inside lane, exposing yourself to the traffic on the outside in order to protect me.

At that moment, I promised in my heart that I would repay all of your love and care after I graduated and began work. I could never have foreseen that God wouldn't grant me enough time for that.

5

Ning, I remember vividly the time I accompanied you to the Xi'an Telecommunication Institute of the PLA.[1] The night before registration day, we stayed at the army hotel in Xi'an. Then, just as we prepared to leave for registration, you panicked.

"Dad, please teach me how to wash handkerchiefs. I have no idea how to do it!" you said.

"You see how spoilt you've been?" I replied with a laugh. "How will you ever be able to live by yourself if you can't even wash a handkerchief? Don't worry, it's never too late to learn." Then I took you into the bathroom, soaked the handkerchief with water, added some soap, washed it, rinsed it, dried it and put it on a hanger. You followed my demonstration exactly, then off we went to the school.

After registration, we found your quarters, unpacked your luggage and met your cadet leader. I was about to leave but you were reluctant to let me go.

"Sorry Son, I need to go back to work," I told you. You nodded and wished me a safe trip. I got on the bus and saw you standing there watching as it faded into the distance. You had hardly ever been away from home by yourself, so this would be your first experience of living independently.

Your mum and I knew it would take you some time to adapt. Back home, we worried constantly about you. Mum couldn't wait to call you to find out how you were getting on. I stopped her. "A man must eventually leave home," I told her. "This is no big deal. He just needs some time to get used to it."

It wasn't long before we received news that you were being commended by your cadre leaders for your excellent performance in military training. At the end of the first term, I asked a friend of mine to arrange a ticket for you on the sleeper train back home. And something memorable happened when I went to pick you up at Beijing West railway station: I went to the sleeping carriage to meet you, but I couldn't see you when all the passengers had disembarked. Fretting, I started to call out your name. Then I saw you, out of breath, running towards me with your luggage from the direction of the seated carriages.

"Why weren't you in your sleeping bunk?" I asked.

You grinned at me. "In Xi'an, I saw a sick elderly man being carried into the carriage. I worried how he would ever handle the journey in a normal seat, so I offered to switch my sleeping bunk with him."

At first I was distressed that you had sacrificed your own comfort like that. But then I was overcome by a profound sense of pride in your concern for others.

"My boy has truly turned into a fine young man," I told you as I patted your shoulder.

Dad, going to university in Xi'an was my official farewell to childhood. Leaving home and being alone in a new world was a shock at first. I struggled there in every way. I was slow in the morning routine, slack in the military requirements, and clumsy in folding my up bedding and cleaning the toilet to the required military standards. That's when I realised you were right about how spoilt I'd been at home. Our squad leader even threw my duvet out of the window several times before I learned how to fold it properly!

Those early days were tough, of course, and I wasn't very happy there. But I soon realised that I would never become a real soldier if I couldn't even cope with the basics. Things soon changed, though, and I started to work harder, up to the standards of my peers. If a man sets his mind to one thing, the chances are he is completely capable of accomplishing it. And so it was with me: within two months, I was able to keep up with my classmates in every respect. It taught me that children mature much faster after leaving the nest.

Another benefit of studying in Xi'an was getting to know this ancient capital city. Historical buildings, relics and anecdotes resonate everywhere in this city, and my friends and I would often travel around the city at weekends and during holidays.

Given my love of history, I found the city fascinating. You had always told me that a man should use his own independent thought and judgment, rather than follow the crowd blindly. When visiting the famous sites in Xi'an, I was not especially excited or proud of the achievements of our ancestors. Rather, I was struck, confused even, by how all the power struggles, the wheeling and dealing, the lust for fortune and women, the pursuit of immortality, and the bloodshed and slaughter, have been repeated throughout history, over and over again. It occurred to me that we learned nothing through the generations, but simply inherited those same impulses from our ancestors.

I also became rather withdrawn and depressed because only the stories of the imperial families had been recorded and passed down. History didn't care about the common people. I also began to wonder whether we should in fact be passing down the accounts of their lives and deeds to our descendants, rather than only recording the history of important people.

Son, I noticed a big change in you during that first summer holiday when you were back from military school. You now projected the air of a soldier. Even your basic mannerisms had changed, such as the way you stood up or sat down and your courtesy in dealing with others. You also became more considerate towards your mum and me. During your high school years, your first priority would be to rush to the computer when you got home, and you would be glued to the screen until dinner was ready. But after your first year of military training, you began to help out around the house, doing chores like grocery shopping or taking out the rubbish. Mum and I were very encouraged by what we saw: our little boy had grown into a fine and dependable young man.

Every year, before the Spring Festival, I would always buy a few pots of flowers. And every year I would struggle to carry them up to our home on the fourth floor. Since the building didn't have a lift it was never an easy task for me. You had never paid attention to this before. At most you would compliment the flowers after I'd brought them home. But on this occasion you stopped me when you saw me carrying those pots.

"Dad, stop. I'll take care of those," you said. Then you took the pots from my hands and carried them all home after a few trips up and down the stairs. I really enjoyed standing and watching you go up and down. My son had finally started to take care of me!

I must say, it's a wonderful feeling when your child begins to look after you.

Dad, as a single child I was spoiled rotten by you and Mum, as well as by my grandparents. But I think my ability to love and empathise was quite underdeveloped. I read once in a newspaper that in some rural areas, children of only seven or eight years old already shouldered the responsibility of housework and taking care of their parents. But I was still a brat even in high school! Everything was taken care of for me. I was rebellious and acted out against you, often doing exactly the opposite of what you asked. I took for granted the hard work you put in to support our family. I didn't appreciate it and did nothing to help. I know I was a handful, and I think it was due to the abundance of love you gave me and the one-child policy.

With an only child in a family, two generations focused on that single child, which of course led to the child being spoiled. It was really an unnatural situation. It's clear to me that multiple children in one family is far healthier. A three-person family just isn't right. Like a house with three pillars, it will fall apart if one is removed. If only you and Mum had given me a little sister or brother. Then I would have been reassured that you and Mum would have someone to count on when I left.

I've read that having four or five children at regular intervals is good for a woman. It can prolong their lives, and it gives them plenty of people among whom to spread their love. They will be more fulfilled and at lower risk of health problems such as hormone imbalances or breast or uterus-related illnesses. In our home town, those women with four, five or even a dozen children, would often live to ninety or older, despite the poor living conditions. On the other hand, many mothers of single children, even those financially well off, often suffered health problems.

History was cruel, however. Your generation was required to make sacrifices and stick to the one-child policy. But there was no way around it, so you shouldn't be so hard on yourself.

Your generation, those born in the 1950s, had a really hard life: the Great Famine of 1959-61 impeded the growth of your bodies; the Cultural Revolution in the 1960s and 1970s contaminated and stifled your spirit; and the strict birth controls greatly affected your family dynamics.

All of these things were reflected in your personality and habits: you were prone to live frugally and stock food through fear of hunger; to be over-cautious and easily spooked by any potential political threat due to the memories of the Cultural Revolution; and to put all your hopes and concerns on your children due to your own difficult upbringing.

Yes, I'm certain that future generations will have sympathy on you and record in the history books that people born in the 1950s had very difficult lives...

Son, you matured so much during your college years. We could see your development each term, as you became more mature and considerate. During the holiday after your second term, you brought home gifts for Mum and me. You gave me a few small replica statues of the Terracotta Warriors, because you knew I was interested in them, and for your mum you brought a scarf and some food from Xi'an. It was the first time you'd ever given us gifts! We knew you'd now learned to show your love and appreciation.

During your third holiday you bought an electric water heater for our kitchen, where we'd always washed the dishes with cold water. Mum was quite touched. "My son really knows what we need," she said with pride.

When you came back for your fourth holiday, you brought home a friend who had a layover in Beijing. You looked after him and helped him to get tickets home. We were so happy that you were making some friends.

During your fifth holiday you started to help us when we had guests to visit, and you also fixed the computer which I needed for my writing work.

During your sixth holiday you brought some nutritional supplements for your grandparents and told us you wanted to visit them. You also consulted with the New Oriental School to sign up for some English classes. We were so relieved that you were starting to plan for your future.

You spent your seventh holiday working on your graduation research and thesis. We really saw how you had matured. I told your mum that the only remaining task for me was to save some money for an apartment to give to you as a wedding present.

After the SARS outbreak in 2003,[2] I scrupulously saved whatever I could from my earnings as a writer, enough to afford an apartment in Beijing. Real estate prices were at rock bottom, and SARS made the future unpredictable. Few people were investing in property, while many were selling. The timing was perfect for me to buy an apartment for you. I didn't think of it as an investment; I just thought it was my duty to provide you with housing when you eventually got married.

During the renovation work, one bannister was to be installed on each step, as normal. Instead, though, I instructed the workers to put two on each step. I was worried that in the years to come, your children may risk falling between them if the bannisters were too spread out. Two bannisters on each step would therefore leave no space for young children to squeeze their head or body through.

One of the workers looked at me, smiling. "But Sir, it won't look as nice, and there's really no precedent for this," he told me. I told him that safety was the most important thing, and that my family was setting a new precedent!

So now we have very child-safe bannisters on the staircase; but where will my grandchildren come from, now that you're gone?

The lesson here is that we shouldn't place too much hope on the future, or rush to prepare for something much further down the road. God may decide to intervene if He considers our dreams to be too fanciful. If He chooses to, He can sabotage our best-laid plans, leaving us with nothing but egg on our face.

Ever since, I have never planned too far ahead, nor allowed myself to get carried away by my dreams for the future. Whatever will be, will be. Always a natural pessimist, I would tend to assume the worst outcome in any situation. After this, I took it to extremes. Every morning, I would wonder in silence, "I wonder what the Creator will take away from me today?"

And so I have been prepared for the worst outcome almost every day, believing that maybe life would take away everything I had. And I know that it could, if it wanted to.

Dad, I'm sorry. I know you were looking forward to having a grandchild. Before I became ill, I noticed that you always so good with any children you met. You always said that your plans for old age were to read, write and play with your grandchildren.

I remember Mum once saying that it was a good thing that fewer young people were choosing to have children nowadays. It was a good way to control the country's population, she said. You weren't having any of it. "That's absolute nonsense!" you cried. "How on earth will our nation survive without the new generation? Who will be there to guard our country? What you're talking about is the propaganda of subjugating the nation!"

Mum was shocked by your indignant reaction. She said you were over-reacting and blowing her casual remark out of proportion. I just laughed; I knew you were worried that Mum's comment may rub off on me, that it might discourage me from having children. Let me tell you, Dad, you needn't have worried. I love children as much as you do. I always planned to have children soon after getting married, so you could have a grandchild to play with. I didn't know that my fate would be sealed well before I could get married or have children. And so I was never able to fulfil your dreams. Before I passed away, it tortured me to think about this.

Dad, Mum, I'm so sorry...

6

Ning, perhaps the most stupid and unforgivable thing I ever did in my life was to break up your relationship with Xiaoyi. I literally smack my head in shame every time I think about it.

During the first term of your senior year, you called to tell us that you'd become involved with a girl. Your mum and I were really surprised. Now you were a real grown-up, with a blossoming romance. At your age, it was quite natural for you to want to meet girls. However, like all parents we worried you might meet someone who wasn't good enough for you. Your mum and I discussed it, and we decided to visit the girl and see for ourselves.

Mum was busy at work and couldn't take the time off, so the responsibility fell to me. In retrospect, if she'd been the one to visit you, perhaps things might have turned out differently. Maybe it would have prevented my terrible mistake and the subsequent fallout. I feel awful about what happened. I behaved like the worst possible father. You and Xiaoyi must have thought I was the most ruthless and cruel parent ever. I'm sure I'm right, aren't I?

I arrived on a Saturday afternoon, and called you after I'd settled in at the hotel. You joined me after dinner. You knew the reason for my visit and were understandably nervous. Fearing my disapproval, you told me a lot of good things about this girl, including that she was from a simple village. I said I didn't care about that, so long as she was a good person. I was a country boy myself, and your grandparents still lived in the countryside. How could I look down on people from the countryside?

I thought that as long as the girl looked nice and had good a personality and character, I would give my blessing to the two of you. You then called Xiaoyi and invited her to join us for breakfast in the hotel the following morning.

You stayed in my room that night. Glancing over at you as you fell asleep, I felt so content. My boy had grown up and now had a girl who loved him. I still remember the dream I had that night: you had a beautiful girlfriend, and all the villagers in our hometown showered you both with compliments.

You got up early the next morning. After washing and dressing, we went down to the restaurant in high spirits. You were happy to be seeing your girlfriend again, while I was looking forward to meeting her. We met her in the restaurant, and you introduced us. The smile on my face froze. The girl's appearance was nothing like I had imagined. She was totally different from the daughter-in-law I had envisioned.

Years later, I realised that I was assessing the girl from the perspective of a novelist searching idealistically for a beautiful protagonist. Of course I was going to be disappointed; no one could have lived up to my ridiculous expectations! Maybe through my work I had developed a tendency to blur the line between fiction and reality, to implant delusions in my imagination. It's no wonder your mum always criticised me for being insensitive and incapable of showing empathy.

I didn't say much that morning other than to encourage the girl (out of politeness, it must be said) to eat more. My stony face must have betrayed my true feelings, though, since I saw you anxiously check my face several times. Everything was polite during breakfast, but I'm sure my lack of warmth and enthusiasm was obvious. You and I had planned for the three of us to go a shopping mall so we could buy a gift for your girlfriend. Instead, though, I decided to go straight back to the hotel, leaving you to see the girl off.

You were in a foul mood when you returned to the hotel. "Dad, what's your problem with Xiaoyi?" you demanded. "Why don't you like her?"

I'm sorry to say that I didn't consider your feelings at all. In my stupidity and vanity, I simply said, "That girl isn't right for you. You deserve someone better, someone who is much better-looking. You should break up with her at once!"

I have regretted those words ever since. They were arbitrary, judgmental and despicable. I never even gave the girl a chance. At that moment, I behaved just like the father in Alexandre Dumas' novel *La Dame aux Camélias*, who sabotaged his own son's happy life. My harsh words must have been devastating to you.

"Dad, don't jump to conclusions!" you said. "You should get to know her first."

I said nothing more, but cancelled my plans to stay for another two days. We never did pick up a gift for the girl. And I took the train back home that night.

I must have broken your heart that day. I saw your sullen face when we said our goodbyes. "It's better to rip off the plaster quickly," I thought to myself. "Better to have a little pain now, rather than more in the future." So I basically made the decision for you.

When I got home I shared my feelings about the girl with your mum. "If you think she's not suitable for him," she said, "then that's that, I suppose." But you wouldn't leave it there. You called Mum and told her all the good things about the girl. You insisted on staying in the relationship and begged Mum to try to convince me. However, I stubbornly stuck to my guns and scolded you over the phone for persisting.

When you were next home for your summer vacation, you'd clearly lost a lot of weight due to the stress of it all. You secretly asked for your mum's permission to invite Xiaoyi to Beijing and meet your mum in order to get her support. Mum agreed, and Xiaoyi came to Beijing to visit our home. I had no idea she was coming, and even though I controlled my displeasure in front of her, I was cold and unenthusiastic during her visit. I couldn't believe you were being this stubborn!

Your mum liked the girl except for a slight concern about how thin she was. However I stood my ground and just hoped Xiaoyi would figure out my displeasure herself, based on my reaction. I didn't smile or laugh once during the girl's stay. She must have sensed my disinterest, and behaved with great caution. Meanwhile I was acting just like the parent of a large family in the old days, trying to arrange a marriage with no consideration given to your happiness.

I remember one Saturday morning I had arranged for you and the girl to visit an English language school in Zhongguancun. You were running late and we missed our appointment. I lost my temper and scolded you harshly in front of the taxi driver and Xiaoyi. I accused you of becoming distracted from your studies by trivial things; that you were behaving more like a playboy than a grown man; that you had lost your focus. Your mum tried to intervene and stop me making a fool of myself, but I persisted. Poor Xiaoyi was so shocked, and your face was pale with embarrassment and resentment.

I was venting my anger, with no consideration for your feelings or self-esteem. Maybe subconsciously I just wanted to undermine you in front of the girl so she would leave you. Remorse floods my heart every time I think of this. I sabotaged the love between you and split you up. I think that your depression over this episode may have weakened your immune system too, and contributed to your illness.

I didn't even leave it there. I asked relatives and friends to introduce you to other girls. I figured that if you met others, you'd realise that you could do better than Xiaoyi. Our relatives and families tried to tell you about other girls, but you weren't interested in meeting anyone else.

And so we found ourselves in deadlock. I was determined not to budge, assuming that in time you'd appreciate my intervention. You were impossibly torn between the girl and me. Eventually you chose me, decided to let go of your love, and were left with a broken heart.

I wasn't there when you saw your girlfriend off. I heard that you bought her gifts. You both cried. You insisted on buying her a computer afterwards to ease your pain. I didn't care about your pain at all; I was just happy with the outcome.

It was only a few years later that I realised the awful mistake I had made. I had lost a good daughter-in-law. I had created a turning point in your life, and deprived you of the opportunity to spend your life with the right one for you.

Only then, with painful introspection, did I fully understand my true motivation behind this: I simply wanted to you have a beautiful wife so that I would have a beautiful daughter-in-law to show off to others. I wanted others to be jealous, to pay us compliments: "Look at the Zhou family's beautiful new daughter-in-law!"

Ashamed though I am to admit it, between your happiness and my own vanity, I chose the latter. I always imagined that if I hadn't intervened, you would have had a wife by your side to lift your spirits and take care of you during your illness. Who knows, you may even have overcome death. I truly believe that. The old couples we visited are proof of that.

However, thanks to my cruel intervention, my son lost the person he loved, and was thoughtlessly and ruthlessly attacked by his father when what he really needed was comfort and compassion.

What kind of father would do something like that?

My stubborn tenacity in trying to break you up was despicable and contemptible. I have always praised love and freedom in my literature; but when it came to real life, I was the one who played the villainous saboteur of romance.

What on earth was wrong with me?

Dad, don't dwell on it – it's all in the past. When I fell in love with Xiaoyi in Xi'an, I wasn't interested in finding the best-looking woman I could find. In fact I preferred to marry an average-looking woman. I once read that average-looking women make the best wives. They are neither too proud nor self-important, and they value relationships with relatives. They are less likely to be coveted by other men, which helps to strengthen the family bonds. Without being too obsessed by their appearance, they place more emphasis on manners, charisma and knowledge, and are willing to keep improving themselves. They can avoid jealousy from other women, and their career path is smoother. I really did want to marry Xiaoyi; I only gave her up because you're my father and I didn't want to break your heart.

I believe that marriage is written in one's destiny. It's like an invisible hand that guides men and women from thousands of miles apart to meet, fall in love and get married. Meanwhile those who may live close to each other and have feelings for each other, are guided apart due to accidents of fate.

What are the odds? Is it all coincidence and accident? Perhaps this can explain one or two cases, or even a hundred cases; but how can it explain tens of thousands? People call it serendipity, but I believe it's an invisible hand that determines whether or not a couple ends up together. If they are fated to be together, they are pushed closer together. If not, they are pulled apart. So whether they end up together or not, it's the will of the invisible hand that decides, not the couple themselves.

To you it seemed that you caused my breakup with Xiaoyi. In fact, it was the invisible hand. To whom does that hand belong? I have no idea. But I'm certain it exists. And we should take comfort from knowing this.

7

S on, I know you were always tolerant, but I really wish you had expressed your real emotions more. But you never really protested nor put up a fight. And you couldn't elope with Xiaoyi because of your job in the military. All you could do was sulk and be miserable. I'm certain that was what harmed your body.

You became quite unwell after the breakup. You had a high fever and stumbled one day into the Health Centre at college. We only found out about it afterwards. You didn't want to bother us with it so never mentioned it. Every time we called and asked how you were, you always said, "Yes, good. I'm fine. Everything is going well."

I made another mistake right after this. I pushed you to apply to graduate school after your college graduation. But your body wasn't really up to it. You'd lost weight during your four years of college because no one was there to take care of you. Perhaps you should have started work straight away? A normal life and proper food may have made your body stronger and your immune system more robust.

Looking back, I wanted you to go to graduate school for two main reasons: first, for your future career – a master's degree would no doubt help your future job prospects. The second reason why I wanted you to go to graduate school, I'm sorry to say once again, was for my own vanity. I wanted that sense of pride that my son had a master's degree. I had no degree at all, so I just wanted you to achieve what I never had.

I remember well the time we sent you off to graduate school. In a dormitory for four people, only one of the top bunks was unoccupied when we arrived. The light was just above your bed, which you said would be convenient for reading at night. I also liked it because I knew you weren't keen on being in darkness. Later, though, I learned that the light ended up being on all the time because your roommates usually went to bed late. That meant you couldn't go to bed early, and you often fell asleep with the light on. As a result you only slept lightly, which no doubt disrupted the melatonin production in your body, a vital element to health. Another threat to your health developed here. I was so regretful. What if I hadn't sent you to graduate school?

Dad, please stop torturing yourself by connecting everything to my illness! In fact, I greatly appreciated my time at graduate school. Those three years were an important time for me, during which I learned all about the Central Plains area where I was born and raised. I knew so little of the history and cultural heritage of the region before.

During those three years I toured all over Zhengzhou. First I visited the ancient Shang Dynasty Ruins, back when Zhengzhou had been the capital of China. Next I went to the hometown of Huangdi, our ancestral home on the Yellow River thousands of years ago. Then I visited the Yellow River itself and learned about people's deep affection for that great river, despite the periodic catastrophic floods. Then I journeyed to Luoyang, where the Han Dynasty tombs, the Guanlin and Baima Temples, and the Longmen Grottoes displayed the glory of the Han and Tang Dynasties.

It turned out that the underdeveloped central area had a glorious history. I visited the town of Kaifeng, which housed the Dragon Pavilion, the DaXiangGuo temple, the Iron pagoda, the memorial temple for Baozhen, Pan Lake and Yang Lake, as well as the street of the Song Dynasty, whose prosperous city scene was depicted in *Along the River* at the Qingming Festival.

All good things come to an end sooner or later, however. Tragically, the city was eventually abandoned by the emperor due to war. The government moved south, along with the country's elite families. The cultural centre of the nation was shifted, a fundamental moment in history when Chinese culture started to expand in the south.

Later on I would visit Anyang, Zhoukou, Shangqiu and Xuchang, each place teaching me something about the Central Plains area. This is when I developed a genuine affection for our hometown. It may be less attractive than the coastal cities of today: the old aristocratic families have moved away and the people I saw there were far from fashionable; but still I learned the dignified glory of its history. I couldn't help but fall in love with our hometown.

Son, I lost my temper with you a few times while you were in graduate school, mainly because of your careless attitude towards money. You had little in the way of savings, although you were subsidised by your school. Sometimes your mum secretly gave you an extra allowance. Quite often I would give you a hard time when we spoke on the phone. It must have been humiliating for you. I'm so regretful now. We could afford it, so why didn't I give you more money? I wish I could spoil you now, but of course I cannot...

Dad, you're right. I was always reckless with money. I would spend all my subsidy and then I'd ask you and Mum for more. I just wasn't careful enough. My money always went on three things: first, dinner with my classmates. Our family was better off than those of most of my classmates, so I was overly generous and would often foot the bill; second, I bought some school books and some electronics. I always had the latest gadget to impress my classmates; and third, I would take my girlfriend on dates and buy her gifts. I had another girlfriend after Xiaoyi. She was good-looking, and you liked her. I often took her to dinner and sometimes I bought gifts to impress her.

I really didn't want to go through the hassle of dating lots of different girls. I took her as the 'one' and planned to marry her after graduation. I had never planned on saving for the future or giving some of my subsidy to you and Mum. I had never really thought about how hard you worked to support the family. I knew you could always write and get published. It was so easy in my eyes, until one day I saw a cheque for 120 *yuan* that had been sent to our home. I was surprised and asked you why it was so small. You said it was the right amount for an essay.

"How long does it take you to write an essay?" I asked.

"A day or two," you replied. I was astounded. I had no idea it took so much effort to make a living.

I knew you didn't care about the money. What you cared about was making me smart about money and finance.

8

S on, you have no idea how thrilled I was at your graduation, especially since you already had a job lined up. I was so relieved; you could finally live on your own and make your own contribution to our family and to the nation. Finally I could take a rest.

I remember the night before you started work, we had a celebration at home. Your mum made a whole table of different dishes, and I opened a bottle of wine. I made a toast: "To Zhou Ning's first day of work! Cheers!"

It was a big day for the family because it finally marked the end of your education. You made a toast to your mum and me. "Mum, after all these hard years, Dad and I are going to give you a good life." Your mum's tears fell into her glass.

I was ready to retire from being a parent. I told your mum the next day, "From now on, all the household responsibilities are on Ning's shoulders, including carrying heavy things, shopping for electronics, making five-year plans for the family, taking out the garbage, and picking things up from the mail office. Please don't send me on those errands any more!"

Your mum smiled. "Look at you, so dependent on your son already!"

I also decided to hand over the family finances to you, so I could avoid making trips to the bank or doing research on new investments. I was happy to leave all those matters to you.

What I didn't expect was the fate the Creator had written for our family. How could I have known?

Dad, working in the Military General Logistics Department was a big step for me. I think I was even more excited than you and Mum! On my first day, I reminded myself that this was an important new chapter in my life, and I wanted to get off to a good start: first, I should be responsible and avoid making silly mistakes; second, I should be proactive and make sensible suggestions, so I could be ready to take on more important tasks; and third, I should get involved in research projects so I can achieve some accomplishments in the field.

I also made an exercise plan: running five laps in the morning, thirty push-ups in the afternoon, and forty minutes of basketball after dinner.

Above all, I wanted to work hard and make you proud of me. I knew I was the one with the highest level of education in our family. But, like you, I had no idea that life had an even bigger test in store for me.

It was as though the wind was howling all around us, but no one heard a sound. And so none of us any reason to be alarmed.

Until it happened.

9

NING, THAT DAY, 28 September 2005, is forever seared into my memory. I remember thinking it was one of the finest days we'd seen in Beijing that year. This ancient city always looks its magnificent best during the autumn, and that year the feeling was heightened by the suspension of construction work that had been in full swing ahead of the 2008 Olympic Games. As a result, the ever-present air pollution had diminished, and some rain a few days before had removed most of the dust, leaving the sky clear and bright. Nothing else disturbed the brilliant blueness of the sky except the faint remains of a few vapour trails far away, left by fighter jets on training exercises.

The windless air was still and silent. Birds frolicked all over the barracks, singing and soaring high into the sky before diving like kites with broken lines, then floating to the peaks of the poplar, locust or walnut trees. Along that whole section of Chang'an Avenue, our barracks proudly stood out as having the most trees and the best-manicured gardens. It created an idyllic sanctuary that was home to numerous birds and just as many of their songs.

Aside from the glorious weather, I was also in high spirits that day because before you left for work, you told me you had finished the first important task your boss had assigned to you: a scientific research report that had taken you most of the past two days and nights. It was clear that you were taking your job seriously, and it made me a proud and happy father to see that you had grown into such a capable young man.

It wouldn't be long, I thought to myself, before you and your girlfriend got married, and my role as a parent would come to an end. Then I would finally be able to write my novel and wait for the arrival of grandchildren to dote on and play with in my twilight years.

I was also happy that day because I had asked for some time off from work so that I could take you and your mum to visit your grandparents in Henan. I'd already phoned them to make the arrangements. I'd always been so busy with work during your school years, and it had been years since the three of us had visited my hometown together. Now we could finally return home for a family reunion with your grandparents on the National Day holiday. What could be better? How could I not be filled with joy?

Unfortunately our Creator doesn't always allow our plans to play out how we hope they will. He likes to make clear from time to time that it's He and He alone who writes our life plan and controls our destiny. He also has a habit of revealing His presence at the most unexpected moments. It wasn't until 28 September 2005 that I truly understood this.

That afternoon, you went with a colleague to watch a National Day celebration performance in the barracks auditorium. Your mum was at work, as usual, and I went to the barber's shop to get a haircut before our trip. So there I sat, in the barber's shop, quietly reading the newspaper as I waited my turn. As I sat there, I couldn't possibly have known that destiny would soon unfold to reveal the Creator's cruel hand.

The prelude to any tragedy is rather reminiscent of a battle: it is quiet, with no obvious sign of anything untoward or unusual.

My phone rang. *Unknown Number.* I almost ignored it. There was only one more person ahead of me in the queue for the barber's chair and I didn't want to miss my turn. But since I was in such a good mood I answered it in high spirits.

"Hello?"

"Director Zhou? I'm a colleague of your son Zhou Ning. I'm sorry to have to tell you this, but he passed out during the show. We've just taken him to the outpatients department at the hospital. Please come straight away!"

I was flustered and panicked, unable to believe what I'd just heard. How was this possible? My son was only twenty-six years old, in his prime. He was an athlete, a basketball player! He was fine when he left for work this morning. How could he suddenly have passed out? Could there have been some mistake?

I didn't hang around as these thoughts raced through my mind. I just got up and bolted out of the barber's shop. I needed to find out what had happened to you. It was only about three hundred metres to the hospital. I ran there in what seemed like a single breath and burst into the emergency room. My worst fears were confirmed: it was indeed you, lying there.

A medical team surrounded your bed, giving you emergency treatment. My heart was in my mouth. "He's waking up," said one of the doctors. Thank goodness! I pushed my way through to your bed, looked at your pale face and met your eyes as they slowly opened.

"Son, what happened?" I asked. "Are you in any pain?"

"Dad, I've no idea what happened," you replied weakly. One of your colleagues who had carried you to the hospital explained what had happened.

"We were watching the show in the auditorium. Zhou Ning was sitting next to me. The speakers were loud and the bright lights swirled around. I heard a sudden gasp from Zhou Ning. I turned to him and saw that his eyes were closed. His body was convulsing and sliding down the seat. I had to move quickly to catch him."

Just then your mother rushed into the room. Seeing that you were awake, she grabbed your hands. "Zhou Ning, you scared your poor mother to death!"

I asked the doctor what could have caused you to pass out. He couldn't be sure; it might have been the stress of work, or possibly some problem with your brain. The only way to find out was to go to a larger hospital for further examination.

I quickly convinced myself that it must have been due to your heavy workload. For two days you had stayed up day and night, sat in front of your computer as you completed your science report. You certainly didn't get enough rest, and you barely ate. Your mother agreed with me, so we took you home, made you lie down for some rest, and prepared a meal to help start your recovery.

You slept well that night. Your mum and I were relieved, though we agreed to take you for a thorough check-up the next day, just to be safe. After you fell asleep, your mum and I started to pack our things for our visit to our hometown.

We couldn't have known it at the time, but the curtain had just risen on the first act of a three-year tragedy, and the director was waiting for the leading characters – you, your mum, and me – to take the stage.

Dad, I was also in a good mood that day. I'd just finished the work project my leader had assigned to me, so I felt a huge sense of relief. Our itinerary for the trip to our hometown was sorted, and soon I'd be able to see Grandma and Grandpa. I also planned to see my girlfriend during the trip.

Everything was so perfect. Before going to the auditorium to watch the show, I detected no sign of the tragedy which had been waiting, lying there hidden within my otherwise happy life.

In the auditorium, I suddenly became uncomfortable. What was the matter? I thought perhaps it was the low temperature. I was really fidgety. Why on earth would I be so restless? This was a show I should be enjoying! I tried to ignore my discomfort, but it was clearly the first sign of distress coming from my body.

On went the show, one performance after another. Applause and laughter came in waves, and all the while I felt worse and worse, the room humid, the lights blazing, the air suffocating. I needed to get out.

Before I stood up, a dazzling blue laser light shot out from the stage. Of course it was only a theatrical effect, but somehow I felt like it hit me straight in the head. Then *bang*. I have no memory after that.

Next thing I knew, I woke up in the hospital. *Why am I here?* I wondered. As I came round I remembered the show, and I seemed to visit a dark, silent place far away. Then I heard your voice and saw your face. I realised I'd blacked out and was in the emergency room in the hospital. Then I saw Mum, looking terrified, with a string of questions: "Son, what's the matter? How do you feel?"

When I first woke up, I felt so weak I couldn't even raise my arms. My strength returned after a while, and my hands and feet warmed up. Later on, you and Mum went home. Before long I felt completely better, back to normal again. I thought the same as you, that this was all because of the long hours I'd spent preparing that report for work. Surely I would be fine after some rest. I had no idea that this was only the start of the calamity.

The countdown on my life had just started.

Son, after breakfast the next day we took you to hospital to get a CT scan of your brain. The scan indicated that everything was normal, and that it had probably just been due to the exhaustion of the previous few days.

We were all so relieved and happy to be told that there was nothing seriously wrong with you. After the scan, I sent you and your mum home, then I went to talk to a senior doctor in the neurology department with a friend who worked there.

The doctor gave me some comfort before I showed him your CT scan. "I'm sure everything will be fine," he told me. "Zhou Ning is young and strong. He can walk and talk perfectly well, and has no resemblance to a sick patient." Naturally, I believed him.

I had interviewed this neurology specialist two years earlier when I'd written an article about him. He had studied at Hokkaido Medical School in Japan and specialised in brain disease.

I showed him a copy of your scan. He studied it for quite some time then looked at me seriously. "Who is the patient?" he asked.

My chest tightened. "My son...it's my son. What can you see?"

"I'm afraid it doesn't look so good," he said, his eyes fixed on the scan.

A chill ran through me and my throat had tightened. "What doesn't look good?"

"It looks like it might be a glioma," he said, pointing to a small shadow on the scan. "A brain tumour."

"Glioma?" My heart sank as the doctor's words hit me. I had heard the word before. A few years earlier a friend's daughter had been diagnosed with one in Nanyang and went to Tiantan Hospital for surgery, where I visited them. It was cancer.

Oh my God! Oh my God! Was this real? The shock of the news hit me almost physically, and my legs began to shake as I struggled to support my weight. I leaned backwards and reached out to support myself with the wall.

"Based on my experience, I'm almost certain of it." I couldn't doubt him; he was an expert in the field.

"But how? What could have caused this? There's no history of this in the family!"

"There's no way to be sure. It may be related to past trauma, possibly radioactive exposure or certain drugs, maybe even stress that has weakened his immune system. Or it might just be genetics. The probability of this occurring in a young male is about one in a hundred thousand."

Oh my God, your condition was one in a hundred thousand!

"What should we do?"

"Take him into hospital immediately. He may faint again due to the build-up of pressure in his brain. An MRI scan should help us to determine the size of the tumour, and from there we can discuss the best treatment."

I was in a blind panic, my mind racing. "OK, OK, we'll go to the hospital."

My friend went to deal with the hospital administration while I went over to the staircase, leaned against the wall, covered my face with my hands, and sobbed. Good Lord, why this fate? Why take my son away? He's my only child. How could you?

I don't know why, but in that moment of despair I suddenly remembered a fortune teller I'd visited in 1993. In the spring of that year, I had gone with a friend to visit Guanlin Temple in Henan Province. Inside the gate, a fortune teller had put up a stand there and had attracted quite a crowd of tourists.

My friend was interested and asked for a reading. I don't remember the details of it, but just as were about to leave, the fortune teller stopped us. "Why doesn't your friend have his future revealed?" he asked, gesturing towards me.

I shook my head. "No, thank you. I'd prefer not to know my fate in advance."

The fortune teller wasn't easily deterred. "Try it once," he offered. "If you're your future is ominous, there's no need to pay. And if it's auspicious, you can give whatever you want."

Now my friend joined in too. "Come on, he's so enthusiastic. Whether you believe in it or not, it can't do any harm to try it."

I didn't want to create a scene or embarrass anyone, so I went along with it. After telling him my birth date, the fortune teller looked at me pensively, before saying, "Your misfortune lies in the direction of the North and the West. It would be wise for you to avoid travelling in those two directions. If they cannot be avoided, then you'd better ask someone to prevent any bad things from happening to you."

Of course I didn't believe his warning. I smiled politely, put a little money on the stand, then walked away. My friend pulled me aside.

"How can this fate be avoided?" he asked the fortune teller.

"It's quite simple," the fortune teller replied. "On a night with no moon, find a crossroad junction near your home. Light three incense sticks in the direction of the North and also the West; burn sacrificial paper, kowtow three times to each direction, and chant, 'To all gods, please bless me.' That's all."

"You should do what he says," my friend suggested. I smiled again and put it all to the back of my mind as we left.

Long afterwards, we moved from Nanyang to Beijing, which of course was to the North. Did our relocation violate the fortune teller's prophesy and offend the gods?

Why did I never follow the fortune teller's instructions? It wouldn't have taken much. Is that why our family was struck by tragedy? Perhaps the Lord had sent the fortune teller to give me a sign. Why didn't I trust him? Why was I so dismissive?

After registering you at the hospital, I washed my face then tried to compose myself before going home. "There was no problem with the CT scan," I lied to you and your mum. "But the doctor suggested you stay in hospital for a while, just in case you faint again". I couldn't bring myself to tell you the truth. Your mum couldn't have handled the devastating blow. You were so young, and she just wouldn't have been able to deal with it.

So what did I do? I classified it 'top secret' and buried it in my heart.

"But now we won't be able to go to our hometown for the holiday," you protested, still thinking about visiting your grandparents.

"No, we won't, at least not yet," I replied. "There'll be plenty of opportunity for that after you've fully recovered."

"Please call Mum and Dad and tell them we won't be going this holiday," your mum told me. "Call Xiaoyun too, and tell her that Ning won't be able to visit her for the time being."

Xiaoyun was your girlfriend, and you were looking forward to seeing her. I nodded and made the calls. Your grandparents were looking forward to seeing us and were disappointed by our change of plans. I didn't want them to worry about you, so I told them it was because of your work commitments. "Yes, of course, work must take priority," they said. "Take care of work first, then come home when you're able to."

After you and your mum fell asleep, I started doing some research into possible treatment plans for you. I also needed to think about how to break the news to you both. The terrifying thought of potentially losing you made me cry again in bed, under the duvet. I realised then that I couldn't share this with anyone; not your grandparents, not your mum, not even you. Our relatives and friends had their own lives to lead, and there was nothing that anyone could do to help the situation. I would shoulder the burden alone.

The next day I started to consult with the doctors. The medical team recommended surgery and chemotherapy as the only viable course of action. Chinese medicine had little effect on malignant tumours, especially when the brain and blood vessels blocked the effects of Chinese medicine. If it worked at all, any effect would be minimal and incapable of preventing the tumour's development. I agreed that surgery was the way forward.

While you were in the hospital, you had further bouts of nausea and headaches. I knew it was the tumour. But I asked the medical staff not to share the truth with you. I couldn't bear the thought of how it would crush you and Mum.

The MRI scan determined the size of the tumour. The senior doctor told me it was malignant, but still early stage – the perfect time for surgery. I resolved that we should proceed with the surgery without delay.

After taking the decision to proceed with surgery, I consulted with my friend about which hospital we should choose for the procedure. Ordinarily, we would have gone to Tiantan Hospital, which specialised in brain disease and had the most experienced doctors. However, I vetoed that option because I had a friend whose daughter had died there after surgery on a similar kind of tumour. I was terrified that the same might happen to us. I soon chose the hospital you would go to, and of course I would insist on the best doctor in their neurology department.

In retrospect, I rushed into making that decision. A specialised hospital would have been much better. I never should have refused Tiantan Hospital just because of one patient's death. Even within the same hospital, not all doctors are the same, and nor are their patients.

As I was busy arranging the details of your surgery, your girlfriend came to visit you with her mother. How could I be in the mood for guests? But since they had come, how could I get out of it? I already realised that your relationship with Xiaoyun was unlikely to go much further. I really wanted to explain everything to them, but I was worried that Xiaoyun wouldn't be able to conceal it from you. She would surely spill the news, alerting you to your situation and possibly making your situation even worse. How could you handle the surgery if you were emotionally devastated on top of everything else? Upon reflection, I decided I would tell them the truth only after the surgery, once you'd made it through.

Since it was so close to the National Day holiday, the date for your surgery was set for the ninth of October, the second working day after the holiday.

Xiaoyun and her mum stayed in Beijing for a few days, and meanwhile I consulted busily with doctors and friends about your surgery and subsequent recovery. I spent hours researching this type of cancer online and also in books. I was also able to force a smile from time to time as we hosted Xiaoyun and her mother.

Mum didn't know the real situation, of course. She thought you were fine, so she put all her focus on Xiaoyun and her mother. She insisted on putting fresh flowers in Xiaoyun's room every day and asked me to drive them around to tour the countryside. How could I get excited about that? But in order to hide your condition from Xiaoyun and not cause any problems, I bit my tongue and did as your mum had asked. As I drove them around, though, I thought only of you. Horrifying possibilities flashed through my mind. I was so preoccupied as I drove, it was a miracle that the tour passed without incident, never mind the fact that I had only recently learned how to drive! Every time I thought about it, the fear still lingered in my heart and in the pit of my stomach.

After Xiaoyun left with her mother, I told Mum about your surgery. At first, I told her you had a benign tumour in your brain which needed to be removed. She was shocked. "But you said there was no problem," she cried. "Why does he need surgery?"

"There's no major problem," I said as I tried to keep her calm. "Just a small one. But we should be cautious and remove the tumour, even though it's benign. It's a routine operation, so don't worry."

"Make sure you ask for the best doctor," your mum insisted.

I nodded and assured her that I'd met with the most senior doctor in the hospital, and that he'd agreed to perform the surgery.

After talking with your mum, I started to think about how to break the news to you. You still had no inkling about any of this and were planning to go back home in a few days. How could I tell you the truth without devastating you? It took me some time to figure it out. I sat by your bed and started to explain.

"Ning, you fainted a few days ago because you were so exhausted. But when they ran some tests, the doctors also found something in your brain."

"What?" You stared at me, wide-eyed.

"A benign tumour."

"How big?"

"Don't worry, it's small."

"Do I need surgery?"

"It's not essential, but if you don't have surgery, they're worried it may cause you to faint again in the future."

"Surgery, then," you said decisively. "To get rid of it for good."

"That's my boy," I replied, relieved. "I knew you'd be brave about this."

I transferred you to the neurosurgical ward that afternoon, where you shared a room with an old man who was waiting for a similar surgery to yours. The man was from the Northeast. He couldn't see anything, but he was very upbeat. After hearing that you were also due for brain surgery, he comforted you by pointing out the scars on his head. "This hospital performs brain surgery all the time," he told you. "They manage them easily. Look at me, I've gone through it twice already and I'm about to have a third. I never take it too seriously. I just fall asleep in the operating theatre, and then it's done."

His words appeared to comfort you, and I think relieved some of your fear. "Yes, that sounds like good advice," you replied. "I'll try to relax."

I think you were as psychologically prepared as you could have been. I'd planned to tell your mum the truth after the surgery. However, it didn't work out that way. The surgeon needed a parent's signature for the paperwork. As it happened, I'd gone to escort out some of your colleagues who had come to visit you, and so your mum was asked into the doctor's room. The surgeon assumed Mum knew about your disease and spoke to her accordingly. "This is cancer," he said bluntly. "The surgery cannot guarantee to remove it once for all. He may relapse after..." Your poor mother blacked out before the doctor even finished his sentence.

I was called urgently into the surgeon's office. Your mum was lying on the floor, pale and drawn. After hearing what had happened, I was absolutely furious. "Didn't I tell you that I would sign the paper?" I yelled. "Why the urgency? Couldn't you have waited for me to come and do this? What if something serious had happened to my wife?" Fortunately, Mum came round after some help from the doctors. She clung to me and wept. Tears streamed down her face. I tried to calm her down.

"You can't cry now. Our son is going to have his surgery tomorrow. We're so close to his room. What will he think if he hears you crying? Do you really want to put this burden on him, too? Our priority has to be to send him into the surgery as relaxed as possible."

Your mum stopped sobbing and walked out of the doctor's office. She went into the bathroom and washed the tears from her face before going back to your room. Your head had been shaved, in preparation for the surgery. Seeing your mum's red eyes, you knew she'd been crying. "Mum, please don't worry," you comforted her. Everything will be fine!"

Mum didn't say a word. She just patted your shoulder and trembled as her tears fell to the floor.

Dad, I saw the gloom in your eyes before the surgery. Mum's eyes were red. I knew she'd been crying, but I didn't expect this to be so serious. I thought you were just worried about the surgery. I told myself that brain surgery was fairly common, and that I was still young. Surely it shouldn't be so difficult for me to come through this? The words of encouragement from the old man who shared my ward also comforted me. If he was still upbeat and optimistic after two brain surgeries, why should I panic and freak out before I've had even one?

I tried to sleep early that night, but I had a restless night. For the first time, self-pity crept in. Why did this have to happen to me right after my graduation?

As I was wheeled into the operating theatre the following morning, I was truly afraid. What if the surgery failed? After all, it was brain surgery. But you and Mum calmed me down. You said you would never put me through something dangerous, and you told me to try to stay calm. I composed myself, and went to sleep under the anaesthetic as the nurses' words faded away.

Son, I'd never experienced surgery being performed on a loved one. I was jittery too. But in the morning, your mum and I agreed to hide all our signs of worry from you. For your sake, we had to appear confident that everything would be fine. You hadn't sleep well, but you looked good. We helped the nurses prepare you for surgery, and we held your hand and walked with you as they wheeled you into the operating theatre. Your mum and I tried to force a smile as we waved goodbye to you. But after the lift doors closed, our smiles faded to reveal our true worry and pain

We hurried to the waiting room, which was one floor down. A telephone connected it to the operating theatre and a nurse attended it, from time to time relaying messages from the operating theatre. Your mum and I could do nothing but sit there helplessly, our eyes fixed on the nurse and the phone.

Crushing fear and anxiety churned inside of me as we waited. This was, after all, brain surgery! Any slight mistake by any one of the medical team might have serious consequences. What if they couldn't completely remove the tumour? I felt my heart throbbing as if in my throat. Mum was beside herself with worry too. She sat there, quietly chanting to herself with her eyes closed.

I needed to distract myself, or else I wouldn't be able to make it through the wait. How could I occupy myself? I settled on contemplating the origin of your illness. It must have been because of my marriage to your mother. If we hadn't got married, you would never have been born, and you wouldn't be suffering like this. I remembered how strongly your mum's father had been opposed to our marriage. I'd always thought it was because I was from a poor family and that he believed I held a grudge against him. Maybe your grandfather was right. Was it possible that he sensed something ominous would befall our marriage? That we would go on to have a sick child?

Your grandfather had passed away by then, so I couldn't ask him for answers. But if your mum and I had followed his instruction to remain just friends, we may each have started our own families and spared everyone from all this pain. It's a pity that we couldn't start all over again, as if life was a simple game of table tennis. We could start a new game, not get married, return to our youth with a new life; a different path, a path which didn't involve any surgery for you, nor any pain for your mum and me.

"Is Xiao Jiayue's family here?" The nurse's voice interrupted my train of thought. "Xiao Jiayue's surgery has just finished. Family members, if you'd like, you can come and see the tumour that has been removed." I rushed over to the nurse, who stared at me. "Are you Xiao Jiayue's family?" I then realised that she hadn't called for me, as Xiao's family came over. The nurse showed them a glass that contained some mushy, bloody tissue inside.

"Was that removed from his lung?" asked one of Xiao's family.

"Yes, please go upstairs. He'll be out soon."

I sunk back into my seat, the image of that bloody extraction still on my mind. The human body is a precision machine. And just like any complex machine, the failure of any single part can affect the entire operation and cause any number of problems. How knowledgeable the Creator is, to be able to build such a perfect and precise machine.

But maybe, I thought to myself, He could have installed zips on the stomach and head, from which any damaged parts could be removed by the patient himself, or through which antibiotics or other treatment could be administered. Then there would be no need for hospitals to train surgeons in neurosurgery or thoracic surgery, which would in turn save enormous time and money, and reduce the risk of surgery.

"Is Zhou Ning's family here?" The nurse's voice brought me out of my daydream. Your mum and I jumped out of our seats and we both ran over to her.

"Zhou Ning's surgery has just finished. He'll be going to the intensive care unit now. You should both go up to wait by the lift."

"Is there a tumour we can see? We saw the other patients had one."

"Glioma are shapeless. They didn't send it down, in order to spare you the worry."

I nodded and led your mum away. At the lift to the ICU, we saw you, still under anaesthetic, your head wrapped in bandages. Your mum and I each took one side of the hospital bed and looked at you. The doctors informed us that the surgery had been successful. They had completely removed the tumour, you had only light bleeding that didn't require a transfusion, and your recovery looked very promising.

Your mum and I looked at other each, and a wave of relief flowed over us. God, thank you for blessing my son and bringing him through.

Dad, after the anaesthetic wore off and I woke up, I was so thrilled to find myself still alive. But the elation soon passed as I realised I was in immense pain. I desperately wanted to touch my head but I found both my hands strapped to the bed. The doctors clearly knew I would try to scratch my head. I called out in frustration. The nurse realised I was awake and came over.

You followed the doctors to check on me in the ICU. I wanted to transfer to the general ward because the ICU was such a painful experience, and I hated being alone in such acute pain.

The most agonising two experiences for me post-surgery were, firstly, peeing. I had a catheter inserted, and every time I peed was like torture. I tried to endure the discomfort until my belly felt distended. Then, each time I peed, my clothes would be soaked with sweat from the pain.

The second was the intravenous drip. I was never fond of the IV, but this treatment was especially horrible. Each drop of the liquid made my internal organs twist and writhe. It's difficult to describe, but it was like a combination of pain, horror, distress and nausea. It was worse than death. I groaned, tossing and turning, for the whole night with that fluid trickling inside of me. You watched me the whole night. I still had no idea what was being put into my body. When I learned the truth about my illness, I figured it must be something to kill cancer cells, with horrible and painful side effects.

I learned two important lessons from my surgery: most importantly, that even though many things in this world are precious, the most valuable treasure of all is our own body; to be healthy frees us from pain. Second, the torment of disease affects not just one person but the entire family. If we love our families, we should do everything we can to look after ourselves.

Son, that night you spent in intensive care, no family members were allowed in the hospital, so your mother and I went home. It was the first time I slept through a whole night since you'd been diagnosed with the disease.

The doctor told us we could see you briefly at ten o'clock the next morning. I went early to wait outside the ICU. I couldn't stop myself staring at the sluggish second hand on my watch. At ten o'clock, the doctor appeared and we followed him to the ICU. You were the only patient in there that day. You were wide awake, able to talk as well as move your hands and feet. I was relieved that the surgery hadn't damaged your nerves or caused any paralysis. The doctor left after he'd checked you over.

I asked you how you felt. "Dad, please get me out of here," you whispered quietly. "This catheter is so painful! And I can't move with my hands and legs strapped to the bed."

I told you that it was necessary to use the catheter, that you just had to try to deal with it. And strapping your hands down was just to prevent you from touching your head. You nodded helplessly, "OK, OK. I'll put up with it."

The pathology test results came back. You were between the first and second stages. It was still quite early, but it was definitely cancer.

The following day you were transferred to the public ward. You had recovered well, but your mum and I struggled to lift our spirits. This was just a temporary victory over the cancer. It could return at any time. We didn't have the power to cure cancer.

You started chemotherapy the night you were transferred to the ward. The chemotherapy drug had been imported from Japan. It was dispensed from a giant black bottle which hung there ominously, projecting an air of horror. You were surprised by this bottle covered in black tape since you only had seen crystal clear IV drip bottles before.

"What is that?" you asked.

I tried to sound as relaxed as possible. "It's medicine to supply you with energy."

You nodded. "It looks strange."

I knew very little about chemotherapy at that time, and I never anticipated the misery it would put you through. After only about five minutes, you started to yell, telling us how uncomfortable you were. When I asked you to describe it, you told me that every part of your body was uncomfortable and agitated. I thought something was wrong, so I hurried to fetch a doctor. The doctor told me it was quite normal to feel like this, and that it happened to everyone. They made the drip slower to lessen the pain. The bottle would last a night, and I spent almost the whole of that night with you. You asked me to help you sit up, then lie down; to rub your back and then your chest; to position you on your side, then onto your back. It was so difficult to watch your agony.

At last, you couldn't take any more. "I feel so bad, Dad," you groaned. "I just want to die. Can you please beg the doctor to stop this?"

I tried to hide my broken heart. "Son," I told you, "the doctor says this is the best medicine. Please try to hang in there. You're a strong man, you can handle this! Your mum and I have faith in you."

You just bit your lip. "Yes, OK I'll try to hang in there."

That night was a real challenge for me, to watch my son fighting the pain alone. There was nothing I could do except wipe the sweat from your forehead and pace back and forth around your bed.

By dawn, the IV bottle was empty and your clothes were soaked in sweat. I wanted to feed you something, but another side effect of the chemotherapy was that it made you nauseous, with no appetite. You managed only a few bites. That awful night lingered in my mind and influenced my decisions for your later treatment. It was another huge mistake that I made.

At that time, I thought that was the worst possible night we could ever suffer. How could I have known that a thousand nights like this or worse awaited us?

Later on, I came to believe that we should never think of a particular period in our life as the worst. It sends the wrong signal to the Creator; it suggests that we are complaining, and that will just elicit even greater horrors in return. The Creator is always able to make His point...

Dad, it's very difficult to truly appreciate what something feels like, if you don't go through it yourself. No matter how detailed the description from others, it's only when you experience it yourself that you see the full picture.

I had heard about brain surgery before. And the old man from Liaoning also told me about his surgery the night before mine, but now I truly understand what brain surgery is like because of that horrifying ordeal.

The brain is the most important part of the body. Just a single tiny error in the surgery can leave you permanently disabled. It can remove your ability to speak, or leave you brain-damaged. In many ways, brain surgery is like a rehearsal of death.

The surgery really affected poor Mum. And after everything you had done for me through my childhood and throughout my education, I graduated then repaid you with this! How terrible that was...

10

S on, someone we knew told us a story about one of her neighbours. This neighbour had had the same cancer as you, at a similar age, and had survived after undergoing surgery, radiotherapy, chemotherapy and some Chinese medicine. He was now about fifty years old, twenty-eight years after his surgery. Your mum and I decided we'd go and pay him a visit, so that we could listen to his story, hear about his recovery and then share his experiences with you.

We went to visit our acquaintance one night after dinner. She had also invited the patient's wife to come. The woman was nice, talented too. She told us how she and her husband had both studied at Peking University. Her husband was very academic and had the top scores in his class, in addition to being a leading figure within student politics.

The couple fell in love. Her husband was selected by the Chinese Academy of Science to go to America for further training before graduation. But right around that time, he started to experience headaches. He was quickly diagnosed with a brain tumour. She was devastated, and to make it slightly less crushing, she told her husband about the tumour, but not the exact type he had.

After his parents learned the truth, they lost hope because of their financial situation. She was the only one there to help, and so in order to look after him she married him, in spite of her own family's objections.

And so, as his wife she went with him through the surgery, radiotherapy and chemotherapy. She also found many ways help him to exercise. In the end, she saved him from death. The couple never had children because of her single-minded dedication to her husband.

Your mum and I cried as we listened to her story. But before we met her husband, she urged us not to mention the cancer in front of him. She had hidden the truth from him for so many years and intended to keep doing so. Of course, your mum and I agreed. Then we talked to her husband for a while. He had a very positive outlook on life as he described his treatment and showed us his exercises.

Your mum and I were deeply touched by this couple's experience of fighting cancer. That man was blessed to have such a good and kind wife. We had nothing but respect for her sacrifices. She really was an extraordinary woman.

Dad, I recovered well after my surgery, but I became very aware of the deeply troubled looks on both your faces. I remember being confused; the surgery had been successful, so why were you both so concerned? Then I thought I figured it out: you were worried about my relationship with Xiaoyun.

I was surprised that Xiaoyun didn't come to see me until I left the hospital. I called her at home and felt she was distant. I thought that's what was worrying you. I had no idea it was actually my life you were concerned about.

Our relationship quickly cooled off. The change in Xiaoyun revealed to me for the first time the mystery of relationships. Love needs to be anchored to something. Left alone, it can simply drift away. Most relationships cannot survive a disaster, especially one that takes such a toll on your body, your emotions, and eventually your love. The way I see it, if the body is crushed, then the love has nothing to attach itself to.

There is such a thing as pure, abiding love. It's rare, though, and I wasn't lucky enough to experience it. The reality of this was cruel to me. What I needed after the surgery was the comfort of love, not the harsh reality; but that's was what I got. I tried to let it go and convince myself it was understandable that her parents weren't allowing her to see me due to concerns over my health.

But deep in my heart I didn't let it go. I just couldn't...

Son, nine days after your surgery, you came home from the hospital. Your mum and I felt little relief, though. We immediately started to look for traditional Chinese doctors to help you to recuperate and get rid of the cancer cells once and for all. After you started the course of Chinese medicine, it dawned on us to call your girlfriend and tell her the truth. We didn't expect her to come and sit by your side through this difficult time, but we hoped she might at least still call you sometimes as a friend, to encourage you. We didn't know that she had already learned the truth and was upset and angry with us for hiding it from her. That's why she decided to break things off with you.

We couldn't say anything to you about this. All we could do was try to comfort you and hope you'd let it go. However, you didn't. How could you, after so many things had happened to you in such a short time? You still thought you would marry her. You were only twenty-six, full of hopes and dreams for the future, but all that awaited you now was the bleak reality. It made sense that you couldn't handle it. You were crushed. In desperation, you said, "Dad, Mum, why am I living such a miserable life? Why am I still alive? I should die." You really scared us.

Your mum wanted to beg Xiaoyun to support you during this critical time. I stopped her. Whether you would be able to pull through this period depended entirely on you.

We tried to console you. "There are plenty of nice girls out there," we said. "After you get better, we'll try to find you a new girlfriend."

"But I don't want anyone else," you replied.

We tried to talk you round. "Many years ago," I said, "when the Russian author Aleksandr Solzhenitsyn was imprisoned for anti-Soviet propaganda, his beautiful wife left him. But after he was released, they got back together. So you see? When you're fully recovered, your girlfriend may come back."

"I am not Aleksandr Solzhenitsyn. I can't become him."

"We know you lost your girlfriend, but how many people lost their home or their family because of trumped-up political charges? They survived. Is your loss any bigger than theirs?"

You were silent. "You're our only child," I continued. "Your grandparents' eldest grandchild. The four of us are counting on you to take care of us, and yet you intend to end your life for a woman? What kind of man are you?"

You sighed, taken aback. "Give me some time," you said. "I will let it go. I'll get over it."

Your mum and I were relieved, for the time being at least.

Later, you needed radiotherapy to kill the remaining cancer cells. We told you it was only a precautionary measure, but we were concerned that you would put two and two together since it was common knowledge that radiotherapy was a common cancer treatment. You believed us, though, probably because you had never known us lie to you before.

We had a choice of where to have the radiotherapy. We could either do it at the original hospital, or else at a specialist cancer treatment centre. This one had more experience in dealing with cancer, but was much further from our home. We thought about it for a while and decided on the original hospital. Years later, I suspected this was another bad decision, and that we should have gone to the specialist cancer centre.

The side effects were serious: your hair fell out, your appetite disappeared, and waves of nausea battered you relentlessly. Every morning, your mum's eyes welled up as we saw the wisps of hair on your pillow. You tried to comfort her by telling her that your hair would grow back after you recovered.

In those days, of course, you were dealing not only with the physical side effects, but also a broken heart. You often gazed at your girlfriend's picture after the nausea hit, and your mum and I would give you some space to be alone. In all, the treatment, including the time between radiotherapy sessions, took more than two months. Then, as it finally came to an end, one morning you put away all the pictures of your girlfriend and told us you would move on. You wouldn't let it destroy your mind and soul anymore.

We felt slightly better after hearing this. You'd made it through another challenge.

A few nights later, you suddenly brought it up while I was helping you to wash your feet. "Dad, guess who I called today?"

"Who?" I asked, smiling.

"My first girlfriend, Xiaoyi in Xi'an."

My smile froze in shock. I'd heard that she had recently got married.

"Can you guess what we talked about?"

"I've no idea," I replied. I still felt guilty about breaking the two of you up. In fact, I felt uncomfortable every time I heard Xiaoyi's name.

"I asked her, 'If we had stayed together and I became seriously ill, would you have left me?'"

"And what did she say?" I asked. I felt I had no choice but to continue the conversation.

"She said, 'There's no way I would have left you. If you abandon a friend in sickness, how can that be called friendship? Never mind the love between a couple. Of course you know my answer. Why do you ask? Is something wrong?'"

"What did you tell her?" I asked.

"I said, 'Yes, you could say that.'"

"Then what did she say?"

"She asked me if she needed to come and visit me. If so, she would leave immediately."

"What about her husband? Would he allow her to come?"

"I asked her the same question," you replied, staring at the ceiling. "She said she would divorce him if he tried to stop her."

I felt a sharp stabbing pain in my heart. I knew you were complaining about my intervention in your relationship. I could do nothing but smile awkwardly. I believed Xiaoyi's words. I knew she loved you with all her heart.

All those feelings of guilt and regret came flooding back...

Dad, please forgive me for bringing it up at that time. I only called Xiaoyi because I felt so dreadful. I'd be lying if I said I didn't feel some resentment about you breaking up our relationship. But I made my peace with that. I'm your only son and I know that everything you did, you did with my best interests at heart. The problem was that you intervened a little too much, never allowing me make my own decision.

In fact, it was I who made the decision to break up with Xiaoyi. Since you didn't like her, it would have been a torment for both of you if I'd kept the relationship going. It would have made me a bad son, and Xiaoyi would never have been happy. It was the right decision, or Xiaoyi's life also would have ended when I died. The deeper the love, the more crushing it is for the surviving partner if one of them dies.

So Dad, you have to stop blaming yourself. Relationships between parents and their children are complicated. You're not the only father who has made a mistake, and you certainly won't be the last. But you made that mistake in good conscience and for my benefit.

11

---

 on, you recovered surprisingly quickly after the chemotherapy and
S some Chinese medicine. Within four months you appeared to be
almost back to full health again. You thought that was the end of the
disaster and were anxious to get back to work. Your mum and I knew,
however, that this was only the first step in your treatment, and that the
road to full recovery would be a long one. Nevertheless, we consulted
the doctor and asked if you could go back to work. The doctor
consented, thinking it would help to distract your attention from the
disease. He did, however, warn that you shouldn't exhaust yourself, for
fear of weakening your immune system.

We agreed that you could return to work, but on condition that you
shouldn't overstretch yourself. You were thrilled, and busied yourself
with all the preparations. Before you went back, I told your mum to keep
your disease a secret from you and everyone else, so as to avoid self-pity,
discrimination and unnecessary stress. Mum, however, wanted
desperately to tell you the truth. She said it was down to you to conquer
your battle with cancer. If you looked after yourself and kept exercising,
she said, surely your immune system could be strengthened. However,
my mind was made up and I gave her an ultimatum: "We should learn
from that wife who kept the disease a secret from her husband. If you
tell him the truth, I will divorce you."

Your mum relented.

Maybe I made the wrong decision. Perhaps you would have taken better care of yourself if you'd known the truth.

Dad, I honestly thought I was fully recovered. After that brief scare, I figured that God had freed me from the torment. None of us could have known that He had only given me a brief moment of respite.

Going back to work was a real pleasure. Only those, I think, who have been close to death can fully appreciate that feeling of liberation. You made the right decision to hide the truth about my disease from me. I didn't have any grief after going back to work. I felt normal and happy. When I saw a bird, I would think of myself as one, flying freely in the sky.

When a person's life is not in danger, they seldom appreciate the pure beauty in it. They take it for granted. Only when it has been threatened do they realise that to live is a blessing...

Ning, I couldn't relax at all after you went back to work. I was still researching ways to cure the cancer once and for all. I enlisted the help of a friend who was studying in the UK, who shared information with me on the development of new medicines. None, though, was guaranteed to be effective. Then another friend told me about a doctor who just returned home to China from the US. Apparently he'd brought back a medicine to treat brain tumours and had started using it on Chinese patients. I immediately called him for a consultation. After explaining your situation to him, he told me that an injection would kill the cancer cells in your brain. A single treatment would be effective for three to four years, he said. It was very expensive, though, and imported mostly for senior officials.

"What's the cost for one dose?" I asked warily.

"Two hundred thousand *yuan*."

I did some mental calculations. If I could earn two million, it would be enough to give you one shot every three or four years. Ten shots could help you to live to about sixty years old. Perfect! The only problem was, I needed to earn more money, at least two million. It was a simple equation: the more money I earned, the longer you would live.

"Whenever you have the money ready, just call me a few days before you want the injection. It's like life insurance for your son. I can guarantee it!"

I almost shed tears of gratitude; he was a lifesaver. After thanking him profusely, I hung up the phone.

My mission in life was now clear: to make money and save your life. I actually believed that money could somehow buy your life!

Dad, I didn't know what you were up to. I just knew that you were busy, making call after call, not home at lot. I was also aware that you'd accepted a contract to write a script for television. I knew you didn't like to write those, for fear of stifling your creativity. I just thought you'd changed your mind and were starting to save up for your retirement. I also began planning in my mind how I would take care of you and Mum after you retired. I really thought you guys didn't need to worry. How could I know that I'd put you in such a dreadful situation, forcing you to resort to doing things you didn't like?

Son, at that time, your mum and I monitored your health while continuing to administer your medicine. One day your mum suddenly recalled an incident from when you were about four years old. I was working in Jinan at the time, and you were living with Mum and Grandma in Nanyang.

That autumn day, they were both making dumplings in the kitchen while you made faces at them from the living room. Your mum pretended to hit you with a rolling pin. Maybe you forgot that there was a glass door between you, and you thought that Mum was really going to hit you. You jumped backward, fell and hit your head on the edge of the table. Your head began to bleed, and you cried. Your mum convinced herself that it was that injury that later developed into cancer in your brain. She was consumed by guilt and self-recrimination. "I should die for this," she said. "Why did I scare our son like that with the rolling pin?"

I tried to comfort your mum and ease her guilt. "Plenty of children bang their head on a table, but how many of them develop brain cancer? Our son recovered quickly then and never showed any sign of any long-term damage. You can't blame yourself for this."

But she was adamant that she was responsible. "It must be my fault," she repeated. "I deserve to die."

Dad, how could I have known that Mum was tormenting herself over this? What child doesn't pick up small injuries when they're young? Why don't they all develop cancer? I'm sure it was just because of a problem with my immune system.

That story reminds me of another episode when I was being naughty. One afternoon Mum wanted me to play in the living room, but I wanted to stay in the bedroom. I locked the bedroom door, then didn't open it for her when she came to get me. She could do nothing but sit in the living room and read a book as she waited for me. After a while, I fell asleep in the bedroom. When Mum needed to go to work in the afternoon, she knocked on the door again, but I was sound asleep and didn't hear her. She worried that I was going to catch a cold, so she broke one of the glass panes in the door and poked me with a bamboo stick. That certainly woke me up...

Son, after you went back to work, we took you for an MRI scan every month. Encouragingly, there was no sign of relapse. The medical doctors said it was because of the surgery, while the traditional Chinese doctor said it was because of the Chinese medicine. Your mum and I believed it was the work of Chinese medicine, and we put all of our faith in its healing power.

We began to feel encouraged that perhaps a miracle would occur after all. Maybe our son truly would dodge this bullet. Maybe everything we had been through was just a warning from God, who didn't intend to destroy our lives after all. Your mum and I heaved a sigh of relief.

We didn't realise yet that we were just being tricked by fate, who was merely testing our faith and our estimation of His power.

I started to write. I had no other skills so writing was my only means to earn a living. Serious journalistic work didn't attract much money: an essay was worth a hundred *yuan*; a long novel, which took one or two years to write, was worth about a hundred thousand *yuan*. It didn't matter. So long as I kept writing, the money would accumulate. I just needed to earn as much as possible so we could afford the imported medicine.

You thought you were fully recovered after going back to work. Although you were still taking the Chinese medicine, you quickly fell back into your old daily routine. You went to bed late, which concerned your mum and me. We were sure that staying up late was potentially harmful, so we urged you to get enough sleep in order to strengthen your immune system.

But of course, you still didn't know the truth about your illness. "How can it be harmful?" you asked, incredulously. "Look at everyone else my age! Who goes to bed at ten o'clock? Most go to bed at one or two in the morning!"

"That's up to them, but you cannot!" I insisted.

"Why? Just because I was ill once? I'm not a child any more. I recovered, and now I'm fine again. Who hasn't been ill before?" you retorted.

I was stumped, and started to question my decision to hide the truth from you.

"Maybe we should tell him the truth, now," Mum suggested.

I wasn't at all convinced. I was terrified the truth would devastate you.

You were working on a research project by this time, and were becoming busier and busier, even skipping meals. Mum and I grew more and more concerned. We kept your disease a secret from everyone you worked with, so they didn't see you as an invalid who needed special treatment. What should we do? If you kept working like this, who knew where it might end?

One night you came home late again. I was mad, and yelled at you. "Why didn't you come home early to rest, like we told you?"

"Dad, don't push me," you replied defiantly. "Do you really expect people my age to have the same schedule as you?" you said.

"Do you know what disease you have?" I blurted out, without thinking.

"Yes! A tumour, and I had surgery to remove it."

"It was cancer," I said bluntly.

There it was. I couldn't take it back now. Your mum nudged my elbow, and shot me a horrified look. How could I have blurted it out like that?

After you went to bed that night, your mum was so upset. "You told me not to say anything, yet you were so harsh in telling him! Did it occur to you how the truth might hurt him?"

I couldn't sleep that night. How would my words affect you? Would you be able to sleep? Would you go to the hospital in the morning to speak to the doctors yourself? What if you collapsed? What if you didn't eat? I pressed my ears to your door a few times that night to check on you. Thankfully you were sound asleep. Maybe you hadn't taken my words so seriously after all.

At breakfast the next day, you came straight to the point.

"Mum," you asked, "Last night Dad said I had cancer. Was he just trying to scare me?"

Your mum looked at me and read my mind. "Yes, he was just trying to scare you," she replied. "But you do need to take good care of yourself. So please make sure you get enough rest. You've just come through brain surgery, after all. You can't live like everyone else does just yet."

"All right", you said, nodding, "I'll try to be careful."

You didn't go to the hospital to talk to the doctors that day. You accepted the story that we were just trying to scare you. How I wished it were that simple.

Nonetheless, after that incident you did take better care of yourself. You ate better, went to bed early, and took your medicine regularly, while doing all the work you were assigned. Those days were actually quite peaceful; if only things had stayed that way.

One day, you told me that a girl you had met online was coming to visit you.

I was a little surprised. "Why would she visit you at home?"

"I've been chatting to her online for a while. We have a lot in common and she wants to visit our home. I just want a girlfriend, Dad, to make my life a bit more interesting," you said.

"Well, yes...of course..." I really didn't know what to say; I knew you'd been heartbroken by the breakup with your ex-girlfriend.

"And I really want to meet her. If things go well, maybe we can even get married."

"Get married? Why the rush? You've only just been seriously ill! It's much too soon to be thinking about marriage."

"I'm doing this for you and Mum."

I stared at you. "What on earth do you mean?"

"If I die one day, then at least you'll have a grandchild to take care of you. That would make me feel better in the other world."

"What are you talking about?" I said, smiling. I pulled you into my arms and patted your back. "How could you say things like that? You have recovered! You should be optimistic about the future!"

"Dad, I just want to be prepared. As the saying goes, you shouldn't put all your eggs in one basket."

The sudden realisation hit me: you must have called the hospital after all. You now knew the full truth about your condition.

I talked to your mum and we agreed to let you meet with the girl. We thought it might lift your morale to have someone to talk to.

One night after dinner, you went to the gate to show the girl in. Your mum and I welcomed her and then went out, to give you both some privacy. The girl looked nice and I really hoped you'd get along. However, about an hour later we returned home, only to find you alone and despondent. The girl had left.

"What happened? Why did she leave so soon?" I asked.

"We didn't have much to say to each other, so I asked her to leave," you replied. "She was just here to check out our financial situation. She was more vulgar than I expected."

"But you said you've been talking online for a while."

"Yes, but when we met in person it was obvious what kind of person she really is."

"Oh well, it doesn't matter," I tried to comfort you.

"Don't take it too hard," said Mum. "There are plenty of nice girls out there."

You didn't reply, and just sat in front of the computer. I looked at you and thought to myself, *Son, maybe you should lower your standards. In this materialistic day and age, even if you're healthy, it's difficult to meet a girl who cares about more than money.*

Nine months passed. Your medical check-up results were completely normal. Was it a miracle? Your mum went to pray in Baiyun Temple in the hope of receiving blessings.

We all became more optimistic about everything. The research project you were part of won a military scientific award, which made us all happy. Even as an atheist, I began to pray in my heart. *God, no matter what you are, if you have any say in matters of life and death, please show your mercy and let my son come through this disaster.*

Dad, I cherished those days too. Before I became ill, I always thought I could be with you and Mum as long as I wanted to. But after my illness, I realised that maybe one day, God would take me away from you both. During that period, Mum was focused on preparing nutritious food for me, and you were busy looking for new medicines. I felt warm, wrapped up and buried in your love. Before, I'd always wanted to leave home to get rid of all the constraints and the nagging. Only now did I understand the meaning of home: a place for me to rest in my weakened state, and a place where I could feel safe and reassured.

It was during that time that I finally understood that your love was unconditional, with no strings attached, even though I had forced you to change your behaviour and compelled you to do things you were reluctant to do.

Ning, your Mum and I thought things would get better with the Chinese medicine, nutritious food and a careful daily routine to help strengthen your immune system.

Ten months after the surgery, you felt completely recovered and were happy to have regained your health. You asked to visit your grandparents in Nanyang. You especially missed your grandma. She had partly raised you, of course, so it wasn't surprising that you had a very close bond with her. Of course you wanted to see her after everything you'd been through with the surgery and the breakup with your girlfriend. Since you were young, you knew your grandma would always listen to you, no matter what you said, never criticising you or making fun. Grandma's arms were a sanctuary for you.

We wanted you to see your grandma too, but she was getting old and wasn't really up to making the long journey to Beijing. But if you went to visit her, we also worried that the travel and the excitement might derail your recovery.

After careful thought, I asked you to wait until the following year, when your body would be stronger. You weren't very happy, but you accepted it. Only later did it become clear that you never would be able to make that trip. As things turned out, that would be your last opportunity to visit Grandma. So despite my best intentions, my plan to delay your visit actually deprived you of that opportunity.

As your improving health raised our spirits, your mum and I started to talk about setting you up on a date. We decided to go ahead with the idea, since you were virtually back to full health. Why shouldn't you live a normal life? Having a new girlfriend might also help you finally to get over the previous breakup. Having someone your own age to talk to might prevent you from being lonely. Our only concern was that a new relationship might disturb your emotional wellbeing. Excitement and worry both were potentially harmful to your body, but maybe they would cancel each other out. We pondered this for a while, and decided to go ahead. I asked a friend of mine to set up a date for you.

My friend was happy to help, and after a short while he told me about a girl he knew who was interested to meet you. I mentioned it to you, and you agreed that we should go ahead and set up the meeting.

The first meeting was in a hotel lobby. Your mum and I took you there. The girl had brought her family too. Both families being there would help both sides to make a quick decision. The girl was a college student, soon to graduate. She made a good impression on us with her looks and her conversation. After the meeting we asked your opinion, and you said that you would be happy to begin dating her, so long as the girl agreed. My matchmaker friend told me that the girl also had a good feeling about you and was willing to date you.

Your mum and I were thrilled! But it still depended on you and the girl to see how things would develop.

After that, you went on frequent dates together, sometimes to the cinema, sometimes for a trip to the park or the countryside. Your mum and I tried not to interfere. All we did was remind you to take your medicine, go to bed early, and not exhaust yourself.

One day I heard you singing while you were playing on the computer. I was surprised; it had been such a long time since I'd heard you sing. I was so delighted by your good mood that I almost started to sing too!

One evening, about two months later, you came to us with a wide grin on your face. "Dad, Mum, she wants to stay with us for a few days."

"Who?" I didn't get it.

"Who do you think? *Her*," you smirked.

Your mum understood immediately, and rolled her eyes at me for being so slow. Suddenly I understood. "Yes, yes, of course we're happy to welcome her! Just tell me what we need to prepare."

"You don't need to prepare anything. She just wants to visit our home and spend some time with our family."

"OK," I replied. "Mum will take care of the cooking. You will look after our guest, and my job will be to make the place look clean and tidy."

You beamed at Mum and me. "Dad's task is both the easiest and yet the most difficult."

Dad, the time when I was dating her was my happiest time since I'd first fallen ill. Like a gentle breeze, her pure heart and laughter always swept away any negative thoughts. She really liked pop music, which I started to listen to with her, and that helped me to relax. She also liked singing shows on television, which we'd watch together. Life was full of fun. She loved taking photos of the scenery and people, and I came to see beauty through her lens. I went back to feeling like I did before I was ill.

Unfortunately, though, I couldn't bring myself to trust her

completely, because of what had happened before with Xiaoyun. Although she was good to me, I couldn't open my heart entirely to her. I was always on my guard, and sometimes I would lose my temper with her over minor things. I reduced her to tears on more than one occasion. I was so regretful that I didn't treat her better. I shouldn't have been suspicious of all women just because I'd been hurt once in the past. I really wish I could express my regret to her. I'm so sorry! But she can't hear me now...

12

S on, your mum and I were delighted when she visited us. Mum prepared a whole table full of different dishes for her. I took out my treasured wine. She didn't drink, though, and we all laughed when you said she was just saving the wine for me!

I could see that the two you got along well and were already close. You were eating and talking with the air of a loving couple. I couldn't have been happier: my son had finally escaped his sadness and found true love!

The girl stayed with us for almost a week. She was full of laughter and enjoyed clapping along with the shows on television as she sat and ate olives. She also liked debating with you. Her vivacious personality brought a lot of laughter to our family, which did a lot to ease the stress we'd all been through.

I gave thanks for the blessing of God, who had given back the happiness He had taken away. Perhaps after all, God couldn't bear to see our misery any longer.

Your mum and I started to look for a job for your girlfriend. She would stay in Beijing after graduation, so I called a few friends and told them about her. They agreed to help and gave me plenty of advice. I sent her CV to some agencies and treated them to dinner. Things started to sort themselves out and one agency told me she could start work there right after her graduation. I was so relieved.

Right then, a journalist from Henan TV called me. He had read my novel and wanted to interview me on his show. He hoped I could visit. Due to your illness, I hadn't been back to our hometown for a long time. But since things had now settled down again, I thought I could go back to visit your grandparents. So I accepted his invitation and went to Nanyang.

The interview went well, but my heart was restless and I felt uneasy for the duration of the trip. I should have been happy to see your grandparents and stay for a few more days. That was the plan, but I was unsettled. I couldn't eat or sleep, and in the brief moments I did sleep, I had a recurring nightmare that something dark was lingering on my head, attacking me all of a sudden. I found it bizarre and tried to calm myself down. I went to help out on the farm, but I kept making mistakes. Was I being absent-minded or just out of practice?

I would sit down to read but found it impossible to focus. I talked to neighbours but was incapable of carrying on a conversation after polite small talk. Your grandparents noticed my apprehension and assumed it was just because of my work. They told me that they were both healthy and had a bountiful life at home. Surely I could see that? I should go back to work, they told me. I sighed. "Yes, I'll go back. I'll visit you again soon, when I have a chance."

I rushed to buy a ticket for the sleeper train back to Beijing. On the train, I was restless, tossing and turning, unable to sleep properly. Usually, I would pass out immediately when lying on the sleeping bunk. I called your mum to tell her of my impending arrival and I asked about you. She said everything was fine, which soothed my anxiety. But still I couldn't shake that unsettled feeling.

Everything was well when I arrived home. Finally, I calmed down. You eagerly asked about your grandparents and other people in our hometown, and I told you they were all fine.

"I should go back to visit Grandma and Grandpa next year," you said.

"Yes," I agreed. "Next year, we'll all go back together on a sleeper train."

The next morning, a Saturday, you told us you planned to visit a friend after breakfast. I was tired from the train ride and planned to take a nap. But right after I went into the bedroom, I heard you make a strange cry from outside.

"Come here, quickly!" yelled Mum.

I rolled out of bed and ran barefoot into the living room. I found you on the floor in convulsions and we immediately rolled you onto your side. My mind went totally blank. You were clearly having a relapse, the thing we feared the most. In my panic I forgot to use the phone and raced off to the outpatients department in our compound. It was the fastest I'd run in my life! I was breathless when I reached the hospital, my pumping heart almost bursting out of my chest.

I described what had happened, and a female doctor and a duty nurse rushed to our home with a first-aid kit and oxygen cylinder. I helped carry their equipment to help them go faster as I led the way. You were awake when we got home. The doctor put you on oxygen and measured your blood pressure and heartbeat. She put you on an IV drip to lower the pressure in your brain, which she said was the reason you had fainted. Then she said that you needed to go into hospital. The dreaded relapse had indeed occurred.

I crouched on the ground and held my head in despair. Without any warning, all our hopes had simply evaporated. I'm certain that this was why I'd been so unsettled during my visit to our hometown. It had proved wrong to rely on your six-monthly MRI scans, to put our hopes on the traditional Chinese medicine and doctors, and to hope that God had spared us from the suffering. As it turned out, He had merely postponed it...

Dad, I do remember not feeling right that morning. I was a bit restless, but I couldn't tell why. The cancer hadn't yet begun to affect my nervous system, but maybe my mind was already sending out alarm signals. I remember sitting on the sofa, putting on my shoes, getting ready to go out and meet my friend. Then, out of the blue, I felt like I'd been struck by a sudden flash of lightning. Then I blacked out, remembering nothing.

My consciousness was like a broken dream, with only scattered images and sounds: a big bang, a swirl ascending towards the ceiling, fluttering clouds, birds screaming, water trickling, the shouting of a crowd, the rocking of a boat.

When I woke up after fainting, I saw you and Mum, and the horror in your eyes. I realised that disaster had never really left, and had caught up with me again. Despair flooded my mind. It seemed I would never escape doom.

The cycle repeated itself: seizure, coma and waking up. Every time I woke up, I'd be paralysed, with no trace of strength, not even enough to open my eyes, let alone talk.

You know, maybe I should have studied medicine instead of computer science. Then I could have studied the human brain, its frailties and the surgery. People always feel invincible when they're healthy. It's only when we're afflicted by sickness that we realise how vulnerable we truly are...

Son, since it was a Saturday, we couldn't admit you to the hospital. Your mum and I decided to keep you at home and wait until we could consult with the doctors. Then, unexpectedly, you had another seizure after lunch, this time a longer one. I was terrified and took you straight to the emergency room in the hospital you'd been in before.

What were our options now?

My first thought was to call the doctor who imported the cancer treatments from the US and ask him about the injection we'd discussed before. I gave him a call. Luckily he was still in Beijing. I told him about your relapse and asked if he would meet me.

Hearing you had relapsed, his tone changed somewhat. He sounded nowhere near as upbeat as he had before. He told me he was very busy, but I begged him to see me. He agreed and asked me to meet him that afternoon.

I went to his office at the hospital. After a long wait, he finally showed up. With my hopes high, I asked him straight out, "That injection for brain cancer you told me about before – can I buy one shot for my son?"

He shrugged his shoulders. "I'm afraid the treatment hasn't turned out to be as effective as we'd hoped. I've stopped importing it for brain cancer patients."

It was a body blow. The instant devastation shivered through my body.

"But don't despair," he continued. "We have a new biotherapy treatment that you can try."

"OK," I said warily. "Tell me more. Where was it invented?"

"A research institute outside Beijing." He passed me a pile of materials containing information.

"Is it effective?" I found it difficult to trust him now.

"Of course. It's not as expensive as the American injection, but it's still not cheap. One treatment costs twenty to thirty thousand, depending on the patient; but more frequent injections are required."

"The price doesn't matter so long as it can cure our son. We'll even sell our apartment if we have to."

"Then admit him to the hospital. The procedure requires him to be treated as an inpatient."

I told your mum about this when I got home. She said we should go to other hospitals first. We went to Tiantan Hospital, where a doctor checked your MRI results. "This patient needs another operation," said the doctor. "Then chemotherapy and radiotherapy to follow. But it's not a permanent solution. There might be another relapse. But in my opinion these are your only options."

Those words sent your mum and me into despair. Next we went to the hospital where you'd had your first operation, but we received a similar answer: surgery, chemotherapy, potential relapse. Your mum and I decided to send you the hospital to have the new biotherapy treatment.

On reflection, this might have been a huge mistake. The doctors in Tiantan Hospital may have sounded harsh, but they were just telling us the truth about the development of your disease. We should have listened to them. But as your parents, we preferred to hear comforting lies than the brutal truth. For in those lies lay hope.

During that period, I was enraged by the absence of a cure for brain cancer. I thought people were trying to destroy our faith on purpose and make us desperate.

We took you to the hospital in an ambulance. The accommodation at this hospital was very luxurious. We booked a single room for you, equipped with a telephone, a television, and a shower. There was also another bed in the room for your mum and me to sleep on. Of course, this place wasn't cheap, but we thought it was worth it to provide you with a good environment where you could eat and sleep well. When you woke up, you looked around the room, wide-eyed.

"It's like a hotel in here," you said.

I forced a smile. "Yes, just think of this as a family holiday. And this is our hotel. Now take a good rest."

Two days passed. But except for a nurse who measured your temperature and blood pressure from time to time, the doctors did nothing for you. I found it strange. Cancerous cells were multiplying rampantly in your brain. Even an hour's delay risked reducing the chances of the treatment's success. Where was the sense of urgency? I went to the doctor's office but found no one. Someone told me he'd gone on a trip. I went to speak to the duty doctor.

"Do you know about the blood-brain barrier?" she asked me.

"Yes, a little," I replied. "It protects our brain, but it also makes it harder for medicine to penetrate into the brain."

"Exactly," she said. "Well, if you know this, why do you think this so-called 'biotherapy' will be effective? The benefits of this treatment are unproven. Even if it is effective, how could it pass the blood-brain barrier and reach the lesion?"

"What? Don't the doctors know?" I demanded, staring at her. She didn't answer me, and simply went off to attend to other business.

I was stunned by her words. It was obvious that she didn't think biotherapy would cure you. I told your mum, who said, "We should go back and talk to her again, rather than waste time being confused and muddle-headed."

This was the third night after you'd arrived at this hospital. No one was in the doctor's office except the female doctor. Your mum and I went in. "You know about our son," I said. "He's our only child. I hope you can understand our desperation in wanting to cure him. We're asking for your recommendation as to what treatment will be best for him."

She hesitated for a while before responding. "Don't trust people blindly," she said. "Go to a reputable hospital and speak to the specialists there. Don't waste your time and money here. Please don't tell anyone else what I've told you."

Your mum and I looked at each other. We understood. The absent doctor wasn't a responsible medical professional. He just saw us as a way to make money.

So, having wasted another few precious days, we decided to transfer you to another hospital. But which one? I searched feverishly online that night for a good hospital to treat your disease. I didn't want to go to Tiantan Hospital because my friend's daughter had died there, nor to the hospital that had performed your first surgery, since you suffered a relapse after that. What would be the point of a second operation? Then there was a traditional Chinese hospital that claimed to specialise in cancer treatment. But I couldn't trust that one either, because doctors there couldn't prescribe Chinese medicines themselves, or they needed to rely on books.

An online advert attracted my attention: *We have received awards for the invention of radionuclides that kill brain cancer cells. We have cured many patients with this treatment.*

I showed it to your mum. "You should check this with some of your contacts," she said. "If what they say is true, we should give it a try."

I agreed and started asking around the following morning. An acquaintance told me that this hospital had indeed won awards for developing this new treatment. Your mum and I immediately decided to transfer you there.

That afternoon, your mum and I carried you into the car and drove to the hospital full of hope. We were oblivious to the fact that we were about to make yet another mistake.

After a thorough check-up, they told us that they would first need to perform surgery to place a radionuclide capsule in your brain, into which they would then be able to inject the isotopes that would kill the cancer cells. I'd originally thought that you wouldn't need more surgery, but it couldn't be avoided. I waited for the day of the operation with trepidation. You were so young. How unfair, I thought, that you should have to endure this for a second time.

On the day of the surgery, I sent you into the operating theatre and waited for you outside. Once again, I experienced the anguish and helplessness of waiting outside the operating theatre, tormented by the passing of each long minute.

A few hours later the surgeon summoned your mum and me into the operating theatre. "The surgery went well," he said brightly. "I was able to move the tumour to one side and place the capsule in the right spot. Once the surface heals, we can inject the radionuclides to kill the cancer cells."

I breathed a sigh of relief and expressed my thanks. Your mum, though, was concerned. "How can you move the tumour?" she asked. "Shouldn't it be removed completely, or not touched at all? Won't a trigger make it reproduce and multiply even faster?"

I defended the surgeon. "Are you questioning the doctor? Don't you think he knows best, whether or not to remove it?"

As it turned out, your mum was dead right. The cancer cells multiplied rapidly in your brain following the surgery. Your condition deteriorated only a few days later. I still remember that afternoon – it was the second day of the May Day holiday.

After your stitches were removed and you went home, you seemed to be recovering well, but you felt uncomfortable, your arms and legs getting weaker. I was about to call the doctor to discuss it when another seizure struck you. It was the most severe one we'd seen, and no matter what the paramedic did, it wouldn't stop. We called an ambulance to take you back to the hospital.

Our apartment was on the fourth floor, and there was no lift in the building. It was incredibly difficult to put you on a stretcher and take you downstairs. You were so tall and heavy, and it took a tremendous effort from me, with help from a few neighbours, the doctor, your cousin and her husband, to get you down the stairs and into the ambulance. My clothes were drenched in sweat, and I almost collapsed. At that moment, I thought helplessly that I was the old one – it should be me on that stretcher, being carried by you!

It took another three or four hours at the hospital for your violent seizures to stop. Then you were taken into the MRI room. During the scan, I held your head in front of the MRI machine. Amidst the deafening sound of the machine, I sobbed and prayed, "God, please bless us just once..."

When the scan was printed, even I could see that the tumour had grown considerably larger. I looked at the scan in despair and realised once again that this was all due to our misguided approach to your treatment. Now what should I do? No other doctors could perform this surgery, so how could we decide what was best for you?

I had to go to your chief surgeon, who by this time was at home on leave. I called him to tell him about your condition, hoping he would be able to return soon. He was surprised to hear from me, but he promised to come back as soon as possible.

Beside ourselves with worry, your mum and I waited restlessly for his return. Since you had first become ill, I'd been nervous every May Day or National Day holiday, when we would have had no option but to wait for the doctors to return if anything happened to you. Unlike most people, I hated every long vacation.

The doctor didn't come back until the ninth of May! I suppressed my anger and begged him for a solution. He checked on you and recommended another operation to remove the growing tumour. Your mum and I had no choice but to agree. At the time, I hated myself for not being a brain surgeon. If I had been, I was sure you wouldn't have ended up like this.

The third operation didn't stop the cancer cells from multiplying, and within a few days the seizures started again. By now you could feel nothing in your arms and legs, and because you couldn't chew or swallow, a feeding tube was inserted through your nose. The only positive was that at least they could now inject radionuclides into the capsule buried in your brain.

The doctor said it all depended on the injection. If it worked, then you might survive. Otherwise, cancerous cells would engulf your brain. They injected iodine-131 into the capsule. Your mum and I watched nervously as we monitored your body's reaction. In the world of medicine, as in the natural world, everything has its predator. And the cancer crumpled under the iodine-131.

The next morning, you were once again able to move your numb fingers and toes on one side. Soon afterwards they injected another shot to kill the remaining cancer cells. The original rampant flame of cancer had been suppressed. Now you could move and swallow again. But it provided little relief to your mum and me. We both knew this would only hinder the cancer, rather than eliminate it. Besides, this treatment carried significant side effects. Healthy brain cells were destroyed as well as malignant cancer cells, which could impair your intelligence or reflexes. The treatment might delay the cancer's growth for a while, but it could never be a permanent solution.

Dad, it's common for those experiencing bereavement to transfer their grief into anger towards the doctors. But I hope that you and Mum can let go of your grudges towards everyone, including the doctors. Don't vent your anger towards them.

I once read in a book that as human civilization evolved, anger levels rose dramatically within the population. Perhaps it's because people gradually developed their own vision of a perfect life, but then later on became disillusioned with the reality. Whatever it was, anger will never solve the problem. Don't all doctors want to cure their patients? Don't they all want positive medical outcomes? Don't they all want to achieve something during their careers?

Limitations in medical knowledge mean that we still haven't discovered the causes and cures of many diseases. Many medicines still wait to be invented. Doctors' hands are tied by these diseases. We just have to face reality. We should be grateful that this hospital prolonged my life as much as they did, even if they couldn't cure me. We certainly shouldn't complain about them for anything they did. To live longer was better than dying, right? It's not their fault. No hospital in the world has a cure for cancer. So how could we have expected them to cure me?

Dad, hatred is dangerous. If you don't let this go, it might make you ill, too.

You know, after I lost control of one hand and leg, as well as the ability to swallow, I was still partly conscious. I could hear your words and sensed your anxiety and panic. I knew you were feeding me through a nasal tube, and I could hear you arguing with Mum.

And as I lay there, I thought to myself that I owed you so much after putting you through such anguish. I should leave this world, I thought, and put an end to your suffering.

13

Ning, we took you home when you were a little more stable. Even though you had cheated death once again, your mum and I were far from happy. We knew that your body was extremely weak after all these treatments. Mum complained about my misguided decisions over your treatment, and she no longer allowed me to make decisions about you alone. Before, we'd often have disagreements about your treatment, but we were always able to discuss it and work things out. Now, even that was impossible. We disagreed and fought over everything. She believed one thing, I believed another – we clashed constantly. I knew we should stop fighting, though, so in the end I agreed to involve her in all our decisions.

I really had no idea there could be such a difference between the love of a mother and that of a father. There are so many mysteries of the human species!

By this point, we felt that we could only put our hopes on Chinese medicine and Qigong[1]. In order to find you a good traditional Chinese doctor, your mum and I read through all kinds of medical books and other materials, and we finally decided to see a traditional Chinese doctor in Dongzhimen. After checking your pulse, the doctor told us about a few cases he had cured, and told us that he could cure you too. We didn't entirely believe him, but at least he managed to lift our spirits.

And so we took you there every month to check your pulse and take some Chinese medicine. Your mum also took you regularly to Yuyuantan Park to learn about Guo Lin's anti-cancer Qigong.

Like people drowning, we were so desperate to grasp every piece of flotsam as we floundered in the churning waters all around us...

Dad, to be honest, I really didn't think I'd survive. I figured it was my time to leave the world, and I felt was almost ready. But perhaps the other world wasn't yet ready for me, so maybe that's why my departure had been delayed again. After all this time, cancer didn't scare me any more. I'd been through so much already by this point – what was there to be afraid of? I only had hatred for it. I hadn't done anything bad in my life, so why me? Was it because I was young and poor? If I'd studied medicine, Dad, I would have fought it with you!

Because of my hatred towards cancer, I agreed to Mum's suggestion to go to Yuyuantan Park and learn Guo Lin's Qigong. The first time I went, I was so depressed because I was the only young person among all the patients. Once again, I felt it was unfair. Why not at least wait until I was older before giving me cancer? Why now?

After only a few days, I felt better. Seeing that I was young and had come to learn Qigong, everyone realised I must have cancer. The care and encouragement from the others who practised there with me made me feel much brighter.

"Don't worry," they would say. "So long as you keep practising, your body will get stronger, and your immune system too. The cancer cells will be killed, and you'll survive."

One man with stomach cancer told me that he had practised Guo Lin's Qigong for five years after his surgery, and now he felt complete normal. Another woman with lymphatic cancer said that doctors had told her she would only live for another six months, but three years had passed since she had started practising Qigong. Now, all her vital signs were back to normal again.

Their encouragement gave me confidence to fight the cancer. I thought that since I already had cancer, fear wouldn't solve the problem.

Cancer may be even worse for those who are weak. Instead, therefore, I should fight cancer. Even if I lost, I wouldn't let it break my spirit.

And so I finally accepted my reality. Many things can threaten someone's life: a car accident, a house fire, a terrorist attack in the shopping mall. My situation wasn't as bad as it was for some people, so I should stop feeling sorry for myself and cheer up.

Above all, I resolved that I wouldn't allow myself to be crushed into oblivion...

Son, by this time you were completely aware of your situation. But despite my worst fears, you remained strong mentally. You had crossed paths with death, but it didn't intimidate you. You fought back ferociously. You took the bitter Chinese medicine twice a day. Sometimes you threw up, but you kept drinking it afterwards. And every morning you would go to learn and practise Guo Lin's Qigong at Yuyuantan Park.

During that time, my driver Xiaopan and I accompanied you to Yuyuantan almost daily. I carried a folding stool, some water and fruits in a bag. You practised Guo Lin's Qigong, set after set. After each set, you sat on the folding stool to rest while I cut an apple or peeled a kiwi fruit for you. The practice was accompanied with walking. At first, it was just a few hundred metres. Soon you could walk further: one kilometre, two kilometres, then three, to intensify the practice. In the end, you could walk a whole loop around Yuyuantan Park, five kilometres in all. I was reduced to panting as I tried to follow you; I had no experience at all of Qigong, but you handled it with ease.

You made many friends with similar experiences there. A woman with breast cancer who took the bus at five o'clock every morning to get there with her husband always checked on your condition when meeting with you, and gave you some encouragement. Then there was the old man with lung cancer who carried his food and umbrella on his bus ride to Yuyuantan every morning, whatever the weather. He had been practising Qigong for fifteen years and had eliminated the cancer cells in his body. He showed you, through his experience, the true strength of the human spirit. Cancer overcame the weak, he told you, and succumbed to the strong.

A beautiful young girl in her twenties who'd been diagnosed with leukaemia came with her boyfriend to learn and practise at the old pedal boat dock. She circled around and practised, her face always serene despite her condition.

Another young woman from Shanxi had the same disease as you. She was in her thirties and couldn't afford hospital treatment. Her husband had left her, but she refused to be beaten. After she had left her child with relatives, she'd taken what little money she had to Beijing to learn Guo Lin's Qigong. The place she rented was a long way outside the city, so she needed to get up early to come to Yuyuantan for practice. She always smiled at you, encouraging you. "Hang in there, little brother," she told you. "You'll get through this."

This was also how we got to know the Anti-Cancer Association of Beijing. Tens of thousands of its members were scattered across various parks, all practising Guo Lin's Qigong. Every year they held a huge gathering, usually in a large auditorium, where they would share stories and experiences. Leaders of the association would present awards for encouragement. Your mum went there once, on your behalf. She was excited to see that many people there had fought cancer for fifteen or twenty years, some even longer. She said they were all in high spirits, with no miserable faces in sight. They gave each other hope and encouragement. You were delighted to hear this, too. "We should learn from them," you said. "We will not allow cancer to beat us!"

People can always find an example to follow in the face of any tragedy. It can be a huge source of strength...

Dad, during the time I practised Qigong, we spent every day together. In my younger years you lived apart from Mum and me, which meant that we never spent much time together. Though we moved to Beijing later on, you were always busy with your writing work, and then I went off to other cities for my university studies.

I never expected us to become so close after I became ill. In those days, I was marching ahead, practising, and you followed, carrying fruits and water for me. After each set, you pulled out the folding stool to let me rest, and peeled some fruit for me. When I was having my fruit break, you would sit and take out a book to read. I thought to myself how nice it would be if God allowed us to stay like this.

Through the ups and downs of my health, I came to understand the precious love of family. I realised how lucky I was to have parents to count on. My illness meant that I was highly dependent on you and Mum. I became nervous whenever you were out of my sight. I would get frightened when you went on trips. Sometimes, you went to the suburbs for a day or two for a meeting. I wanted to call you as soon as you left home so I could ask you to come back. My sickness made me as helpless as a child...

Son, I sensed you changing during those days. When I went to Shahe for a meeting, your mum called me right after I arrived and said you wanted to speak with me. I was a little worried and asked your mum to put you on the phone. To my surprise, though, you simply said, "Dad, I miss you. Please hurry home after your meeting."

Warmth surged in my heart. "Don't worry," I replied. "I'll come home as soon as the meeting is over." I turned down almost all meetings after that and devoted all my time to you. Sometimes, I wished I could carry you on my back like I did when you were young; to carry you everywhere I went and not be apart from you for a single moment.

Since you'd been practising Guo Lin's Qigong, you were growing stronger, putting on some weight and regaining some colour in your face. Your mum and I couldn't be complacent, but we were happy with the improvement. Mum prayed to Buddha every day, wishing for your health to keep improving. She heard that setting animals free could elicit blessings for a loved one. And so she started to buy a few fish to set free in the lake at Yuyuantan. If she was busy, I would carry out this duty.

One day, Mum gave me a fish at noon, when it was blazing hot. I drove to the park alone, which was empty due to the scorching sun. I was dazzled by the sunlight, and when I crouched down to put the fish into the lake, I almost fell in too! I fell down on the ground and wished

Buddha could see our efforts and give you blessings that you would stop being tortured by this disease. If only Buddha would bless you with a healthy life, then I would gladly come to set fish free every day, forever...

Dad, I did feel much better during those days, but I knew you and Mum weren't taking anything for granted. Every few days we'd go to a private Chinese doctor near Dongzhimen. After registration, we'd queue up on the first floor to wait for my turn to check my pulse and get my prescriptions. Then we would go to the second floor to take the medicine. The three of us and our driver Xiaopan would be there together. Although the waiting was boring, I felt warmth in my heart. We had never been together for anything like this before.

Sometimes when I got hungry you would go to the workers' canteen close by to buy a few steamed dumplings. Once, I got really hungry when you were talking to the pharmacist, and I snuck out with Xiaopan to buy *baozi*. I was hungry and ate all three *baozi* with Xiaopan. I couldn't stop burping on the way home.

"Why couldn't you control yourself?" you chided. "Since you bought so many, couldn't you have at least saved one for me?"

Mum laughed and said to me, "How selfish of you! What about me?" Mum's joke cracked us all up. It was the first time I'd laughed so hard in ages...

14

S on, eventually my worst fear was realised. One overcast morning, we went for yet another MRI scan. Anxious as always, I stood in front of the screen, concerned about the progression of your illness. I noticed the doctor's eyes fixed on the screen, and the mouse pointer stopped at your brain lesions. It was with a deep sense of foreboding that I later took the scan to your doctor. Sure enough, the cancer had progressed to a point where it could no longer be controlled. My heart sank into the abyss. My world was spinning, everything dulled: the lights on the ceilings dimmed, the green plants faded, the red flowers on windowsill swirled into a smudge of blood. Everything changed before my eyes.

I pulled myself together in order to go and consult your doctor in another hospital. He looked at the scan. "The tumour is too large," he said. "We can try, but I cannot see any way to control it." Desperation seized me. I got home and saw you on the couch, anxiously waiting for the results.

"Nothing's wrong, good as usual," I said light-heartedly. You fixed your eyes on my face for a second, and then moved them away.

"Dad, have some lunch," you said.

How could I eat anything? I pulled your mum into another room while you were taking a nap and showed her your scan results. Her tears began to flow before she'd even finished reading them. I could find no words of comfort. I just held her in my arms and we wept together.

It seemed that fate never did us any favours. Whatever we did, this demon simply wouldn't leave us alone...

Dad, I read something in your eyes that day. Despite your words, I could sense your despair. I knew my cancer had got worse. I didn't ask you for more details, though, because I knew you wouldn't tell me. If I'd pressed you, it would only have made you withdraw further, and that would have made your pain even worse. I think that's when I, too, realised that the devil would never let me go.

Later that day, I lay in bed and started to plan for the remaining life I had, to see what I could accomplish. I had no financial savings or debts; I had accomplished little at work, but neither had I neglected my duties; I hadn't lived a perfect life, but neither had I done anything seriously wrong.

All things considered, I felt I could pass over into the other world with my head held high.

Son, that night, your mum proposed that we burn some yellow paper at a crossroad junction to cast the devil's spirit out of you. I knew by now that she was desperate and seeking some kind of comfort. I agreed and said that we should all go together. At around ten o'clock that night, your mum and I helped you downstairs. Our compound was large, but it took us a while to find a suitable intersection, because there was so much traffic. Finally, we arrived at a remote junction. By now it was almost eleven o'clock and very quiet everywhere. The streetlamp was off. Your mum lit the yellow paper, its flames brightening the night. I was very concerned; what if a car passed by? This was fire, after all. You looked around, keeping watch while we listened to your mum praying.

"God, please end the misfortune brought upon our son. Please, I beg you. He has suffered enough. Please now allow him to recover."

On the way back, you broke the silence. "Even if I am guilty of something, hasn't my punishment already been enough?"

I looked at you, feeling your resentment towards fate. An outcry burst from my heart too. "God, you have been tormenting us for so long. Time and time again. When will it stop?"

Dad, that was my denouncement of fate, my refusal to accept what the disease had in store for me. I couldn't give up. I kept practising Guo Lin's Qigong every day, even when one of my legs went numb. I still remember those days when I went to Yuyuantan Park every morning. I practised Qigong with help from you and Xiaopan. Even walking was hard for me by then, but I swore in my mind, "Cancer, you may beat me up, but I will never surrender."

Other patients in the park offered their encouragement. "Relapses are common," they would say. "Hang in there. Victory is just a little further down the road!" And I really was expecting a victory then. I couldn't give up, I had to keep on fighting.

As the cancer progressed, however, it started to affect my nervous system. Eventually my entire left leg became paralysed, and after that it became very difficult to go to the park. But still I continued to practise in our compound with your help. At nine o'clock in the morning and three o'clock in the afternoon, we would show up at the track, me limping around with your support. I thought to myself, if there's a God, wouldn't He be touched by our efforts?

Son, your mum and I were so proud of your perseverance during that time. You must have felt your relapse looming. And yet you clenched your teeth and stood up to face it head on. For your numb left leg and foot, we took you for some acupuncture in order to stimulate your nerves, and we asked the therapist to make you a plastic support for your leg to help you rehabilitate. The first time you put on the leg support, you cried out for pain, but you didn't give up. You put it on and walked for a few steps in the room. I could tell each step was agonising for you. Your eyebrows tightened, your body staggered, but you said nothing. You rested a little bit and kept walking.

I'd always felt that your mum and I had been neglectful in not instilling in you a sense of grit and determination, but how you proved me wrong! You had plenty of willpower and stamina, which had developed during your seven years at university. We just hadn't seen it before. When you interned in the Lanzhou Military Region, you never skipped exercises or physical training at all, even when your ankle was sprained. That kind of experience cultivates a strong constitution.

Dad, I always had bizarre dreams. Sometimes I would be riding a tiger, then flying away like a bird from one tree to another, or across mountains; sometimes I was riding a boat on the dusky river with the howling of wolves coming from the bank, passengers sitting still in their seats and watching the back of the boat captain. I watched closely, and realised we were sitting on a snake; sometimes, I was running on a track with a dozen soldiers. I was jaunty, but they were all panting. When I turned back to them, they all became old with white hair and beards. Then the track became covered with white painted numbers, eights and threes; another time, I saw a flock of sheep in the snow, all following the lead sheep except one, who left the herd and went in the opposite direction, soon disappearing into the storm.

I only remember these among all the strange dreams I had because they came to me repeatedly. Not until later did I realise that they were warnings about my destiny. I used to think that many things in life occurred randomly: airplane crashes, car accidents, robberies. Many things happened by accident. But those ominous dreams made me realise that, in fact, many things may be predestined by fate to occur at a precise time and place.

Son, I've spent a lot of time thinking about how the world works, but to be honest, there are so many things I don't understand. For instance, one man who takes good care of himself, who doesn't smoke or drink, might be in rude health one day, but then might die of a sudden illness. Then someone else who is sick and visits the hospital regularly, who smokes and drinks, might go on to live a long life.

Some brilliant and well-turned-out men were trapped in poverty and were never able to prove their value to society. Meanwhile, others who were untalented and dishevelled-looking tried their luck and were able to climb the social ladder and dictate over others.

Some beautiful and kind women married abusive husbands and suffered until death; yet other average-looking and wicked women married good men and were taken care of and enjoyed bountiful and blessed lives.

How can all this happen? Why is the world like this? It's so difficult to explain. *It's such an unpredictable world,* I thought to myself. *What's the point in trying to figure it out? Maybe it's better to live in a confused fog.*

When I read books by theologians and philosophers who have tried to explain the rules of the universe, I would find it a rather pointless pursuit. In any event, how can anyone know if their explanation was correct? Could it ever be proven? How can this world, that no one truly understands, be so easily analysed?

Dad, after my condition worsened, I know that was the hardest time for you and Mum. During the daytime, you needed to take me to the track to help me exercise; you fetched the Chinese medicines at the hospital and prepared them for me; you went grocery shopping so you could cook special meals for me. At night, you helped me shower, helped me to bed, and helped me to get up and pee at night. By then my left arm and leg had gone completely numb. I was like a child in the shower. You helped remove my clothes, put me in a chair in the bathroom, put soap on me, rinsed me, dried me and got me dressed again. I had regressed to being an infant, completely dependent on my parents again.

In the early stages, I woke you and Mum up twice a night to pee. But as the tumour developed, adding pressure on my nerves, I needed to pee more often. Sometimes you were only able to lie down for an hour before I woke you up again. I could tell you were exhausted. I really didn't want to wake you, but neither did I want to wet the bed. Looking at your red eyes and unsteady steps, I hated myself for bringing all this trouble down on you.

Dad and Mum, I brought so much misery to your life, and I couldn't even let you sleep properly...

Son, we never gave up, never lost hope that the Chinese medicine and Qigong would kick the cancer away. But eventually it was the cancer that gained the upper hand. It kept getting worse, until eventually you couldn't walk at all. After you became wheelchair-bound, your mum and I panicked. We believed in anything that promised to save your life.

Your mum heard that an old lady from Henan who was selling vegetables in Beijing had a special ability to communicate with the gods and had cured some seriously ill patients. Mum looked into it and invited her over. She was an illiterate, ordinary country woman. I had my suspicions about her, but I kept them to myself. I didn't want to disappoint your mum, so I just hoped for a miracle. In any event, you should never judge a book by its cover. So many things can't be explained by science, so maybe she was one of them. What if she really was able to cure you?

Your mum went to great lengths to treat the woman well, and then she asked her to try to cure you. You were sitting on the couch. She came up to you, stretched out her arm, palms down, circled your head a few times, then appeared to grab something out of your head in her clenched fist, then cast it into the air. She repeated this a few times.

"Good," she said. "I have pulled out the tumour and thrown it away. Your son should recover very soon." Your mum thanked the woman profusely. I looked at her suspiciously. Was that little performance supposed to cure you? If I had witnessed this scene elsewhere, I would have accused her of being a charlatan. But here in our home, in front of you, I didn't dare say a word. I even convinced myself that perhaps she really was a psychic who could cure you. Things sometimes work out if one truly believes. What if my doubt destroyed the atmosphere she created? I was a very superstitious person at that time. Any claim that you could be cured could convert me into a believer.

Before she left, she said, "In three days, it will take effect. You will see a miracle!" Her words lit a glimmer of hope and delight in my heart. I sent her downstairs in gratitude, and gave her a gift.

Three days later, your condition hadn't improved at all. In fact, it had got worse.

Much later, I came to understand why people are superstitious: it's a coping mechanism, an instinct in times of desperation, a last resort in a helpless situation. People who haven't been through disasters find it hard to believe in superstition. But for those that have been affected by disaster or tragedy, I feel sympathetic towards them. I can try to explain the truth to them, but I don't think we have the right to make fun of them or treat them with contempt. They have enough misery in their lives already...

Dad, after I could no longer walk, I still needed to go up and down the stairs at the hospital or to get some fresh air outside. Since there was no lift, it fell to you to help get me to and from the fourth floor. It broke my heart, listening to you struggle every time you carried me up or down the stairs. I was twenty-nine years old. How could I do this to you? Sometimes I insisted on walking on my one leg that was less paralysed, but you couldn't bear to see me struggle and so you carried me on your back again.

I tried to comfort myself: maybe God felt that you never carried me much when I was a child, since you worked in another city. Maybe He had put us into this situation to make it up to me. But I couldn't bear it!

Son, I remember those days when I carried you up and down the stairs all the time. And even though it was exhausting, it was satisfying to know that I was at least physically up to it.

Once, though, when I carried you upstairs into a restaurant after an excursion outside the city, my legs suddenly started shaking. I rested for a moment and then continued to carry you up. When I put you down, I was panting, my mouth open and my heart pounding. I was scared; what if there was something wrong with my heart? How would you and Mum cope? Who would take care of you both?

I stopped carrying you after that. Fortunately, your cousins, uncle and friends from the military were able to help. Only then did I realise the value of a lift and the inconvenience of living on the fourth floor.

There was one thing from that time that I regret deeply: one morning, I helped you to sit at the table for breakfast. I put chopsticks in your hand, sat next to you and began to eat. But I didn't realise that you weren't able to support yourself fully in the chair with your half-paralysed body. You bent forward a little to eat, then lost your balance. Your whole body fell to the floor like a dead weight. I jumped up to catch you, but I wasn't quick enough. The side of your face landed on the floor. I knelt down on the ground, my face only a few inches from yours. My heart was broken, but you gave no word or sign of complaint. I pulled myself together and helped you up. I blamed myself for not getting you a chair with solid arms.

"Dad, don't be hard on yourself," you said with a smile. "You and Mum have already done so much for me. Maybe God is just testing my reactions now."

Your words brought tears to my eyes...

Dad, I could feel my world becoming smaller and smaller during those days, little by little, day by day. First, one of my legs couldn't move, and I couldn't go to Yuyuantan Park to practise Qigong. Then I lost control of the other leg. That meant I couldn't walk around the playground in our compound. Next my arms went numb, making it even harder to go downstairs. And now I was totally confined to our apartment.

I started to understand that, besides physical force, another constraint on man is disease. Disease is a truly ferocious enemy of human beings. We always seem to be alert to the threat of aggressive regimes and militaries, opposing organisations and individuals, which we might consider enemies in our daily lives; but we should never stop being vigilant against disease, which can completely control and then torture us. The risk from disease is as serious as an attack by an entire army!

Sometimes, our worst enemies are inside our own bodies...

15

S on, as your condition worsened, I rushed around, consulting doctors everywhere I could. I spoke to the leading authority on brain tumours in Tiantan Hospital, who looked at the MRI scan I showed to him.

"I'm afraid there's nothing more we can do for him," he said, shaking his head.

I shook my own head in disbelief, tears flowing. "But he's my only child," I replied. "How can I just give up?"

I went to see a prominent chemotherapist in the tumour hospital near the Second Ring Road, but he told me the same thing; I went to another tumour hospital on Fushi Road and asked the doctors there if they could help. They also studied the MRI scan and shook their heads; the PLA Navy General Hospital performed a gamma knife treatment on you, which had no discernible effect; and neurosurgeons from Xuanwu Hospital and the PLA's Air Force General Hospital said that to discuss any treatment options was futile at this point.

During that time, I took your MRI scan to every hospital and every doctor I could find, praying to meet a miracle-worker. Each time I left disappointed.

In my despair, I developed a genuine hatred towards our Creator. Why didn't He make a spare organ for each body part, like a spare tire for cars, so we can simply replace the old parts with new ones? Shouldn't it be possible to replace the human brain? But no, He clearly wanted to gloat about His omnipotence and make the human body as complex and mysterious as the universe. To figure out how the human body worked was just as laborious as learning about outer space.

It took a medical student a lifetime to learn about just a single organ. If the combined efforts of countless medical schools, hospitals and doctors around the world couldn't find the cause of cancer and control it, then who was to blame? In my mind, it was obvious: it was the Creator who was negligent in not creating spare organs.

Creator, you have made so many people suffer. You are the cruellest force in the world!

Dad, don't blame the Creator. You'll only infuriate Him. We don't have any right to blame Him anyway. We should be thankful for His efforts in creating human beings at all! If not for those endeavours, Earth would be such a boring place, and no one could experience the joy of life.

We should also appreciate that He made the human body so intricate. It's a wonder that our brains can produce such sophisticated feelings. Other animals may have emotions, but nowhere near as complex as ours. Think about a couple in love: they are reserved and observant at first; then they start to make small talk, hinting at attraction with subtle expressions; then they go on a first date, then progress to kissing and touching each other's bodies; and then eventually they get married. Their relationship goes through so many intricate stages, together intertwining to create a beautiful arc.

The Creator deserves enormous credit and gratitude for all this. Don't take it away just because I'm unwell. Think about our amazing bodies: the digestive system, the circulatory system, reproductive system, respiratory system, and the neural system. How much amazing work has the Creator done to make such a complex body?

So be grateful, Dad. Don't complain about life just because of me.

———

Son, by that stage your disease was destroying my mind. I had a growing antipathy towards the world, and I complained about everything all the time.

One day, Mr Zhang, who was in the same hospital as you, heard about your condition and offered to coach you to learn the Buddhist text *The Heart of Prajna Paramita Sutra*, which he thought might help to keep you relaxed. He stressed the importance of remaining calm in the face of adversity.

"To peacefully accept reality makes one suffer less," he said. I agreed with him, so he scripted a version of the text in calligraphy for you, framed it in glass, and taught you to read it.

After that, you would read *The Heart of Prajna Paramita Sutra* a few times every day. You soon memorised it and could recite it accurately by heart. I would watch you reciting it with your eyes closed, without any trace of pain or grievance on your face. I wondered at its power, and started to read it myself. I even marked the punctuation of some paragraphs according to my own interpretation.

Avalokitesvara Bodhisattva
when practising deeply the Prajna Paramita
perceives that all five skandhas are empty
and is saved from all suffering and distress.
Shariputra,
form does not differ from emptiness,
emptiness does not differ from form.
That which is form is emptiness,
that which is emptiness form.
The same is true of feelings,
perceptions, impulses, consciousness.
Shariputra,
all dharmas are marked with emptiness;
they do not appear or disappear,
are not tainted or pure,
do not increase or decrease.
Therefore, in emptiness no form, no feelings,
perceptions, impulses, consciousness.

No eyes, no ears, no nose, no tongue, no body, no mind;
no colour, no sound, no smell, no taste, no touch,
no object of mind;
no realm of eyes
and so forth until no realm of mind consciousness.
No ignorance and also no extinction of it,
and so forth until no old age and death
and also no extinction of them.
No suffering, no origination,
no stopping, no path, no cognition,
also no attainment with nothing to attain.
The Bodhisattva depends on Prajna Paramita
and the mind is no hindrance;
without any hindrance no fears exist.
Far apart from every perverted view one dwells in Nirvana.
In the three worlds
all Buddhas depend on Prajna Paramita
and attain Anuttara Samyak Sambodhi.
Therefore know that Prajna Paramita
is the great transcendent mantra,
is the great bright mantra,
is the utmost mantra,
is the supreme mantra
which is able to relieve all suffering
and is true, not false.
So proclaim the Prajna Paramita mantra,
proclaim the mantra which says:
gate gate paragate parasamgate bodhi svaha
gate gate paragate parasamgate bodhi svaha
gate gate paragate parasamgate bodhi svaha.

Your mum also started to read *The Heart of Prajna Paramita Sutra*. She studied it more carefully than I did, and soon she was able to recite it together with you. Watching you both focused on reading and reciting definitely distracted you from your inner pain, and I felt tremendous gratitude to the great Buddhist who wrote it. He had truly keen eyes to penetrate the superficiality of the world: *That which is form is emptiness, that which is emptiness form...No ignorance...no old age and death...No suffering, no origination, no stopping, no path, no cognition...without any hindrance no fears exist.*

But I was no Buddhist. I had no ability to transcend, confined as I was by my earthly pains...

Dad, Buddhism teaches us in *The Heart of Prajna Paramita Sutra* and other scriptures that people close to death should try to reduce their attachment to their bodies:

Life and death are a cycle;
Deal with it with a peaceful life and liberate oneself by practising;
Life is a prison;
Death breaks the shackles of the body;
Death is a relocation for the body, from a shabby house to a grand one,
*   like replacing worn clothing;*
Death is not the end, but just the start of a journey to the western
*   blissful lands.*

So relax, Dad. Don't get hung up about it all, don't be afraid, and don't hold any grudges. By then I already knew my disease couldn't be cured. I read *The Heart of Prajna Paramita Sutra* to rid myself of my desire to cling to life. I just wanted prepare myself and wait calmly for the final moment to arrive.

But Dad, it was really difficult to stay calm and relaxed, despite the guidance of scripture, despite all the support from you and Mum, and despite my efforts to let it go. I was still afraid of the afterlife I was going to. I knew nothing about it...

Son, no one in this world has any idea what the afterlife is like. In this, the gatekeeper of the afterlife has done an outstanding job. No one has ever been allowed to visit before their time, regardless of their power or money, their talents or social status. It's almost inhumane in its inflexibility, but it protects this mysterious world. Trying to speculate about it can terrify anyone. You were no exception, and we both understood that. That's why we never gave up on your treatment.

It wasn't long before you were unable to eat by yourself. Your mum, your aunt and I took turns to feed you. We also tried another therapy in hope of providing some relief. Every morning at three o'clock, your mum and I struggled to wake up in order to feed you a kind of fortifying medicine. But it didn't work. Your condition just continued to deteriorate.

You also lost your control of your bowels. You must have sensed the time was close. One day after I gave you some water, you grabbed my hand.

"Dad, I think I may be leaving soon," you said. "I'm so sorry."

Tears streamed down my face as I grasped your hand. "Stop saying that," I said. "Mum and I will find a way to cure you."

You shook your head. "While I can still talk, promise me one thing."

"Of course, anything you want."

You fought to contain your tears. "When I leave this world, I'm not so worried about you. I know you're strong. But I am worried about Mum. Please take good care of her."

Reduced to sobbing, I nodded. "Don't worry, Son. How could I not take care of her? We've come through so much together during our marriage. We've always pulled through, despite all our trials. We may quarrel sometimes, but we've always supported each other through life. So don't worry."

You clenched my hand. "Thanks, Dad. I'm happy to hear that."

I shook your arm. "There's one thing you need to promise me, too," I said. "You can't give up on yourself now. You should fight the cancer together with me. A miracle may happen. I've read in books that seriously ill patients can sometimes still recover for inexplicable reasons. You must believe in miracles. Your mum and I are still counting on you to take care of us."

You didn't say a word, but tears rolled down your cheeks.

Dad, after this conversation with you now, I'll have no other concerns left on Earth. You can take care of my grandparents with the help of my aunts, uncles and cousins. I'm sure they still have a few good years ahead of them. Just don't tell them I've passed – we both know they won't be able to handle it. Just tell them I married a foreign girl while working abroad, and that I'm unable to visit them because she became sick.

You know, I always had a feeling that my days were numbered.

I told you not to ask for anything from the military unit I was working for. Not because of my pride, but out of guilt. I became ill not long after I started work. I achieved so little, yet my colleagues still visited me constantly in hospital.

Oh my comrades, I'm sorry I was unable to repay your kindness. If I ever upset you, please forgive me. If I said anything hurtful, please excuse me.

Dad, do you know what the most painful thing was for me at that time? It was that you and Mum had to take care of my toilet visits. Every time I needed to go, it took a few people just to get me in there! Later, I soiled myself all the time, just like a baby. Eventually, you had to put nappies on me, removing what little dignity I had left. The disease was so vindictive that it was able to take away any last bit of freedom and dignity from my life, just like a brutal dictator.

Who gave it such power? Why are there no limits on its ability to destroy?

Son, I saw the bitterness in your heart, and the suffering your loss of dignity caused. Your mum and I could see that your condition was getting worse every day. Knowing that the treatment of balancing *yin* and *yang* wouldn't be effective, we decided to try a head patch for removing tumours. I went with your MRI scan to consult the doctor for that. "No problem," the doctor said. "Bring the patient in." Your mum and I didn't entirely trust him, but what could we do? We were counting on a miracle. What if it had worked?

We had to believe there was hope.

Back again we went to the hospital. We didn't know then that this would be the last time you were at home. You wouldn't go home again after that. As we were leaving, I remember that you turned back to look at the unlocked door while Uncle Wang, who was carrying you downstairs, took a short rest. I thought maybe you'd forgotten something. "Don't worry," I said, "Everything has been packed for you."

I later realised that this was your farewell to our home, the place that had witnessed both joy and sorrow.

In the hospital, the nurses undressed you and put incontinence pants on you. "How utterly embarrassing," you muttered in disgust. I could find no words to console you.

I really didn't expect those to be the last words you would speak. Your very last words! You soon lost the ability to speak because of the build-up of fluid on your brain. After that, we could no longer communicate verbally. Your last sound was just a sigh, a final protest to the disease.

The miracle for which your mum and I held out hope never materialised. It seemed that the gods had ignored all of our prayers and entreaties, and refused to stop the unrelenting and aggressive disease. The tumour kept growing and the patch treatment led to a serious build-up of fluid on your brain. This impacted the part of your nervous system that regulated your body temperature. You were stuck with high fever of forty degrees.

And then you lost consciousness.

That tiny glimmer of hope in our hearts evaporated, and once again we were thrown in an abyss of despair and panic...

Dad, that was the first time I'd ever had a persistent high fever. The pain it caused was tremendous, much worse than the seizures. With those, I'd always lost consciousness so never felt any pain. The doctors tried to bring my temperature down as I drifted in and out of consciousness. In my brief moments of lucidity, it felt like I was being roasted in an oven. I tried to escape, but had no way to make even the slightest movement. An image of a roasted duck flashed before my eyes. It was as though I was that duck, set on an iron shelf. The roasting wouldn't stop until I was completely burned.

Sometimes I would open my eyes and look at you and Mum. My

eyes begged you to remove me from the fiery hell, but I knew there was nothing you could do. I kept my eyes firmly shut after that; I didn't want you to feel my agony and worry about me. Maybe it was God's intention to put me through this to atone for some earlier mistake I'd made. If so, let it be, but let me take the punishment alone. There was no reason for you and Mum to suffer too.

As I endured this punishment alone, I quickly lost the will to live. I just hoped for it to end, to be released from this torture, to be allowed to enter a new world.

For the first time I truly understood the advocates of euthanasia. In fact, euthanasia is a kind of ecstasy...

Son, I didn't accept that your high fever couldn't be stopped. I just thought this hospital was incompetent. Your mum and I decided to transfer you to the best hospital in the city. I called for an ambulance and begged the president of the other hospital to admit you. Their doctor checked on you.

"No drugs will be effective," he told us bluntly. "They can use ice therapy to cool you down physically. But it's a treatment of the symptom, with no real effect on the disease itself."

I didn't want to believe it, but I knew he was right. "So long as it alleviates my son's pain, please do what you can."

Son, that ice treatment was a further torment for you. You lay on the cold bedding, with ice bags wrapped like pillows and placed under your armpits. Anyone else would have done anything to be away from those ice bags, but even with them, your body temperature still only fell to thirty-seven degrees. On those days, I stared at the thermometer all day long. If it was thirty-seven or below, I could manage some food. But if it rose above thirty-seven, I panicked and lost my appetite.

You needed meticulous care: regular nasal feedings, changing the side you were lying on, cleaning and massaging your arms and legs, checking on your IV drip, and constantly watching your vital signs monitor. Our relatives and friends offered to help. Your mum and I took care of you during the day, while relatives and nurses took the night shift.

The beeping of your vital signs monitor was always in my head. The readings of your blood pressure, heartbeat, and oxygen levels kept flashing in front of my eyes. The rhythmic beeping and flashing were engraved on my mind. Even years later, some similar rhythm would catch my attention and I would look around involuntarily for a monitor that wasn't there.

There are two sounds in life that I truly loathe: one is a train whistle at night, which reminds me of all the times I had to take a night train, fighting to get tickets, the hustle of the crowd going through the ticket entrance to get on the train, and the soreness from cramming into the seat or even on the floor because there were no sleeping bunks available.

The second sound I loathe is the beeping of a medical monitor, which brings flooding back the memories of you in that hospital bed and the anguished look on your face. I cannot bear it...

Dad, I was in a deep sleep during those final few days. Except for the occasional scattered dream, I don't recall much at all. My ears fell deaf – I could hear nothing; my nose was impaired – I couldn't smell; I couldn't move my tongue; and I lost my sense of touch. They were all signs that my body was slipping away, step by step closer to death.

Son, that experience clearly showed that a life doesn't disappear with the flick of a switch. It's a gradual process. First your motion was limited, and then you were confined to bed. Next your body became paralysed, and you were completely dependent on others. Then you lost the ability to talk, your senses failed, and finally you fell unconscious into a peaceful state. This was all preparing you to enter a new world.

This is the opposite of how a new life takes shape. Each life begins in silence with no consciousness, and over time starts to acquire senses and form reactions. Gradually it gains independence with the freedom to get out of bed, communicate, and move around through free will.

The end of life is just the mirror image of how it begins.

Dad, in that unconscious state, I felt a relief I had never experienced before. There was no pressure on me. It was as though an invisible hand had removed the burdens from my shoulders, one after another. The relief was enormous.

You always talked about looking forward to a relaxed life after your retirement. I thought this must be similar to that. In death, we can finally relax. In death, no longer do we need to do our boss' bidding, nor worry about being late for work or making careless mistakes. With work, though, there's always some unrelenting pressure that never really goes away. For instance, you may need to fight for certain compensation in retirement, worry about your children's family and work, or the development of your grandchildren.

But in my final moments, I had only one question to deal with: when should I leave?

16

Son, your coma threw your mum and me into a panic. Of course, we knew what it meant. Mum wanted to stay with you through the night, instead of going home to get some sleep. But I couldn't allow it. After enduring days of this torment, her own body was close to breaking down. Even one night in the hospital might have left her hospitalised.

"If you're so worried," I told her, "let me stay overnight instead." This persuaded Mum to go home for the night. In fact, my own body was on the verge of collapse as well, like a bottle of water that is nearly empty, just a few drops remaining. For your mum's sake, though, I willed myself to stay strong and settled in for the night shift.

Something was wrong with your catheter the next morning. Even then I couldn't go home to get some rest! At lunchtime, I really wanted a bowl of noodles from a guesthouse on the east side of the hospital, about two hundred metres away. I could see people coming in and out of its doorway, but I simply didn't have the strength to walk over. I feared I would collapse. Then what would happen to you and Mum?

In the end I bought two unheated buns at the hospital's grocery store, then stayed around the corner from a staircase to eat them. If an acquaintance had passed me at that moment, he would have been surprised by the way I sat and ate; perhaps he wouldn't have recognised me at all. I didn't even have the strength to pick up a newspaper and put it under my backside to sit on. I just sat on the bare floor, leaned against the wall and ate with my washed hands. At that moment, I ate simply to sustain myself so I could go back to your bedside. After I'd finished eating, I remember sitting there for what must have been twenty minutes before I could summon the strength to stand up and walk again.

Dad, I'm sorry for dragging you and Mum down. Even while I was in the coma, I could still feel you and Mum around me. I could sense your smells, your voices, and your footsteps as I drifted in and out of consciousness. Perhaps it was because of the mysterious connection of blood ties. As I was fading, hearing was the last sense I lost. As I drifted further and further away, I could still hear some vague, fragmented sounds, but I could no longer discern their meaning. I wished I could tell you to give up and let me go, to accept that any further effort was pointless. But despite my wishes I couldn't speak.

Even if I could have spoken at that moment, and even if I had talked to you, I know now that you still wouldn't have given up. Among all the relationships in the world, only those between parents and their children are truly pure and unconditional. It's human nature. Other close relationships, including those between grandchildren and grandparents, husbands and wives, siblings and even close friends can withstand awful difficulties as well.

Dad, please tell Mum that, even after all the pain, it was your love that made me see that the world is truly a beautiful place.

Son, the moment that your mum and I feared the most finally came. At ten o'clock that night we fed you some water and administered your medicine. We checked the medical machines you were hooked up to and handed you over to your cousin and nurse for the night as Mum and I prepared to leave for home. She paused at the door, as if struck by a sudden thought. "I think I should stay here tonight," she said.

"But you've been here the whole day," I protested. "Now you want to stay the night as well? How will you have the energy to take care of our son tomorrow?" Reluctantly she agreed and we left together, though she clearly still had doubts.

How could I possibly have known that this is how we would part? If I had known, of course I wouldn't have encouraged your mum to leave the hospital. If I'd known, of course I would have spent the night at hospital with her.

It was three o'clock in the morning when my phone suddenly vibrated. I woke up. It was your cousin's number. My heart was pounding. He knew how exhausted I was and he wouldn't have woken me up unless it was urgent. As soon as I picked it up, I heard your cousin's frantic voice.

"Uncle, please come quickly! Ning's blood pressure has dropped suddenly. He's been sent to intensive care!"

I didn't want to frighten your mum, so I kept my voice low. "OK, I'm coming," I replied.

I grabbed my clothes and opened the door, which woke your mum. She ran to the door and grabbed my hand. "Where are you going?"

"Ning's blood pressure is a little low," I replied as calmly as I could. "I'm going to the hospital to check on him."

Your mother turned to get her coat. "I'm coming with you."

I wanted her to get more sleep. "Let me go first," I told her. "I'll call you if it's serious."

I ran out of the compound, gasping for breath. I didn't wake up the driver. He was tired too, but I knew I couldn't drive in this frame of mind. In the darkness, I ran to the street to hail a taxi.

When I reached the hospital, your cousin Shanwa was waiting anxiously in front of the intensive care unit. He told me they were still trying to resuscitate you. I watched doctors rushing in and out. I grabbed one and asked if I could come in. The doctor shook his head.

"We're still trying to save him," he told me. "You can't do anything to help in there, and you may bring some bacteria in. Please wait here for now. We'll let you know when we have any news."

I paced back and forth outside the ICU until the morning light broke. There had been no updates at all from inside. I slouched downed to floor and fixed my eyes on the door of the ICU. Finally, your doctor emerged. I stood up quickly.

"How is he?" I asked. The doctor didn't reply. He just removed his lab coat and gestured for me to put it on. He then led me into the ICU.

"Come and say goodbye to your son. I'm sorry, but we just lost him."

Like an explosion, the rock hanging over me suddenly fell. I was seized by a violent headache. My body wobbled and I struggled to hold on to the wall. I took a deep breath, and stumbled towards the ICU.

Dad, when the doctors and nurses wheeled me into the ICU, I was ready to leave the world. I was tired of living with this illness, with no quality of life. Living wasn't only torture for me, but it had placed an enormous strain on you and Mum. It was time to bring it all to an end.

I once watched a film in which a man became a paraplegic following a swimming accident. Eventually he became so tired of being looked after by other people, that he went to extraordinary lengths to find someone who would help him take his own life. At the time I couldn't understand him; now, though, I completely empathised.

Living isn't effortless, especially living with a hopeless disease that creates a enormous burden and sucks all the pleasure out of life. So if living causes me to suffer, why shouldn't I free myself?

While the doctors were working on my body, my soul was watching coldly from the side, without offering any help. At that moment, all I wanted was to leave, to leave behind the fever, the ice bags, the cold bed, the debilitating seizures, the feeble limping, all the restrictions of the human body and the human world...

Son, when I rushed to your bedside, there you were, lying perfectly still; it was clear that you had stopped breathing. I leaned down to kiss you. I kissed your cheeks, your forehead, and your hands. Your body was still warm, and there was no trace of pain or distress on your face.

I dared not cry. I had heard that if tears fell onto a deceased family member, it might make their soul reluctant to leave. So I fought back the tears and seized the last chance to massage you. I massaged your shoulders, to make them flat; your arms, to make them relaxed; your legs, to allow them to stretch out more comfortably; and your feet, to restore them back to their state in the days before you were sick.

Gradually your body was getting cold. In desperation, I tried to massage you more vigorously to warm your body, but it didn't work. I knew you were definitely leaving this world. I turned to the sky to pray, hoping that God would give me some more time to continue massaging your body and be with you; but the clouds rolled in at that moment, with God behind them. He was determined to ignore me and take you away. As your body grew colder, you drifted further and further away...

Dad, when you came to my bedside, my soul had just risen off the ground, not far above your head. I saw you kissing and massaging me, but I felt neither. I heard you sobbing to yourself and saw how devastated you were, but I couldn't console you and Mum any more.

I'm sorry, Dad. You and Mum gave me all your love, but all you received in return was the pain of parting. In the next life, in the other world, I promise I will do my best to repay you...

Dad, I felt so relieved and comfortable when my soul was finally freed from my flesh. I could float anywhere, overlooking your world. I once read a report in a science journal about near-death experiences. An experiment was carried out in which a particular design was put onto the beds of patients who were on the verge of death and who couldn't possibly have seen the design. After they were resuscitated and brought back to life, almost a hundred patients said they could recall the pattern. I had my doubts when I first read this, but now I understand.

I couldn't go far, however. A lady with a white veil pulled me off the ground, and whispered that I shouldn't stray too far away from you, that I was still in the early stages of bidding farewell to this world. In the past, I'd heard old people talk about death, saying that when someone dies, two ferocious ghosts come to take away the soul. Now I know this to be wrong. It was a lady with a white veil or scarf who came to me. I couldn't make out her face, but I could feel her gentle kindness. She mostly used gestures to communicate. When she did speak, her voice was soft, almost like a whisper. She seemed very cultured and elegant, and I wasn't afraid of her at all.

Of course, I didn't want to go far, anyway. Before, I had grown resentful of life and had no desire to cling to this world. But when it came to it, when it really was time to leave, I was reluctant. After all, I had spent twenty-nine years in this world, during which I had grown up, gone to school, and worked in military service. This world where you and Mum still lived, as well as Grandma and Grandpa, all our other relatives; my classmates from all the schools I went to; my peers, colleagues and friends in the military. In the end, it was so difficult to leave you all.

I had also grown attached to many of the places I lived in or visited: Zhouzhuang, Qulin, Dengzhou, Nanyang, Jinan, Zhengzhou, Xi'an, and Beijing. It made it very uncomfortable to leave them all behind.

Son, when the staff from the hospital morgue came, I helped them to move you from the bed. This was the last time I carried you. I remembered how I held you when you were a child, and how I carried you many times after you became unwell, even though you were taller and heavier than me. In the past, each time I carried you, I felt warmth because you were my son, the continuation of my life. This time, however, my heart was overwhelmed with pain and despair.

As I carried you out of the ICU room, your mum, aunts, uncles, and cousins huddled around you. Mum burst into tears and came to hug you. I was afraid that her tears would fall on you, so I hurried to place you on the trolley. I had no idea why I insisted on escorting you from ICU to the morgue. I held your hand tightly, to protect you from being scared.

Son, in the natural order of things, I should leave first, then Mum, and then you last. It should be you escorting me. But this had been reversed because that was God's will. I can hardly find the words to describe how heart-wrenching that was.

After I sent you to the morgue, I went home to gather your clothes and some other things for the funeral. My heartache was beyond control. Days of sleep and food deprivation had given me a headache and dizziness. At that moment, I really just wanted to leave this world together with you. But your mum had already collapsed in bed, crying. I couldn't just abandon her. I needed to pull myself together and support our family during this time of crisis. I braced myself and contacted people to arrange everything for your funeral. Fortunately, with the help of your cousins, I managed to get everything done.

It was 3 August 2008, the date that changed the history of our family. I don't know why God chose that particular day. All I know is that we will never be able to speak to you again...

Dad, while you were preparing for my funeral, the lady in the white veil who had pulled me off the ground signalled for me to follow her. I really didn't want to, and she didn't say where we were going. I was worrying about you and Mum, and didn't want to let you out of my sight. However, she moved her finger just a little, and a sudden great force pushed me to follow her. We didn't use our legs to walk. We just floated as if on a cloud. I faced the direction she pointed. Then a howling wind sent us flying.

In the blink of an eye, we were in another place, with surging, turbulent water below. Countless people were crying and struggling in the water. Suddenly, I became nervous – what was this place? I bent down instinctively to try to reach the struggling people, but the lady lifted her hand, and I couldn't move at all.

"Why won't you let me save them?" I shouted at her. She didn't answer, but gestured at me to keep watching. "What am I looking at?"

Still she was silent. The number of people struggling in the water dwindled. At this moment, she took my hand again and motioned for me to follow her again.

We travelled the same way as before. I opened my eyes as soon as the hum of the wind stopped, and the sight was even more frightening. The ground beneath my body had cracked. The cracks were gushing out fiery magma and sand; houses were collapsing, people were crying and running away, many people were trapped in crumpled houses, and countless others had fallen into cracks in the land.

"What is this place?" I asked her in horror.

She didn't answer; she just gestured at me to keep watching.

I leaned over to pull a man from one of the cracks, and once again she froze me with the flick of a finger.

"Why can't we save them?" She remained silent. "Why are you showing me this if I can't do anything about it?"

Still she didn't answer. I could only stare at her in disbelief...

17

Ning, early on the morning of 5 August 2008, I went to the morgue with your mum, your uncle Liu, and your cousin Shanwa. We asked the staff to dress you. This was the first time you'd worn the new 2007-style military uniform. You were quite ill when the uniform had been sent to you, so you'd asked me to put it away until you got better. No one could have foreseen that the first time you would wear it would be at your own funeral.

Seeing you in the uniform, my heart was torn into pieces. Just a few short years ago you were full of vim and vigour on the basketball court. How could your life have been turned into this? Why couldn't it have taken another path?

Before placing you in the coffin, I kissed you again. It was my last chance...

The hearse pulled into the Babaoshan graveyard. You were placed in the funeral parlour. Your leaders, colleagues and friends came to bid you farewell. At that moment, I worried that your mum and I would collapse there and then. But we hung on so you could go in peace.

At the end of the farewell ceremony, I took you to the back room, but the staff wouldn't let me go any further. I knew it was our final moment together. I threw myself on top of you and kissed you one last time.

Farewell, Son...

Then your body was cremated, and an hour later I put your ashes in the urn with my quivering hands. Your mum, uncle, cousin Shanwa and I took you to the Laoshan Hall of Ashes to stay temporarily.

I had always intended that you would live out your life in a large home; instead, here you were, aged only twenty-nine, bound to a shrine of just two square feet.

When I left the Laoshan Hall of Ashes, I finally allowed my tears to flow. The trees on the hillside, the birds in the trees, the clouds in the sky, and the Creator in charge of our fate; all of them should hear my cries!

Son, why was life so callous to us? Why were you struck down by this disease? Why didn't this disaster befall me, instead of you?

Why?

Dad, I followed you that whole time in the farewell room at Babaoshan and in front of the crematorium in Laoshan. Seeing the grief on both your faces, how badly I wanted to reach out and wipe away your tears! But the woman in the white veil prevented me again. I could only watch your pain, unable to offer any comfort. Let it go, Dad! I'll always be your son.

I didn't feel sad when my body was cremated. On the contrary, I was relieved to be unshackled from it. The human body has many desires: appetite, lust, fortune, material things, power, fame, success, immortality. Each pushes people to strive forward, out of breath, and to live insipid and unfulfilling lives. Sometimes people burn with anger, or gnash their teeth with hatred, stamp their feet in frustration or cry out in pain.

What is the meaning of a life controlled by desire? So long as the body exists, why is that so few can see beyond the wants of the flesh? I was finally able to part with my body, and with it, all my earthly desires.

I was no longer a slave to my physical form. Finally, I was free.

Son, when we got back from Laoshan, we saw reminders of you everywhere in the house. Your mum and I couldn't stop ourselves from crying. From that day, we always feared the nights, when we missed you the most; from that day, we feared holidays, which reminded us that our family was incomplete; from that day, we feared going to weddings of our friends' children, where the bride or groom would remind us of the wedding you should have had; from that day, we feared meeting up with friends, because they would naturally talk about their children, when we had none...

One day, your mum held the clothes you left behind and sobbed. "It's not right to leave Ning's ashes in that hall. We need to find a cemetery for him where he can rest in peace."

"Yes," I agreed, "I'll take a good look at all the cemeteries in the city." Starting the next day, I ran around the city to inspect the various cemeteries I'd found online. I must have visited almost all the cemeteries in Beijing!

After an exhausting day, I finally decided that Tianshou Cemetery was the best; not just because it was where many scientists, educators and artists rested and could keep you company, but because it was a beautiful park with green grass, persimmon trees, flowers, fountains, long galleries, pavilions, and stone carvings. There was a long walk adorned with statues of monks, and people roamed freely inside.

A sense of leisure permeated the grounds. The site was well-managed too, with security guards all day long and maintenance staff carefully wiping and tending the tombstones. Music reverberated throughout the park every day. I wanted this to be your final resting place. I went home to tell your mum, who went to see for herself, and she agreed.

In the cemetery, as well as single tombs, there were tombs for couples, tombs for families of three, and tombs for several generations of family members. I asked your mum if we should reserve places for our own graves, since this was an ideal place to rest. Your mum agreed. It was common in this graveyard for parents to buy graves so they could one day rest with their deceased children. They just left their own tombstones blank until they were needed.

The next thing was to choose a location for your grave. We walked through the cemetery and picked a spot beside the corridor in Ark Park. Here, a young girl who had died of an illness was on your left, a young man was on your right, and a teenager who had died in a car accident was just behind you on the right. You would at least have others to talk to and not feel lonely.

A separate tomb for your mum and me was next to yours. You had one, and we a larger one. The tombstone was in the shape of a book and so were the lids of the two tombs, but your book wasn't completely finished.

We all loved reading. Even in the afterlife, books can accompany us. We had three lines engraved on your tombstone:

His character is moral and kind
His work meticulous and exemplary
Mum and Dad love you forever

Dad, I saw the cemetery you chose for me, the location of the tomb, and the gravestone you and Mum picked out. I was very pleased. Of course I was happy that you and Mum had a tomb next to me. One day we would all be close to each other again. My only concern was that it might be an unlucky omen. After all, you were still alive.

I wanted to tell you that on that day, when the tombstone was arranged to be engraved, I actually went with you, and I wanted to be there all the time. However, the lady with the white veil who shadowed me pulled me away. She took me to another place, a city I'd never seen before. It was bustling with skyscrapers and the interweaving flow of cars and people. But I couldn't see anyone's faces or read the words on the billboards. I couldn't even tell which city or country this was. I thought she just wanted to show me a prosperous city scene.

Suddenly, the peace was broken by sirens. Ambulances screamed down the street, one after another. Dozens of ambulances pulled up, and anguished cries rang out as people ran in a panic through the streets. Then, in a flash, people began to fall to the ground, with more screaming all around. A moment later, the noise died down. More cars and ambulances pulled up. The whole city fell deadly silent.

"What just happened?" I asked, shocked by the scene below me. The lady was as silent as she had always been. I wanted to go down to the ground and see what was going on, but she pulled me back and left me frozen. I stared at her face under the veil and struggled to understand why she had shown me this strange and macabre scene...

Son, it's not a bad omen to pick out tombs and gravestones ahead of time. Your grandparents in the countryside chose wooden boards to make into coffins long ago, and the location of the tomb in our family graveyard, which set their minds at ease. Ever since your mum and I decided on our tombs and gravestones, I have had peace of mind, with nothing to worry about.

The date of your burial was set for a weekend so as to be convenient for friends and relatives who wanted to pay their respects and say farewell. According to your mum's wishes, we also invited an abbot and a few monks from the nearby temple to chant prayers during the funeral ceremony.

The ceremony was held in a special hall in the cemetery. After your mum and I placed your urn into the hall, the monks played Buddhist music, lit candles and incense, saluted and began chanting the scriptures aloud. After the chanting and saluting, an honour guard placed your urn in a coffin, which was later carried by four members of the honour guard and taken to the graveyard under the guidance of another honour guard bearing the national flag.

It was a gloomy morning in early April. Your mum and I walked behind the coffin with friends and relatives as we headed towards your final resting place in Ark Park, amid the sound of mournful music. No one could have felt the grief in my heart. I had written about burials several times in the past, but only then did I realise that the anguish I had written about was far removed from reality. Only those who have experienced the burial of a loved one can truly relate to the inner torment of people who have experienced loss like this: the feelings of futility and panic, of helplessness and pain, of desolation and gloom.

My eyes lost focus, my legs wobbled, and my body trembled with pain...

———

Dad, I was watching as you and Mum put a mobile phone, an MP3 music player, watches and a few other things in my grave. You also burned paper money, clothing, cars, houses, furniture, and household appliances outside the cemetery. You had carefully planned all the things I would need in the afterlife. Still close to you at that time, I hadn't completely passed on to the next world, and I didn't understand what life was like there or if these things would even be useful. Still, I was deeply touched. You took care of me no matter what. Even after I had passed, you were still trying to make my situation as comfortable as possible.

My ashes were buried, completing the first leg of the journey the Creator had charted for me. I had started from nothing, acquired a physical form, then returned to nothing.

That's what people often say: that in life, people are bred by their parents, who eat the grain from the earth; and in death, so they must return to the soil. To do otherwise would anger God.

Sometimes I think that life is a game, like the clay dolls we used to make as children. We would blend clay with water and mould them into dolls. Then we put them neatly on the classroom window sill, and we'd talk to them and play with them. Suddenly, heavy rain leaked through the window and over the window sill. It melted the clay dolls, mixing them once again with the soil beneath the window. The dolls returned to the earth...

Man comes from nothing and returns to nothing. It's a cycle...

Son, if life is a game, it should follow a fundamental rule of all games: that people playing it must do so voluntarily. I don't want to be a part of this game. In fact I hate it! A game should never be so cruel as this one. People play games for fun. Where's the fun in this game? It's absurd for the Creator to have designed this game and set the rules for it. I protest strongly against it. I would rather not be alive. In fact, I wish I'd never been born!

If I hadn't been born, then I wouldn't have suffered all the pain of life and death. I really want to suggest that the Creator should ask a man's own will before He decides to bring him into the world. If he agrees, then he will be born. If not, he will not. Surely, that's the only way to be fair?

But with the Creator's game, regardless of whether or not you want to be born, regardless of whether you will be able to endure the pain of living, the Creator only asks for your parents' opinion. And sometimes not even theirs! It just makes no sense at all...

Dad, don't be so dramatic! Don't lose respect for the Creator just because you lost me. Every parent has the right to have children, and the Creator must honour that right. Imagine if the Creator hadn't allowed me to be born after you and Mum were married. You would have been angry with Him and thought that was also unfair!

Please calm down. You are suffering from losing me, but you are not the only one who has experienced this kind of pain. Remember that car accident in the suburbs of Beijing? A family of four was hit and only the mother survived. Didn't she lose more than you did?

A man has to accept his destiny in life, good or bad, happy or miserable. Destiny lies in the hand of the invisible God, who alone is responsible for determining the fate of man. No matter what you get, you should just accept it with grace. There's no sense in complaining.

I lost my life, and you lost your son. I am trying to convince you as well as myself to accept this. Do we have any other choice?

18

Son, not long after your funeral, I dreamed about you one night. In the dream, you rushed into my arms.

"Dad, do you still remember me?" you asked.

I was stunned. "Son, how can you ask this?" I replied, patting you on the shoulder. "How could I possibly forget you?" Then I suddenly remembered that you were no longer with us. "Have they sent you back?" I asked. You nodded. I became emotional and wanted to hug you again.

Suddenly I awoke from my dream. I lay there wistfully for a while, trying to interpret out the meaning of this dream. Did it mean that you missed your mum and me?

And why would you have asked me that question?

Dad, your dream was just a reflection of you missing me. When you were dreaming about me, I was actually far away. After my ashes were buried, the lady in the white veil turned to me.

"Now you can come with me," she whispered. I nodded. All earthly matters had been settled, and I understood that I couldn't linger here forever. She handed me a piece of black cloth. "Cover your eyes," she instructed. As soon as I did that, the wind whistled in my ears. I felt her pulling my hand and, before I knew it, we were flying.

I don't know for how long or how far we travelled. But eventually I heard a man's voice. "Everybody stand here!"

The lady and I stopped, and the black cloth on my eyes fell away. I saw that we were on the bank of a great river. There were no buildings, only trees and grass. The river was shrouded in thick fog, and its other bank was not visible. The flow of the river was fast and smooth, its dark green colour implying its great depth. No seaweed could be seen, nor any reeds on the bank. A light wind rustled the grass and leaves. No cicadas could be heard; in fact it was eerily quiet.

On the riverbank stood other newly arrived souls just like me, each with their own white-veiled lady as a guide. Only then did I realise that everything I'd seen wasn't for me alone. All souls who came to this world were accompanied by an escort who guided the way between the two worlds.

Eventually, I mustered up the courage to talk to my companion. "Can I see your face now?"

She shook her head, though I sensed she was not offended. "I am not permitted to remove the veil. Please forgive me," she replied.

"Then can you tell me your name?" She shook her head and gestured for me to look ahead.

"Welcome to Heaven," said man who had just called us. He stood in front of us on an oddly shaped tree stump. His voice boomed. "Heaven is immense and is divided into many kingdoms, or fields. This side of the river belongs to the Field of Judgment, where you will be screened and sent to your respective destinations. The Field of Judgment is very large, and contains many gateways. This is Gateway 333339. Most of the souls we receive here are from China. You can address me as 'Gatekeeper'. Think of me like an immigration officer from your old life. After the screening process I shall send you all to your different destinations.

Dad, I was in the Kingdom of Judgment in Heaven! It was difficult to take in, but I leaned forward, eager to listen to the Gatekeeper.

"What you see before you is the true nature of Heaven," the Gatekeeper continued. "Here you will find many things that existed on

Earth, and some things that did not. Look around this kingdom and acquaint yourselves with it."

I looked around. My companion who had brought me here turned to me. "This is the bank of the River Styx," she whispered. On the bank were all kinds of trees: willow, elm, plum trees in blossom, and trumpet vines. I could see boats on the river and stones on its banks. My eyes were full of wonder; was this really the Kingdom of Judgment in Heaven?

"There are four steps to complete before you can cross the river!" The Gatekeeper announced loudly.

I turned to the lady in the white veil. "Why don't we just fly across the river?" I asked quietly. "Why go to the trouble of taking a boat?"

She shook her head. "No one can fly across this river," she whispered. "It is a natural barrier. The only way across is to take a boat. It is God's will. Whoever dares to disobey shall fall into an abyss from which they can never be rescued."

I silenced myself and continued to listen.

"The first step is to verify your identity. I will announce your age, how you came to arrive here, and the destination where your soul shall reside. You will be able to double check for yourselves, in order to avoid confusion."

The Gatekeeper held some kind of register and called out the first name. "Xiao Jiaxiao."

"Here." An old man stepped forward.

"You are seventy-nine years old. You died of liver disease, and your soul is truly rotten."

Xiao Jiaxiao looked devastated. "Why is my soul rotten?"

"When you were twenty years old, you stumbled upon a girl being raped in a corner of the factory where you worked. You failed to intervene and later denied having witnessed the incident.

"You had three marriages and five children. When you were fifty-two years old, you beat your second wife to rid yourself of her. Your persistent domestic violence eventually drove her to hang herself. To hide the truth, you made an excuse that she didn't get along with your children from your previous marriage.

"These are the reasons why your soul reeks of filth."

Xiao Jiaxiao was shocked, dumbstruck. He stared blankly at the Gatekeeper as he struggled to find his voice.

"Am I perhaps mistaken?" The Gatekeeper gazed at him, and turned to the crowd. "If I am wrong, please tell me now. I wish not to level false accusations at anyone. Xiao Jiaxiao, need I repeat the testimony?"

Xiao Jiaxiao said nothing, and simply lowered his head in shame.

The Gatekeeper turned to the next page. "Jiang Weilan," he continued.

"Yes," answered a young woman.

"You are a soul of slight impurity."

"But my soul is untarnished," she protested.

"You quarrelled with a classmate from a poor family when you were seventeen years old, and deliberately knocked her calculator to the ground.

"When you were twenty-four, you posted an anonymous story online about a college student working as a prostitute at a hotel because you were jealous of her beauty. This story caused her and her boyfriend to break up.

"When you were twenty-seven, you complained about your mother-in-law and had frequent altercations with her. You threatened your husband with divorce in order to remove her from your house. And you refused to allow your husband to visit her at weekends, leaving her stricken with loneliness.

"I repeat: you are a soul of slight impurity."

Jiang Weilan was silent. I was shocked by how precisely the Gatekeeper appeared to know everyone's deeds in the human world.

"Lin Wenhao."

"Yes," a man in his forties replied.

"Lin Wenhao, forty-five years old. You burned yourself to death. After your house was designated to be demolished, you refused to leave because you thought the compensation offered was unreasonable. You refused to relent even when the developer cut off the electricity and water supply. You were stubborn, even when the developer hired people to bulldoze your house. You set yourself on fire in front of them as a protest. Your soul bears injustice."

Tears flowed down Lin Wenhao's cheeks.

The Gatekeeper turned over another page. "Chen Dongchang."

"Here," answered another man.

"Chen Dongchang, forty-one years old, died of a heart attack. You were the chairman of a paper mill which dumped pollutants into the water. During the inspection by the environmental protection agency, you would activate the decontamination equipment and promise not to discharge any pollution. You would then immediately turn it off after the inspection in order to reduce costs. The drinking water for tens of thousands of people was contaminated. Many mothers gave birth to deformed babies, and children died of pollution-related diseases. Whenever anyone tried to report you to officials, you bribed them and threatened those who rejected your offer. Your soul is guilty."

"But I paid so much in taxes to the government every year," Chen Dongchang protested loudly. "I'm not only innocent but also virtuous!"

The Gatekeeper glared at him. "Taxes or human lives: which is more important?"

"Because of my contributions to the local economy, three mayors from the city were promoted."

"Do you truly understand the meaning of the word 'contribution'?" The Gatekeeper narrowed his eyes.

"You have no right to judge me," said Chen defiantly. "You weren't there. So many people attended my funeral, which was presided over by the secretary of the municipal party committee. I was honoured as a role model for entrepreneurs! A memorial hall will be built in my name! My biography is to be written by a professional writer! My name will be immortal in my city!" he said proudly.

"Believe that your name shall be immortal, if you must."

"Luo Daodong," the Gatekeeper continued swiftly.

"Here," answered a man who looked a little older than me.

"Luo Daodong, thirty-seven years old. You arrived here because of infections that resulted from burns that you received. You were idle at home, and always argued with your wife. You even slapped her on occasion.

"One day a neighbour's apartment caught fire, and firefighters arrived to fight the blaze. You managed to get out of your apartment, but you rushed back into your neighbour's without hesitation when you heard a child crying from within. The fire engulfed you quickly. The neighbour's child was rescued, but you died of the infections. You are a compassionate soul, despite minor flaws."

Luo Daodong smiled. "Thank you for the compliment."

"Tan Lisheng," the Gatekeeper continued as he read from the register.

"Here," a man called out.

"Tan Lisheng, fifty-nine years old. You hung yourself before being detained and interrogated. As a high-ranking officer in the Commission for Discipline Inspection, you worshipped money, and you tried every means imaginable to acquire wealth. You ordered your subordinates to send money to you and collected red envelopes[1] from them on various holidays. If anything happened in your family, like a wedding or funeral, or even someone being hospitalised, you would ask your secretary to inform your subordinates, expecting them to give their condolences with offerings of red envelopes. If someone didn't show up, you would ask your secretary to threaten them with impeachment, and scare them into sending you a red envelope. You embezzled tens of millions over the course of your life. Yours is truly a greedy soul."

"Liu Huihuang," the Gatekeeper continued.

"Yes," said a young man.

"Liu Huihuang, you are thirty-eight years old and lived a good life with your family. You should have enjoyed your life, but you opened an illegal coal mine. Several landslides buried workers underground, and you always found excuses to cover it up. When another miner was crushed to death by a landslide, you secretly burned the body and refused to pay compensation. The miner's family had no choice but to report you. The coal mine was closed down. You were determined to retaliate against the whistleblowers using explosives. Many innocent people died in the explosion. You were cruel and had lost your humanity. Even when you were sentenced to death, you were unrepentant, and claimed still to be a hero even after twenty years. Your soul is so contaminated, a soul of crime."

Li Huihuang stared at the Gatekeeper. "What can you do about my atrocities?" he sneered. "Are you going to sentence me to death again?

Mark my words, I shall be a monstrous ghost and haunt people's lives for eternity!"

"Good, very good. Very bold indeed," the Gatekeeper said, almost humouring him.

"Did you think I am scared by you, by this?" Li twitched his lips in contempt. "You must be kidding me!"

"Jiao Danzhu," the Gatekeeper continued.

A white-veiled lady raised a baby in her arms. "Yes," she answered.

"Jian Danzhu, you are only three months old. You came here due to a high fever. You were never tarnished, nor did you commit any crimes against the law or morality. You are truly a pure soul."

Jiao Danzhu didn't seem to understand and gave a short cry in response.

"Wang Meili," the Gatekeeper continued. A woman stepped forward.

"Wang Meili, fifty years old, you have arrived here following a death sentence. As a political officer, you abused your rank to trample over other people's lives. Your son once liked a girl and tried to rape her. The girl fought back but he killed her in the ensuing struggle. You are a parent yourself. You must have understood the girl's parents' grief. They desired retribution and sought to send your son to prison. However, you accused them of not disciplining their daughter, whom you claimed provoked your son in public, and induced his mental disorder. You purported to obtain medical proof of your son's mental disorder, which exonerated him from all charges. In fact, your son had no such disorder. The girl's parents pressed for prosecution. You couldn't suppress them even with all your power. Then you murderously contracted someone to pretend to be drunk and run the girl's parents down with a car. An entire family was wiped out. Your soul is covered in complete darkness, stained with evil and sin."

Wang Meili sneered. "Ever since that incident with my son, all I have heard is criticism about what I did. I became numb. I have lost my life. You have brought me here. What is there to be scared of? What more can you possibly do to me? Sentence me to death again if you wish!" she retorted.

The chief narrowed his eyes and stared at her. "Very good," he said after a while. "Such a heroine, very impressive."

The Gatekeeper commented on each soul lined up according to his register. I was the last one, I think because I'd only just arrived.

"Zhou Ning, twenty-nine years old. You come here after a brain tumour. You lied to your parents many times when you were a teenager because of your addiction to video games. You are a soul with slight blemishes." I was shocked. Did they really record such trivial matters?!

Dad, I'm sorry that I was so addicted to video games back then. I always went to the internet café after school and lied to you, saying that I'd stayed at school to do my homework. I'm sorry to say that the Gatekeeper was correct: I did lie to you.

Most souls that arrived at Gateway 333339 were similar to my own judgment: souls containing slight blemishes. Only five souls were considered evil while in the human world.

I remember two other cases in particular: one man was accused of rape and murder. He just happened to pass by a murder scene, went to check on the victim, but left his fingerprints and footprints at the scene. He was convicted and sentenced to death. The real murderer was only discovered long afterwards.

The second case was a young girl who had worked in a government agency; a girl whose beauty attracted her boss to try to seduce her. She refused his advances and reported him for sexual harassment. Her boss held a grudge and hired someone to follow her and film her on a date with her boyfriend, which was later portrayed on the internet as an act of prostitution. She took a drug overdose and ended her life.

After the identity screening, the Gatekeeper put down his register and addressed the gathered crowd. "Now we shall take the second step. You must bathe and change." He pointed at the river bank. "Men are to bathe under the locust tree three hundred metres to the left. Women are to bathe under the oak tree three hundred metres to the right. All souls, please now go and bathe yourselves. You will find your new clothes on the bank: blue robes for men, and white dresses for women. Discard your old clothes. Then return here afterwards. Is everyone clear? Please make sure you bathe near the shore. Do not venture too far out."

Everyone nodded as the men and women walked to their respective sides. Before I moved with the other men, the one with a soul of crime, the illegal coal mine operator, pointed at a few of the other souls. "Do we all need to bathe and change?" he asked the Gatekeeper.

"Yes, of course," answered the Gatekeeper. "Just wait for a moment."

We men came to the locust tree on the left, undressed, and washed ourselves. The light was dim, but the water was clear. It was cool, yet bearable. There was no trace of weeds, nor fish. As we bathed, the water felt as if it were expanding. Fog rose from the middle and drifted across the river, blocking the view of the other shore. It was dead silent, with no other sound except us. It was nothing like any river I had ever seen before. There were no fish bumping into my legs, nor frogs croaking on the bank.

After we finished bathing, we found a pile of blue robes on the shore. Our guides, the ladies in the white veils, were waiting on the shore as well. Perhaps because we didn't possess physical bodies anymore, they didn't shy away. They helped us to pick up our robes and get dressed.

After a few moments, we were all dressed in the blue robes, which were quite pleasant to look at. The women came back in their white dresses, like angels in the heavens. The Gatekeeper asked us to stand by, and turned to those who hadn't yet bathed: Chen Dongchang, Tan Lisheng, Liu Huihuang, and Wang Meili. "Now it's your turn. As before, men on the left side under the locust tree, women on the right side under the oak tree."

"Why didn't you let us go with them? What's the point of separating us since it's the same place. Why the extra fucking effort?" Liu Huihuang grumbled and scoffed.

The Gatekeeper didn't seem upset at all. "For different experiences."

"How? It's the same river. Can you boil the river? It's mystical nonsense!" Liu Huihuang continued to grumble.

They were clearly all upset about having been separated from the rest of us, but they had little choice but to follow their instructions.

The rest of us waited. I thought to myself that there was no sense in dividing us up, since we all bathed in the same river. Perhaps it was all just for show. By now we could see them in the water. They seemed as though they would finish very soon. Suddenly, Liu Huihuang and Chen Dongsheng broke the silence.

"Oh God!" someone screamed.

Everyone was startled. "What happened? We were just there." Before anyone could respond, Wang Meili shrieked from the right.

"Oh my God!" she shrieked.

We looked at the Gatekeeper, who just stood there calmly and watched.

Out of curiosity, a few other souls and I ran to the locust tree to take a closer look. We gasped in horror. A dozen or so crocodiles appeared to be attacking the bathers. They struggled to get back to the bank, but failed in the face of the ferocious attacks. They bobbed up and down, helplessly trying to dodge the attacks of the crocodiles, their hands covering their heads, screaming for help.

A few of us pulled some branches off the tree on the shore and tried to help them by attacking the crocodiles, but the Gatekeeper stopped us. He waited until they were exhausted and stood in the water, frozen with terror, then waved his hand. Surprisingly, all the crocodiles swam away on cue. The Gatekeeper signalled for us to pull them out. Since none of us possessed physical bodies any longer, they weren't wounded, just horrified. They woke up and stared at us in terror.

"Let this be a warning to you all," stated the Gatekeeper coldly. "Do not make the mistake of assuming we can do nothing to you here. Now you have experienced being hurt. It doesn't feel good, does it? All the crimes you have committed in the human world indicate the disintegration of your souls. You are animals, and so it is only fit to put you in the same place as cold-blooded animals, to subject you to the realities of the laws of the natural world. When you bullied those weaker than yourselves in the human realm, you inflicted similar horror and pain on them. Unfortunately, you no longer have a body with which to experience real pain. So, do you wish to try again?"

"No, no, no..." they cried, shaking their heads in terror.

Two women in white dresses ran towards us. "Gatekeeper, please save Wang Meili! She's being strangled by snakes!"

The Gatekeeper walked to the river bank but said nothing. Curious, we followed close behind him. After getting closer, we gulped in fear. Wang Meili had crawled to the river bank. Many snakes entangled her, hissing and licking her face and neck. Her eyes were shut, her face pale, and she had no strength to fight back.

We watched the Gatekeeper nervously. He raised a hand, and the snakes suddenly dispersed into the water. A white-veiled lady held out a white robe towards her.

"How does that feel?" the Gatekeeper asked coldly.

Wang Meili opened her eyes slightly before sobbing uncontrollably.

"Now you know the meaning of desperation. Don't you? You were too feeble to fight against that horrendous attack. That is exactly the kind of torture you inflicted on that couple through when you hired someone to run them over after their daughter died. You asked what I can do to you here. Now you have seen it with your own eyes. Would you like to try it again?"

She shook her head.

"Get her dressed," the Gatekeeper instructed.

We all made our way back to where we had been gathered. The atmosphere had changed significantly. An intense tension hung over our heads; the scenes we had witnesses had been horrifying.

"Thus we conclude the second step," the Gatekeeper announced. "Now the third step: you must all drink the soup."

"The soup?" we all wondered.

Four assistants carried buckets and stacks of bowls towards us.

"First, the unjust souls, please come forward," instructed the Gatekeeper. Lin Wenhao and a few other souls came over, took a bowl of soup from the assistants, and drank.

"The soup you drink is called Forgetful. You will forget all the wrongs in the world, and only beautiful memories will remain. Now you will be able to live at peace here."

Sure enough, the grievances on their face faded.

"Those souls guilty of crimes, those who bathed separately, please come forward," the Gatekeeper instructed.

Liu Huihuang and Wang Meili approached warily and drank the soup as the assistant passed by.

"You are drinking the soup of oblivion," the Gatekeeper explained. "You will completely forget your families and start a new life in another field of Heaven. Even if your family comes to Heaven in the future, you will not recognise each other. You will live alone, as is the will of Heaven."

They were shocked, open-mouthed, but said nothing because of the dire warning they had just experienced.

"Now it is the turn of those souls bearing impurities, slight or heavy," the Gatekeeper continued.

An assistant passed a bowl of soup to each soul in that group. "You are drinking the purifying soup," the Gatekeeper explained. "This will cleanse your soul and allow you to live in pleasure in Heaven, as well as retain your memories of the world."

These souls looked visibly relieved after hearing this.

"Now for those souls of compassion, but with slight blemishes, please come forward." The Gatekeeper smiled. It was the first time I'd seen him smile properly. The assistant passed each of us a bowl of green soup. I drank it in small sips. I couldn't tell what flavour it was, though it wasn't unpleasant. Neither salty nor spicy, sweet nor bitter, savoury nor sour.

"This soup will help you to retain your memories of the human world and also your emotions attached to it. After your families come here, you will be able to meet them and live happily together in Heaven."

It was a huge relief to all of us to hear this.

"Now for the fourth step," the Gatekeeper announced. "Self-reflection."

We all looked at each other, confused. Self-reflection? The Gatekeeper didn't explain; he just pointed at the forest. A huge mirror, at least twenty metres tall by ten metres wide, appeared from nowhere. Never before had I seen a mirror this large.

"Please line up in front of the mirror as though you are taking a photo, to leave a record of your soul's information in the soul library."

We all looked at each other, a little surprised, and then lined up in order as the Gatekeeper had instructed. I tried to stick my head out to see what was in the mirror, but I couldn't see anything.

"Only when it's your turn will you be able to see what is in the mirror," the Gatekeeper explained.

My turn came. I expected to see only myself in the mirror, but instead I saw quite a few men and women reflected in the mirror with me. Confused, I was surprised to see some similarities among us.

"Those are your ancestors," the Gatekeeper explained. I looked back into the mirror and noticed clear resemblances between us all: long eyes, long eyelashes and large lips; the second toe on their feet was long and slim. It turned out they were my great-grandparents, my great-great-grandparents, and other relatives!

"Can I talk to them?" I asked the Gatekeeper with delight.

He shook his head. "No, not yet. You will have a chance later."

I was surprised to see a string of symbols suddenly appear on my robe in front of the mirror. "These symbols on your robe are the code for your family," the Gatekeeper explained. "You can memorise them if you want to. They are for the managers here in Heaven, and don't mean much for all the souls residing here."

I was delighted as I left the mirror. I had seen and would be able to meet my ancestors! It was so exciting!

After we left the mirror, we talked amongst ourselves about the codes and family members we had seen in the mirror. "My mother came here just a month before I did," said one man excitedly. "I didn't expect to see her here. She looks exactly the same, apart from her white dress. I hope I can be with her forever in Heaven."

"You have now completed all the procedures of Gateway 333339," the Gatekeeper declared, "and I have completed my duties. Later, the assistants will take you to where you belong. I have just one more instruction: please be quiet on the boat and listen to the captain's instructions to make sure you disembark in the correct place. If you do not, tragedy will befall you."

Then we were on a boat, sailing to a place unknown.

19

S on, even though I'm an atheist and don't follow any religion, I do believe that Heaven exists. Many scientists have lectured to me on our current scientific understanding of the universe and have denied that Heaven is real.

"Please don't kill my belief in Heaven," I would beg them, "regardless of what science has discovered. I am trapped in this fate and have no choice. But I want to believe that there is something beyond this life. Please let me believe there is another world after this one, and that people can transcend time and space. Please don't destroy this hope..."

So Son, your story gives me such great comfort. Heaven really does exist!

People conjure up many different imaginings of the afterlife and tell many stories about it. I used to hear the old people in your grandparents' village say that dead people will pass over the Naihe Bridge to cross the river. But now you have told me about this river, and that people take a boat to travel, rather than walk.

I have so many questions, after hearing all this. How was the journey? Where are you now? What's on the other side of the river? How is your life there? Is it similar to here?

Your mum and I have been praying for you to go to Heaven after your death. Now you're really there! I don't know the route of the river or if there are challenges or obstacles to overcome, but I believe in you. With your intelligence and perseverance, you'll be well-equipped to handle any difficulties that could arise during the journey. I know you'll reach your destination...

Dad, it was quite an unusual experience on the river. There's no sound at all, not even from the boat cutting through the water. Many boats come and go in sheer silence. The captains greet each other with a silent nod when boats pass. The boats are made of wood, with sails. They sail purely by the wind; there's no engine or other machinery on board.

I reached down into the water and felt a strong current in the river. The captain warned us that nothing could pass here except for the boats on the river; not even things flying in the sky. He told us to be very careful while we drifted along the river and not to touch anything.

Just then a red lotus flower drifted towards us. A middle-aged man sitting in front of me reached down his hand to it out of curiosity. As soon as he touched the lotus flower, a savage man's face appeared at the surface of the water and tried to pull him into the river. The man cried out and we tried to help him, but we couldn't stop him. He was sucked into the water. We all turned to the captain, who just sighed.

"He broke the rules," he said matter-of-factly. "He has no choice but to stay here and guard the river."

After that, no one dared move a muscle. We just stared at the river, still in shock at what we had just witnessed.

I had assumed we were sailing straight to the other bank, which shouldn't take us long. Then we learned that it would take a whole day because we were stopping at other islands along the broad river.

Many long and narrow islands lay close to each other, running through the centre of the river. It took us three hours to arrive at the first one. We thought we had stopped there for a rest. Unexpectedly, the captain announced, "Tan Lisheng, criminal soul, please disembark."

Tan Lisheng was surprised. He hesitated, but left the boat. As soon as he went ashore, four men in black robes and scarves circled him and tied a black belt around him. They took him to the centre of the island. He stopped and looked back at us, but a black panther rushed out of the grass and flung himself onto Tan Lisheng's shoulders. He cried out for help as the panther's tongue touched his neck.

"These islands are for punishment in the afterlife," the captain explained to us. "All the souls of criminals are sent here. It is called Island 71116. Please come with me and observe."

We all looked at each other. No one said a word. We disembarked in silence and stepped onto the island. It was no more than three kilometres wide, but its length stretched much further. It was covered by tall grasses and shrubs, barely allowing any light to penetrate. Some animal cries echoed faintly to our ears, and the smell of large animals burned in our noses. I couldn't help but tremble a little.

The scope for punishment is large; so is Island 71116. The captain led us along a trail through the grass and introduced the island to us. We saw many large stone pits, perhaps three meters across, each one sinking down some five or six metres. In each one was a person counting money, some accumulating knives in place of money, some gathering cloth, some counting copper coins, some silver ingots, some gold bars, some British Pounds, some US Dollars, some Euros, and some Rmb.

"Those are the embezzled proceeds of corrupt officials from every dynasty throughout history. Their punishment is to look back and recount everything they embezzled in the world of the living. Here is the famous Pit 198003. Please take a look." The captain raised his hand and pointed at the man in the pit.

We directed our eyes there. An old man on a futon was counting a wall of stacked silver ingots. He must have felt our eyes, for he bent his head forward as if ashamed.

"Do you recognise him?" The captain raised his voice, then answered his own question: "He is the renowned He Shen of the Qing Dynasty."

I examined the old man again. He truly was the infamous He Shen, known to be richer than the emperor himself! I noticed a poem on the wall of the pit, the very one he wrote before he hung himself.

What night is tonight?
Another year starts after the Lantern Festival.
The moonlight, casting the sombre people.

It really was him!

"Why is he here?" asked one of the souls.

"Where else would he be?" the captain asked scornfully. "This is where he belongs. Counting money every day and sleeping beside his stacks; this was his only goal."

We visited many similar stone pits, which housed corrupt souls from China and elsewhere. The infamous corrupt officials we all learned about from Chinese history were all placed close to each other.

On the left side of He Shen's pit sat Liu Jin, the eunuch from the Ming Dynasty who owned three hundred and thirty thousand kilograms of gold and more than eight million kilograms of silver ingots. On the right side of He Shen sat Liang Ji, a general from the Eastern Han Dynasty, who embezzled over Rmb 3 billion worth of silver. Behind He Shen was Xiao Hong, the younger brother of Emperor Wu in the Liang Dynasty, who embezzled Rmb 300 million worth of silver. They all had their heads lowered, counting their money mechanically.

Before we left, the captain led us to visit Tan Lisheng, who was already sitting in his own stone pit and had started to count a large sum of money. A black-robed assistant told him, "Tan Lisheng, this is the Rmb 87.15 million you embezzled. You must now count it out one hundred thousand times. You will be supervised by shifts of assistants. They will record each time you finish. For every mistake you make, you will need to count an additional ten thousand times as punishment."

"Ten thousand times?" Tan Lisheng was startled.

"Yes, so count them carefully," the black-robed assistant said coldly.

We were all astounded. How long would his punishment take to complete?

On the way back, one of the souls asked the captain, "What if they escape from their pit?"

"Where could they go?" replied the captain. "As soon as they leave the pit, they are on an island full of hungry predators like lions, tigers and panthers."

Upon hearing this, my eyes shot around the grass and shrubs that surrounded us.

Son, what you have described sounds more like Hell than Heaven! I heard people talk about it when I was young. If men committed crimes on Earth, they would be sent to another world for punishment after death. I thought it was underground, but it now seems that it's also located in Heaven, on an island, a particular section within Heaven.

This isn't at all what I expected...

Dad, we took the boat to another island after this. This time, Wang Meili was told to disembark. She didn't dare object, and submissively left the boat. A few men in black robes scarves took her away. The captain took us out for a tour again.

"This is Island 874253." he explained, "The place where murderers are punished." The captain clearly wanted to show us how they are punished.

We followed him silently. It was a completely different scene. Nothing grows on the flat ground there: no grass, no trees. It's like the training ground at a military complex, just one huge boundless stretch as far as the eye can see. Small glass houses only a few square metres in size housed criminal souls.

"Their punishment," the captain explained, "is to listen to the dying cries of their victims over and over again." A women's tragic weeping burst out from a glass house nearby as the captain finished. We were all shocked and jumped to look at the house, where a man covered his ears. The cries penetrated the house, but there was no visible source of the noise.

"This is House 59000831," the captain announced, pointing at the number on the house. "He was driving while drunk, hit a girl, and drove off. The cries are the girl's screams and her mother's sobbing. He will listen to these cries every day, non-stop. That is his sentence."

I shivered. People go mad even if they listen to the same piece of music too many times! Imagine what horrific torment it must be to be forced to listen those screams again and again...

We passed quite a few similar glass houses, each one infused with the sobbing and weeping of men and women, young and old. The souls inside tried to cover their ears and free themselves from the torture.

At last, the captain led us to Jiang Meili's house. She immediately lowered her head upon seeing us. A man dressed in black robes and a black scarf told Jiang Meili, "You killed an innocent couple on Earth. Their elderly parents were heartbroken because of what you did. Now it is time for you to pay the consequences." As he finished his words, the mournful cry of an old couple resounded throughout the house.

"Our poor son." As soon as it sounded, the cry of another elderly couple could be heard.

"Our poor daughter."

Wang Meili trembled, and we all trembled with her. She immediately raised her hands to cover her ears.

"It will not work," the black-robed man sneered. "The cries can reach to the deepest parts of your brain."

"Let us go now," said the captain. "We should leave Ms Wang to listen to this alone. She must atone for what she did on Earth."

The captain signalled for us to board the boat again and visit the next island. On this next one, the punishment was to live out one's victim's experiences and go through all their suffering.

We went to the island, and the captain asked Chen Dongsheng, whose paper mill had emitted lethal pollution, to disembark. A few black-robed assistants led him away. A dreadful smell hung in the air. Sewage and garbage floated everywhere. It looked like the end of the world. There were no houses on this island and no places to sit. Iron bars enclosed some open spaces, with ten criminal souls in each one.

"The residents of this island," explained the captain, "are those who have polluted the land, the water or the air during their time on Earth."

We went directly to Chen Dongchang's place. The number 873210 was carved into one of the bars. Chen Dongchang had just arrived there, and he was looking around, taking in his surroundings with an air of panic. He nodded awkwardly when he saw us.

An assistant appeared with a bowl of dark liquid. "Cheng Dongchang," he said, "I shall send this water to you three times each day. You must drink each bowl to the last drop."

"OK," Chen replied. "It's only water. I can manage that." He took the bowl but instantly recoiled as he brought his lips to the bowl. "It smells disgusting! There's no way I'm drinking that!"

"So *now* you care about the water?" the assistant scoffed. "This is the water polluted by you yourself while you were on Earth. Meanwhile you drank nothing but bottled water. Now it's your turn to taste the water you polluted. If you spill but one drop, you will need to drink another bowl. If you refuse, we will help you to drink it." Three more black-robed men appeared. Two took his arms while another pulled back his head to expose his lips.

"Stop, stop!" Chen cried. "I'll drink it," and he lifted the bowl to his lips.

After that we went to the fourth island, where the coal mine owner Liu Huihuang, who was responsible for an explosion and many resulting deaths, left the boat. "This is Island 694356," the captain said, "the punishment area for truly criminal souls, who will be locked in a completely dark stone room. You can see many of these stone huts everywhere. None contains a window, only a black iron gate and a few small vent holes. These criminal souls have lost all compassion and will remain here in isolation forever."

When Liu Huihuang was led to one of the stone huts, he remained defiant. "I'm not afraid of you at all," he cried. "I tell you, I don't regret a thing I did on Earth! If I go back there some day, I will blow the whole world up. I will kill as many people as I can!"

As we heard these words, a few black-robed men pushed him into the room. The door slammed with a chilling boom.

20

S on, the scenes you witnessed sound terrifying, but I'm comforted nonetheless, for they confirm to me that everything we do here on Earth is observed and recorded. We will always face in the next world the consequences of our actions in this.

I have seen so many people enjoy honour and prestige in life, even though they're ruthless and go against reason and nature. I can't stomach it. I've always complained about God's unfairness. I understand now that I've been short-sighted in hoping for karmic retribution to be exacted within someone's lifetime. For even if someone escapes retribution in this life, he shouldn't feel fortunate.

For in Heaven, justice will be done.

Dad, the captain explained that the Field of Punishment is very large, with many islands for different kinds of punishment. It would be impossible to see all of it, but he showed us those four islands to give us a general idea of how God punishes the guilty.

Finally, our boat was approaching the opposite shore, where everyone who remained on the boat would disembark. As we approached, our moods were lifted as the gloom cleared and the light became brighter.

Finally, the boat pulled in and we disembarked one by one. The captain and the assistants who'd accompanied us didn't join us, though. Instead they turned around and set off again. I hadn't even seen the face of the lady who had accompanied me this whole way. I waved to her, and she waved back.

"May you find joy," she said.

How could I be joyful here? I wondered.

Everyone heaved a sigh of relief. We had finally made it! The lingering mist dispersed, to reveal a pure blue sky. The sun hung overhead, radiating warm and brilliant light. The green grassland stretched endlessly, and white rabbits hopped here and there. Birds tweeted from afar.

The air was filled with the sweet fragrance of flowers, which was not only pleasant to the nose, but uplifting to the spirit. I was filled with an urge to dance, and I noticed that all the souls were also in high spirits.

"Welcome!" called a man wearing a blue scarf on his head. "This is the entrance to the Cleansing Field of Heaven. I am responsible for receiving new souls. You can call me Ah Liang."

"Ah Liang, what is this place?" a girl named Wenhao hadn't heard clearly.

"The Field of Cleansing," he repeated. "Congratulations on making it here! This is the closest spot to your ultimate destination in Heaven, the Fields of Joy. We are currently on the north border of the Field of Cleansing."

"The Field of Cleansing? What are we supposed to do here?" Wenhao was very direct, her questions to the point.

"This is a mandatory field through which every soul must pass," Ah Liang explained. "Each soul must stay here for almost one month. During that time, the soul must do only one thing: cleanse itself. Each of your souls is tarnished; some only slightly, others more heavily. You will each need to cleanse your soul in order to render it pure again. For, of course, a soul cannot be cleaned with water.

After you leave here, you will enter the Field of Study, to study the rules of Heaven and the skills that can make you happy. After that, you will then enter the Fields of Joy, to enjoy the bliss that is promised to each soul. You can also enter the Holy Field through there, which is where the gods live. Every year, each god will select some souls to meet and talk with."

"Great, that's wonderful," Wenhao replied, rather sarcastically. "So how do we cleanse ourselves?"

Ah Liang smiled patiently. "There is no rush to start the cleansing. First, I will take you to your accommodation so you can rest. Everyone who arrived on this boat will stay at Station 16111. You will each find your name on a door. Now, I will restore your ability to fly." He waved his hand, and we all rose into the air.

"Good. Now, please follow me." We flew after him.

We landed on a slope, on which were scattered a few trees and some flowers. The bottom was covered with dense shrubs. A dozen or so wooden houses were on the slope.

"Those are cedar trees," Ah Liang told us, pointing at the trees. "Those are heaven lotus flowers, and those are heaven thorns." Then he gestured towards the wooden houses. "There is a house for each of you. Find the one with your name on it, then go inside and take a rest. I will return tomorrow to help you to begin your tasks. Please be reassured: the Field of Cleansing is an absolutely safe place for you to rest. Nothing will disturb or harm you here."

21

Son, I'm so relieved to hear that you arrived safely. What does it look like, your house? Is it similar to houses on Earth, with windows and walls? Are there beds, tables and chairs inside? I hope it's comfortable. Your mum and I provided many things for you in the afterlife: a fridge, a television, a car, air conditioner, phone, MP3 player, and clothes suitable for all seasons, plus some money. We burned them all close to your graveyard, so I hope you received them. Put them all to good use.

Are there rules about communication in Heaven? Can you talk with each other? If so, be kind and sincere. Share your things with others, as you did on Earth. If you run out of something, you can tell me and your mum in our dreams. Do try to get along with your neighbours. I know you have a big heart, always willing to lend a hand to those in need. So let us know, and your mum and I will burn more paper money for you.

Is there a distinction between day and night there? Do you need light or candles? What about food? Do you eat according to the schedule on Earth, or is there just one meal a day? What's the trend for clothing? Luxury brands or something simple?

Is the Field of Cleansing large? We have continents and countries on Earth. How is it divided there? Are there names, or just numbers? How do you travel from one place to another? If you drive, please be careful! Do you a job or some duties in the Field of Cleansing? Your mum and I tell ourselves that Heaven needs talents like yours for specific tasks, and that was why you left us so early. We thought it might be because of your passion and talent for computer science. That was why God chose you and took you away from us.

Dad, the houses here are not built out of concrete or bricks, but from logs and sticks, mudbricks and hay. Their design is quite different from what we're used to on Earth. They are of different sizes, depending on the size of the logs used to build them. The walls are not painted, but covered with mud. The furniture is made of bamboo or wood, also with no paint or varnish. They are very comfortable to stay in, though, with an earthy fragrance, similar to what we used to have in the fields in late spring.

My house is not overly spacious, but large enough for me to have a good rest. The window frames the view of the slope, with its ancient giant trees, idyllic sheep and rabbits, and birds circling in the sky, like a painting of a pastoral scene. I feel very content here in my home. I guess this is something I could never find on Earth, where I was forever burdened with stress. I was always busy and had no opportunity to enjoy myself like this.

That night, I fell asleep quickly from exhaustion, and didn't wake up until late. The sun was already in the South when Ah Liang called us all to have some soup.

The food is very simple here, probably because we don't have a physical body to sustain. We just had some green vegetable soup. Ah Liang then sat with us on the grass in the sunshine, and passed round a pair of glasses to each of us.

"From now on," he said, "you must wear these glasses during your time in the Field of Cleansing. You will each see different things whilst wearing the glasses. They will help you to look back over your life and cleanse your soul. Once you feel that your soul has been purified, please tell me. I will then take you to the Door of Purity for examination. If you pass the test, then you will be able to enter the Field of Study.

"No one is a saint," Ah Liang continued. "Impure thoughts, contemptible ideas and awful mistakes happen in life. If the glasses bring back one of your memories, and you find that you need to talk about it, please come to me. If you don't want to talk about it, that's fine too. My house is just over there on the right."

We were all curious to try out these glasses, and we quickly put them on. Everyone shouted in wonder. After I put on my glasses, I was immediately surprised to see a scene of me as a toddler flash before my eyes. Then I was in primary school and eating tofu puddings; then I was addicted to video games in Grade Three; then I was squeezing the acne on my face in junior high school; then I was hit in the face while playing basketball in high school; then I was kissing my girlfriend in college; then I was lying in the hospital, depressed.

These glasses were so magical! How did they work? Who made these and what was their purpose?

Ah Liang tapped my shoulder. "Come with me," he instructed." I removed my glasses and followed him into the forest. "Do you have any questions?" he asked.

"Yes," I replied, "I'd like to know how the glasses work."

"On Earth," he explained, "you are often told that God watches your every deed. It is not merely rhetoric, but fact. Human instincts are very perceptive. God watches everything and keeps a detailed record of your behaviour. Those glasses are the eyes of God."

"My goodness, can it be true?" I asked, incredulously.

"Rest assured," Ah Liang replied. "You have no major blemishes in God's eyes. Of course, that doesn't mean that you were immune to temptation. According to God's will, you just didn't have enough time to become corrupted. Since you are a pure soul, we wish to ask a special favour from you."

"We?" I asked. "Who else is there with you?"

"I speak on behalf of the delegates of Heaven."

"What would you like me to help with? I'm a newcomer. How could I possibly help you?"

"Very soon, the other souls will approach me to tell me what they have seen in the glasses and to confess their deeds to me. I would like you to record these accounts, not with words, but with this." He put something that looked rather like a hair dryer in my hand. There were a few buttons on it. "You will need to learn how to use it. Do you need my help?"

"No, it shouldn't be difficult," I replied. "I have a background in computer science and programming. It should be easy for me to figure it out." After a few minutes, I'd learned how to use it. It was rather like some kind of video recorder with built-in editing software that could transcend time and space. I don't know how it worked, but it wasn't complicated to use.

"May I access the video content inside the device while I play with it?" I asked Ah Liang. I certainly didn't want to break any rules in Heaven.

"Yes," he replied, "of course you can watch. I have given it to you, and I won't keep any secrets from you. Now, off you go. I'll tell you when I need you."

Heartened by the trust he'd shown in me, I started to wander around the Field of Cleansing with my glasses and the recording device. I wanted to get to know the area. My goodness, I was amazed by how big it was! I walked for a whole day along the bank of the River Styx. The flat slopes stretched for miles, long and unbroken. Many houses like the ones we stayed in were scattered about here and there, each numbered, each with a soul living inside.

Each station had a delegate wearing a blue headscarf, just like Ah Liang. They were all very pleasant and welcoming to me. I ran into other souls during my stroll through the grassland, flat, and forest. We nodded politely to each other in greeting, and each soul passed along quietly.

Eventually I returned to my house, exhausted. Before bedtime, I played around with the machine Ah Liang had given to me. Since he said it was OK, I started to browse through the confession videos it contained. A former official's video caught my attention:

"Ah Liang, through these glasses I have come to know that God has seen my every deed. I am shocked. I thought I hid my wrongdoings well, and that many things would remain secret forever. I believed that no one would know or judge me for what I have done, let alone that it would be recorded in history. I had no idea that a pair of eyes was always watching me from Heaven.

"I am very nervous to look back over my life. To read one's own biography is a painful journey. I am ashamed, and I need to confess.

"One awful thing I did was to collect evidence of my fellow officers' embezzlement. Even though much of their misconduct was well-hidden and secretive, as an insider, how could I not have known? It wasn't difficult for me to secretly record their activities. My motive was the pursuit of justice. But even though I told myself this, I never sent the evidence to the discipline-inspection commission afterwards. Instead, I held on to it, using it as a weapon against any of them who competed with me for a position. Whenever this happened, I would report their behaviour so they couldn't be a threat to me.

"I remained undefeated. There was nothing wrong with it legally, but it wasn't right. I felt fortunate that no one discovered my deception, but I am restless now. One time I learned about a senior official who was to have the final say on a promotion I was up for. He was apparently the model of moral rectitude, and never took gifts or bribes. I wanted to befriend him in order to pave the way for my promotion. After a long period of observation, I noticed he was fond of interactions with young female colleagues. I devised a plan.

"A friend's daughter, pretty and ambitious, had been working for me for a while. Her father had called me a few times to ask for a favour in the form of her promotion. I decided to take her with me when reporting to the leader, and I left a few times to use the bathroom during the meeting to give them some time alone. I'd instructed the girl to invite the leader out for lunch with us, to which he agreed. Again I left from time to time on the pretence of making phone calls, so they could talk privately. Sure enough, they exchanged numbers while I was gone.

"I made the girl responsible for all contact with this leader, and soon she hinted she would be able to secure a promotion soon if I obtained the leader's consent. The girl was smart, and later they checked into a hotel together.

"The girl and I both received a promotion, and they were happy together. No one was a victim in this case, and I didn't incite any punishment on anyone. But I felt guilty that I had used both of them to achieve my own ends."

I was stunned by what I had seen and heard.

The next morning, Ah Liang asked me over to help record the confessions of a few souls in our station. I agreed and took the machine with me. Shortly afterwards, an elderly woman, around eighty years old, came into Ah Liang's house. She began to speak, and I started to record:

"When I put on my glasses, I found that something was missing. I will confess anyway for peace of mind. In the autumn before I died, my youngest son brought his family to visit me. My husband was already dead by then, and I lived in the countryside with my eldest son and his family. My younger daughter-in-law worried there wouldn't be any snacks for her son in the countryside, so she brought some pastries and biscuits for him. There was one type I'd never seen before, which was called Qilianxue, and my four-year-old grandson shared one with me.

"One morning, my younger daughter-in-law took her son outside to play. Those pastries caught my eye. I really had a craving for them, so I put one in my mouth. But that was just the start; I couldn't control myself. As the saying goes, 'Old people revert to childhood.' That was me! I thought my little grandson wouldn't notice since there were plenty of other kinds of snacks. But my grandson cried for Qilianxue when he came back inside, and my daughter-in-law found that they had all gone.

"'Who ate my son's pastries?' she asked. I was too embarrassed to tell the truth, and she directed her suspicion toward my eldest son's two daughters and questioned them relentlessly. Of course they denied having eaten them. 'Then it must have been a ghost,' she scoffed sarcastically. My older son didn't want the situation to escalate, so in the end he admitted that he had eaten the pastries. It stopped my younger daughter-in-law's questioning, but she was very unhappy.

"I am so sorry about this episode. I should have told the truth..."

"Yes," Ah Liang said, "a confession will make you feel better. But God will not blame you for this."

The following was from the confession of an old man:

"Ah Liang, I was a prison warden before. One thing didn't show up in the glasses, and I need to confess it. In my fourth year as warden, my former rival for the position of deputy director of the Justice Bureau, the current deputy director who had beaten me to the job, was sent to my prison because he had killed someone in a drunk-driving accident.

"I was thrilled, and immediately visited him in prison. With a solemn face, I told him, 'Boss, I couldn't help you in the trial, but I will take care of you while you're in here.' I arranged a shower for him and a table full of nice food for later. Then I asked a trusted subordinate to 'take care' of him. He understood the implication. He transferred the deputy director to a two-man cell with an aggressive criminal who had a history of violence towards his cellmates.

The next day, the deputy director was covered from head to toe with cuts and bruises, and had three broken ribs. I pretended to be furious and put the criminal in chains, and then I sent the deputy director to the hospital. He was so touched that he shed a few tears."

Ah Liang nodded his head thoughtfully. "Yes, we knew about this," he said, "but we misinterpreted the event. We thought you had genuine compassion for him."

Next, a middle-aged woman came in:

"Ah Liang, I was an obstetrician and came here because of a brain haemorrhage. I was among the best in the obstetrical department, and many families requested my services. Almost all of them would send me a red envelope out of tradition.

"To reassure the pregnant women, I would normally take the gift from them, then return it to them after the successful delivery of the baby. Once, the daughter-in-law of a high-ranking official came to our hospital, which caused a big fuss. My bosses told me again and again to be extra-careful with her case. This troubled me greatly; I was careful with every one of my patients!

"While the woman was giving birth, many people waited outside. When I glimpsed the fat red envelopes in their handbags, I was even more indignant that they believed that money could somehow influence my level of medical care. So when the pregnant woman gave me a red envelope containing five hundred kuai, I took it without hesitation. I took my daughter to a restaurant and spent all five hundred. I felt no guilt at all. Maybe I thought that five hundred kuai was not a substantial amount. Maybe God didn't record such trivial matters, but I still feel that I need to confess it now."

Ah Liang smiled. "Your attitude toward bribery was interesting. You were indignant at others, yet you still took your share when you had the chance. Perhaps you thought that since everyone accepts bribes, it would be OK for you to take one too. Fortunately, you didn't take much. You are forgiven in the eyes of God."

Next came a young woman:

"Ah Liang, I was a prostitute, and was stabbed to death in a robbery. I appreciate that God has allowed me to enter the Field of Cleansing. But actually I am very guilty. I didn't become a prostitute because life had left me no choice, as others did. I just didn't want to endure a low-end job like sewing

or cleaning or babysitting. Prostitution was a way to earn money quickly and live a comfortable life.

"I was worried about being shunned by society, but I found men were more accepting of vulgar activities when they came at night, no matter what they claimed during the daytime.

"Anyway, one of my clients had requested a fake invoice from me, for office supplies, so he could be reimbursed. What could I do, except go to those who create fake invoices? Those men were no better than us."

"Don't judge others," Ah Leung interrupted her. "Focus on your own story."

"Yes, sorry. Back to my story. So, on my second day working at Paradise, two men asked me to join them for a drink. From their conversation, I learned that the fat guy was a government official, and the slimmer one was a businessman. The official said, 'Many people are asking for this grant, but I'm in favour of securing you as a friend.'

"'I know you're looking after me,' replied the businessman. 'You are my saviour. What could I accomplish without your help? Big brother, rest assured. For every kuai *I make, half is yours! Let's spend the night here. I need to go to deal with some business. I'll be back soon. Here's my wallet.'*

"He never came back. That was just an excuse, so the officer could have me alone in the room. We had sex for almost the whole night! That guy's energy was scary! We had sex again and again. Before he left, he took the businessman's wallet to give me the tip. We had a rule there that tips should never be more than five thousand kuai*. But he had so much money! He wouldn't blink at giving me more. I told him he should compensate me for my extra work. So I asked for seven thousand.*

"'That seems fair,' he said, and gave me the money. I didn't see this episode in the glasses, but I feel I should tell you about it. I did not earn that extra two thousand kuai *honestly."*

Next was a man of about forty:

"Ah Liang, I need to confess to you something that wasn't recorded in the glasses. When I was a financial analyst, many people called me 'The Prophet' because of the accuracy of my share price predictions. One day, a girl I was fond of came to see me and asked me to recommend a particular stock. She hinted with her eyes that I could get anything I wanted from her in return. I

hesitated because it broke all ethical codes, but I simply couldn't resist her. All I needed to do was to say something I didn't believe in. I agreed to her request.

"She shunned me afterwards, always with different excuses. Later I discovered that many people had bought the stock I'd recommended. The share price rose, of course, her company took the opportunity to sell shares and make a fortune, and then the share price collapsed.

"God didn't record this, probably because He thought it was just due to my inaccurate analysis. I used that excuse too, to justify my actions. I hadn't taken advantage of anything; my analysis was just inaccurate. I need to confess now that my actions cost many people their savings."

I recorded the confessions of a dozen souls with the machine that morning. I thought that was a lot. But after the lunch break, Ah Liang called me over again. "You need to record more confessions this afternoon." I nodded in acknowledgement. It wasn't a chore for me, but rather a chance to listen to and learn from different stories.

The first one to come to Ah Liang in the afternoon was an eighty-year-old man:

"I had a small business selling pot-stewed meat. I give thanks to God, who has kept a full record of all the good and bad deeds during my life.

"When I was in my fifties, my friend Liu Xiuhua's husband died. I thought it an opportunity for me. Though Xiuhua was almost forty, she was still beautiful. Her face was young and fresh-looking, and her breasts bounced when she walked. I had admired her greatly for a long time, but of course she was married. Now that her husband was dead, there was nothing to stop me pursuing her.

"I went to see her every two or three days, and brought her some stewed meat. She received me very warmly each time and poured me tea. After a few times, I thought the time was right. I cleaned my hands thoroughly with a new soap I had bought and put some perfumed oil on my face. I really thought she would fall for me. I went to touch her breast immediately after I brought her home. She quickly dodged my advance. 'No, we can't do it,' she objected.

"I was angered. 'You have taken so much meat from me,' I said. 'Are you just leading me on? If you're not interested, why did you accept my gifts?'

"I persisted for a while, but I couldn't change her mind. I was agitated and thought of a plan to take my revenge. I put a piece of old and spoilt meat in the stew and took it to her to apologise. 'I'm sorry,' I said, 'I shouldn't have been so

forward with you the other day.' My face was red with feigned embarrassment. Just as I'd hoped, the woman fell for it. She ate the bad meat and had diarrhoea for three days. Finally, she went into town to get some medicine for it.

"I was very pleased with how my plan had worked out. But it was wrong. And now I need to confess to God."

The following was a young man, just a little older than me. He had been an army platoon leader:

"One morning, my platoon was on duty on three bus routes running across the city centre. My commander told me that there was intelligence that a group of terrorists was planning to blow up a bus. We didn't know the details, but we were placed on the buses, to beef up security. I assigned thirty-seven soldiers from my platoon into fifteen groups, for the fifteen buses running on the three routes.

"We were all fully armed, to present a show of force and hopefully deter the terrorists. I boarded a bus with two other soldiers. I stood in the middle of the bus, one soldier stood at the front, and another in the rear. We watched every passenger getting on and off the bus, but couldn't identify any potential suspects.

"The whole morning, we saw no one suspicious. My concentration levels dropped. Maybe the intelligence was wrong; perhaps we had scared away the terrorists; or maybe our bus wasn't the intended target.

"The whole morning had exhausted us all, and I signalled for my two colleagues to take a seat when we pulled up at a large shopping mall. It was the busiest stop on the route, where lots of passengers got on and off. I watched each of them, but I was also tired and my earlier alertness had faded. Yes, I was still on duty, but I thought the likelihood of an attack actually taking place was very low.

"Suddenly, my eye began to twitch. My heart started pounding and a girl with a large backpack caught my attention. She stood out, first because no one else getting on at this stop had a backpack as large as hers; second, she was wearing a pair of dark sunglasses – few women wore glasses like that; and third, a nervous look flashed across her face when she saw me. Yes, that was definitely a look of fear. Common sense said that passengers should feel comforted, not fearful, when they saw us on the bus.

"I started to move towards her as the bus started to move again. She put *her backpack on the floor and looked forward. 'Excuse me, can I check your backpack?' I asked. She looked at me and gave me a big smile.*

"'It's so hot on the bus, don't you think?' she asked. She started to unbutton her shirt, revealing her white skin. One of her breasts caught my eye. She wasn't wearing a bra! We were standing close, face to face, and my eyes were fixed on her breasts. They were so beautiful.

"I didn't realise that she had put one hand into her pocket and hadn't answered my question. Not until she gave the smile of victory did I realise that she was up to something. She took out a remote control and pressed the button. She had distracted me, and it was too late for me to do anything except throw my body over the backpack.

"I was blown to pieces and deemed a hero. But I know the ending could have been different: if I hadn't been lured by her breasts, if I'd done my job properly and neutralised her in a timely manner, that explosion could have been avoided.

"I fell for the oldest trick in the book, and have the responsibility for all those other lost lives on my shoulders. I am so sorry..."

"Don't be too harsh on yourself," Ah Liang comforted him. "You did what you could to minimise the loss of life. God will understand."

Dad, that soldier did so well. The enemy identified his blind spot and used it to inflict carnage. She's the one who really needs to confess.

Son, I didn't know about the Field of Cleansing before, or the glasses or the confessions. To be honest, there's something I need to confess too. I remember when I reported to the southern border, two soldiers were ordered to escort me and three other colleagues to the border. I was very nervous, afraid that the enemy would jump out and ambush us from the grass, or that we would step on a landmine, or that we would be caught up in gun fire.

I was thirty-four years old then, with the rank of deputy colonel. I was armed too. I should have insisted on leading the way so as to protect the younger soldiers. But I remained silent, waiting for the young soldiers to escort us. When one of them offered to lead the way himself, I was relieved. They were on escort duty, after all.

Fortunately nothing happened that day. However, I know in my heart that I put my fellow soldiers' lives in danger to protect my own.

Dad, it's not your time to confess yet. Let me tell you what happened next, so you can have a better understanding of Heaven and the place where your soul will be cleansed.

Women's confessions took up the rest of the afternoon. The first one was around forty years old; she welled up with tears when she saw Ah Liang.

"*I hung myself. With the glasses I saw myself going through the mill to take care of my husband and children. I am ashamed, though. I had always been very competitive ever since I was young. After getting married, I started to compare my husband with other girls' husbands. At first, my husband got promoted quickly, first to deputy section chief, then to section chief, deputy division chief, and division chief.*

"*People came to visit and sent us gifts around the holiday season. I felt proud and gloated constantly to my girlfriends. After my husband had been division chief for a while, I thought he had stopped working hard, especially when I saw others' husbands continue to rise to positions such as director-general or even mayor. I complained that he was good for nothing.*

"*'We need to offer bribes if I'm to get promoted,' he told me. 'A director-general's position costs about a million* yuan. *We just don't have that kind of money.'*

"*'Then let's take out a loan,' I suggested. He shook his head resolutely. 'If we take a loan, I'll need to embezzle money afterwards to pay it back. A little bribe won't cover it, but a substantial sum will send me to prison.'*

"*I knew he was right, but I was still upset. I never showed him a happy face, and didn't allow him to touch me at night. Once he reached for my breasts, but I slapped his hand away. He sighed. Eventually, because I had pushed him so hard, he borrowed more than one million yuan from a businessman and then started to bribe the leaders with gifts. It really worked, and soon he was promoted to deputy director-general.*

"*The night before his first day in his new job, I made a reservation for two tables at a posh restaurant and invited relatives and friends over to celebrate.*

His businessman friend also said we didn't need to pay him back. I was so thrilled!

"After he took office, our house had never seen better times. People sent us all kinds of gifts: food, clothes, daily necessities, even flowers and house plants. Some also sent bribes for promotion. At first, I didn't dare open the fat envelopes. I just took the thin ones with one or two thousand inside. After a while, though, I didn't worry so much. Fat envelope, thin envelope, gift cards, I took everything that was sent to us. Everyone was doing the same thing we had done! How unlucky would we be if somehow we were caught? He was just a deputy director-general, and he had all these gifts sent to him. The director-general would have even more, so I just took it all. One person wasn't significant in this corrupt system.

"After a while, I'd collected so much money that I bought two apartments in the same complex of the same size: both over one hundred and sixty square metres, one each for my parents and my husband's parents, in different buildings but both on the eighth floor. I was completely fair to both sides of the family.

"My husband was afraid that it would attract attention. 'What are you afraid of?' I retorted. 'Being a good son? Well, you're setting an excellent example to your subordinates on how to be a good son!'

"Later I was afraid the money would depreciate in the bank, so I bought another apartment of one hundred and eighty square meters for my son who was in middle school at the time, as a future wedding gift.

"I thought I was managing the family finances very well. Bank interest rates were so low, but the property market was rising so much. I was so delighted by everything and wanted to make love with my husband at night. However, by this time he had lost energy and interest, falling asleep straight away at night. No matter how I tried to seduce him, he wouldn't respond.

"I thought his lack of interest was due to fatigue from his work, until one day a young, pregnant woman knocked on our door and asked for my husband. I immediately understood everything. How dare he? I fully planned to make a huge scene at home, but before I had a chance, the anti-corruption department made a sudden visit to our home.

"You know what happened afterwards. I forgave him and visited him every week in prison, took care of our son and both families, and even helped the pregnant woman to have an abortion.

"I was a good wife and a good mother, but I felt so sorry for him..."

The second woman to visit Ah Liang was young, perhaps a little younger than me.

"I am here because of an plane crash. I thought it was so unfair, because I had a pure soul. But after I saw what was in the glasses, I found that there were many things I need to confess.

"In my second year of college, my friends started to date and form couples. It was common among them to have sex on the first date and enjoy life, no matter if they had found the right one or not. Soon my classmates started going to hotels or living together in rented apartments. I was intrigued. One classmate had asked me out a few times. I was hesitant because he was very short. A girl came to me and scolded me, telling me that I had stolen this boy, her boyfriend, which really angered me.

"'Well, since you want him so badly, so do I!' I thought to myself.

"I went on a date with the boy immediately and had sex with him as revenge against the girl. I didn't really like him though, especially after we had sex. I spoke with him frankly.

"'You're not the person I'm looking for,' I told him, 'but we can still be friends." He wasn't angry with me, but he asked for three thousand kuai *as compensation for the time he'd spent with me. I counted out the three thousand, threw it in his face, and left.*

"A month later, I found out I was pregnant. But during that time I'd fallen in love with a poet, so I decided to get an abortion. The doctor told me that I was likely carrying a girl, based on her experience. But I didn't care. Girl or boy, it made no difference; I didn't want it. I just wanted my poet and my happiness.

"After four days, I went on a date with the poet, attending one of his poetry readings:

Don't waste a minute.
Don't miss the one you love.
Don't be scared of being hurt.
Don't think of your body as a sacred temple.

"I have two reflections about this: first, I shouldn't have taken another's boyfriend; second, I shouldn't have taken a new life."

Next was a girl of about thirteen or fourteen:

"I shouldn't be allowed to enter the Field of Cleansing. I should be forced to stay in the Field of Punishment. I murdered someone. God must not have seen that. I thought I could slip through at first, but I have decided to confess my sin and accept whatever punishment God chooses for me.

"When I was four years old, I was abducted and trafficked from Sichuan to Hebei. I was sold to a single man in the countryside of Hebei, who took me in as his own daughter. He took care of me and sent me to school. I remembered nothing about my own parents and family, so naturally I came to consider this man my father.

"As I grew older, my body matured into that of a young woman, and my foster father began to see me differently. The affection in his eyes changed into something more sinister and frightening. One night, he crawled into my bed and raped me. I was scared and in agony. I decided to drink pesticide and end my life. Before I drank it, I put some into my foster father's porridge. I hated him and wanted him to die.

"On reflection, I had no right to end his life. He had hurt me, but I still had no jurisdiction over his life. I have sinned and have no right to be here."

Ah Liang shook his head. "You should not blame yourself," he said. "Although your foster father did die from drinking pesticide, it wasn't because of you. He came home and found you unconscious. He understood immediately. He was regretful and didn't know how he would ever explain to the neighbours what had happened to you. So he decided to end his life too. He found another bottle of pesticide and drank it, rather than eating the porridge. So you are not a criminal. The soul of a criminal cannot arrive at this place."

Son, I cannot imagine this. We seldom think about the purity of our souls whilst in the world of the living. Every day is filled with mundane matters. We're always so busy setting goals for ourselves and striving to achieve them. No matter what position we hold, we always seek a further promotion. We make efforts to win the trust of leaders and get nominations; to gain the support of our peers or find ways to sabotage our competitors.

We labour over planning where to take leaders to dinner, over which connections might favour us the most. No matter how much money the businessmen have, they always want more. And so they busy themselves with nurturing connections with officials in key posts; with how to get their support and secure contracts; with how to obtain more loans from the bank; and with how to hide money overseas.

Scholars constantly strive for new discoveries to secure fame for themselves. They fixate on what to research, their path to authority in their field. All for a bigger reputation and greater academic awards.

Even ordinary people will strive for something: when to rebuild their house; when to marry off their son; when to buy a television; or when to send their grandson to university. So long as we're alive, we are led by our goals, panting and sweating at every step along the way, until death finally catches up with us. We simply don't have the time or inclination to worry about the purity of our souls. We should give thanks to God for allowing us some time in Heaven to take care of these things.

Dad, before long, nearly all the souls in Station 16111 had confessed their sins to Ah Liang. Some talks were short, others were long. And my role in each of these confessions was to record the details of what people said. The confessions varied, but overall I was startled by the impurity of the souls here. There are so many temptations in life. It's impossible for anyone to maintain a completely pure soul. I only stayed in the world for a short time. If things had been different, maybe my soul would have become contaminated, or worse.

After talking to all the souls, Ah Liang took back the recorder he gave me and gathered everyone together. "No matter how tarnished your souls were," he said, "so long as you have made a confession, your sins are forgiven. You are now ready to go through the checkpoint and enter the Field of Learning, where you will start to learn about all the rules and regulations here in Heaven. I will accompany you there tomorrow."

We were all delighted to hear this.

The next morning after breakfast, everyone was lined up, forming two lines in the field. "Please keep silent and fly with me," Ah Liang instructed. Full of curiosity, I rose into the air and overlooked the houses while imagining what the Field of Learning might be like. There are so many fields in Heaven!

After three hours, we arrived at a majestic gate. Four words were carved on it: *Door of Pure Souls*. The number *16111* was written on both sides of the frame. Four men dressed in yellow robes and yellow headscarves stood to attention on each side. They looked like the guards at a government building, but they were not armed, allowing them to project an air of peace and solemnity. They welcomed us with a gentle look.

"Now we are at the Door of Pure Souls," announced Ah Liang formally. "This door connects to the Field of Learning. Please line up and walk through one by one. If you hear a crisp tweet, it means your soul is clean. You can move forward and enter the Field of Learning. But if you hear the roar of a tiger, then impurity still lingers in your soul. You will then need to return to the house you have stayed in for the past few days and do more self-reflection in the glasses. After you confess to me again, you will come here with the next group of souls for another test."

"Oh my God, how strict!" groaned an old man.

I could see a high wooden doorstep covered with thorns, to prevent souls from passing. But I couldn't see any speaker or sound system from which any tweet or roar might come.

We lined up according to Ah Liang's instructions and passed through the doorway, one after the other. Everything went smoothly. More than sixty souls in front of me elicited a tweet with their passing and walked through the doorway. I also heard the bird tweeting when it was my turn. A doorman signalled to me to keep walking through.

A sudden and long tiger's roar shattered my elation. The woman behind me was pulled back so suddenly that her legs flailed wildly in the air. The sudden withdrawal almost threw her to the ground. I was shocked. *My Goodness,* I thought. *It really can identify unclean souls!*

"But I confessed everything!" the woman protested. "My soul is pure!" She tried again to pass through the door, but two guards immediately seized her arms and escorted her back outside. Ah Liang walked over to her.

"Don't cry for injustice," he said. "This place has never wronged a soul. Do you not believe in God's judgment?" The women was silent for a while.

"Please let me confess here and now," she pleaded. "So I can go with everyone else and enter the Fields of Joy."

Upon hearing this request, Ah Liang took one of the guards aside and discussed the matter. After a while he turned back to the woman. "Yes, we will allow it," he said, "but I didn't bring the recorder. You will need to confess before everyone. If you still cannot pass the test after your further confession, you need to return with me, with no more complaints."

The women nodded and began to talk. "I was a singer before, and I did hide one thing from God. When I first entered show business, I wanted to land an important role so badly that I bribed the director with a red envelope containing thirty thousand *yuan*. He implied that I should stay and spend the night with him. His appearance repulsed me, and I had no intention of getting close to him. But to get the job, I gritted my teeth and stayed with him. *You can't make an omelette without breaking a few eggs*, I told myself. If I couldn't get onto the stage, how could I ever become successful?

We had sex for the whole night. On the second day, he demoted another singer and gave me a solo opportunity, which was the career break I needed to become famous. This is embarrassing to admit, yet common in the world. That's why I didn't mention it with my other confessions."

Souls on both sides of the door had listened to the woman's story. No one reacted, no one made fun of her.

"I know such an open confession will make people look down on me," she sobbed, "But I just want to enter the Fields of Joy and live a peaceful life."

"This is not a secular world," Ah Liang replied, "where some are privileged and true equality is hard to achieve. People have even used different phrases to describe the deaths of people belonging to different classes, from emperors to dukes and princes, down to ordinary people. Funerals were also classified. So was the size of the graveyard, funeral objects and even the material used for the gravestone.

In Heaven, however, no one is privileged. Each soul owns nothing but itself. There is no power here, no wealth, no fame, no possessions, no moral high ground. After the Field of Cleansing, each soul is pure and equal. You can be assured: if you have nothing left to hide, you may try the door again."

The woman hurried towards the door after Ah Liang's words. This time, a crisp bird tweet rang out when she crossed. She burst into tears of joy and came over to join us. Two other men failed the test after her, but they didn't request an on-the-spot confession, so returned with Ah Liang to Station 16111 in the Field of Cleansing.

We entered the Field of Learning. Guided by a young woman in a yellow robe, we came to District 910333, which was similar to District 16111 in the Field of Cleansing, with houses dotted everywhere. The rooms here were larger, though, allowing people to sit and talk around a large table.

"Welcome to District 910333 in the Field of Learning," said the woman in the yellow robe. "My name is Xiaozhen and I am here to help you all. We have two kinds of housing here: the smaller ones are for you to live in; the larger ones are where you will come and learn together. You will stay here for half an hour and learn two things: first, the rules of the Fields of Joy, including all aspects of living and communication; second, you will learn a job skill as well as some general skills that you will need in Heaven. For example, if you would like to knit, you can learn how to knit; if you would like to draw, then you can learn how to draw; if you want to farm fish, learn how to do it; if you like paper cutting, learn it; if you like embroidery, you can learn it here."

Then Xiaozhen started to distribute the house numbers. I was assigned to house 1055, which I was very happy with when I entered it. The layout of the rooms was similar to where I had lived in the Field of Cleansing, and with similar furniture. The sun shone through the windows, a breeze passed through the door, and the room was warm and clean. A few yellow birds chirped on the willow branches. The air was filled with the scent of fresh leaves.

On the second day, we began our official learning.

First we started with how to communicate in the Fields of Joy. Xiaozhen was the manager and teacher in District 910333. She told us that there was no single common language in the Fields of Joy. Since we hadn't drunk the water of oblivion, our memories were intact and we could still use the language we knew to communicate with each other. Souls could understand each other if we were from the same country.

We would also have a translation device to understand other languages. She handed a device to each of us, which was rather like a large wristwatch. Easy to operate, it could translate any language for us with the words being displayed on the face of the watch. Xiaozhen taught us how to use the device, and switched the language she used from French, to Kutu, to Hezhe, and lastly to Romanian.

Then we started to learn how to live in harmony. Xiaozhen gathered together all the souls from Station 16111.

"All souls are equal in the enjoyment of Heaven. It is not so only on paper or in words; there is absolute equality. We have the same standards for all in terms of food, clothing, housing, and transportation. Even God follows the same standards, with no exceptions. No violence is permitted in Heaven. The common practice on Earth is that those with power make the rules, but not here. Each soul should be harmonious with each other. When we meet one another, we should put our right hand on our right ear to greet each other. When we discuss something, we should sit down together and talk openly. In the event of any disagreement, a panel of seven souls will serve as judges, and their final judgment must be respected. When we say goodbye, we should bow to each other, shake hands or place one fist into the palm of our other hand. Then finally, we should turn around after taking three steps and give a final smile to each other."

We spent some time practicing the new procedures for greeting others. Despite some similarities with the conventions on Earth, we laughed as we awkwardly tried them out on each other.

The next lesson was about clothing. "Each soul can wear any style of clothing he or she wants. There is no change of seasons. You can go and pick out whatever you like from the clothing bureau. There are many rooms filled with different styles of clothing for all different ages. You can choose from the pictures hanging at the door of each room, and then walk in. When you walk out, you will be in the clothes you have chosen. The fabric used for each style is similar, very light and soft. Black for men's clothing and white for women's clothing. If your clothes become torn or dirty, you can go there to change them, with the same procedure: just go through the door and come out with a new outfit on. Nudity is not allowed in Heaven. No matter what style you are wearing, you need to cover up before leaving your house."

After learning the rules about clothing, we moved on to food and eating. "Since there is no burden of the body in Heaven," Xiaozhen explained, "the purpose of eating has changed. Eating is not for pleasure, but for the nourishment of the soul; to keep the soul active in Heaven. The food here is different from what you ate on Earth, mostly juices and soups made from fruits and vegetables. We have two meals a day: one in the morning, and one at noon. If you pick up the bowl, you need to finish it. You don't need more, or you will become too sluggish to move."

"Now onto housing," Xiaozhen continued. "In the Fields of Joy, each soul has a similarly furnished house. There are more toiletries in the woman's housing. Souls can visit or live with each other if there is mutual consent, regardless of gender. Since souls have no physical bodies, sexual intercourse is not possible; but souls can kiss and cuddle each other, all of which is derived from love rather than desire. As long as it's mutually consensual, no one will interfere. You can move in with each other. Some couples will want to stay together, which is totally fine.

Some souls have all their family members together in the Fields of Joy. They can apply to live in a few houses close to each other, or move in with their father or mother, brother or sister. If anything becomes damaged in the house, you can get a replacement from the storage building. Volunteers will come to perform repairs on your house if there is something wrong with it."

"There are a few rules concerning travel in Heaven," Xiaozhen continued. "There is no mechanical transportation in the Fields of Joy. Each soul can walk, run, or fly around. You can fly anywhere you want to. You won't bump into each other while flying; souls can sense where to go and avoid clashes naturally. Your speed is determined by your own will. You can fly as fast as you would if you were travelling by a car on Earth, or you can drift slowly like a floating cloud. When you wish to fly, you just need to touch your right ear, and then you will ascend. Many souls live in the Fields of Joy. All souls that have come into existence since the start of human history are there, except those being punished, but not many souls like to wander around. No matter if you walk, run or fly, you cannot cross the border back to the Field of Cleansing or the Identification Field, nor to the Field of Learning or the Holy Field without permission. Otherwise, you will be banished to the Field of Punishment."

"We will learn for half a day, then relax in the remaining half. You can read books in any language with the assistance of the language converter. I have many books on different skills in my home. You are welcome to borrow them any time. Or feel free simply to wander around. The Field of Learning is a long, narrow island, like the Field of Cleansing. It borders the Field of Cleansing and the Fields of Joy, with a wall which separates them. It stretches infinitely, but its width is a few thousand kilometres across. Different sections in the Field of Learning connect to each other, each containing souls undergoing learning. You can wander around and enjoy the scenery in the meadows, the forest, rivers or hillsides, each with birds tweeting, flowers blooming, brooks turning and twisting. No one will impose limitations on you, so long as you don't interfere with other souls."

I walked too far away once and arrived at Section 99743021, where souls from Sweden lived. Luckily I had the language converter on my wrist, or I would never have been able to communicate with them!

Later Xiaozhen told us that in the Fields of Joy we would need to make our own entertainment. We could do nearly anything to enjoy ourselves, such as hiking, climbing trees, playing with dogs, singing, dancing, listening to music, playing basketball, or playing poker. There is no gambling here though, mainly because pure souls have no desire for money, but also because gambling will frustrate the losing side, which contradicts the fundamental philosophy in the Fields of Joy of happiness for all souls. There are no prostitutes here, either, because human desires no longer exist. Romantic relationships here are mainly about the mind and kinship of spirit.

"There is only one rule about entertainment," Xiaozhen emphasized. "Do not interfere with or upset other souls."

Our daily routine was quite different from when we were alive. On Earth, we were stuck in a perpetual loop of resting to restore our physical strength, then using that energy to work for money. In the Fields of Joy, both rest and work served the purpose of enrichment, of fulfilment. Each soul works only on the things he or she likes. No one will push us to do anything we don't want to do.

If we choose, we can also just rest and not work at all. However, everyone prefers to be engaged in some sort of fulfilling work, rather than rest all the time and do nothing. We remember those emperors on Earth who ignored their political duties and spent all their time on pleasure – they eventually lost their happiness in life. Like the body, souls need exercise to remain active and sharp.

22

S on, after your description, I very much look forward to the Fields of Joy. All the rules make sense to me. The stories of Heaven are well-founded. There are good reasons why people kneel down before God in sorrow. All the toil and suffering on Earth matter and will be rewarded.

In the past I have always feared death, resenting it as the end of everything: life, body and soul. I regarded it as ultimate darkness and emptiness. But I am so relieved, Son, after you have told me it is not like that at all!

I now have a completely new understanding of death. The demise of the body is just preparation for us to enter a new world. I'm so relieved by this idea. The looming fear of death has now evaporated.

Dad, after the first period of learning, we started to practice according to Xiaozhen's instructions. Then she tested us after a few days. We answered her questions on a range of different topics. I found the test quite easy and I passed with flying colours. After the test, we started the second period of learning: choosing a skill to learn that interests us and benefits others.

It was a difficult choice for me, Dad. You know I enjoyed many things on Earth. I wanted to be a professional basketball player, but sports are just for fun in the Fields of Joy; I wanted to be a software engineer and work on computers, but computers don't exist in Heaven; I had also wanted to open a toy store with my classmates, but there are no shops or even money in Heaven. If a child needs something, they just register to get it. What, then, would I do with myself?

After serious thought, I decided to pursue writing. I always liked to write because of you. Do you remember those essays and science fiction pieces I wrote when I was in middle school? Do you remember when I got published in the *Nanyang Daily*? I can vaguely recall my idea of Heaven from that time. I was very young, but I believed in my heart that there was something above the sky. Yes, I decided I wanted to be a writer for all the ardent readers in Heaven.

We were given two weeks to decide what we wanted to do. Then Xiaozhen asked us for our decisions. People wanted to do all kinds of things, which fully occupied Xiaozhen's notebook. One woman wanted to look after babies, one man wanted to be a dentist; someone wanted to be a wedding photographer, another a monkey trainer.

If someone wanted to do something not permitted in Heaven, Xiaozhen would explain the situation patiently and ask them to consider other options. For instance, souls in Heaven have no bodies, so why would there be need for a dentist?

After I told Xiaozhen my idea, she smiled. "Wonderful! We hoped you would choose something like that."

I was surprised. "With so many souls in Section 910333," I asked her, "do you really have expectations for each one beforehand?"

She shook her head. "Only for a few souls. You should know that the Fields of Joy are millions of times larger than the Fields of Identification, Cleansing or Learning. Only God knows their exact size. But just by rough estimation, you can get some sense of their scale.

"Managing the Fields of Joy is no simple task, being even more complicated than the intricacies of human society. Many service providers are needed. The management board will pay attention to the talented ones with potential even while they are still on Earth. Your article *Thoughts Above the Sky* caught God's attention. He was impressed by your intuitive understanding of Heaven. And so we watched your life, your body, your personality and your disease, until you arrived here."

I stared at her as I tried to digest her words. "Does this mean that it was you who ended my life early?"

"I don't know about that. None of us knows God's intentions. But you must be aware that His design can never be revealed to mortal ears."

I didn't press her further. What was the point, since I'm already here, and nothing can change that? But I was still curious about their expectations. "You just said my choice was close to your expectations," I said. "What exactly *are* your expectations?"

"You should write neither fiction nor prose," she replied. "Instead, you should focus on writing the biographies of elite individuals who have passed, and their contemplation of life. Most didn't reveal themselves completely on Earth, probably due to being consumed by trivial daily matters, the fear of power, or the pressure of human relationships. Now, they are completely free here and able to speak without restriction. Therefore, God wants to send you and a few other select souls to meet them, interview them and write down their thoughts."

"What's the point of collecting these accounts?" I laughed. "We're in Heaven, and this is a one-way journey. Thoughts and contemplations on human affairs don't matter any more. Who can be guided by this wisdom? Not the souls in Heaven. It's valuable for people on Earth, but how can we relay the message? There's no return from Heaven to Earth!"

"It's natural for you to think like that. For you are an ordinary soul, and you forgot about God in Heaven in the Holy Field, who keeps his eyes on the Earth and enjoys the freedom of moving between the two realms. Do you understand?"

I stared at Xiaozhen in shock. I had no idea that a message can be transferred from Heaven to Earth. Isn't it a one-way journey?

"Don't just stand there with that blank look on your face!" she chided me. "Since you chose to be a writer, you must prepare yourself!"

"If I am to record the experiences and thoughts of others, isn't that like being a journalist in human society?" I asked her. "If I just need to write down what is said, what more is there for me to learn? I am literate and can write. You shouldn't treat me like a child who's just learning to read and write. I earned a Master's degree while I was alive. Shouldn't writing down a conversation be easy enough for me?"

"I admire your confidence!" Xiaozhen replied. "Let me share some background information regarding the elite people you will meet in the Fields of Joy, each of whom was a prestigious figure in their time. Imagine the conversation you might have with Lao-tzu. If you don't understand his philosophy, how can you ask any questions of value?"

Lao-tzu? I was shocked. I grabbed Xiaozhen's hand. "Isn't he the author of *Tao Te Ching*?"

"Whoever else could it be? Do you know of any other Lao-Tzu?"

"Is his soul in the Fields of Joy?" My eyes widened.

"Of course! Every soul from Earth, as long as they are not condemned to the Field of Punishment, enjoys their afterlife in the Fields of Joy. Now do you see why it's necessary to prepare yourself properly?"

"Yes, of course." I was embarrassed. "If I'm to speak with the most respected souls like Lao-tzu, how could I not want to learn more?"

"We will assign a few teachers to you. They will teach you the necessary skills. Of course, this is not the most important part. To be successful will depend mostly on your own efforts. You need to prepare to learn a great deal in the Field of Learning. Compared with others who will learn to plant flowers, you will need to put in much more time and effort."

I bowed to Xiaozhen. "Please rest assured: I shall not fail."

Son, what you have told me is beyond my imagination. It seems you are learning new things there every day! I simply cannot imagine that there is such a rigorous system, and that the Field of Learning holds you accountable for things. You are living in a different space, but life continues.

You must spare no effort in living up to the trust placed in you. I am going to tell your mum about this to pull her out of her tragic sorrow. Your life continues in another space. It's like we sent you abroad for further study.

Son, this is such a tremendous comfort to me. My heart is nowhere near as heavy as before.

Dad, before we started our formal learning, Xiaozhen sent relevant books to every soul, as well as our assigned teachers from the Fields of Joy.

My first teacher was an elderly man from China with white hair. After I greeted him, he was quite direct with me. "I'm no expert," he told me, "just an intellectual. But I hope you will gain an exceptional comprehension of the world. In order to have a dialogue with elite minds in the Fields of Joy, you first need to become elite yourself. The first lesson I am going to give you is on the realm of thinking."

"The realm?"

"Yes, the place where people's thoughts can form and develop. All topics can be categorised into one of nine domains: Heaven, Earth, God, society, nation, race, people, things, and soul.

"Heaven relates to weather, the formation of wind, rain, snow, lightning and hail, as well as the movements of celestial bodies such as the sun, the moon and the stars. Earth consists of the movement of the crust which forms the land. God is in charge of Heaven, Earth, and people. Shifts in the weather, the transformation of Earth, and the design of the human body direct us to God.

"Society concerns the communities and social groups formed by people. Nation sets up the borders and space within which people communicate and interact. Race refers to the evolution of the family, the clan and ethnicity. People is about process of birth, growth, and aging, illness and death, and different lifestyles and values. Things are materials that are needed for survival and development. Soul is about peace of mind and the afterlife.

"The realm of thinking is unlimited. A person finds it hard to understand one category in isolation, but this is the scope of reference for your interviews in the future, no matter how you phrase your questions."

Lesson eight was about society. He said society is the aggregate of human activities. Among all the social animals in the world, humans have the most reliance on society. A wolf is still a wolf even if it leaves the pack, but a human is no longer truly human if he lives outside of society. Instead, he becomes like an animal. Society is neutral, but the institutions that people design create divisions. Institutions that allow their members to participate in social affairs and enjoy freedom of speech as well as benefit equally from development are beneficial to society, and vice versa.

Lesson ten was about humans, which he said were the greatest, wisest and most industrious animals in the world. However, cruelty and evil can transform individuals to another species if they are not contained. That's why God set up the Field of Identification at the entrance of Heaven and the Field of Punishment for those that deserve it. The elites from human society have forever discussed, contemplated and tried to rationalise the uncertainties of life.

Lesson fifteen was about things. Things included everything except Heaven, Earth and people. People use them to live, yet are manipulated by them. They are the cause of laughter, crying, complaints, protests, even violence. Things have driven life to be both more interesting, but also more horrifying.

He was a responsible teacher and would stay in my room for a while after our lessons. Sometimes he would close his eyes to get some rest. Other times he would open his eyes to supervise me. Each time I asked a question, he would open his eyes and say, "Try to figure that out by yourself first. I will respond after you tell me your ideas. Learning happens when you think and reflect."

At the very end, I asked, "Can you please tell me your name, Master? I would like to know more about you, since you have taught me so much."

"It's not worth your effort. But if you insist, I will tell you. My family name is Wang, my given name is Bo'an. I am also known as Yangming. I used to teach at the Zhongtian Pavilion on Earth. I was a teacher in life."

"Wang Yangming?"

"Yes"

"From the Yuan Dynasty?"

"A Wang Yangming who taught during the Yuan Dynasty; was there more than one?"

"Oh my goodness! You are Master Wang Yangming?" I recited his poem:

The rich and noble are like wine,
Five buckets make one wasted.
Rather lost in mountains and rivers,
With no fame in mind.

"A few of my thoughts have done well to reach you after so many years. I am touched," he said.

"I am so fortunate to be your student!" I replied. "My father taught me to read your work, *Xiang Temple*, in which you explained your philosophy that everyone can be taught. Later, I read several more of your books: *Knowledge and Practice*; *Meditation*; *Truth*; and *Roses All the Way*. I didn't understand all of them, but I was deeply affected by your insight. The conscience you emphasised is so meaningful to human society."

"Well, those are my old works and thoughts."

"You believed that conscience – compassion, honour and shame, reverence, right and wrong – was instinctive to people. That these things are innate in human nature always made sense to me."

"Yes, honour, shame and gratitude comprise the conscience I wrote about."

"Unfortunately, many people have lost their conscience," I said. "Milk with melamine, poisoned pork, processed food with reused oil, steamed bread dyed with noxious additives, carcinogens dumped into the water, the hit and run incidents that happen to children."

When Master Wang heard what I'd said, he suddenly burst out laughing.

Son, I cannot imagine that you talked with Wang Yangming and became his student! Master Wang was the founder of the philosophy of the mind. He pursued ultimate happiness in life and emphasised the beauty in experience, which had a profound impact on Chinese philosophy.

You should seize this opportunity and learn as much as you possibly can from him. The more you understand, the broader your mind will become, and the more comfortable your life can be. I really hope that one day I will also get to meet him and hear more about his thoughts on conscience.

Dad, classes here are not as stressful as learning on Earth. There's no material purpose or objective. Education here is just to make us fulfilled and enriched in the Fields of Joy. If someone isn't able to master a project he or she chooses, they can just switch to a simpler one. No one will blame you for that. There are no tests, no rankings, no first place, no criticism, and no rewards.

Learning is always stress-free. Whenever you feel tired, you can just go back to your house for a rest. The teacher won't be angry with you. It suited me just fine. Usually, I spend the mornings in lessons or reading books, then in the afternoons I go for a walk. It's amazing to walk around in the Field of Learning. Sometimes I walk, sometimes I fly. I travel here and there, stopping to rest or to have a look around at my leisure. It's just like taking a relaxed vacation on Earth!

One afternoon, I walked into another district and saw a dozen or so young men and women learning to dance. Their teacher was a young woman in the traditional dress of the Tang Dynasty. I recognised this dance from a performance I once saw in the Shanxi Grand Opera House in Xi'an. The students were fully engaged, following each move precisely. The teacher paused sometimes to offer some assistance.

I was fully captivated by the woman's dance and watched for a long time. She was well-proportioned, with a dignified and beautiful face. Her movement was lithe and graceful, and each expression shone with elegance. I was enchanted by the teacher. On Earth, she must have been a prominent dancer at the China Opera House. They stopped for a rest before I left. One of the girls asked, "Miss Yang, how long did it take you to learn this dance during the Tang Dynasty?"

"I designed the choreography while dancing. Including the time spent on teaching the maidens in the palace, it took about one month," replied the woman.

Miss Yang? The palace? These words stopped me.

"And why did you create this dance?"

"To please Li Longji. Everything I did back then was to please Li Longji. Not like here, where we can dance purely for enjoyment."

Li Longji? My goodness! Was this Yang Yuhuan? I asked a young man nearby, "Is she—"

"Miss Yang Yuhuan? She is. Have you read *Song of Eternal Sorrow* by Bai Juyi? It tells the story of Miss Yang. She is our dancing teacher now. She is an amazing dancer. Do you want to learn to dance? Miss Yang, I think we have another student here!"

Yang Yuhuan walked over to me with a smile on her face. "And which district are you from?"

I immediately waved my hand, embarrassed. "I don't want to learn to dance. I just stopped by to take a look."

"Then please sit down! No ticket is required for watching. Dancers love to have an audience. The more, the merrier!" she said, smiling.

My courage began to rise. "Did you have many audience members in the palace?"

"Yes, of course. It was officially just for Li Longji, but there were always maids, eunuchs, and soldiers in attendance as well."

I was watching her neck while she talked. I knew she had hung herself from a pear tree on Mawei Hill. I wondered if there was evidence of that incident on her neck. Ominously, she wore a scarf around her neck.

"Young man, are you checking my neck? I know what you are looking for. That tragedy damaged my body and left an imprint on my soul, but the scar cannot be seen. See for yourself," she said as she removed her scarf.

I was embarrassed, and my face reddened. I took a glance at her neck and moved my eyes away immediately. There was nothing there. Her neck was smooth and unblemished.

"I appreciate that Li Longji taught me what men desired on Earth; how quickly love fades; and about the uncertainty of royal life. Unfortunately, he was sent to the Field of Punishment. I will never see him again, or I would ask him to touch my neck, to remind him how he repaid my love."

Son, during Yang Yuhuan's time, it would have been impossible to meet her even if you were from a noble family, let alone an ordinary person! Wherever she went, she was guarded by soldiers, followed by droves of maids and eunuchs who encircled her, making a wall of people.

It seems that equality does indeed truly prevail in Heaven. You can talk to her, and she can teach everyone to dance. It was good for you to meet her. She can help you to understand that glory is as transient and ephemeral as a passing cloud. Don't let it make you conceited. Don't complain if you never had it. A peaceful life has its own meaning, too. People come into the world naked. Then society dresses them up into different identities, some achieving glory and others not.

No matter what our lot is in life, we leave it all behind when we leave the world of the living.

Dad, the second teacher Xiaozhen assigned to me was a communications expert. My job was to interview the elite individuals in the Fields of Joy, so it would be important to improve my communication skills.

He was an elderly Frenchman who spoke only his country's native tongue, but the translator helped me understand him effortlessly. He told me that conversation was charming, that successful dialogue can entice and bewitch people. This was why some people become professional speakers, he explained. A tactful conversation can secure many gains; meanwhile, careless talk can create missed opportunities. The way we converse can earn respect or disdain. Words are powerful. They can end a war or sustain a happy marriage. They can take you to higher positions in political office or make you a beloved leader, a champion of the people.

He taught me four essentials to having a successful conversation: first, compliment your partner; second, be a good listener; third, be sincere with your partner; and fourth, be humorous. The first few moments are critical to when speaking to someone for the first time. You must let them feel your respect and warmth, your empathy. You need to prepare for an interview, to familiarise yourself with the experiences and personality of the interviewee in advance; you need to craft your words carefully and maintain eye contact during the conversation; you need to lead the conversation and make sure to steer your partner to the desired topics. In the subjects you know little about, be frank and honest. When your interviewee loses their train of thought, don't panic. Deftly switch to another subject and regain their interest. The biggest taboo in conversation is to interrupt the interviewee or to correct them with a harsh tone. The conversation should end with grace, so as to leave a good impression on the interviewee.

The two of us also had a practice discussion about social system design to practice my skills, which went very well thanks to his guidance. I shook his hand when we parted that day. "I'm so fortunate to have met you," I told him, "and to have learned the art of conversation from you."

He smiled kindly at me. "I'm no expert, but I am recognised as such by the delegates in Heaven. My conversations on Earth weren't so successful. When I talked to King Friedrich II of Prussia in Berlin, to persuade him on liberal politics, we ended up quarrelling. I didn't stay for lunch, left in anger and moved to the border of France and Switzerland."

"The Prussian king? You talked to the Prussian *king*?" it was a struggle to process.

"Yes, he invited me speak with him."

"The Prussian king *invited* you? Then who are you?"

"I was a writer."

"A writer. What is your name?"

"My name is François-Marie Arouet. I was better known on Earth as Voltaire."

"Oh my goodness! You're *Voltaire*?" I was shocked. "I've read several of your works: *Candide, Treatise on Tolerance, The Maid of Orleans, The Age of Louis XIV*."

"Those works mean nothing to me now," he replied, "but I do appreciate that they had at least one reader in China. I didn't expect that my words would travel so far across the world! Most probably you are aware of this, but I was a big admirer of Confucius' philosophies on Earth. I advocated for natural religion, with no trace of superstition or fanciful folklore, no blasphemous reasoning and no naturalist dogma, which of course was very similar to the teachings of Confucius. I have never been to China. According to my understanding of Confucius, it must be a place of equality and benevolence. That's why I accepted the invitation of Xiaozhen to teach you conversation skills today."

"Thank you for teaching me how to converse. I want to tell you that your books still have significant influence in the world. I am so honoured to have been taught by you. Do you know you are still revered as the king of French philosophy, the finest poet in France, and the conscience of Europe..."

23

Son, how lucky you were to speak to Voltaire himself! I read his books when I was young, and his ideas have always stuck with me, especially the value of human freedom, and freedom of speech in particular.

Voltaire lived in an age of primacy and autocratic monarchy, and he witnessed first-hand the anguish of people who lost the freedom of speech. In fact he was a fierce proponent of human rights. I didn't know he was an expert in the art of conversation, but of course he is a respected philosopher from the Age of Enlightenment. God has granted you a huge honour, to be able to talk to people like him in Heaven.

Dad, to mark the end of the fourth month since our arrival in the Field of Learning, Xiaozhen arranged a performance for us to demonstrate what we had learned. It was like a test, only without scores, ranking or criticism. It was a bright morning; all the souls were lined up with whatever equipment they needed in two lines, facing each other with a large space in between. We watched those in the other line as they performed what they had learned.

A middle-aged woman stood opposite me, showcasing her weaving skills: a little duck, a puppy, a rabbit, a kitten; she created each as vividly as if they were real. Then she used bamboo strips to make baskets and buckets, and then a straw mat. She was so skilled that I thought she must have been trained before, whilst on Earth. Only when I talked to her did I realise that she had in fact been a college chemistry professor. She said she didn't want to continue working in the chemistry field, but rather perform some less challenging but more fulfilling labour. Weaving was a skill she had always wanted to learn when she was younger. I asked her why she hadn't continued to use her experience and expertise in chemistry. She shook her head, and said that it was difficult to anticipate the consequences of chemistry's development.

"Some new discoveries or developments," she explained, "have caused untold damage to the world, instead of improving it. Take the invention of plastic bags, for example. The convenience it brought to society was at the expense of the environment. If you take a train anywhere in China, you will see the trees littered with plastic bags, hanging like some artificial and eery fruit. Plastic bags dance in the wind in both the city and the countryside alike. It takes more than two hundred years for plastic bags to decompose. There are countless plastic bags buried underground, destroying the permeability of the soil, and compromising the Earth's ability to sustain plant life. Livestock can also die from obstruction of the digestive tract if they consume debris mixed with plastic bags by incident. Let's assume each person uses thirty thousand plastic bags during their lifetime. When these non-biodegradable plastic bags accumulate beyond a certain point, then what can be done?"

"Maybe we can figure out a way to decompose them?" I offered.

"But why should we invest so much effort and money to solve this problem? Wouldn't it be better if the plastic bag had never been invented in the first place? Why can't we just carry things the way our ancestors used to, making weaved straw baskets or bamboo baskets from nature?"

"We're always trying to find more convenient, more economic solutions. Plastic bags were one such solution."

"Then our desires dragged us towards danger. We need to learn to control our desires."

"Desire is innate," I suggested. "It's difficult to go against our nature."

I hadn't intended to invite a debate. I just want to understand her ideas better.

"Desire up to a point creates a stimulus to work hard and innovate. But taken to excess, it will lead people towards danger and desperation. For example, a healthy amount of desire for power will encourage people to work harder in order to get promoted. But unchecked and without restraint, desire can push people to assassinate competitors and rivals, which will destroy the self."

I had no idea Xiaozhen had recorded everything in the performance. Later I was told that my conversation with the former chemistry professor showed that I had mastered the basic skills of conversations. Dad, I was so happy to hear this! But even though the evaluation of my performance was good, I knew I still had much to learn.

Son, there is no skill that can be mastered in a day. You had a conversation with a chemistry professor and talked openly and on level terms with her. That in itself was a big achievement. Elite people in every field have their own understanding and contemplation of life and society. It's a wonderful opportunity for you to let them talk to you. So keep at it – I have complete faith in you.

Dad, every fifteen-day period became a learning cycle. There was then a three-day break, with no classes. People could do whatever they wanted and go wherever they wanted in the Field of Learning. During one of these breaks, I roamed into an area called the Origin of Desire. The land was boundless, flat as a mirror, and scattered with low, unfamiliar plants with beautiful octagonal leaves and cherries hanging from the branches. The fruit was like jade: glossy, brightly coloured and with an enticing sweet aroma, which made people helpless to resist the urge to take the fruit. Some visitors couldn't resist the temptation and put a few into their mouths, one after the other. I watched them and couldn't help but pick one myself. Just before I put it into my mouth, a few of those who had eaten the fruit fell down and started to roll around. They had somehow been transformed into wolves!

"My goodness, what just happened?" I shouted, horrified at the scene before me.

An old man with a white beard approached me and a few other visitors. "Are you shocked? This is a test devised by God to test each soul's will to resist temptation."

"I'm sorry, who are you?" I asked warily.

"I look after the Origin of Desire."

I pointed at the wolves. "What has happened to them?"

"Souls in the Field of Learning should have no desires since we have no physical needs here in Heaven. However, people are accustomed to pleasure, so some desire remains and there are souls who are unable to resist temptation. God set up the Origin of Desire as a reminder. Look at these few who couldn't resist the temptation of those beautiful fruits. Their earthly desires have resurfaced. What might they do if their desire was even stronger? What might they do if they do not learn how to control themselves?"

"So what should they do?" I asked.

"Any lingering desire in the soul in the Field of Learning can fester and corrupt souls if not contained, just as on Earth. Are there not plenty of examples of that? Take the farmer's son, once compassionate and ambitious, who rose to be the owner of a milk factory. He couldn't resist the temptation of fortune. The desire to make more money drove him to poison the milk produced by his competitors. Children died from that poisonous milk. Wasn't he a wolf?"

"But these souls weren't to know this was only a test," I protested. "They weren't prepared for this."

"Desire is a choice," he replied. "I will forgive them this time, since they have not yet completed their learning." He raised his hand towards the wolves and turned them back to who they were before, but they were struck dumb.

Son, I am fascinated by the idea of a testing ground for souls in Heaven. Maybe we should have similar places of warning on Earth, too. People have many desires here: desire for fame, power, fortune, beauty, housing, food. Many find it difficult to control themselves in the face of all these temptations. Most criminals in jail are there because of temptation. It's important to control our desires in the face of temptation.

Once, a businessman coveted a singer and wanted her to be his mistress. He sent someone to the singer with an offer: if she joined him for a week in Hong Kong, he would pay her two million *yuan*. The singer smiled in contempt and left. A second offer was made: seven days together would net her five million *yuan*. The singer paused for a moment and left again. A third deal was proposed: one week, *ten* million. The singer thought for a while and then left. The fourth time, the middleman came to her and promised fifty million *yuan* for seven days together with the businessman. She nodded her head.

We can't really blame the girl too much. Self-restraint can become very difficult under increasing temptation. The only way to resist all temptation is to stick to your principles at all times and try to endure any suffering.

Dad, we spent six months in the Field of Learning. Xiaozhen met with each of us, and upon hearing that we had all learned something, said, "Now that you have finished your learning and can keep yourself occupied in the Fields of Joy, you are ready to leave. I will take you there tomorrow."

"There's no test?" I was surprised.

"No," she replied. "I have observed you all throughout the process. You have all learned enough to enter the Fields of Joy."

All the souls were thrilled to hear we would be leaving for the Fields of Joy. We chatted excitedly about what they might look like, and how we would adapt to living there. I knew in my heart that the Fields of Joy must be the Heaven that we imagine during our time on Earth. But what would it really look like?

The next morning, Xiaozhen called us for breakfast soup and lined us up. "Please fly with me to the southwest," she instructed. We did as she'd asked, floated up, and flew with her.

We flew at low speed, with the Field of Learning passing by below us. After about half a day, a shimmering barrier in the air stopped us. I didn't know what made it, but it obstructed our view. Xiaozhen signalled for us to land on the ground at a golden gate with the number *173595* printed on the frame. Two lines of delegates guarded the gate, though they appeared to have no weapons.

"Welcome, everyone!" Xiaozhen raised her voice. "We are at Gate *173595* of the Fields of Joy. You are now entering the most coveted area in Heaven. I am so happy for you all. Please wait until you hear the angel call your name, then cross the threshold and walk upstairs onto a flat platform where angels will meet you. Please remember, don't fly up. Take the staircase on foot. Keep your eyes forward. The staircase is high. Don't fall down. I look forward to seeing you again. I must stay for another six months in the Field of Learning, and then I will join you in the Fields of Joy. I look forward to meeting you all again!"

We all bade our farewells to Xiaozhen while an angel started to call out names. I was number thirty-nine on the list. When I heard my name I answered loudly, then crossed the threshold, after which I could see a high staircase facing the gate. The staircase was long and steep, more than six hundred steps, and ascended into the sky.

I followed the thirty-eighth person up the stairs, step by step. From the first step, I could hear music in the air, soft and melodic. I didn't recognise the instruments in the song, but it was so refreshing and pleasant, like the music from the film *The Song of the Phoenix* I watched when I was back in the world of the living. It was like being in a wonderland! I heard people behind me making similar comments as we climbed. A refreshing fragrance also hung in the air, providing further comfort and relaxation as we climbed in tranquil silence.

Finally I reached a broad platform, almost like a playground, enclosed by tall poplar trees where white doves nestled and cooed.

In the centre of the larger platform was a small raised stage, on which stood an elderly man in a pale green robe. Two rows of young men wearing similar robes flanked him on either side. The men on the left had odd numbers written on boards they were holding, while those on the right had even numbers on their boards. Behind the old man was a large billboard on which was a map with numbers written all over it.

After everyone from the Field of Learning had reached the platform, the old man stepped forward to address the assembled group.

"Welcome to door 193595 in the Fields of Joy," he began. "Congratulations on starting your new life in Heaven. I am most delighted to welcome you here. The Fields of Joy are many times larger than Earth. Most souls live here after departing from Earth. This is a place of ultimate freedom, and it contains souls of all different nationalities, races, religion, and languages. The different regions and districts here are for administrative purposes only. The conditions in each region are exactly the same.

"First, you must get yourselves settled. You can choose where you want to live. The delegates on either side of me will send you to your preferred living area. Take some time to look at the map and talk with the delegates before you make your decision."

I hesitated. There were so many delegates. Who should I talk to? What if I didn't make a good choice the first time? Would it be possible to switch later? Luckily, a neighbour of mine from the Field of Learning, Fang Jin, pointed at the map.

"Look," she said, "District 22967, the central area of the Fields of Joy, looks quite similar to your hometown in Henan on Earth. Let's talk to a delegate and enquire about living there."

We approached the delegate closest to us. I was anxious to ensure the first choice I made in the Fields of Joy was a good one.

"Yes," the delegate confirmed, "District 22967 will be quite suitable for you. Most souls who live there are originally from China. If you have decided, I can take you there now."

Fang Jin and I looked at each other, and nodded. The delegate signalled for us to fly with him to the west.

After about two hours, we saw another delegate flying toward us. The delegate who had accompanied us came to a stop, as did we. "The delegate from District 22967 has come to take you the rest of the way," he said. "My job is complete. Please follow him now."

"Welcome to District 22967!" the new delegate greeted Fang Jin and me enthusiastically. "My name is Cody. I come from France on Earth. My job is to welcome newcomers. Our district is located in the centre of the Fields of Joy, and has a population of three hundred million." Cody smiled at us.

"Three hundred *million*?" I was surprised.

"Yes, but compared to other districts, we're not so large. Most souls here are from China, and we are the closest district to the Holy Field."

"Where are the other souls from, besides China?" asked Fang Jin.

"We have souls from more than fifty countries on Earth. They speak many different languages. Some even lived on Earth before the common era."

"Oh. Is it OK for us to speak Chinese?" Fang Jin continued.

"You must have learned about the language converter while in the Field of Learning. So don't worry about communication here. Go ahead. You won't regret coming here."

Cody waved goodbye to the delegate who had brought us here. Fang Jin and I did the same.

We followed Cody and continued flying west. The sheer scale of the Fields of Joy was beyond comprehension. We flew at a very high speed, but we still hadn't left District 99991.

"My goodness! It's huge!" Fang Jin exclaimed.

"Of course it is! How many souls on Earth have come here after death? How many individuals have been born on Earth? After they live their life on Earth, almost all of them come to the Fields of Joy. How could we not have enough space for them all? All of this was taken into consideration in the Fields of Joy. Take District 22967 for example – we plan eventually to accept more than thirty billion souls," Cody explained.

I stared at him. "My goodness! How much space does that require?"

"You'll see when you arrive."

I wasn't sure how long we'd been flying, when Cody finally said, "Here we are." We landed on some flat terrain, crisscrossed by streams and shaded by trees and fragrant flowers. Villages and houses were nestled among the trees.

"There are no cities in the Fields of Joy," said Cody. God believes that cities are not ideal places to live, because of their hustling and bustling nature. Most souls prefer the tranquillity and spacious living area found here. You can both live over there, not far from me." He pointed to a few houses not far away. "Come, let's walk."

The roads here were not wide, since there are no vehicles in Heaven. Roads twisted along the streams and trees. Fish leapt from the water, birds tweeted among the branches, and sometimes little rabbits hopped out from the grass and stared at us before quickly hopping away whenever we walked too close. Fang Jin and I followed Cody and enjoyed it all as we took in our new surroundings. How could we not? After all, these were the Fields of Joy! Everything was so idyllic.

A wooden sign that read *Fragrance Corner* stood at the edge of the village. "This is the name of our village," Cody told us. "Most people who live here come from northern provinces in China. You'll fit in nicely."

Fang Jin and I found our assigned houses. I lived in house 699, and Fang Jin lived in 698. Both were new houses. Cody explained that most new souls in the Fields of Joy get a new house, but that we can move into an older house later on, if we choose to move. The houses weren't large, each around sixty square metres, with a simple layout of a living room and a bedroom. Each house had a garden in which grew flowers I hadn't seen before. Their fragrance permeated throughout the house. The bed, tables, chairs, and cabinets were all made of wood with no paint on them, simple but beautiful. My house was at the end of Fragrance Corner with the forest on one side and Fang Jin's house on the other. It reminded me of our hometown in Zhouzhuang village.

Cody lived in the centre of Fragrance Corner, in house 377. He told us we could go to him for help with anything we needed. He said that the villages in the Fields of Joy have no particular management personnel. Souls simply took turns to do whatever was needed. After making sure that Fang Jin and I were happy with our new homes, he said, "Why don't you both take a rest now, before you start to enjoy life in Fragrance Corner? I know you learned all the rules about living here while you were in the Field of Learning. If you have any questions or need to ask anything, feel free to come to me or any of your neighbours. Don't worry, you'll be fine! OK, I'll be off now."

After Cody had left, Fang Jin and I visited each other's houses and made sure we had everything we needed. By now it was approaching dusk, but Fragrance Corner was not hectic and rushed, as Earth would be at that time. It was very peaceful, with no one in sight. Fang Jin and I were excited by our new environment. We didn't want to sit in the house, though, and we weren't hungry, so we decided to go and introduce ourselves to some of our new neighbours.

We knocked on the door of the house next to Fang Jin's. An old lady opened the door. "Are you newcomers?" she asked kindly. "Welcome!"

Fang Jin and I introduced ourselves. After learning my hometown on Earth was Nanyang, the old lady smiled. "I'm from Shangzhou in Shaanxi," she said, "not far from you. What a coincidence! I'm glad we're going to be neighbours here in Heaven too." She took our hands and led us into her home, which was similar to ours. Hers had some paper cut-outs on the windows for decoration.

"Did you make these yourself?" I asked, admiring the paper decorations.

"Yes. I wanted to learn paper cutting when I was young, but I was from a poor family. Each day I needed to help my parents in the fields and around the house. I had no chance to learn. After I got married, I started to help around my husband's home. We had six children later. Each day was like a long, tiring journey. I completely forgot about my wish to learn paper cutting. I never expected to learn it until I arrived in the Field of Learning. If I'd known, I would have come to Heaven sooner! Looking back at my last days on Earth, I was tortured by cervical cancer and scared to death. It's funny, really. All my days on Earth, I endured a busy and hard life. Only after I came to the Fields of Joy have I been able to live for pleasure."

"So now you do paper cutting every day?"

"Yes. I have nothing to worry about in the Fields of Joy. I can go out for walks, I can talk with my neighbours, I have no other commitments. I can cut paper for as long as I please, which makes me happy and at peace."

"What do you do with all the paper cut-outs you make?"

"I usually send them to my neighbours. They all like my work. A few days ago, Cody took a batch and sent them to souls living to the north in Green Corner. Souls here all have their own speciality, so we can share the results of our work around. We are all very content."

Dad, the lady's kind smile reminded me of Grandma. How is she, by the way?

Son, Grandma is fine. She misses you, though. We lied to her and told her that you went abroad. She always calls me to ask about your life abroad and wants to call you. I'm always having to come up with new excuses! Sometimes I want to tell her that you're in Heaven, but I'm worried that she won't be able to handle it. She's eighty-seven now, after all. You have to remember how difficult it is for people on Earth to truly believe in Heaven. Most people are afraid of death, and know nothing about the Fields of Joy.

If Fragrance Corner is your home now, then be nice to your neighbours. Your mum and I know you are polite and kind-hearted. We're sure that you'll fit in well and be popular there. After we reach the Fields of Joy ourselves, we'll find you and then we can finally be together again.

Dad, I had a good night's sleep that first night. There's no electricity here, so if you need light at night, you go to the fireflies in the garden and ask if any of them would like to help. One firefly will follow you into the room at your request, providing light for whatever you need, especially reading. Then, when you want to go to bed, you can just say, "I'm going to bed now. See you tomorrow." Then the firefly will fly away through your window.

That night, after the firefly left, I fell into a deep sleep until the morning, with no dreams disturbing me. The morning light and tweeting of the birds woke me up. I had some soup after I got up. There's no problem figuring out what to eat in Heaven. All the soup powder was assigned to us beforehand. We need do nothing but boil some hot water and make the soup. It's very convenient.

I was wondering what to do in the morning after my soup, when a young woman's voice appeared outside. "Mr Zhou? May I come in?"

I was surprised. "Yes, please come in," I called out. A girl in a long dress came in.

"Cody told me we have two new neighbours," she said pleasantly. "I am very pleased. You've just arrived and you must be curious to find out more about your new home. My name is Bo Linlin. I became a tour guide in the Field of Learning, and now I also live here in Fragrance Corner. Would you like me to give you and Miss Fang a tour? I'd be very happy to show you around."

"That would be wonderful!" I replied. "Thank you so much." I followed her outside, where Fang Jin was waiting for us.

"She was so welcoming that she woke me up very early this morning!" Fang Jin complained sarcastically in a hushed voice. I gave a look that told her to stop. After all, it was just a friendly gesture from the girl.

"Do you know why it's called Fragrance Corner?" asked Bo Linlin.

"I don't know," I replied. "Something to do with the pleasant smell?"

"Yes, I assumed that when I first came here. But it's more than that. Many different kinds of flowers grow here. Unlike on Earth, we have a nine-month season here in Heaven when flowers bloom. The fragrance flows into the air, and weaves itself into the clouds. That's fragrance for the eyes as well as the nose."

"Oh, really?" I reached out to grab a cloud. Sure enough, the fragrance was denser for a moment, and then drifted away in streaks of vapour.

"Why don't we live in the village, but in the corner?" Fang Jin asked.

"Most of the living areas are called 'corner' in Heaven. It's God's will. The Fields of Joy are vast."

"I see."

"Do you know this river's name?" She pointed to a stream flowing in front of Fragrance Corner. We shook our heads. "It's called Fragrance River, a branch of Tianmu River, one of the five major rivers in the Fields of Joy. Come, you can smell it."

Fang Jin walked down the bank, cupped her hands and lifted out some water. "It's delightful!" she said.

"The water has a fragrance too?" I asked dubiously, walking towards the river so I could see for myself. Why, yes indeed! It smelled wondrous, like roses on Earth. "Who put the flower extract into the water?" I asked.

"Do you think Heaven is like Earth?" Bo Linlin chided me gently. "That everything is man-made? You see that grass on the bank? Some grass leaves fall into the water. It is called fragrant grass, and it infuses the water with its fragrance. If you take a bath in the water, the fragrance can linger on your body for more than three days. It smells better than any man-made perfume."

"Have you bathed in the river?" Fang Jin asked.

"Why don't you come and find out!" replied Bo Linlin, raising her arms. Fang Jin shied away. "How uncivilised!" Bo Linlin pouted. "This is Heaven. We don't have bodies or desire. There is nothing wrong with smelling me." She signalled me to go and smell her.

I didn't want to offend her, so I walked over to smell her. Sure enough, a trace of fragrance wafted into my nostrils.

"I took a bath right here three days ago. If you want to smell good, just bathe here every few days."

"Yes, yes," I replied, not quite sure how to respond.

"Do you see that open space beyond the trees on the other side? There's a high platform there, where people gather every morning and evening. Many residents play instruments in Fragrance Corner: the erhu, flute, violin, cello, trumpet. Look! Three people are performing there now!"

I looked, and two men and a woman were indeed playing on the stage. The music carried through the air.

"Do they play songs we know on Earth?"

"Not entirely. Because people's memories of Earth life aren't erased, there are some elements of earthly music. But people like to listen to and play new songs. One resident here was a composer on Earth, and learned more about it in the Field of Learning. He is our composer here. He is very young, and came here because of HIV."

"People with HIV can stay in the Fields of Joy?" I was a little surprised.

"Yes, HIV is just an illness, and people who have illnesses are not guilty," she replied.

"You're also young," I said. "Why are you here?" I immediately felt embarrassed after I'd uttered the words. We'd only just met her, after all.

"Leukaemia. Because of a high-pressure lifestyle and environmental pollution. Many young people die of diseases like this." She answered matter-of-factly and didn't seem upset in any way.

"Were you married?"

"No. My ex-boyfriend is married to another woman now."

"Aren't you upset?"

"No, it's just unfortunate. Very unfortunate."

"Because you didn't marry him?"

"No, because he married another girl only six months after my death. It was a little too fast. He promised to love me forever. I thought it would take him longer to find another relationship."

"Do you doubt his love for you?"

"I just don't believe in true love on Earth. I believe it just satisfies our physical and material needs. It's just a game. Love is just a label that disguises that truth."

"So you don't believe in true love between a man and a woman?"

"There is none on Earth. At least, not that I ever saw. Maybe true love can exist in the Fields of Joy. Without desire for pleasure or material things, without the pressure of reputation, people are attracted to each other by pure thoughts. This, I believe, may nurture true love."

I stared at her. I hadn't expected that this seemingly happy and innocent girl could have gone through such ordeals.

"Am I scaring you?" she asked, grinning. "If you did meet someone who truly loved you on Earth, then I'm happy for you."

I shook my head and thought of the girl who had left me after learning of my disease. Did true love really not exist on Earth? Or had I just been unlucky? Had Xiaoyi truly loved me?

Bo Linlin pointed into the distance. "Do you see that pavilion over there and the people around it? They're playing games."

"Games? Let's go and take a look," I replied. Fang Jin and I were excited to see, so we all walked towards the pavilion.

Four men were engaged in a writing contest. A slim young man had carved on a bamboo plate: *Kindness is a treasure that will bless you for three lives.*

A larger man wrote with a brush: *Virtue is the farmland that will nurture many generations.*

An old man with white hair wrote with a pen: *Whether Rich or Poor, to be content is what matters.*

A short middle-aged man typed on a typewriter: *Mountains, rivers, bamboo, flowers; leisure is a blessing.*

When they had each finished, a girl put each of the four inscriptions on the four pillars of the pavilion, and handed a flower to each spectator.

"Please place your flower under the piece you like the most."

Bo Linlin winked at us. "So, which do you think will receive the most flowers?"

"I think the older man," I replied quietly.

"Which older man?" Bo Linlin asked.

"The white-haired man, of course."

"Do you know when that slender young man was born? He was born in the Han Dynasty when Liu Xun first became king. That was in the year 73BC. How old is he now? The larger man was born during the Tang Dynasty, in the first year of Li Zhi's reign. That was AD650. So how old is he? The white-haired man was born in the fifth year of the Republic of China, which was 1916. The man who is typing was born in 1966. So which of them is the older man?"

"Oh my goodness! Then why does he look so young if he was born in the Han Dynasty?"

"Heaven allows the soul to remain at the same age as when they first arrive here. So in the Fields of Joy, it is not possible to determine a soul's age by their appearance."

I was immediately reminded of having met Wang Yangming and Voltaire. It made complete sense.

"Look, they're announcing the result," Bo Linlin said as she gestured for us to watch. Audience members went forward to put their flowers at the writing piece they liked the most. In the end, the larger man from the Tang Dynasty received the most flowers. People started to clap and cheer as a Caucasian woman went over to kiss him.

"That woman is Cody's neighbour in Fragrance Corner. They were friends on Earth and died together in a car accident," Bo Linlin told us. I looked at the woman and thought that despite the tragedy of the accident, they were blessed to be together in Heaven.

Later, Bo Linlin showed us the library in Fragrance Corner. It was a large building, stocked with books in different languages.

"Those are books written by the residents of Fragrance Corner," she explained. There are two sets: one is here and the other is in Heaven

Library, which has a branch in each residential area. Libraries are open to everyone here. If you can't find the book you want in your local library, you can try in Heaven Library."

"Are there also copies of all books from Earth here?" I asked Linlin.

"Almost. Most writers end up in the Fields of Joy. Only a few went to the Field of Punishment, where their books are also kept."

Dad, Linlin showed us so many places and I quickly became familiar with the area. Fang Jin and I became quickly entranced by this place. So you and Mum can rest assured: I have well and truly settled into my new home in the Fields of Joy.

24

Son, it's difficult for me to conceptualise everything you've described. I am reminded of Blake's words, that imagination is proof of another kind of existence. It was another truth: rationality binds people in reality, but imagination frees us to transcend worlds.

From your experiences, the Fields of Joy is the ultimate goal that people pursue, where our souls can begin a new life. They can have friends there, play games and enjoy the company of others. Many souls will live very happily there.

It's a huge comfort to me, as I know it would also be to anyone else who has lost a loved one. If only they were aware of it...

Dad, a few days after I arrived in Fragrance Corner, I was reading at home when I heard a knock at my door. I opened the door and saw an elderly couple, both with silver hair.

"Are you Zhou Ning?" the man asked.

I nodded my head.

"Were you from Beijing? But your hometown was in Zhengzhou, Henan?"

I nodded again, shocked. How could he possibly know?

"Were you from Zhouzhuang Village, three kilometres from Goulin County?"

"Yes. How do you know all this?"

"And was your father Zhou Daxin?"

"Yes, but sorry – who are you?" I assumed they must be volunteers in the Fields of Joy.

The couple looked at each other and smiled. "Finally, we found you!"

"You were looking for me?"

"You are our great-grandson."

"Great-grandson?" I stared at them and remembered the image I'd seen in the identification mirror.

"Yes, we are your father's grandparents. We passed away in the 1950s when he was very young. But we have been watching you all from Heaven. We watched as your father grew up and got married; we watched as you were born and grew up; and we watched as you became ill and passed away. We tried to estimate when you would arrive in the Fields of Joy. The place is so large and it took us a while to find you. But finally we're here together, and now we'll be able to spend time getting to know you!"

Imagine my shock, Dad! You had never told me anything about my great-grandparents, but there was a clear family resemblance in their faces. The genetic code couldn't be wrong. I was in no doubt whatsoever that they were indeed my relatives. I invited them in and made them some soup.

"I will be able to take care of you both from now on," I told them.

"You don't need to do that," my great-grandfather replied. "We have everything we need here in the Fields of Joy. We just want to see you regularly and enjoy the happiness of our family reunion."

They told me they were living in Plum Corner in District 774856, but they would apply to move to a house here in Fragrance Corner.

"Won't that be difficult?" I asked.

"Not really. You can stay anywhere you wish in Heaven. You just need ten days for the application."

We talked a lot that day. They asked me a lot about our life on Earth, and I asked them about the different fields in Heaven. Although I had never met them before, I immediately felt very close to them. Our blood ties were natural and strong. And after a few days, they would move to Fragrance Corner...

I asked my great-grandparents how they knew about me. They told me there was a window in each residential area in Heaven, through which souls can observe people on Earth. The window was only open for a single day each month, when souls can line up to watch the Earth. The window was able to help souls locate the place they wanted to see. I found it difficult to comprehend this, so later, after my great-grandparents had left, I went to see Bo Linlin and asked her where this window was.

"Why the rush?" she replied. "It's not open today, so there's no point in checking it now."

"But I really want to see it," I insisted.

She had little choice but to take me to an open area in the east side of Fragrance Corner. She pointed at a large stone slab under a broad locust tree. "There it is."

I approached and knocked on the stone. It was solid, cold and still.

"This is the window?" I looked at Bo Linlin in disbelief.

She didn't reply immediately, but started to count on her fingers. "In seven days the window will be open again. You'll be able to line up here and watch the world. It gets busy, though – make sure you come early."

I still found it difficult to believe, but I made a note of the date. When it came, I got up early and went straight to the locust tree. I was sure I would be the first one there, but there were already a dozen or so residents lined up. *So it must be true,* I thought to myself. I took my place in the queue and it kept growing longer after me.

After sunrise, I heard a cracking sound come from the stone slab, and one side was lifted slightly by the air, revealing a square opening. I came close and peered into the cloudy abyss. It clearly wasn't the first time for the first man in the queue. He kneeled down and adjusted the telescope that was there in the window. People waited behind him and watched a meter on the stone, which started to count down from ten minutes, the time allocated to each person. Then it was the time for the next one. The first man reluctantly left the window, and a second came forward.

Soon it was my turn. I couldn't wait! I hadn't expected Linlin to be here too. She must have worried that I wouldn't know how to operate the telescope. She told me to direct it firstly to Asia, then to China, to Beijing, then to locate our house among all the streets. Adjusting the telescope, I followed her instructions and, oh my goodness, I saw everything! I saw the garden, the building, and even our apartment! I saw Mum bringing groceries home, and you taking the garbage out. You seemed quite down. Was it because of my leaving? And Mum was putting medicine in her mouth. What was that for? Was it from vertigo? I'm so sorry I can't be there with you. Please look after yourselves.

But Dad, Mum – I saw you! I really saw you...

25

Son, I don't know if you're just trying to comfort me, or if there really is some kind of window through which you can observe us. It sounds too good to be true, but I hope it's real. How wonderful it would be if you can still see Mum and me! Even though we cannot see you, knowing there is at least some connection between our two worlds is such comforting news.

God was very careful. A window between Heaven and Earth was such a good idea. We all believed that your death was the end, and that no communication would be possible after that. No one on Earth expects there to be a window. It was God's design. He must be aware of our suffering to be parted and was so thoughtful.

God, even though you cannot hear me, I would like to thank you from the bottom of my heart!

Dad, the next day, I decided to go and look for Grandpa. Since my great-grandparents had been able to find me, I was fairly sure that I would be able to find him. I still had some clear memories of him. When I went to No. 15 Primary School in Nanyang, Grandpa picked me up every day after school. He always stood prominently at the side of the gate so I could see him right away. His chunky body and bald head made him stand out too, and I always spotted him in no time.

Grandpa would take my hand as we crossed the busy street to the other side, and then he would let me run ahead as he followed behind. Sometimes in the evening, he would buy a toy or some snacks for me from the street vendor: a mechanical dog, a magic cube, a sweet potato, or an oven roll. I still remember the little mechanical frog he gave me once. After I wound it up, it would bounce around on the ground for ages. I would follow it and clap my hands. Grandpa would smile as he watched me. I was still very young when he passed away, and I had no comprehension of death back then. I always regretted not seeing him off in the cemetery, so it's important that I try to find him here.

I went to find Linlin and asked her how to go about finding Grandpa. She told me that the first step was to make sure he was in the Fields of Joy and not the Field of Punishment. I told her that Grandpa valued his reputation more than life itself, and he did many good deeds throughout his life. There could be doubt that he was in the Fields of Joy.

"Well," said Linlin. "If you're certain he's here, then you could go to the Archive Centre. That's where every soul's records are kept. You can find anyone's information there."

"My goodness!" I exclaimed. "Then how large must it be? So many souls throughout human history must have entered the Fields of Joy."

"You'll know once you're there," she replied, and with that, she beckoned me to follow her into the air, and we flew there together.

After about two hours, we arrived at a place that was set apart from the residential area. It reminded me of a huge supermarket. Many houses and buildings were divided by a river. Unlike cities on Earth, there were only few people out on the street. A large sign stood in the central plaza. It was written in many languages: *Archive Centre*.

"Here we are," said Linlin.

"Good Lord!" I exclaimed, scarcely able to take in the sheer size of the place. "It must be several times the size of Beijing!"

"How could it possibly house everyone's records if it wasn't so large?" she replied. "Let me explain how it works. Each city or district is named by its name on Earth, for example Versailles, Xinyang, or Melbourne. Each street is named by year, like 5000BC, 4300BC, AD121, and so on.

Each block is then named in months and days, like 1 January, 7 March, 13 December. Each house is named in hours and minutes, like house 0:00, 3:23, 10:50. You can locate anyone here by pinning down their address on Earth, and the date and time they passed. Then you can find their information in that particular house."

"How wonderful to have such a complete archive," I marvelled.

"Indeed it is," Linlin agreed, "but it's not like the records we kept on Earth, of school or work achievements. The information here is just where you're from, why you're here and where you live. Its only purpose is to help friends and family find each other here. It's for every soul's convenience, according to God's will."

"How thoughtful!"

"Your grandfather lived in Nanyang, China. So let's start with Nanyang district." We flew up high and found Nanyang first, then the street for 1992, then the block for 7 April. I didn't remember the exact time when he passed away. Bo Linlin looked at the code on my robe and found his record in house number 1440. Only when I entered the house did I realise that so many people had died in exactly the same minute in Nanyang. It was a house full of people's names! I went to a board on the door and, following Linlin's instructions, wrote down Grandpa's name. A name tag brightened up. I went over, and it was Grandpa's name tag: *Yang Qingjun, came here on 7 April 1992 at 05:13, from Zhenxi Street, Goulin County. Lives in Maple Corner, District 561892.*

Dad, I met Grandpa that morning! I asked Linlin to accompany me to District 561892. She had been so welcoming since I'd arrived, and had helped me with every little request I'd had. I was so grateful. If not for her, who knows what problems I might have encountered? I told her so on our way to District 561892.

"Thank you so much for being my neighbour, and for all your help."

"You have enriched my life here, too," she replied. "We haven't had too many new souls in Fragrance Corner recently. I'm so happy that you and Fang Jin joined us."

We arrived at Maple Corner around noon. The sun shone directly above the maple trees enclosing the area, and butterflies flew around everywhere. I was amazed by Grandpa's home. Many souls were outside, some playing chess or cards, others attending to plants; some were taking a walk, others practicing opera. I knew Grandpa was an opera fan, so I paid special attention to that group. Then I saw him, performing in high spirits:

Hair on end and shoving my hat,
In wrath I lean on th' balustrade,
While th' rain leaves off its pitter-pat.
Eyes fixed skyward, I sign long and loud.
A hero's fury fills my breast.
At thirsty, nothing achieved, unknown,
– but these to me are light as dust –
I've fought through eight thousand li
Holding the field, under cloud and moon.
What I do mind, is not to let
My young head turn white in vain,
And be gnawed by empty sorrow then...

"Grandpa!" I called over to him.

Dad, imagine his shock! He stopped and just stared at me. After a moment, he came to take me in his arms. "Zhou Ning, why are you here? You should be with your parents at home."

I explained my story, and Grandpa took me into his arms. "My boy, I didn't expect this for you. However, in many ways you are fortunate to have come here so early and be spared from all the suffering on Earth. Come home with me."

He noticed Bo Linlin. "Are you two together? Is she your wife, your girlfriend?"

I didn't want Bo Linlin to be embarrassed. "No, she's my neighbour." I explained. "We met soon after I arrived here. She is a most wonderful guide!"

Bo Linlin showed no sign of embarrassment. "Hello, Mr Yang. My name is Bo Linlin. I didn't know Zhou Ning before, but we have become good friends."

Grandpa smiled. "I'm happy for you, Zhou Ning! It's lucky to have good friends in the Fields of Joy. You won't be lonely here. Now, come on, won't you please come home with me?"

Grandpa gave us each a cup of soup as a greeting. A middle-aged woman came in, who I thought must be Grandpa's partner. Grandpa introduced us. "Zhou Ning, this is your grandmother. She left the world earlier than I did, which is why she looks younger. I found her in the Fields of Joy and now we live together again."

I was so overjoyed! I had heard about Grandma many times from Mum, who had told me she passed away young because of sickness. I don't remember her at all. Our reunion was completely unexpected. "Grandma!" I cried as I rushed towards her.

Grandma took me into her arms and her eyes filled with tears. "My boy, I left so early and never had a chance to hold you. Come and give me a hug now."

While we were all overwhelmed by our tears of joy, a man knocked on the door. "Is this the home of Yang Qingjun?"

"Yes, who are you? Oh, my goodness! Wenben, my son! What are you doing here?"

I was surprised too. My uncle? Was he also in the Fields of Joy? I went to the door and saw my uncle standing there, weeping. I ran into his arms.

I learned that Uncle had died just a few minutes after me because of a heart attack. Now he lived in Beauty Corner in District 357892.

"It's OK," Grandpa said, placing his arm on Uncle's shoulder. "You no longer need to suffer on Earth, and now we can all be together again."

Linlin and I talked with Uncle, Grandpa and Grandma until dusk. I loved my grandparents' openness and Uncle's humour. I also liked Maple Corner, which appeared to be lit up by red maple leaves. I asked Grandpa, Grandma and Uncle to move to Fragrance Corner with me. Grandma was happy to, but Grandpa was concerned there were would be too many of our relatives living there together. He suggested we stayed where we were, but visit each other regularly.

"Yes," Linlin agreed, "it's very easy to fly and visit each other. There's no need to move in together."

———

Son, I never realised you would be able to meet so many of our relatives! You know, Grandpa really loved you. When you were little, he and your mum took you to visit me in Jinan and Xi'an. You needed to be carried all the time. At that time I couldn't afford tickets for sleeping bunks for you all. Sometimes I couldn't even get a ticket for a normal seat! So they had no choice but stand in the aisles, taking turns to carry you. Your grandpa was overweight, and when he carried you in his arms, he often grew short of breath. I felt very sorry to put that burden on him. But now you have met him in Heaven!

It gives me great comfort that you can now repay his kindness and take care of him. In fact, you should try to take good care of everyone. I know it will be a heavy burden for you, but I promise that I will share it with you when my time comes...

Dad, my great-grandparents moved to House 469 in Fragrance Corner a week or so later, after their application was approved. The original resident also moved to another place so they could be near their family, too. In Heaven, moving is simple. They didn't need to bring any luggage. Cody, Fang Jin and Linlin came to help as we prepared the house for their arrival. We did a thorough cleaning, dusted everything and wiped the floor. Linlin was very considerate to bring a few pots of flowers with indulgent and soothing fragrances.

Great-Grandma was very happy. "Zhou Ning," she told me, "You must cherish Linlin. She is so considerate."

"Great-Grandma, don't make fun of us!" I replied, embarrassed. "She's just my friend, not my wife."

"Maybe one day she'll become your wife," Great-Grandma said, mischievously. Linlin's face blushed.

"But there's no marriage in Heaven," I told Great-Grandma. "There are only soul partners who have deep affection and respect for each other."

"Well," Great-Grandma continued, "you can both live together, and have that affection and respect."

Linlin shied away. Fang Jin and Cody laughed, then joked, "Your great-grandmother is right. Why don't you move in together and take care of each other?"

Then Great-Grandpa chided Great-Grandma, "Don't meddle, Dear. This isn't Earth, where marriage can be the product of power or fortune. Things are completely equal here. No one is superior to anyone else. Love is just about affection and one's own will."

One day shortly afterwards, Linlin took my great-grandparents to see Tiankuang Lake, which she said was the most beautiful lake on Earth or in Heaven, and well worth a visit. Strangely, although my great-grandparents had been here a long time, they had never heard of it but were glad to pay a visit.

Linlin was our tour guide. It took us three hours to reach the lake, which was immense. Even the great lakes on Earth such as Lake Ontario or Dian Lake cannot compete with its majesty. The most famous attractions here are lotus flowers and dancing fish, and the Heaven maids scattering blossoms. The lotus flowers here bloom every day at noon, with gorgeous petals as large as a basketball court! At noon, the huge petals slowly open, and their fragrance disperses through the air.

It was like a fairy tale! Then the fish started to dance. First, storks screeched on the lakeside, then the fish started to splash in the water. It was spectacular, like a choreographed dance. We were amazed. The maids scattering blossoms was an entertainment arranged by Heaven. Thirty-six beautiful maids were picked from different districts, each carrying a bamboo basket filled with magnolia flowers. They stopped a few metres offshore, and then began to sprinkle the petals of the sky orchids on the lake. A flower-shaped waterfall formed for a moment on the lake. Everyone was captivated by the wondrous spectacle!

Every day I was having new experiences and learning more about Heaven.

My life was becoming so enriched. I really appreciated that Bo Linlin kept offering to be our tour guide. She was a true professional and all the tours with her made my great-grandparents so happy. But I was growing concerned that we were taking up too much of her time. I hadn't even known her very long!

One day, Great-Grandpa wanted to visit Heaven Theatre, which I knew nothing about. I had no choice but to ask for Linlin's help again.

She lived in the centre of Fragrance Corner, not far from Cody. She answered the door immediately. I had to admit she made me excited and happy. Had I fallen for her already? She was a little surprised to see me. "Hey, it's you!"

I felt a little deflated. "Are you not pleased to see me?"

"Yes, of course I am! It's just that you seldom come to my house. It's usually me visiting you all the time. Come on in!"

Her house was very comfortable. The layout, the furniture and garden were the same as mine, but she'd clearly put a lot of thought and effort into decorating it. In the small courtyard, she had designed a small stream. The water was lifted by two self-elevating buckets, then introduced through a hole on the fence, flowed through the courtyard, then returned to the river. She had planted flowers on one side, and beautiful birds landed on the tree.

Inside she had a reading table covered by books of tortoise shells, bamboo slips, seals and paper. Her own embroidery was on the bed. The fragrance of books and flowers complimented each other. Nature and culture were in harmony.

"Such a beautiful nest!"

"Wrong word!" She immediately corrected me. "It's a beautiful home!"

"Of course, such a beautiful home. I'm interested in having something like this."

She pretended not to understand. "What do you mean, you're *interested*?"

"I mean, I'd like to live in a place like this," I replied

"Really? Well, you'll need to apply for that!"

"Apply for what?"

"To move in with me."

"And would you approve it?" I laughed.

"That depends on your motivation," she said rather formally, but smiling. "If it makes sense, then it's possible that I will approve it."

"Well, in that case I shall give the matter serious consideration," I replied, with equal sarcasm. We both laughed. "But I could really use a favour from you today: I'd like to take my great-grandparents to see Heaven Theatre."

"Yes, of course!" she replied, enthusiastically. "But why are you inviting me?"

"I would like you to show us the way. You are the tour guide, after all."

"Oh", she seemed a bit deflated, "Yes, of course. I'd be happy to take you there."

What a wonderful day we had! I thought Heaven Theatre would be something like the National Theatre in Beijing. I was completely unprepared to find it thousands of times larger, with so many different theatres inside for dramas, operas, ballets, musicals, even burlesque shows! All kinds of performance can be found there. For Chinese opera alone, there are more than four theatres: Beijing Opera, Yue Opera, Huangmei Opera, Hebei Bangzi, operas from all different places and eras; you name it, it's there!

The first thing we did was take a tour of the theatre. The magnificent architecture and distinctive gates dazzled and amazed us; this was Heaven, after all. Its grandeur, beauty and sheer magnificence is unrivalled anywhere on Earth. There were posters on each gate, providing details of all the performances. I glimpsed a musical performed by Marilyn Monroe and asked Linlin about it. She said it was common because God didn't like films or television shows in Heaven. Marilyn Monroe wanted to continue to be an actor, so now she performed musicals. A performance by Charlie Chaplin was taking place in another theatre.

I was amazed to see that Shakespeare's new play Terror was being staged too. Apparently, Shakespeare never stopped writing after he arrived here, and many theatres competed to host his new plays. Olga Lebeshenskaya's Swan Lake was being performed here too. She was revered as a 'Dancing Soul' on Earth, which was now literally true here in Heaven.

Fascinating though it all was, my great-grandparents were not interested in these productions. They asked where the Henan Opera performance was. Great-Grandpa said he had been a fan since he was young, and he knew all the plots and even the lines by heart. So we searched for the relevant theatre, and finally arrived at Theatre 6786, where Mulan was being performed.

The show had already started when we came in, and my great-grandparents were immediately entranced. They nodded their heads in time with the music. Linlin and I smiled at each other.

"I'm jealous of them," she whispered in my ear. "How wonderful that they're able to stay together in Heaven. So many couples on Earth ended up in resentment or divorce, never wishing to see each other again."

I didn't know how to respond. I thought of all the couples I'd also known who fought constantly. What would it be like if they met each other again in Heaven? Might formal marriages become a thing of the past as human society evolves?

Son, it's so good to know that there are theatres in Heaven. I've always loved local Henan Opera, ever since I was young. It must run in the family. When I was a child, I would go and watch performances in neighbouring villages, no matter how many miles away they were. With no electricity in the villages at that time, the local people put cotton thread in kerosene for lighting. Strong winds would distort the shape and shadows of the actors and even interrupted the singing on occasion. Even then, I was mesmerized, watching from beginning to end. I memorised and can still recite some verses from those operas, even today. It was the most relaxing thing for me, being lost in the rhythm and the music. I hope I'll be able to enjoy those performances again in Heaven some day. It would be a big comfort to me, after I depart this world.

Son, these operas were not very popular among your generation. I must say, I'm surprised that you had the patience for it! Actually, I find it very touching...

Dad, something surprising happened in Fragrance Corner one morning that I wanted to share with you. After breakfast, a beautiful young woman came to look for Cody. I led the way for her, and wondered if maybe she was Cody's sister. They didn't really look alike though. Perhaps she was Cody's girlfriend, and Cody would be thrilled to see her?

Unexpectedly, however, when I knocked on Cody's door and he saw the woman, he was visibly shocked. "Why are you here?" he shouted.

The woman didn't seem upset, however. "My dear, why shouldn't I visit you? I've been looking for you ever since I arrived after a tsunami. Let's get back together. I'm so lonely here."

"I don't want to get back together with you. I don't love you any more. Please leave me alone!"

This was a completely different Cody from the one I'd come to know. This Cody was cold and frosty.

"How could you do this to me, Cody? Have you forgotten your promise to me? Have you forgotten how you pursued me and showered me with flowers and gifts?"

"That's all in the past. I'm sorry but I don't love you any more. So please leave."

"You don't even want to catch up with me after all this time? How can you be this cruel?"

"Look, if you don't leave, I will request a formal judgment."

"Please, I beg you, Cody. Forget any unpleasant things that happened before, and let me stay. I love you and will take care of you just as I did when we first fell in love."

Cody turned to me. "Zhou Ning," he said, "please invite seven people here. I am requesting a formal judgment. Since you're my friend, you're not allowed to take part."

I had no idea why Cody was so being cold to her. This really wasn't like him, but I had no choice but to agree to his request. And so I gathered together seven neighbours and brought them to Cody's house.

"I, Cody, request the initiation of a formal judgment process to solemnly proclaim on the matter of Lisa wishing to move in with me. Please hear my statement first.

"I met Lisa when I was twenty-one years old, during my first year at college. I pursued her and quickly fell in love. She soon became my girlfriend and we were married five years later. Just after our honeymoon, I was diagnosed with pancreatic cancer and went into hospital. She cried so much, not so much for my sickness, but because she felt that I had somehow deceived her. In fact, I decided to let her go when I learned of my illness. I planned to talk to her after my surgery, but she stopped visiting me in hospital when I needed her the most.

"I then learned from my sister that Lisa had started dating another man, and I signed our divorce in hospital. She married the other man the day before I died. I gave her my blessing, even though I was privately devastated by how quickly she had abandoned me.

"And now she comes here because of a tsunami, and asks to move in with me? Sorry, but I cannot accept this. The pain of what happened before is just too much to bear. Therefore, I request a judgment, which I shall accept and abide by."

"Lisa, please tell us your version of the events Cody has described," said one of the judges.

"I admit that Cody is telling the truth. But I have my reasons. Everyone knows how dangerous pancreatic cancer is. There is no hope of recovery. The doctor told me that Cody would live only for six months at most. After learning this, my parents urged me to leave Cody immediately. I agreed because I needed to get on with my life. Why should my life be ruined by his disease?

As it turned out, another man began pursuing me right away, and I took that opportunity. I hoped that by coming here, Cody would understand my decision back then. Didn't he want me to have a good life? Didn't he wish me happiness? How could he hate me now? What kind of man is he, really? Now I come to him because I know we can get back together. Who has any right to say that we can't be a happy couple again? Who?"

After they had both said their piece, the seven judges left for a discussion. I couldn't walk away because I had brought Lisa here and I also wanted to know the outcome.

About half an hour later, the judges returned. One of them announced, "I have been entrusted by everyone to announce the result of the judgment: Lisa had the right to abandon her marriage with Cody and start a new life on Earth; equally, Cody has the right to reject Lisa's request to live together in Heaven. Accordingly, Lisa, you are requested to leave immediately."

Lisa snorted angrily and left. Cody looked mightily relieved...

26

Son, this judgment system in Heaven sounds very interesting. It protects everyone's rights, and everyone has the right to be a judge and have their opinions heard. It creates a level playing field. The system works in Heaven because all souls have been purified and are free from desires. On Earth, the same system can become badly corrupted due to bribery or conflicts of interest.

Dad, as I became settled in the Fields of Joy, my initial excitement began to wane. I either stayed at home, or visited relatives, or wandered around. I became restless, even a little bored.

It occurred to me that I hadn't yet had any chance to practice the skills I had learned in the Field of Learning. Would there be some sign for me to do this? Had God forgotten about me?

It turned out that He hadn't. One morning while I was daydreaming, Bo Linlin knocked at my door, together with another girl.

"Come on, it's time for you to start working. We don't want you to become bored and unfulfilled."

I asked how she knew. "It happens to every newcomer. After the first stage of excitement, souls can get bored. This lady is the delegate from the Holy Field. She has a task for you," she said.

"Mr Zhou, my name is Darya, a messenger from the Holy Field. We think the time has come for you to start to do something productive. But you can keep enjoying your time if you are not yet ready."

"Yes, yes, I'm ready," I nodded eagerly. "I'm already getting bored! Please tell me, what would you like me to do?"

"You have learned communication skills in the Field of Learning. God hopes that you can interview certain elite souls here and record their thoughts on life."

"Yes, but I wonder what's point of doing that? We don't have physical bodies now. How can their thoughts help us here?"

"Your interview reports will be sent to God. I don't know His intentions. No one does. You should just follow His wishes."

"But do you have any idea what God's intentions are? So I will have a purpose, instead of giving up half way through."

"I suppose He is hoping to understand people's thoughts, their reflections of nature, life, and society. Maybe He has other intentions. I am just a messenger, so I cannot tell you any more."

"But I never found out in the Field of Learning who I'll be interviewing."

"Yes, you couldn't learn that in the Field of Learning. Here are the first few names." She handed me a piece of paper on which were written three names:

Charles Darwin

Harley

Li Changda

"Oh my goodness!" I exclaimed. "I know hardly anything about Darwin's theory of evolution. And I don't even recognise the other two names!"

"You don't need to know them. You can find out about them."

"Well, Darwin was certainly an elite on Earth, of that there can be no doubt," I replied. "As for the other two—"

"God has his own definition of 'elite'," Darya interrupted sharply. "Just follow His instructions. Here is your equipment. It is an integrated camera, recorder and transmitter."

"Where do I need to transmit to?"

"You don't need to ask. Just do what you are told to do."

"Is there any deadline?"

"It's up to you. Your priority here is to enjoy yourself. Your job is a means to helping you find your purpose and make your life more fulfilled. It is not about earning money or carving out a career."

"Thank you, I'm relieved to hear that. Can I bring someone else along to the interviews? Like Miss Bo Linlin here. She is an experienced tour guide who can help me a lot."

She smiled at Linlin. "It's up to the two of you. You don't need my permission."

"And how should I contact you after I finish the interviews?"

"Use this," she said, giving me a small device. "Just press this button and I will come to you. You can call me by my name, Darya. Actually, we have met before."

"We have?" I replied, surprised. I tried to recall all my experiences in Heaven, but had no idea who she was.

"I'm sorry," I said, embarrassed that I didn't remember her. "Where exactly did we meet?"

"You really don't remember me, do you?" she replied, amused. "Let me give you a clue." She put a scarf on her head.

Of course! She was the delegate who had brought me to Heaven from the hospital. She escorted me through the Field of Identification, the Field of Punishment and the Door of Purity.

"Yes, it's really you!" I cried, grabbing her arms.

"You asked for my name before, but I couldn't tell you then. Now you know! I am Darya."

"But Darya, when did you become a messenger in the Holy Field?" I felt a strong bond to her. "What a wonderful surprise!" I continued to hold her hand.

"Just now. My first assignment is to inform you about your interviews. I am pleased to see you again, too."

I was still buoyed with excitement after Darya had left. "Will you join me for the interviews?" I asked Linlin.

"Yes, but only if you give me a formal invitation," she replied, laughing.

Son, God has placed His trust in you. You must complete your task well. It was always one of our family values, to honour our commitments. You must therefore focus all your effort on completing this important task.

I must admit, I am rather concerned that you're too young and inexperienced. How could you talk to those elite souls? They might see through you; they might even ignore you completely! What if they don't consider you someone sufficiently worthy to share their thoughts with?

Son, please moderate your expectations and be prepared for disappointments.

Dad, what worries you also concerned me. But I wanted to give it my best shot.

I decided to find Darwin first. I borrowed all his major works from Heaven Library and devoured them all: *On The Origin of Species, The Variation of Animals and Plants, The Descent of Man, The Expression of the Emotions in Man,* and *The Power of Movement in Plants,* all of which comprised his lifelong research and discoveries.

Speaking of Heaven Library, it was the size of Zhengzhou! The catalogue room alone took up three whole streets...

Later, Linlin helped me to find Darwin's address. We flew directly to Joyce Corner, where he lived. When we arrived, he was in his garden, studying what appeared to be two types of grass, and measuring their length. He looked the same as when he left the world at the age of seventy-three, similar to the picture I saw in the textbook.

He seemed upset by our interruption. "I'm not expecting any visitors today," he said, rather gruffly.

I started to explain. "Please forgive us—"

"Please leave. I have made prior arrangements today." He was very blunt.

"Sir, we would never have met you if we required an invitation. You had departed the world for almost one hundred years already by the time I was born. I am nobody, with no academic achievements worth mentioning. You could never have heard about me, nor had any reason to offer me an invitation. But I am a true believer and advocate of the theory of evolution. I would very much welcome an opportunity to hear your wisdom."

He turned round to look at me directly. His face had softened now, less serious. "Is that so?" he asked. "In that case, you'd better come in."

"Thank you," I replied, hugely relieved that we had made it past the first obstacle. "I read your biography and am aware that you come from a prestigious family of doctors. And that the same career path was planned for you. My own story is not so different. My father was a military man, and I also became a soldier."

"But I never really liked medicine," he lamented. "So when my father sent me away to medical school in Edinburgh, I would often go to the sea to collect specimens, to observe and classify them."

"It was the same with me," I said. "I never wanted to be enlisted. I loved basketball. It was my favourite thing about army life."

"Later, my father sent me to Cambridge University to study theology," Darwin continued. "But I had no passion for that, either. However, I did make some friends there and learned the skills for locating and identifying mineral specimens."

"Passion is a most vital quality in young people," I said. "I believe that parents should respect and encourage their children's passions, which may lead to a greater chance of living a fulfilled life. I envy you for persisting with your passion. I, on the other hand, gave up my basketball under pressure from my parents."

"Opportunities are also very important," he said, becoming more animated now. "At the age of twenty-two, I was given the opportunity to set sail on board the HMS Beagle as naturalist for a five-year scientific expedition. I travelled to many different places all around the world and researched countless local species of plants and animals."

"I learned about evolution from my teachers at school, and read your books in college. *The Origin of Species* is known to almost everyone on Earth. May I ask, was the book conceived during that voyage?"

"Who cares about *The Origin of Species* here in Heaven?" he asked sarcastically.

Of course, I didn't tell him that God had sent me here, which may have given him second thoughts about talking to me.

"Please enlighten me," I replied rather formally. "My soul is curious, and I fear becoming bored in Heaven."

He smiled at me. "Very well, I admire your curiosity. Before that voyage, I still believed that God was the Creator. But many things that I saw during the voyage challenged my beliefs. In South America, I found the fossil of an ancient armadillo. It was quite similar to the armadillo of the modern age. Had they evolved from the ancient ones? In the Galapagos Islands, I observed the different features of the birds in different islands, which I believed could be explained by evolution.

"After that voyage, I collected more evidence by visiting farmers, owners of plant seeds, and those who raised livestock and poultry, who showed me the changes in plants and animals throughout the process of domestication. I even raised some pigeons myself for observation. And over time, my beliefs leaned increasingly towards natural selection and evolution.

"I wrote the book *On The Origin of Species* which marked the denouncement of God as the Creator. Later on I began to study the origin of the human species. With the foundation of *The Origin of Species* and after a period of research, I proposed that humans evolved from apes. I published my research in the book *The Origin and Choice of Human Beings*. Humans, I postulated, had undergone a long evolutionary process. Everything originated as a primitive single-celled micro-organism, then evolved into multi-cellular organisms, then into lower organisms in the oceans, shellfish, fish, amphibians, reptiles, birds, mammals, primates, and then finally we evolved into apes and humans. This theory was developed by others later. The evolution from apes to human was then divided into five stages: *Ardipithecus Ramidus*, *Australopithecus Afarensis*, *Homo Erectus*, *Homo Heidelbergensis*, and *Homo Neanderthalensis*.

"Your theory was quite revolutionary at the time."

"Yes, it was quite natural to find opponents in a theory that challenged conventional theology. What truly surprised me was that even some scientists were against it. Their reasoning caught my attention too. For instance, some argued that cockroaches had been living on Earth for more than five hundred million years, far longer than humans. Why had they stopped evolving? What made them survive the process of natural selection? Why didn't duckbills and rabbits keep evolving or die out over the Earth's long history? Some zoologists pointed out that fossils found in the Earth's crust layers indicated that some advanced fish appeared earlier than less advanced ones. I knew there was still much to be proved in my theory."

"Did you ever question yourself? Were you affected by self-doubt?"

"It was not a matter of questioning or self-doubt, dear boy. But there was a sense of pity, of regret, that I could not actually prove the theory of evolution. I felt impotent. Helpless."

"Helpless? In what way?"

"One human lifetime passes in the blink of an evolutionary eye. It is nigh on impossible to gain a full understanding of the fields of biology and zoology within a single life. So very difficult. Many problems remain unsolved."

"Did you believe until your death that humans had evolved from the lower species?"

"Yes, fervently. I would never renounce my theory. But many things remained to be proved, and at that time I had no more answers. It caused me considerable distress. There were moments when I regretted ever feeling compelled to investigate the origins of human beings. I perhaps could have chosen a different, a less...divisive path."

"You may have had a choice as an individual. But as the human species, surely we were compelled."

"Indeed. Humans needed to explore this. But someone other than I could have done it."

"So you were chosen for the role?"

"No, I made myself the chosen representative. It was my own choice."

"Do you regret this choice?"

"It brought much agony and stress upon my wife and me."

"Yes, your wife Emma. I believe she was a devout Christian."

"After my works were published, the church castigated my theory because it denied the Creator. My wife then found herself in a very difficult dilemma, between her life as a Christian and her role as my wife. Her life was impossibly challenging."

"But you never compromised?"

"How could I? This was my life's work!"

"I know you have received monumental acclaim, but I must tell you how much I admired your work. Your research made a unique contribution to human knowledge."

"Thank you. I am very happy to hear this, even here in Heaven."

"According to your research, humans evolved from lower species. Does this mean human beings will continue to evolve?"

"Of course they will! It will never cease."

"And do you have any predictions for the future of human evolution?"

"I do, but it's pure speculation. I believe that people will grow smaller in stature in the future, perhaps only half of the average size today, because humans no longer require physical prowess to survive and fight in nature. Our brains will continue to advance and intelligence will continue to increase. Humans have benefited from making labour-saving tools, and they will continue to do that. Meanwhile, the reproductive capability of humans will slowly degrade because raising children is increasingly regarded as a burden; furthermore, the natural environment is a source of destruction of the vitality of male sperm and female eggs."

"You said that the human brain will evolve further, with intelligence levels rising ever higher. Can you predict to what level, ultimately?"

"High enough to build technology capable of destroying not just humanity, but Planet Earth itself."

"Do you mean nuclear weapons?"

"No, nuclear weapons are still manageable. The magnitude of an explosion remains under human control. Some countries are conducting research into weapons of deterrent, such as biological and genetic weapons. Such weapons are capable of being carried into other countries by infected birds and rats, thereby infecting entire countries. These viral agents are not containable. Who, therefore, can guarantee that they will not mutate and infect the entire planet? Perhaps their inventors may have thought of solutions for these problems in advance. But natural variation is uncontrollable; solutions have no guarantee of success."

"You paint a disturbing picture," I said, genuinely troubled.

"So long as evolution progresses and human intelligence grows, the day will inevitably come when people will lose control of the technology they invent. Can you not foresee it?"

"This is indeed a horrifying prospect," I said, sincerely.

"And the final act will be the destruction of humankind."

"It's unimaginable!"

"Perhaps. Maybe I'm just too pessimistic."

"If you could still communicate to people on Earth, what would you say to them?"

"If things do not evolve as I fear, then so be it: humans will survive. However, great care must be taken. A system must be in place to manage the invention and use of advanced technology. Otherwise, I fear the future of the human species is bleak indeed."

"Is this the most important lesson you can offer to those on Earth?"

"Most certainly. We must take great care of ourselves, and remain vigilant."

Son, I think that everyone has an urge to investigate their origins. When I was very young, I remember asking your grandma where I came from.

"I gave birth to you!" she replied.

"So where did you come from?" I went on.

"Your grandma gave birth to me."

"But where did Grandma come from?"

"From your great-grandmother."

"Where did she come from?"

"From our ancestors in Shanxi."

"But where did our ancestors come from?"

"You cheeky little boy!"

Those were the only answers Grandma could give me. Fortunately, I eventually read *The Descent of Man*, and *Selection in Relation to Sex* by Darwin. Those books taught me that the common ancestors of all humans were in Africa, and that those early humans had evolved from apes. I was reluctant to accept this deep in my heart, but Darwin proved it beyond any reasonable doubt. I'm glad I learned about it.

But Darwin's dystopian prediction for the future of human

civilisation has shocked me. Could human beings, even Earth itself, really be destroyed? Was it actually possible?

Dad, I went to visit Dr Harley next. It took me out a long time to figure out which Harley I should look for, because there were so many people with that name. With Linlin's help, though, the task was much easier.

Dr Harley lived in Love Corner in District 88653. He had been a professor of history in France. He was reputed to be something of a ladies man, having had seventeen wives, but apparently no children.

In the Fields of Joy he occupied himself by painting pictures of female nudes. As we met, his eyes were focused on Linlin, which unsettled her a bit. I wondered whether he still lusted after women even here in Heaven.

He came straight to the point. "You have a pretty face and nice hips," he told Linlin. "Your boobs are a little small, but I'm more of an arse guy. I think if we were on Earth, I would wish to marry you, my dear!"

These really were his very first words to us! Linlin was embarrassed, but I must admit it was rather funny.

"I understand that you had seventeen wives on Earth. Why so many?"

"Men are always attracted to beautiful women and want to marry them. It's only natural," he replied jovially. "Now, have you come here to be painted? You are most welcome! More and more people have been coming to me recently – which is much needed if I am to improve my painting skills."

He welcomed us into his house. Oil paintings of nude women in every pose imaginable were laid out or hung everywhere.

"Did you paint all of these?" I asked as I looked around at all the pictures.

"Yes, this is what I learned in the Field of Learning. I have no interest in human history. No one really cares about it in Heaven. I regret having taken it as my career on Earth. But enough of that; what do you think of my paintings? Aren't they beautiful?"

"Yes, they're very good." I couldn't lie; the female bodies he had painted exuded natural beauty.

"I gives me endless happiness and fulfillment to create so many works of art. Now I truly understand God's joy when He created man."

"Do you believe that humans were created by God?" I shifted the topic to what I was really interested in.

"Who else could it have been? The structure of the human body is so precise, so complex: the muscles, bones, blood vessels, ligaments, nerves, heart, spleen, kidneys, lungs, stomach, and intestines all interconnect with each other and are perfectly aligned. Who else could have accomplished such a complex project, if not God?"

"What about the theory of natural selection, of evolution?" I asked.

"That's Darwin's theory. But it's a lie. Whom can he delude with it? Certainly not me. Did he ever produce evidence to prove it? But I *do* have the evidence of his lie. It is clearly stated in the Bible:

"God created mankind in his own image, in the image of God he created them; male and female he created them.'

"God blessed them and said to them, "Be fruitful and increase in number; fill the earth and subdue it. Rule over the fish in the sea and the birds in the sky and over every living creature that moves on the ground.'

"But for Adam no suitable helper was found. So the Lord God caused the man to fall into a deep sleep; and while he was sleeping, he took one of the man's ribs and then closed up the place with flesh. Then the Lord God made a woman from the rib he had taken out of the man, and he brought her to the man.'

"This is what Christians believe," Harley said. "And it's not exclusive to Christians," he added. "There are many similar stories in other cultures. In Māori mythology, for example, Tiki created the first human by mixing his own blood with clay, and then breathed life into the clay man.

"In Australia, the aboriginal story of creation is that the Creator cut two pieces of tree bark and put some clay on top of each one. Then He carved a man's shape on each of them, and put hairs on them from the fibres on the bark. Then He blew the air to the figures and infused them with life.

"In the mythology of the Shilluk people of Africa, the Creator, Juok, came to the land of the Shilluk, and finding there black earth, He created black people out of it. Juok moulded all the people of the Earth.

He gave them legs to run, arms to farm, and eyes, mouths and ears to survive.

"The Dayak people of Borneo believed that their god Sakarra made man on the orders of Heaven. He first created a stone man who could not speak, then He created an iron man whose tongue was even harder. The third time, He made a man of clay. The man spoke as soon as he was made.

"According to Pima legend of the Native Americans, the creation story considers the Earth Doctor to be the Creator. Once the creosote bush had been created, the Earth Doctor tried to cultivate it, but was unable to do it successfully. Man was created, but they didn't get sick or die naturally. They fought with each other and destroyed everything on Earth. The Earth Doctor was upset and crushed everything to dust by pulling the sky downwards. He then cut a channel through the Earth by pounding His stick, then travelled to the other side to create mankind.

"In China, people believed that in the beginning, there was nothing in the universe except a formless chaos. This chaos coalesced into a cosmic egg and Pangu woke up from the egg. Pangu began creating the world: he separated Yin from Yang with a swing of his giant axe, creating the Earth (murky Yin) and the Sky (clear Yang). Then Nu Wa came to Earth before there were any people. Nu Wa became lonely and decided to make copies of herself from mud in a pool. The figures she created came to life and wandered off to populate the Earth.

"In Ancient Greece, people were believed to be created by the gods on Mount Olympus. The golden age was the first and the one during which the golden race of humanity lived, when there was no fear or sadness in the world. After the first age came the silver age, when people lived happily too. The Bronze Age followed, when people were imbued with desire and lost the blessing of the gods; and finally came the Iron Age.

"Arabic creation mythology was very clear that God sent Azrie to create man. He created a clay figurine and dried it slowly. Then, after forty days, God gave life and soul to the dried clay figurines.

"The holy book Popol Vuh of the Mayan civilisation reads:

"*In the beginning, there was nothing. Only the Creators, Tepa and Gukumatz, who created all the animals. Then they made a person out of mud.*

Although this person could speak, he had no thoughts. The Creators destroyed him and made another man with grains and gave him a soul. Men started to populate the Earth.'

"Why are these legends so strikingly consistent?" asked Dr Harley. There can be only one explanation, and that is that they are the truth: people were created by God."

"I don't agree that your conclusion is inevitable," I replied. "Something is not true simply because many people believe it."

"And what do *you* believe?" he asked me, a little irritated. "That all those people are wrong and only Darwin is correct? If you believe only in him, why have you come to see me? I think perhaps you should leave now; I should return to my painting." He waved his hand dismissively at us.

"Please accept my apologies if I have upset you," I said, bowing to him. "I am nobody's disciple; I wish merely to learn from prominent thinkers."

My compliment calmed him a little, and he seemed embarrassed for his sudden short temper. "Why am I so obsessed with this?" he asked no one in particular. "No matter," he said, "but I really should return to my painting now."

"Dr Harley, if God truly made man, do you think He is proud of His creation?" I continued.

"Not necessarily."

"Could you elaborate?"

"I mean, I think God may very likely regret His creation of man."

"Why? Don't you credit God's work?"

"I credit it because of people's appearance, but not people's souls, which are so dirty and unworthy."

"What do you mean?"

"For example, people are inherently self-interested. Many are single-minded and vicious in their efforts to amass material wealth for themselves, while relishing in the pain or poverty of others. In their pursuit of power, men are capable of despicable deception, or even killing each other. In their pursuit of women, men will employ any means possible to achieve their ends. Driven by jealousy they set traps and ambushes for each other; they hide sharp claws within velvet paws.

The same applies to nations: bullying, vicious games, leading ultimately to war, death and destruction. But God is not blind to human activity. And what must He think when He sees all this? So yes, I think He may well regret having created man. And He must regret not being able to control people's souls"

"Do you really believe so?" I was shocked.

"Yes," he replied. "I hear God's confession too: 'I was wrong. I should not have created man.'"

"Really?"

"Probably."

"Probably?"

"I probably hear that."

"Can you tell me a little more?"

"Well, human beings are still in their infancy."

"Could you explain that, please?"

"Most people have not learned how to get along with their peers and to coexist with nature. Without the police and prison system, the world would be such a terrible place."

Son, Dr Harley's words surprised me. He believes that God created man, yet He regrets His own work? I don't know if God really regrets it, but I am very dissatisfied too. First, because of all the discrimination and inequality that exists in the world: in wealth, power, race, social status, sexual preferences, nationality, appearance, and education level. In the real world, there's no such thing as equality.

Second, because of the way humans are destroying the planet. Just think of all the pollution of the air, the water, the land, and all the radioactive material we have created.

And third, because of the all the fighting that occurs among couples, or between work colleagues, politicians and even nations. Consider the conflict between Israel and Palestine alone: how many people have died as a result?

———

Dad, after we left Dr Harley's house, Linlin and I went to visit Li Changda. It turned out that he was a Chinese lawyer who lived in Beauty Corner, District 55832. He came here at the age of fifty-one due to sickness.

He liked to collect stones. He would go out and about all over each field to accumulate a large collection. At his home, stones were laid out in all different shapes and patterns. It was like a stone world! He didn't ask why we had come to see him, but instead he introduced his us to his stone collection. It didn't really interest me, but I was struck by his passion. He had constructed all kinds of objects from stones: a dog, a tiger, an egg, a boat, a building.

He smiled as I looked around. "Do you like them?"

"I do," I replied, nodding. "Was this your passion on Earth?"

"Yes, it was. Such a pity that I couldn't bring my collection here with me. I had an extremely precious one shaped like a man's genitals!"

"Really?" I laughed.

"Don't laugh! It might be a piece from outer space."

"I see. Do you believe that men were created by visitors from space?" I was intrigued.

"Yes," he replied, without a trace of irony. "About fifty to sixty thousand years ago, a group of aliens visited Earth as part of an exploratory mission to locate a new home. In the end, they decided that Earth was not the place for them. But while they were there, they conducted an experiment of splicing and combining genes from apes, wolves and some marine animals to create a new species: mankind."

"Is this your opinion?"

"Not just mine," he replied. "It was also the theory of Daniken, who worked for NASA and researched this topic. He published a book *God Is An Alien* in 1968, in which he claimed that the god in the Bible was actually the commander of alien spacecraft and the angels were aliens too. Other people published the same theory too.

"Is there any evidence to support this argument?"

"The first evidence is in the Bible. God said, 'We created mankind in our own image.' These words refer to 'we'. But according to Western religious belief, God is unique, the only one, so how could He say 'we'?

Who was God talking about? Clearly there were other extraterrestrial beings with him there."

"That's how you explain 'we'?"

"How else could it be explained? For further evidence, consider the human body. The face looks like an ape, the greedy and selfish nature is like a wolf, and seventy per cent of the human body is water, like aquatic life. And human skin is smooth. Isn't that like a dolphin's?"

"But can't that be explained by evolution?" I asked.

"I don't buy that," he scoffed.

"Is there any other evidence?"

"Yes, the third one is from a French reporter by the name of Claude Fleurien. On 13 December 1973, he felt an impulse to drive out to a volcano where a red light shone through a thick fog. He claimed that a man, four feet tall, emerged from a space ship, who claimed he was Jesus. In June 1983, a book about him was published in Taiwan entitled: *I Have Been To Outer Space*."

"Could that Frenchman have simply imagined this event, like some kind of vision?"

"Whenever something extraordinary occurs, it is natural to be sceptical. But why would a reporter have lied about this? What would have been the point?"

"Well, I'm not sure it constitutes strong evidence."

"Other evidence comes from some ancient Chinese books. In *Tao Te Ching* by Lao Tzu: '*The Dao is the underlying principle behind the creation of myriad things. The process giving rise to the myriad things began with the Dao producing a kind of generative force.*' So what is the Dao? It must be a way to create things."

"Do you really think it can be interpreted in this way?"

"I believe it's the perfect explanation!"

"Well, let's suppose that your theory of aliens is correct. What are your thoughts on the future of human civilisation?"

"I confess, I am not optimistic."

"Why? In what way?"

"I mean that humans control everything. We have already developed cloning technology for animals. Human organs are probably the next thing. When people get sick or have an accident, they will easily be able to have an organ transplant. Technology will fundamentally change ethics, the basic rules of human society, and the whole picture of life on Earth. But who do you think will be upset by this?"

"Who?" I asked.

"The aliens, of course! They were the Creators, and they must remain in control. The change will upset them greatly."

"Do you think so?" I couldn't help but let out a laugh.

"Why are you laughing?" he demanded, clearly irritated. "If you're here to make fun of me, you might as well leave! I didn't invite you here."

I had broken one of the taboos of conducting an interview: I showed open disdain for the interviewee's opinion.

"When I was on Earth, I was particularly irritated by self-righteous people, those too stubborn to accept new ideas. I certainly didn't expect to meet the same kind of people here. Please leave!"

"Sir, please forgive me," I said, trying to recover the situation. "I am not laughing at you; these ideas are just so fresh to me."

"Is that so?"

"Yes, of course! Please, let's continue. I would like you to share your wisdom with me. So what do you think the aliens will do if they are upset with mankind?"

"Their reactions might be many. They could destroy us with earthquakes and tsunamis; or else they might set asteroids or even stars crashing into the Earth."

"That's a horrifying thought," I replied.

"Destroy first, then rebuild."

"My goodness."

"I hope I am worrying too much."

"I respect that you are a firm believer that mankind was created by aliens. Is there anything else you would like to share with me?"

"Don't feel too confident in yourself, or you will be punished. The same goes for humankind."

27

S on, I've heard those stories about aliens over the years, but I've always doubted them; there have always been so few witnesses and no reliable evidence. But I do believe that technology has the potential to destroy human civilisation.

Human cloning is very likely to happen, and I'm very concerned about the possible consequences. The foundation of human society is the nuclear family unit, and all ethics are based on that. Cloning may well lead to the disintegration of families, and what might happen then? In my view, it could all end in chaos.

Dad, I really don't know if this was what God expected from me, and I had no idea if my interviews had been valuable. But I dutifully recorded them all and sent them over to Darya.

The pager clearly worked, since Darya came to me an hour later and handed me a list of names for the second batch of interviews. There were three more: *Wei Yuan, Li Shutong, Albert Einstein*. Einstein was familiar to me, the others not.

"Darya," I said with trepidation, "I have no idea if my first set of interviews met God's expectations. Please take back the interviewing tool. I would like to hear God's opinion after He watches all of these. Then I can continue my work."

Darya smiled. "I mentioned to you before that it was an instant transmitter. God has already seen everything, so there's no need for me to take it away. God does have one message for you, though: don't be a passive listener. Try to be more proactive and don't be afraid to get into a debate."

I nodded my head. God already knew everything!

"Do you have anything else to tell God?" she asked me before leaving.

"No."

"Very well. Good luck."

I hoped Linlin would accompany me again for the next set of interviews. Truth be told, I didn't want to be apart from her. She laughed and replied, "Well, it helps me pass the time. But I want to ask something from you in return."

"Of course! What is it?"

"It's a secret."

Our first interviewee was Wei Yuan. He lived in a district adjacent to us. After the first round of interviews, it was easy to locate him. Before the interview, I went to Heaven Library to do some research on him.

Wei Yuan was born on 23 April 1794 in Shaoyang, Hunan. He studied Chinese philosophy at the age of seven, obtained a provincial degree in the Imperial examinations at twenty-eight, and subsequently worked in the secretariat of several prominent statesmen.

He wrote *A Military History of the Qing Dynasty* at age forty-eight, and wrote his best-known work, the *Illustrated Treatise on the Maritime Kingdoms*, which contained numerous maps and geographical details of both the western and eastern hemispheres. In that book he recommended that the Chinese learn from the superior technology of the so-called barbarians (in his day, Western countries seeking trading rights), so as to be strong enough to deal adequately with their challenges.

Wei passed away at his retreat in Hangzhou in 1857, leaving behind an important body of scholarly works, including some of the earliest explorations of 'the encroaching Western world,' which profoundly influenced the reformers that followed him.

Linlin and I met him one morning. He was slightly built and lived alone in a place called Willow Corner. He had converted to Buddhism and refused to see guests for a long time. Our visit clearly took him by surprise. "Have you come to the wrong place?" he asked. "I am Wei."

I bowed to him in the manner of the Qing Dynasty. "Yes, Sir," I replied. "We are here to visit you."

"Really?" he replied, curiously. "And you are?"

"We are interested in your *Illustrated Treatise on the Maritime Kingdoms*. We were hoping you might be willing to discuss it with us."

"That's a very dated work," he replied. "But thank you for showing interest. Please, do come in." So we did, glad to overcome the first obstacle. The second was to show interest and build a rapport with the interviewee.

"Your book was the first systematic world history ever written in China," I said. "Its contribution to isolated China's understanding of the wider world was of immense value," I said, repeating the words I had memorised. I looked around at the vast collection of books in his house. Besides his own works, many appeared to have been borrowed from Heaven Library.

"After the Opium Wars, we were so worried and strove to learn the technology from the West in order to better deal with the challenges they posed. I was quite narrow-minded back then."

"Your *Illustrated Treatise* had a profound influence on later reformers, such as the Self-Strengthening Movement, the Reform Movement of 1898 Led by Kang Youwei and Liang Qichao, and the Meiji Restoration in Japan."

"Thank you. You may be a young man, but you certainly know how to flatter a writer! A compliment for one of my books is the best gift I could possibly receive. But I suspect that's not your only reason for visiting me today."

I was a little embarrassed. "We have come to hear your wisdom and your observations on life," I said. "You must have a unique understanding of life, given all your experiences. Would you be so kind as to share some of your insights with us?"

"But we're in Heaven now. What's the point of discussing this now?"

"It's just curiosity. People's lives are full such of suffering and misery, and yet they struggle to keep on living. I would like to understand why."

"Oh well, I suppose it can't do any harm to share my thoughts on the matter."

I was relieved that he didn't reject me.

"I regarded it as one of my greatest achievements, to understand life better, besides the *Illustrated Treatise on the Maritime Kingdoms*. The impulse to survive is a natural instinct of humans, as it is for all animals. No other reason is needed."

"So it's purely a survival instinct?"

"Yes, for the most part."

"What about a desire for the pursuit of good things in life. Could that also be a reason?"

"Yes, good food can be a motivation when people are younger. The promise of good food would make a child happy and excited. Love and marriage can also be a purpose later on, then raising a family, pursuing material wealth and comfort. People find purpose in their desires."

"That is so true. During my own life I talked to many young men in the countryside and asked them about their purpose in life. 'To find a wife,' they would answer.

"'What will you do after you find a wife?' I would ask.

"'To have children,' they replied.

"'And then?'

"'To build a house. To find wives for our children. To have grandchildren.'

"Life is an endless cycle. This is just human nature. So is it all about instinct?"

I remembered Darya's reminder from God to be more proactive and to provoke some debate.

"Of course, there are other reasons in addition to instinct, especially in the face of adversity. Some find their purpose in their family. They live for their family, worried they couldn't survive without them."

"Exactly. I really wanted to live long enough that I could take care of my parents and grandparents. I really wanted to be able to look after them. My grandmother always said she lived to such an old age so she could ensure her family had a good life."

"Yes, but we are all interdependent. Our family needs us, and we need our family."

"Yes, and some people elevate themselves to the broader picture, to make themselves part of society, the nation and the world. They devote themselves to activities which can contribute to society and make the world a better place. In this way, they can overcome the adversities of life. Lin Zexu is an example of someone I admired greatly. During the Opium Wars, he fought for the benefit of all people in the Qing Dynasty."

"You mean that was his vocation?"

"Yes. Professions can take many forms. Religious people take preaching as a career. Doctors take saving lives as a career. Pottery craftsmen take craftsmanship as a career. All these people can live for their profession. It is their calling."

"So does that create a purpose in life for humans?"

"That is not a simple question to answer. It's a dilemma for humans. Not all questions can be answered. Parents are familiar with the situation when their young child keeps probing on one particular question. No matter how knowledgeable the parents are, they will always run out of answers. So what should humans do? We should do what parents do. Tell the child to stop searching for answers. And that's what I am telling you now."

I couldn't believe my ears! He was telling me to stop searching for answers, even though he was so knowledgeable!

I nodded my head.

"Don't keep pursuing. Life is full of mystery, so let it be."

I looked at Linlin and hoped she would join in the conversation.

Linlin took the hint and smiled. "I think Mr Wei is telling us to go back to reality, and not ponder on the mysteries of life that are so far away as to be unreachable."

"Exactly!" Wei exclaimed. "We must balance the pursuit of our dreams against the constraints of reality. Only then we can live a happy life. But of course, this doesn't apply to souls here in Heaven."

Son, I've never really thought about it that like that before. Neither did your grandparents. We just became caught up in our mundane lives. As a youngster, I always wanted to go to university and get a job in the city. That dream was shattered during the Cultural Revolution, however, so I enlisted in the military as a way to get out of our hometown.

In the military, I worked hard to become an officer and earn a salary to help our family. Then I wanted to get married. After your mum and I had you, we tried to send you to the best primary school, then the best middle school, and then we moved to Beijing to give you better education opportunities.

Right after you graduated, I tried to get you a job in Beijing. When you became ill, I wanted to cure you. That was my whole life. I had practical goals and worked hard to achieve them. But I didn't pursue the bigger meaning of life. Compared with the elite high achievers, my life was wasted...

Dad, don't put yourself down. Most people on Earth lived their lives the same way you did. Every life has its own purpose and value. So don't compare yourself with others. In fact, that's exactly what Li Shutong said when Linlin and I visited him.

Li Shutong lived in Birdsong Corner in District 77985. When we found him, he was bareheaded, and greeted us in the traditional Buddhist manner. His house was also full of books on Buddhism.

"So, why have you come to see me?" he asked Linlin and me.

"I have just arrived here," I replied. "Although I only lived for only twenty-nine years on Earth, I enjoyed your poem *Farewell*:

Outside the resting arbor, beside the ancient thoroughfare;
The fragrant grass so green, stretching to meet the sky afar.
The evening breeze brushing the willow, the flute sound lingering;
The setting sun beyond hills and mountains.
At the verge of heaven, at the four corners of the earth,
My bosom friends are half-gone and no longer seen.

With a gourdful of turbid wine, enjoy the last moment of pleasure;
The parting dream turning cold this very night.

"So of course I wanted to meet you. How could I miss this opportunity in Heaven?"

"Thank you for your compliment," he replied. "That was indeed my work in the earthly world. But I don't believe it's widely read here in Heaven." He was warm and humble.

"You are so modest. The poem *Farewell* is about departure, and about sincere friendships in life. I find that it helps me to get away from mundane life. I believe there was also another reason why you wrote this poem?"

"Yes, it was a snowy winter's night. A friend of mine, Xu Huanyuan, called my wife and me into the yard. We went outside and he told me that his family was penniless and he had come to say goodbye. He didn't even come in. I stood in the snow, watching him mournfully from behind as he left. I wrote that poem in tears that night."

"You had a splendid life: your calligraphy was praised for its style; your poems were passed down through generations; your oil paintings and carvings were admired; your theatrical performances were recognised; and your musical compositions were revered. No one can compare with your achievements in the arts over the past century. I do have one other question for you, though."

"I certainly don't deserve all that praise. But I'll gladly answer your question."

"Do you think the value of people's lives can be compared to one other?"

"That's a very difficult question to answer."

"But I believe you must have considered it. If you don't mind, please share your wisdom."

"How can lives be compared to each other? First of all, each of us is born into different situations. Wealthy families can provide a comfortable lifestyle; some families are able to educate their children and give them every opportunity in life, while other families in remote and impoverished areas barely have enough to support their children's growth and development. So people become unequal in every aspect.

How can their lives be compared? Take me, for example: my father gained a degree in the Imperial examinations and became a government official. Later on, he became the richest businessman in Tianjin. My education started in school at a young age, where I even learned English and carving. Could a street vendor's son ever have the same opportunities as me?"

"I can see your point," I said, nodding.

"Second, people have different lifespans and reach their peak at different ages. I lived for sixty-three years, yet you lived for only twenty-nine years. How can we compare our two lives? You couldn't understand what I learned at the age of sixty-three. Is it because you're not smart? No, of course it isn't."

I nodded again.

"People on different career path have different accomplishments. Officials obtain power, researchers make new discoveries, teachers educate people, artists create art, and farmers cultivate the land. How can we compare their achievements to one another? How can we compare a skilled farmer with a senior official? Will the official have a better life? Probably not. Will he be happier? Not necessarily."

"Some people do think it's possible to compare the value of each life; that the value of a life can somehow be quantified. It seems very strange to me. How can we possibly quantify the value of a life? Is a governor's life worth more than an educator's? Is a soldier's life worth less than a scientist's?"

"So you believe it's impossible to compare the value of different lives to each other?"

"Well, I think God has it absolutely right. Whether a soul ultimately enters the Fields of Joy is not determined by the person's age, the job they had, or their achievements. As long as the person worked hard, made a contribution to society, didn't hurt anyone, they can come to the Fields of Joy. This seems both equitable and fair".

Dad, I know you and I both agree with Master Hongyi's belief that we shouldn't compare ourselves with others, but in real life people compare themselves with each other all the time: Zhang is more successful than Li, Ma's life is better than Wang's, and so on. For the past twenty-nine years of my life, that was all I saw and heard every day. I was so confused by the reasons for this. Fortunately, I was able to understand it better during my next interview.

It was with Albert Einstein.

Einstein lived in the most remote area in Heaven, called Unknown Corner. It was said that he had specifically requested to live in the most far-flung place. Delegates pondered for a long time whether he should be placed there. It was the furthest point from the Holy Field and far removed from other places as well. Only three souls lived there.

Even with Linlin's help, it still took a long time to find Unknown Corner. We found his house, knocked on the door and were surprised when he answered it immediately.

He was clearly surprised, too. "I thought it was my ex-wife," he said. "I'm expecting her. Are you here to discuss the superluminal phenomenon on Earth? How many times do I need to tell you that I don't care about that at all. I really have nothing to say on the matter, so please leave me alone! I just want to live a peaceful life. Is that too much to ask?"

Bo Linlin and I didn't know what to say. Certainly, neither of us knew anything about any superluminal phenomenon.

"Yes, I know I said nothing can travel faster that light, which moves at 300,000 kilometres per second, in my theory of relativity. Recently, the Italian National Research Centre in Gran Sasso found empirical evidence of the neutrino at the European Centre for Nuclear Research, which travelled faster than light. Many scientists in the Fields of Joy came to tell me this, because it cast doubt on my theories on relativity. But what can I do with this knowledge? How could I have foreseen this decades earlier? Yes, this new discovery may well lead to new theories. But how does it affect me? I'm in Heaven, and I shouldn't concern myself with human affairs. I couldn't even if I wanted to. Why have you come to disturb my peaceful life? Please see yourself out, and leave me alone!" By now Einstein was emotional, angry even.

"Sorry, but that's not why we're here. We don't care about any of that either."

"Then who are you?"

"We are admirers of yours."

"Why do you admire me? I'm not someone you should admire, and I certainly don't want your admiration. I'm just an ordinary soul like you. Please leave. I'm waiting for my ex-wife Mileva, and I don't appreciate uninvited guests. And I don't need any admirers. Thank you and goodbye!"

"Sir, would you please hear me out?"

"If I must. But please, make it short. I don't like long stories. I am not a patient man."

"Sir, before we came to the Fields of Joy, we lived in China. My primary school teacher told stories about you when I was ten years old. 'Albert Einstein was the greatest scientist in the world,' he would tell us. 'He once visited Shanghai on his way to Japan in 1912, where he sang high praises for the art collection housed at Zi Garden. He was a friend of the Chinese people. You should read his books and aspire to become a great man like him.'"

"He even put your picture on our classroom wall to remind us of your greatness. And now, thanks to God, it's remarkable that I can meet you in person today."

"So, you're from China? Yes indeed, I enjoyed Shanghai very much. But you must be very disappointed to see me in the flesh. I am not handsome at all! I am just an ugly old man. I suggest that you don't try to visit other celebrity souls while you're here. The reality may disappoint you. Just as they were once ordinary people on Earth, so they are ordinary souls here in Heaven. Don't make the mistake of magnifying their worth in your mind. I do appreciate your visit today, but I have plans today to meet Mileva. I'm afraid I can spare you no more time. Perhaps we could arrange a meeting some other time?"

"Oh yes, of course." I was embarrassed, since of course we had showed up uninvited. We hadn't made an appointment and I didn't want to upset him again. Before we said goodbye, though, I heard a woman's voice from behind us.

"Albert, why don't you let our guests in? It's very impolite to make them stand in the doorway. You really are quite inconsiderate when you're busy."

Linlin and I turned around and saw a graceful young lady.

Einstein shrugged his shoulders, embarrassed.

The lady stared at Einstein. "Albert, aren't you going to introduce us?"

"Oh, yes, these two visitors are from China. I didn't have a chance to ask their names. This is my wife, Mileva."

Mileva shook our hands. "Albert is mistaken," she said. "I am his *ex*-wife. It's a pleasure to meet you. I don't have many Chinese friends. Please do come in."

"Thank you, Miss Mileva," I said. "I know you have things to discuss with Dr Einstein. I only have one question to ask, but we can easily come back another day."

"No, don't leave. Please do come in and sit down. I don't need him for very long. He'll be free soon enough."

Linlin and I entered the house. The layout and furniture in the room was so spartan. There was nothing there, really, except a few chairs and a violin.

"Do you think our home is too simple?" Mileva asked as she noticed our eyes scanning the room. "That's him – he has very low expectations of life. He is always so focused on his work. He's been like it ever since we met. Isn't that right, Albert? Don't you agree?"

Einstein smiled and sat in a chair. "I'm not committed to any research right now and I have decided not to read any books. The room looks so much larger without books! Now, I play the violin from time to time, or I take walks along the river. I hike in the mountains, sometimes, too."

"So why have you come to see Albert today? asked Mileva. "We're in no hurry, so we have plenty of time. There are no limitations on time in the Fields of Joy. So go ahead, please."

This seemed like our best opportunity to conduct the interview, and I grabbed it immediately.

"We came here today to ask if Dr Einstein can shed some light on one problem that plagues human society. Humans constantly compare themselves with each other, creating jealousy and depression, and sometimes even driving them to murder, suicide or to create some other kind of turmoil in society. Why do you think it is that people seem compelled to compare themselves to each other?"

"What a good question!" said Mileva. "I always felt miserable when comparing myself with others. You may not know this, but Albert and I had a daughter, Lieserl, who died when she was only a year old. I always wondered about the reason why my daughter died so young, while other women became mothers and grandmothers. It made me very upset to compare my life with those of other women."

"Yes," Linlin said. "We would like to better understand the impulse that drives us to make such comparisons. We were hoping that Dr Einstein might be willing to share his experiences with us." Now that Mileva was here, our visit seemed to be going much smoothly.

"You have asked the wrong man," said Einstein, smiling. "I studied and researched natural science. You could ask me about the theory of relativity, photoelectric effects or quantum mechanics. But questions about human beings? Well, that's a subject I know little about. When Israeli President Chaim Weizmann died in 1952, the Prime Minister Ben Gurion asked if I would be willing to accept the presidency. I had to decline. I told him that I knew only about science, about objective matters. I knew very little about humanity. How could a person like me become a president?"

"We know you studied physics," replied Linlin, "but this question isn't profound. We would just like you to give us your opinion, based on your own life experiences."

"Yes, come on, Albert," Mileva chimed in. "They have come here to talk to you because of your reputation on Earth. As the girl says, this isn't a profound question. So why not share your opinions with them? Why do you put on this detached air? These are the Fields of Joy in Heaven! When did you become so lofty? Did your second wife make you like this?"

"If you want to hear my opinions, I will share them. However, I wish to make it perfectly clear that these are just my personal thoughts. They're based purely on my experiences on Earth. There's no scientific rationale behind any of it.

"I do believe that there is a natural instinct for mutual comparison among humans. The rules of the natural world prevail on Earth, which means that the strong prevail over the weak. A strong body can help you to earn more money through physical labour; superior intelligence can help you to achieve more in academic pursuits; good looks offer more choices in relationships. So yes, all of this drives people to compare themselves with each other so they can find their own position in life.

"Besides that, society even encourages this behaviour! The driving force behind the evolution of human society is the unsatisfied needs of individuals. What are these unsatisfied needs? They come from competition and comparison. Indoctrinated in children from a very young age. Kindergarten children are praised for better performance in singing competitions. Bureaucrats only get promoted if they meet all the criteria. Scientists are awarded scientific prizes and research funds only if they make meaningful contributions to scientific development. People are compared and selected by the rules imposed by society. How could everyone *not* fall into this trap?"

"So you think it's unavoidable, inevitable even?" I pressed. I was all ears.

"Yes, I do believe it's unavoidable. And I understand your concerns. You believe that this constant competition and comparison causes much pain. But I'm not sure that's necessarily the problem. What matters most is *what* you compare."

"What you compare?"

"I believe there are two areas to which we should be focusing people's attention: first, happiness in life. We have only one life, which means that the ultimate goal for the individual should be to be happy and fulfilled, regardless of power, fame or material wealth. If people cannot feel as happy as others, then their quality of life is compromised.

"Second, the richness of the soul. Your physical body was given by your parents. You have no say in it. You cannot interfere with fate either, but you are the master of your own soul. No matter what your individual circumstances, if one person is good in nature, then to other people he has a pure soul. Otherwise, his soul is contaminated, and his life has less value."

"But how can we compare those two categories? They are so subjective," asked Linlin.

"Yes, that's a very good question. Happiness is an emotion. It cannot be measured. In the same way, it's also very difficult to determine the richness of one's soul. These things are invisible on the surface, yet the comparison in both areas is constant. Do you remember reading of complaints by Chinese emperors that their life wasn't as good as those of the general population, because by comparison, they knew they weren't as happy as others? Mother Teresa of Calcutta did great deeds all her life. When she died, the whole world paid its respects to her. Wasn't it because her pure soul added value to her life?"

28
———————

S on, Einstein makes a lot of sense to me. People simply cannot stop comparing themselves with each other. It's part of human nature. That's how people find fulfilment or the motivation to move forward. I totally agree that this can lead to either agony or desperation.

But imagine if people stopped doing this – what would happen to the world then? It would surely become stagnant, with little progress or innovation. But competition and comparison are not what determine the value of a life. No one can be certain of their life's value. That requires the involvement of others, and is done mostly after one's journey on Earth is at end. Only then will a man's deeds and misdeeds finally be judged.

Dad, the morning after the interview with Einstein, God's messenger Darya came to my house again. Her knock was so gentle that I almost missed it.

"Is it because Miss Linlin is here and you are shy to let me in?" she joked as I opened the door.

"Maybe one day we will ask you to conduct our marriage. It would be so meaningful to have an angel do this," I said, smiling at her.

"My goodness, when is that? I would love to!"

"I'm just joking. I haven't asked Linlin yet. Anyway, let me tell you about my interviews."

"There's no need," said Darya. "With the help of the interview recorder, it's as though we were present in person. I came here today to give you the third interview list." She handed me a piece of paper, with three names on it: *Yuan Shikai, Socrates, Xue Tao.*

"Do you know these people?"

"I know the name Yuan Shikai. He was also born in Henan. We're from the same place. The other two I don't recognise," I answered honestly.

"Socrates was a philosopher in Ancient Greece. Xue Tao was a poet during the Tang Dynasty. That's all I can tell you. But you can do some research in the library."

"Yes, of course."

Linlin and I went to the library that morning and found some basic information about all three. Then we went to look for their addresses.

I could never have imagined that Yuan Shikai lived in the same place as me! Linlin and I were both so surprised to discover that he lived only five houses away! I had passed by his house and greeted him so many times. I knew his family name was Yuan, and I called him Mr Yuan. Little did I know that he was the celebrated Yuan Shikai, the first official president of the Republic of China!

"Hello Mr Yuan," I greeted him. "I'm so sorry, I had no idea you were such an important person on Earth!"

"What do you mean, important?" he replied. "You and I are the same: ordinary souls in Heaven, both ordinary residents in Fragrance Corner." He gave me an honest and sincere smile.

"I mean all the stories about you on Earth. You had the power to shape the whole of China in the early twentieth century! I learned all about you from history books when I was young. You were fascinated by Sun Tzu's *The Art of War* from a young age, and you collected and learned about many different political and military strategies.

"At the age of thirteen you wrote a poem entitled *Talk of Ambition*:

Confronted by dragons and tigers one cannot struggle against,
casting murderous looks to the heavens,

275

I long to open my mouth wide to the sky,
so that I may swallow up the chosen ones.

"At the age of twenty-three, you were stationed in Korea as the minister of trade and governor of Korea, then you founded the new armed forces in Tianjin, then you founded Shangdong University, developed industrial and mining enterprises, built the Beijing-Zhangjiakou railway, established the parole police, forced the Qing emperor to abdicate, and worked to build the republic using the principle of Five Races Under One Union."

"I did all that. But it was all in vain."

"Why? It's all recorded in history."

"Indeed, but many other stories of mine were also recorded in history. Young man, it's very nice of you to mention only the good things I did in my life and not speak about my betrayal of Tan Sitong, which caused him to be beheaded in Caishikou; or how I authorised the assassination of Song Jiaoren; or my claim to be emperor; or that I had many wives."

"Which of us committed no mistakes during our life?" I replied. "Let alone the fact that you were involved in politics, at a time when bloodshed was rife."

"Thank you for your understanding. This is the first time I have heard such a sympathetic assessment of my life. To tell the truth, while I was on my way here, I fully expected to be sent to the Field of Punishment. Were I to tell you I wasn't scared, it would be a lie; I was terrified! To look back on my deeds, when did my personal battles ever stop? If I had been sent to the Field of Punishment, what could I have done about it? I thank God that He and His delegates were judicious and forgave me because I didn't kill anyone by my own hand. My soul was tainted by filth, but I was permitted to enter the Fields of Joy in spite of it all. And finally I am satisfied. Very satisfied indeed."

"Mr Yuan, have you ever considered that you could have had a life of glory?"

"What do you mean?"

"I mean when you became interim president of the Republic of China. If you had acted within the law and not fallen into dictatorship; if you had consolidated the congress and election systems, and relinquished the presidency after a two-year term, might China have become peaceful afterwards? Maybe there would have been no warlords to plunge people into misery and suffering. You could have been the first legitimate president of the Republic of China, and your role in history might have been remembered in a completely different light."

"How could I have seen that at the time? All I learned during my whole life was how to grasp power tightly in my own hands, which was the cause of everything that was to happen later. If anyone else had been in my shoes, they probably would have made exactly the same choices. At that time, no one was immune to the seductive lure of power, except maybe Sun Yat-sen."

"Please forgive me for speaking so frankly. But it seems to me that your ascent to emperor was not such a wise move. It went against the principles of the time, and destroyed your reputation. Indeed, it was perhaps the biggest mistake of your life."

"It's not something that can be explained so easily. But, since we're talking about this, I will make a few points clear. First, I was selfish. The president's power was limited, after all. Only an emperor could have absolute power that could be inherited by my son and grandson. I wasn't prepared to hand that power to anyone else. You were young and never held such power in your hands. But with power like that, you can have anything you want and decide other people's fates. The temptation was so hard to resist! So hard.

"Second, the encouragement of Yang Du and Yan Fu had a negative effect too. Although I wanted to be an emperor, I needed to consider the government and public opinions. Yang Du and Yan Fu talked to me time and time again to persuade me that the public was in favour of a constitutional monarchy, like those in Britain and Japan. It gave me the confidence to try to do something similar in China.

"Third, my son, Yuan Keding, pushed for it. He was my eldest son and wanted to be the prince and inherit the country. So he forged a copy of the Shun Tian Times, and made me believe that Japan supported this move. My second son, Kewen, and my daughter, Shuzhen, discovered the truth later, but by then it was too late. Deding lied to me and betrayed the country. My treacherous son..."

"It's all in the past. Mr Yuan, don't get upset about what is done."

"Yes, but my mind is still not at peace. Every time I talk about these events, it upsets me. Many souls from my family are here in the Fields of Joy. They have asked to move here with me, but I have rejected them all. I just want to be alone and live a peaceful life, and to leave my history on Earth behind."

"Why do you torture yourself? You experienced so many monumental historical events. There are many reasons for you to cling to them. Even an ordinary a soul like me gets upset about my past experiences on Earth, too."

"Thank you. You are very considerate, for one so young. You know how to comfort me. I am touched. But I'm sure you're not here to comfort me. What is the nature of your visit?"

"It's nothing serious. We're just passing some time, and we're curious about your reflections on life."

"Well, well, well, I do have an awful lot to say about life. You two really came here today for this?"

"Yes, Sir. We did."

"Well, this *is* unexpected. I thought perhaps you were descendants of my enemies, here to humiliate me. I wronged too many people in my life, so I am prepared for the ignominy. But if you're here just for this question, I will be honest with you: if I had another life, I wouldn't live it as I did. I would avoid politics completely.

"Ever since I got involved politics during my time in the military, it was stress-free for a while, but it was all too short. Each time I was promoted, I was so proud, but only for a brief moment. Then I quickly became depressed. I was scared of losing my life if I didn't get things done right. During the Reform Movement of 1898, led by Kang Youwei and Liang Qichao, my head hung and my body was limp every day. Everyone knew the horrifying disposition of the Empress Dowager. If she had even the slightest suspicion of my intentions, I would have been beheaded. Every time I met her, my heart froze. Of course, there were advantages to being a high-ranking official. You could get anything you wanted to eat or drink; you could live in a spacious house; you could marry any girl, or girls, you wanted. I had ten wives altogether in my lifetime, and I know many men were jealous. But in the high-pressure world of politics, I couldn't take much joy from it. They all started to compete with each other and complain to me all the time, which became such a burden."

"The many different factions, and all the deception and fraud exhausted me, too. Behind many a smile lay hatred. One may wish you good health in person, but curse you to be dead the next day. Anxiety and worry are a part of everyone's lives, but more so for people in officialdom. We worry about losing support from higher up, about the betrayal of peers, about incompetent subordinates who may cause problems for us.

"Take the festivals, for example. Common people just need to prepare food and drink for the holidays. We, on the other hand, agonised over what gifts to give to our superiors, which needed to be to their liking. If a higher-ranking official loved South Sea pearls, but you sent him gifts from Suzhou and Hangzhou, you were asking for trouble. You needed to rack your brain to remember your bosses' preferences. It was torture.

"People were snobbish too. There were a number of people around you who would pay their respects and send you gifts. They were flatterers, even by calling you brother, uncle or father. But as soon as you were removed from your position, they all scattered like chickens looking for food in other places. They would try every means to avoid you, or even swear curses on you. What was the point of being in that business?"

"Then why do you think that, even today, Chinese people encourage their children to become government officials?"

"First, because in China, people are valued according to how much power they have. Only when you are a senior official are you respected and admired. Only then is your life deemed to be successful.

"Second, officials in China control all the local resources, which makes it the most effective way to look after their own family's interests.

"Third, a few people work for earnest political aspirations, to serve the country and the people. They are few and far between, though.

"And finally, the rules of officials remain a secret to outsiders. No one ever talks about them. Ordinary people only hear the stories about the opulence, but rarely about the dark side that goes with it. That's why they fought for positions, time after time, one after the other. If you do a little research, you'll find that the second and the third generations of political families tend to go into business, rather than continuing to fight in political circles."

"I don't know," I replied. "I'm not entirely convinced. People in other countries besides China like to become politicians as well. In other countries' elections, people also fight hard for senior office."

"Yes, and that shows that part of it is human nature. The desire to control other people is instinctive, just like in the animal kingdom. Monkeys fight to be the dominant one, and wolves have the same urge to become the alpha within a pack. But like I said, there are a few that go into politics out of idealistic aspirations, rather than for selfish purposes. They genuinely do want to govern the provinces and the country."

"Did you have these insights while on Earth, or after you came to Heaven?"

"I had a life of almost fifty-seven years, and a great deal of that time was spent in political office. Do you think it took that long for me to understand?"

"So why didn't you pack it in, do something else?"

"As I've explained, the temptation was too much to resist. As long as I had power, I had people around me. I could control the forces of nature, I could control the fate of others, and I could stockpile all the resources under my control. That sense of achievement, satisfaction, pride and comfort was quite intoxicating. It was like opium. And for as long as you have access to it, it's impossible to give it up. See for yourself: do some research and tell me how many officials in China and elsewhere have left office of their own will."

"If you could live your life for a second time, how would you like to live it?"

"As a cowboy."

"A cowboy?" I couldn't believe my ears.

"Yes, a cowboy. I would sell cows in exchange for food and clothes. Cows are loyal. They won't betray you, set you up for failure, or humiliate you. The life may be poor, but I would feel safe and comfortable..."

Son, your talk with Yuan Shikai sounds very interesting. If and when I make it to the Fields of Joy myself, I would very much like to meet him. As someone also from Henan, he should have been our local hero, but he turned out to be the opposite. I really want to tell him how shameful it was that he wasted the opportunity to be a great man. He should acknowledge his mistakes, but the land that nurtured him should also take some responsibility. He grew up here, after all.

The poison in this land got into his body through the water and food, which formed his character and ambition. I can understand him now. His whole life was defined by his wrongdoings in later life. Our twilight years are so important; they can determine our entire legacy. We can work hard for our whole life and get so close to our destination. But in the end, poor choices can consign us to the abyss, our lifelong reputation floating away, leaving us with nothing but misery and regrets.

Yes, it was in that final chapter of his life where Yuan Shikai failed.

Dad, Linlin and I visited Socrates one afternoon not long afterwards. Linlin said she was looking forward to meeting the philosopher who had been forced to take his own life by poison in 399BC.

He lived very far away from us, perhaps because he had come to the Fields of Joy such a long time long ago. It was approaching dusk when we eventually found him at Universe End. He was tending tulips in his garden in long robes and bare feet. The garden gate was open. He saw us and assumed we were neighbours who had come for flower seeds.

"I'm sorry," he said when he saw us, "I only have these four or five tulip plants."

"They should be fine," Linlin replied. "How much do they cost?"

Socrates was shocked and stopped to look at us. "Is it not inappropriate to associate flowers with money? Flowers are the supreme expression of natural beauty. Money stands for material wealth. There can be no equal exchange between them. Why do you still think as if on Earth?"

Linlin and I both smiled. Realising that we were not, in fact, there for

281

flower seeds, Socrates rose up from his flowers, stroking his beard. "Who are you?" he asked.

"We wish to learn from you, and we have come here today to pay our respects. Please allow us to help you with your flowers." Linlin and I immediately helped him to plant the rest of the flowers.

"I haven't had visitors for centuries. How did you find me?"

"We found your address in the Archive Centre."

"Thank you for remembering me, a useless old man. Two thousand four hundred years have passed in a blink of an eye since I came to the Fields of Joy."

"But your name is immortal on Earth and also in Heaven. Your conversations and debates in the markets and streets are still studied by people. You originated so many thoughts and produced so much wisdom." I repeated the comments I had learned during our research.

"What wisdom? All of my thoughts are common sense to people nowadays."

"But so many of your words from two thousand four hundred years ago still guide people's lives today. For example, *The hottest love has the coldest end*; *The less we need, the closer we are to God*; *People who want to control the world must first learn to control themselves*; *Men live by forgetfulness, women live by remembering*; *Within every person there is a sun. Just let it shine*; *What else do we need in this world except sunshine, the air and a smile?*; *People can make mistakes, but not the same one twice.*

"Young man, I am so happy you still know all those clichés! If my words can help people today in even the slightest way, I would be so happy."

"From what I read, I understood that you lived a frugal life on Earth. You wore the same coat for a whole year, and you didn't even have shoes. You didn't care much for food. It seems that you spent all your time and energy talking to other people in pursuit of truth and wisdom. I am curious to understand what drove you."

"Now that is a very good question. No one has ever asked me that before. As you can see, I am very nondescript in looks. Almost ugly, you might say. I have a flat nose, fat lips, protruding eyes and a clumsy body. If I couldn't think and talk, what else could I have contributed to Athens and to other people?"

"If you believe you did good for the people of Athens, why didn't you fight back when you were accused of defying religion and corrupting democracy and youth? When you were sentenced to death, why did you agree to drink the hemlock?"

"In those times, it served no purpose to argue. I didn't want to sacrifice my pride and become a beggar. All I could do was follow the laws of Athens and face death."

"And now, today, what do you consider to be the most important truth for people? Could you explain your true feelings?"

"There are many truths in life. I don't know which is the most important. But if I were forced to pick one, then it would be that uncontrolled desire brings disaster."

"All kinds of desire? The desire for food? For sex, wealth, power, fame, immortality, development, supremacy, exploration. All of them?"

"Yes, I believe so."

"And could you tell me if you were satisfied by your life on Earth?"

"No. Most of the time, I was not happy. But I didn't really have any other choices except thinking and talking."

"Really?"

"Yes, I may have been able to delude myself, but not others."

"What do you mean, delude yourself?"

"Sometimes, if you are committed to only one thing, you need to find a justification for it. In my case, I felt compelled to tell myself constantly that people needed me to keep thinking and talking."

"But people really *did* need that. You weren't deluding yourself."

"But after my death, people continued to live their lives as before. So in reality, they didn't need me at all."

"Yes, but because you laid the foundations, people were able to continue to develop your thoughts."

"Thank you for your words of comfort."

"So if you could live your life again, what would you do with it?"

"I think I should like to be a farmer. To plant crops, vegetables, and fruit trees, to produce all the essential food for people."

"Why?"

"Those basic things can help people to understand themselves and others."

"Do you still want to understand yourself?"

"Of course! To know both yourself and nature is essential. If I could live again on Earth, I would write down my thoughts, but I wouldn't talk to other people. As for writing them down, I think I would give that task to my student Plato."

Son, I know very little about Socrates, but a friend of mine used to write his words in a notebook. Proverbs such as:

Don't win friends by giving gifts;
Fate is merely opportunity in shadow;
If all human disasters were shared equally among everyone, most
  people would gladly accept their original share;
Less expectation is closer to happiness;
Be quiet when you are angry, for fear of making things worse.

Socrates was a truly wise man in my eyes. His thoughts were inspirational and enlightening. He won so much respect from people. I cannot imagine that he was not happy with his life. I would really like to meet him in the future. You must remember his address so you can share it with me when I'm there.

Dad, the final interview with Xue Tiao was quite relaxing. She lived close to us in Green Willow Corner. Linlin and I flew there quickly. When we arrived, we read the words in her entrance: *Chanting House*. Linlin and I smiled at each other. It must be the right place.

We knocked on the door and could see through the window that she appeared to be writing. She put down her brush to open the door and frowned when she saw us. "Yes, can I help you" she asked brusquely. It appeared that she didn't welcome the disturbance.

"We are here to visit Miss Xue," replied Linlin with a smile.

"Please come back another time," she replied. "I don't have time for visitors now." She looked like she was about the close the door. Linlin was taken aback by her directness and stood open-mouthed, blushing.

"We're so sorry," I said quickly, before she closed the door on us. "We thought for a long time before coming to visit you. We do not wish to disturb you, but we will be living together soon. We understand that you were one of the most famous female poets from the Tang Dynasty, and we wanted to hang one of your poems in our living room."

Xue Tao's face softened slightly. "Well, you should really have made an appointment first."

"Yes. It was inconsiderate of us. Please accept our apologies. We should not have come unannounced." I bowed to her.

"Well, why don't you come in, then? I was in the middle of writing a poem, but your knocking interrupted me."

"We're very sorry." I took Linlin's hand to lead her in, but she was still reeling from the cold greeting we had received. She looked like she wanted to leave, but I pulled her in.

"You two really do look like a couple. Yours, I think, would be a happy marriage on Earth, and also a happy story here too." Her tone was much warmer after we went into her house.

"Thank you for your compliment. We decided to live together so as not to be alone," I replied.

Xue Tao wore the style of robe that was common in the Fields of Joy, but her hair was tied up in the Tang style. One of the books I had read said she liked to dress in the Taoist style and tied her hair up in her later years, when she built a house in Biji to live a tranquil life.

"Don't listen to him, Miss Xue," said Linlin. "I haven't decided to move in with him just yet."

"Well, don't take too long to think about it. He seems like a good man. If you lose this opportunity, how long might it be before you have other one? What if some other girl takes him away?"

"Another girl? Well, they are welcome to try!" Linlin replied, smiling at me.

"Don't say that! It's obvious you like him. But other girls may like him too. If you don't cherish this gift, you may lose him to another girl. I have seen it happen so many times."

The small talk lightened the atmosphere.

"So would you be able to write a poem for us?" I asked again.

"Yes. Since you want to put it in your house, I shall write one for you." She walked to the table and took out a brush and a piece of red paper.

The full bloom of flowers bursts out for the yearning of love.

The jade hangs in the mirror, waiting for the spring breeze.

"Those are words from one of my poems. I give them to you as a blessing."

We were pleased with the meaning of the poem, and her calligraphy was very striking, like the one written by Wang Xizhi. Linlin and I smiled at each other. "Thank you, so very much, Collator Xue."

"Don't call me that. I was never officially given that title. It was just some praise from Wei Gao. Please don't call me that."

"Yes, but I came to know that name from Wang Jian's poem:

"To Collator Xue in Sichuan.

Collator Xue lived by the bridge, in the Pipa flowers.

Many talented men visited, but couldn't match with the spring breeze.

"Then, after you came to Heaven, the Sichuan official Duan Wenchuan wrote the epitaph for you and gave you the title Collator."

"I don't care about that. Here in the Fields of Joy, just call me Miss Xue."

"Yes, Miss Xue. Of course. We appreciate your poem, and we shouldn't disturb you any longer. But as two fans of your poetry, could we please have a short conversation with you?"

"A conversation? How could we have anything in common to talk about? You must have come here very recently. We lived on Earth a thousand years apart."

"We have a common interest in poetry, which transcends time and place," replied Linlin.

"Well yes, of course. OK, let's talk about poetry. Who is your favourite poet?"

"I liked your poems. In *The Departure*, you depicted so vividly a dog who had been parted from his owner."

"Oh, you flatter me," she said, waving her hand dismissively.

"It's not flattery, I really like it!" I replied. "I also like Yuan Zhen's poems. Especially *The Summer Palace*:

In the faded old imperial palace,
Peonies are red, but no one comes to see them...
The ladies-in-waiting have grown white-haired
Debating the pomps of Emperor Xuanzong.

"A profound feeling was poured into the scene of the sorrowful ladies in the palace, which represented the poet's feelings of the fall of the Tang Dynasty."

Xue Tao gave a slight smile after hearing Yuan Zhen's name. She sighed. "His best poem is *Moon Night*:

I am waiting for the moon to rise, and leave the door open.
The shaking of flower's shadows makes me think you are coming.

"I like his *Departure*," said Linlin.

No water's enough when you have crossed the sea;
No cloud is beautiful but that which crowns the peak.
I pass by flowers that fail to attract poor me,
Half for your sake and half for Taoism I seek.

"I need to thank you both on behalf of Yuan Zhen. He would be most pleased if he knew you enjoyed his poems."

"Have you met him in the Fields of Joy?" I asked. "I heard about your touching love story."

She forced a weak smile. "What's the point? I heard he lives with his wife, Wei Cong. I hope they enjoy their days in Heaven."

"Miss Xue, you wrote so many beautiful poems that are still recited by people today. Can you tell us your reflections on life?"

"I don't see the point. I left the world more than a thousand years ago."

"We are just curious. Please could you share some insights?"

"Just try to live a normal life while you're alive."

"Does that mean you regret the life you lived?"

She nodded. "If I had another chance, I would certainly take a different road."

"What would you do?"

"I would marry an ordinary man and have many children. I would become a wife and be content with a mundane life. A happy and simple life. I wouldn't be a singer or a poet to serve officials. I could choose to write after a day's work, or not write at all. I wouldn't need to bear the bitterness of love or other people's attitudes. That life was so difficult..."

29

S on, I can't imagine that Xue Tao lived unhappily. She was so highly revered. I remember her poem:

> Apes shriek in the temple, the haze brimming with grass and wood
> fragrance.
> Green mountain is commemorating Song Yu; the water is crying King
> of Chu.
> Mornings and evenings under the balcony; the State of Chu fell in
> cloud and rain.
> Willows grow melancholy in the temple, waiting for the spring breeze.

She was truly a legend. I really looked up to her and believed that only through her way was life worth living. I had no idea that the truth was so different.

Dad, after the interview with Xue Tao, I told Linlin that I wanted to take a break from interviewing, so long as Darya didn't have any new messages for me. I'd been so busy running around, doing research and conducting interviews every day. It had all been quite exhausting.

Linlin smiled. "And how would you like to spend your break? Sleeping at home? Maybe a trip to Heaven Theatre, or perhaps we can take a tour somewhere?"

"Well, since Miss Xue gave us the poem, maybe we should make it official and move in together."

Linlin was silent for a while, before asking, "Are you serious? Do you just want someone for company, or do you really care about me?"

"You must know I have strong feelings for you."

"I need to remind you this is not the secular world. Although perhaps you think I look pretty, I don't have a real body to kiss or caress. All you can have is my soul. Are you sure you like my soul? I know the drive for a man to get a woman is primarily physical attraction and desire. Only later might he become interested in the woman's soul."

"There's no need to explain it to me, I replied. "You don't have a real body, and neither do I. So yes, I care very much for your soul." I smiled at her. Her wariness was endearing. In fact, though, living together was very common between couples in Heaven.

"It's important that you realise things are different when we're just souls. I don't want you to be disappointed if we move in together."

"Yes, I know that. I am certain I won't be disappointed."

"OK. Do you want to move in with me, or shall I move into your place?"

"It's up to you. You decide."

"Then you should move into my place. Then if you get bored with me, you can move back and the neighbours won't talk about it too much. But if I move in with you, then you get bored and kick me out, it would be awful. I would be so sad."

"It won't happen," I tried to reassure her. "But if it concerns you, I'm happy to move in with you."

"Would you like Darya to be our witness? Should we go to and tell her?"

"No, I'm worried she'll give me another list of interviewees. I won't be able to relax with something on my mind. I want to be completely relaxed when we move in together."

"OK. Then let's go and tell your great-grandparents first."

"Yes, let's move in together and then we'll invite them over."

"OK," Linlin agreed.

I moved a few things over to Linlin's house the next morning. Before I left, I put a note on the door, "Please visit me at Bo Linlin's house." Then I left. In the Fields of Joy, even if I moved in with Linlin, my house would be kept the same, so I could come back at any time.

Linlin's house and garden were much cleaner than mine. After I unpacked, I hung the poem Miss Xue Tao gave us in the living room. Then I put one red towel and on yellow towel on each side of the gate, a sign that two people are living together in Heaven.

Linlin and I embraced each other for a long time. I smelled the fragrance of her soul. For the first time since I'd been in Heaven, unbridled happiness surged through me.

While we were still locked in our embrace, the song of an erhu started outside. Surprised, and went outside to take a look. A slight man was playing the erhu near the door. Were there beggars here in Heaven?

"Uncle Liu!" said Linlin. "Please come in!"

"Who is he?" I asked Linlin.

"He's a neighbour who lives on the west side. Uncle Liu, he plays the erhu."

"I saw the two coloured towels in the yard," said Uncle Liu jovially. "So I realised we must have a new couple in Fragrance Corner. I thought I would come and play a tune on my erhu to celebrate."

I'd always loved the erhu, and could play a little myself. "What else can you play?"

"What would you like? *Leisure Life, Good Night, Walk into the Light, Birds in the Mountains*, or *Shadows of the Candle*? Take your pick from any of those."

"Are you serious? You can play all of Liu Tianhua's music!" I was amazed.

Linlin rolled her eyes at me. "Uncle Liu *is* Liu Tianhua," she said.

The penny dropped. "My goodness! You're really the famous musician Liu Tianhua?" I could hardly believe it!

"Do I not look like him?"

"Well, yes...of course." I was almost lost for words.

"Well, since you're a fan of the erhu, I will play a few songs for you. You can listen to see if it's the same music played by the musician Liu Tianhua." He started to play and the music flowed.

"Oh my goodness! This is the most beautiful version of *Good Night* I have ever heard! Linlin, why have you not introduced me to Maestro Liu before?"

"I only knew he played the erhu," said Linlin, smiling. "I didn't know he was famous! I never listened to music much."

Applause followed the music. I turned to see that a small crowd of neighbours had gathered outside, attracted by the music. Uncle Liu seemed very pleased to have an audience, and started to play *Birds in the Mountains*. I was entranced by the beautiful melody and closed my eyes. My head moved with the rhythm.

"*Bo Linlin*," a man suddenly shouted. The music stopped, and the joyous scene was shattered. "You cannot move in with Zhou!"

A young man shoved his way through the crowd and came towards Linlin. "I came to find you as soon as I arrived," he said. "Finally I have found you here in Fragrance Corner. You can't move in with someone else. We can't miss this opportunity to be together again."

Linlin was startled, clearly recognising the man. "Why are you here?"

"I was caught in a mudslide in Taiwan. But if I had arrived any later, we would have missed the chance to be together again." He took Linlin in his arms as he said this. Linlin sobbed. I was completely shocked. I didn't know who he was, and I was lost for words.

The neighbours quickly dispersed, and Liu Tianhua left with his erhu. What an embarrassing situation! I certainly hadn't anticipated anything like this.

"Zhou Ning, this is Wan Tianxing, my fiancé on Earth. And this is Zhou Ning, my partner in Heaven." Linlin pulled herself away from his arms.

"It's nice to meet you," I said, forcing a grin.

"I'm sorry, but I'm going to have to ask you to leave," said Wan Tianxing. "Linlin and I shall be living together now." He waved his hand at me, dismissively.

Linlin's face turned so red I thought she was going to explode. "How *dare* you?" she yelled at Wan Tianxing. "You think you have the right to send him away? He is my partner here. I can have nothing to do with you now. Do you understand?"

Wan Tianxing looked stunned at her outburst. He clearly hadn't expected this reaction. "So what should I do then?"

"You should wait for your *wife!*"

"How long should I wait? I didn't even like her that much. She became lazy after we got married. Except for her face and manicures, she didn't care about anything else. We fought all the time. She wasn't satisfied with me at all. Even if she comes here, I don't think I could live with her."

"So you came here for me instead? Do you know how much you hurt me back then? I had only been gone for half a year. You completely forgot about me and you even burned my pictures! Do you think I don't know this?"

"That was according to your own will!"

"My own will?"

"Before you left the world, you held my hand and told me to burn all your pictures and find another girl to marry. You told me to forget you. Do you not remember?"

"How could you have taken my words literally?"

"You didn't mean it? I was so devastated, but I respected your wishes. If I didn't do that, how could I have survived? Even after my marriage, I never stopped thinking about you..."

"Really? Oh my goodness..." Linlin started to cry again.

Silently, I gathered all my things together and moved back into my own house. Dad, it was torture, and I couldn't think of a way to deal with it. I didn't want Linlin to be upset again. It was clear they really loved each other on Earth, and now they had a chance to be with each other again. There was no longer any place for me. I wished them good luck...

Son, I can't really help you with this. Just follow your heart. In my experience, once a woman loves a man, her heart doesn't have any space for someone else. If she can accept someone else, it means she didn't love the first man enough. There are no financial or other material concerns in Heaven. If Linlin really loves you, she will come back to you.

Son, I don't want you to get hurt by this. You've been hurt so many times by other relationships. Just accept it.

Dad, I didn't sleep well that night and got up really late the next morning. Just as I opened my eyes, I saw Darya by the window.

I immediately put on clothes and went outside, "I'm sorry, I said. "You should have woken me."

She shook her head, "I wanted you to have a good sleep. I heard about Linlin's fiancé. I'm sorry."

"It's OK, I'm fine," I replied, forcing a smile, "Luckily we didn't ask you to witness the ceremony, or you would have felt embarrassed too."

"I want to make you feel better. When something bad happens, something better will be waiting just around the corner for you."

"Really, and what is waiting for me?"

"I don't know yet. But I'm going to give you this." She gave me another note with three more names on it:

1. *Li Nanxing – Pomegranate Corner, District 77777*
2. *Nora – Red Beauty Corner, District 667798*
3. *Wolfgang Amadeus Mozart – Persimmon Tree Corner, in District 338819*

"Are these interviewees?"

Darya nodded her head. I looked at the three names. I knew only of Mozart, but at least I had all their addresses. And I wouldn't need any help from Linlin.

Later, I went to do my research on them in the library.

Li Nanxing had been a farmer. He had lived to 103 years old. He was from Wudang Mountain in Hubei, and had been a scholar when he was young.

It wasn't difficult to find him, especially when I saw his white hair and beard. When he saw me, his face creased.

"I have been in the Fields of Joy for many years," he said. "You are the first one ever to visit me. Heaven is satisfactory for the most part. It's just a little short of neighbours to talk to. People in Pomegranate Corner mind their own business, not like the village I lived in on Earth where people liked to gather together and talk. Please, won't you sit down?"

"Perhaps you could look for your family members in the Fields of Joy and live with them," I suggested.

"There's no need," he replied. "I had some problems with them when I was alive. It's better if I live alone. If it gets too lonely, I can always make some straw rope."

"You could always look for someone from your hometown too."

The old man stroked his beard. "From your accent, I can tell that you're from my hometown."

"I'm from Zhengzhou in Henan," I confirmed. "Not even one hundred kilometres from your hometown."

"So why did you come here today? For my straw ropes? I don't wish to brag about my skill, but my rope is of the very best quality."

I smiled. "No, not for your straw rope. I just wanted to talk to you. I heard that you were a scholar on Earth. Why did you not become a government official later?"

"No. To become a scholar was just the first step of the exams. Some people kept working their way up. My family really wanted my two brothers and me to keep taking exams and become officials. My father was the owner of a shop which sold mountain products, and my family was doing well then, and could support the three of us."

"Did you keep taking the exams?"

"No. If I had followed my family's wishes, perhaps I could have become an official. Both my brothers continued their exams, and they were not as talented as me. Still, our teacher often praised me, not them."

"So what happened? Why didn't you?"

"I already had so many things at such a young age: a wealthy and loving family; a healthy body; a scholarly identity. I preferred to be content and give something in return. Rather than keep wanting more and more, I preferred to make myself busy. With all three of us studying for the exams, my family would have needed to work even harder to support us all."

"What did you do then?"

"I became a private teacher for another large family. I earned a good salary every month."

"Was your father happy?"

"No. My parents and grandparents all wanted me to keep studying so I could follow in my brothers' footsteps."

"What positions did your brothers hold?"

"My eldest brother was an official under the Wuchang county magistrate who administered lawsuits; my second brother was a cavalry officer."

"They must have taken care of you?"

"They didn't have the time. The revolution of 1911 broke out. My second brother died in the battle, and my eldest brother died later in the retreat."

"I'm sorry to hear that. Did you get married in your hometown?"

"My parents were opposed to my marriage also."

"Why?"

"At that time, there were three families that asked matchmakers to come to my door. One was Huang, the family of a wealthy businessman in Xiangyang City. The father had read some of my articles that had been published in the Xiangyang News. He thought I was talented so he sent someone to check me out. After discovering that I was still single, he sent someone to propose a marriage to his daughter.

"Another one was a large family, Guo, in the nearby town of Danjiang. The father of the family knew I could keep accounts, and he also wanted to give his daughter to me.

"The third one was the Shan family from our neighbouring village. Mr Shan was also a private teacher. His family background was quite ordinary, but he knew me very well and trusted me.

"The daughters of all three families looked good. My family believed that men struggled upward while water flowed downward. Accordingly, I should marry the Huang girl from Xiangyang City, or Guo's daughter from Danjiang. I shouldn't even consider Shan's daughter from the neighbouring village, they told me.

"The backgrounds of the Huang and Guo families were so much better than mine, I thought. If I married their daughter, I would need to be careful all the time, and they may look down on me. On the other hand, if I married Shan's daughter, I could be at ease. Because of this, I agreed to marry the Shan girl. And because of that, my parents had a big fight with me and didn't talk to me for a long time.

"What I believed then was that there was no reason that I should have so many advantages. I would surely pay the cost in the future. It turned out I was right. Huang's house was searched, and their property was confiscated for political reasons. Guo's daughter was kidnapped by bandits, and they spent their entire fortune to get her back. But even then she wasn't returned to them. She was tortured to death by the bandits."

"And did you have a happy marriage?"

"Yes. My wife was very virtuous, and she took care of the family. Our children were born one after another. She spent all her time devoted to them. Meanwhile I founded a small school with another teacher. We got by."

"You founded a school?"

"Yes. After I'd saved some money, many people, including my wife and my parents, told me to buy more land and build a house for the family. But I didn't need more land or a larger house. I sent my children to study in Wuhan. My partner in the school withdrew his money for a larger house later on and left to tend to his land. During the land reform, however, he was classified as a landlord and suffered. Meanwhile I donated the school to the government and they appointed me as headmaster, a middle-class peasant."

"For how long were you the headmaster?"

"For just over a year. The county government asked me to be the director of the bureau of education, which made my children so proud. But I was over sixty years old, and I didn't feel up to it. So I declined this honour and retired. Many people were competing for the position, and the county government didn't ask me to reconsider."

"I am wondering, why did you keep passing up these opportunities?" I asked.

"It wasn't passing them up. I just tried to remain sober and not be greedy, despite all the temptations. It's important to know when to stop. My whole life experience has boiled down to this philosophy: don't overindulge in too many good things, or trouble will inevitably follow."

"If you had become the director of the bureau of education, you would have been a senior civil servant."

"Well, I heard that the director of the bureau of education died in the Cultural Revolution."

"Really?"

"After I retired, I went back to my village. My children wanted us to move in with them in Wuhan for a better life. My wife had worked hard her whole life and it was time for her to enjoy life. But I didn't want to go with her. She scolded me for being too stubborn. I started to learn how to be a farmer in the village, to grow wheat, broad beans, peas, corn, and sweet potatoes."

"Did you find it hard? The farm work."

"I'd be lying if I told you it was easy. I needed to irrigate the fields in dry weather and drain the water in the rainy season. I worried about the wind and the hail stones. From sunrise to sunset, I needed to keep working whatever the weather. But it kept me physically healthy. I was strong, and not bothered with the problems like high blood pressure, blindness, or deafness. My brain was clear. My wife moved to the city with a better environment but less physical work. She died young of a heart attack. But the hard work in the fields helped me to live a longer life."

Son, Mr Li's attitude towards life reminds me of the common phrase in our hometown: 'Quit while you're ahead.' In other words, don't get greedy. I never really paid too much attention to it, but Mr Li's story showed me how true it is. In fact, it is very difficult for people to refuse good opportunities that are put in front of them. People prefer to compete instead of quitting. Only a few are able to act with restraint. Even I wasn't. Mr Li was indeed a wise man.

———

Dad, the next person I saw was Nora, who had been a cleaning lady in a German factory. She later ran an orphanage and adopted many children. She came to the Fields of Joy a few years ago, at the age of seventy-one. When I found her in Red Beauty Corner in District 667798, she was making model cars out of cardboard. She did this to pass the time, so she said. Once in a while, she would send the toys she made to children in No Worries Corner. She gave one to me, too. The model cars she made were so lifelike, even having windscreen wipers. I asked her which factory she worked for on Earth.

"Audi," she replied.

"I'm curious," I said. "Why is the logo for Audi four connected rings?"

"It was first used in 1932 when Audi was formed by the merger of four companies, Horch, Audiwerke, DKW and Wanderer. The four interlocking circles symbolised that merger."

"And where did you have cleaning duties at Audi?"

"The lobby on the first floor."

"Did you do this job voluntarily?"

"I was an orphan. My parents died in a gas explosion when I was eight years old. I wasn't at home then. I dropped out of school afterwards. Because of the explosion, my neighbours' property was damaged. I was the one who paid for it. My relatives refused to take me in, so I went into the orphanage. I lived there until I was eighteen years old. What I learned there couldn't help me find any other work except cleaning jobs. I met my husband, Gore, two years after I started working at the company."

"Your husband also worked for Audi?"

"Yes. He was responsible for installing car doors on the assembly line."

"How long did you know each other before getting married?"

"Just over a year. He was an excellent worker on the assembly line. He was so familiar with the processes, and so much better than most of his fellow workers. He could do the job with his eyes closed! Once, he went to the office area and fainted in the bathroom I was about to clean. I saw him and woke him up. That was how we met each other."

"You must have had a happy marriage."

"Yes, but only for a short time."

"What do you mean?"

"Not long after I became pregnant with our daughter, he fainted again on the assembly line and he hit his head on a car on the assembly line. His blood gushed, but when I reached him it was too late. He only managed to finish one sentence: 'Take care of our child...'"

"My goodness, how awful!"

"Once again, another of my loved ones had died. What should I do? I cried my eyes out, but I had to move on. I buried Gore with my company's help, and after that I took care of the baby in my belly. I knew Gore liked children, and I needed to take care of my baby. A few months later, I gave birth to a girl. I wanted to raise her in the way that Gore and I had planned. But when she was three years old, she began to faint like her father had before her. I took her to doctors everywhere, and finally learned it was an incurable genetic condition that ran in Gore's family. It even caused the patient's brain to stop developing. That's what happened to my daughter. Her intelligence gradually became stunted and she remained as a young child."

"Life was so cruel to you."

"It struck me so hard, but I couldn't leave her alone. She was a baby, and I needed to make sure she was taken care of. I couldn't continue my old cleaning job because she required so much care. Without a salary, I couldn't even afford to eat, and then I came up with the idea of earning a living by providing care for other mentally disabled children. After I posted an advertisement, two other families came to me to send their mentally disabled children and paid me to look after them. Finally, I had found a way to support my family."

"I'm so happy for you."

"The news soon spread and many families sent their disabled children to be looked after, and before long my house was full. The news reported my deeds, and the government and two wealthy investors gave me the funds to build a new dedicated building for foster services. In this way, my Beautiful Children School officially opened.

"By the time I left Earth, more than one hundred and twenty mentally disabled children had attended the centre. Oh, but forgive me.

I was so focused on my story that I forgot to ask why you came here today. Is there anything I can help you with?"

"No, thank you. I just came here for your stories and insights."

"There is little to learn from the stories of my time on Earth. I just lurched from one disaster to another. I hope no one ever has to live a life like mine."

"I disagree. When disaster struck, you faced it head on, instead of giving up. This is something to be proud of."

"Thank you for your comforting words. I knew there was no use in feeling sorry for myself. People may sympathise with you at first, but constant complaining will just make others lose respect for you. Instead, I should stand up, be brave and say, 'Come on, then, give me everything you've got! Let me see what you can throw at me!' By confronting fate, I think it's possible to ward off bad luck."

Dad, I used to think that my life was full of misery and regret, that my life was so bad. But when I met Nora, I realised that the Creator actually took some pity on me. The world is full of so much pain. He may even have protected me on occasion. If there had been any more pain in my life, I wouldn't have been able to bear it...

Son, I also sympathise with Nora's experience. I didn't know there were other people that bore greater hardships than us. I wonder if God have could have given some compensation to Nora after so much suffering and pain. Could she live again? So many things can start over again. Why not life?

I believe the Creator didn't think very carefully when He designed the rules of the universe. There is only a single, irreversible and unrepeatable opportunity, which too often is filled with many regrets. If only we could amend the rules to allow Nora a second chance; then, perhaps, I might feel that life is fair.

Dad, the next person I interviewed was Mozart. You and Mum liked Chinese folk music, so I never had much interest in Western music. I knew that Mozart was a musician, but that was about it. I didn't know anything about his music or his life.

In Heaven Library, I learned that he was born in 1756 in Salzburg, Austria. His father, Leopold, was a violinist and a composer in the archbishop's orchestra. His mother loved music too, and played cello and violin.

Mozart was the seventh child in his family. At the age of three, he had shown his natural gift for music by playing musical compositions on the piano. When he was four, his father returned home one day with a friend, and saw him writing musical composition on a sheet of paper. His father asked what he was doing. He replied in a serious manner that he was composing. His father laughed with his friend. They thought it was just child's nonsense scribbled on the paper, but when his father looked closely at the notes, he suddenly burst into tears. "My dear friend, come and see how beautiful this is!"

At five years old, Mozart could identify the notes and even chords by ear accurately no matter what instrument they were played on, and could easily tell the pitches of cups, bells, and other objects when they were struck. He had perfect pitch, something rarely achieved even by professional musicians over a whole lifetime. He was truly a musical prodigy.

From the age of six, he began to perform with his ten-year-old sister on a tour of Europe. Throughout his life, he created a total of more than five hundred pieces of music, including twenty-two operas, forty-one symphonies, forty-two concertos, and sixty sonatas, as well as chamber music, religious music, and other serenades and waltzes. He made extraordinary contributions to the development of European music.

When I found him in the Persimmon Tree Corner in District 338819, he was playing the piano. I pushed the door open and listened for a while. I couldn't tell what music he was playing, but I could feel the purity in the music, which reminded me of when I played with my friends on the grasslands as children. I was touched and became lost in the music until he finished and came to ask who I was, which woke me from my daydream. I bowed to him.

"I heard your music and couldn't help but come in. You play so beautifully!"

He smiled. "Thank you for your compliment. You are very clever, to find a way to listen to free music. Perhaps I should charge you an entrance fee!"

"Of course. How much?" I laughed at his humour.

"Ten thousand."

"But there is no money here. What should I do?"

"You'd better go and talk to God!"

We both laughed.

I had read during my research that Mozart was a typical artist. He loved life, was poetic, and had rich feelings. He was simple and cheerful, sensitive, emotional, and had a feminine tenderness. He had child-like curiosity. He was so open and funny. His gregarious demeanour and youthful face made me feel closer to him. My fear disappeared.

"I would be delighted for more Chinese people to like my music," he said. "When I was alive, I told my wife that I wanted to do a tour in China. But other commitments and the huge expense made that impossible, not to mention the fact that fate didn't allow me much time on Earth. I didn't expect that a Chinese soul would come to hear my music today. I am very happy to see you!"

"Thank you. You are such a warm person. I thought you might put on airs since you are so famous. I met some Chinese musicians on Earth who were very distant and unapproachable."

"I want to know, what do you think of my music?"

"You shouldn't have come to Heaven so early. You should have stayed in the world longer, where so many tragedies happen every day. Your music could comfort people and make life easier for them."

"Wasn't that my wish? But for some reason, our family was pursued by death. My parents had seven children. Only my fifth sister and I survived. The others all died young. I always sensed that I wouldn't have a long time, and so it was: I only lived for thirty-five years."

"Did you feel the looming threat of death?"

"Yes, after I had a conflict with the Archbishop of Salzburg, I felt that death was stalking me."

"When was that?"

"1772, when I finished my tour and returned to Salzburg, where I had served as the leader of the archbishop's orchestra. Although I received great honours on the tour, the archbishop regarded me as his slave and scolded me all the time. Every time he did so, I felt humiliated and pained. I didn't sleep well and hardly ate. I began to feel that my health was declining. A black shadow occasionally flashed past me."

"Really?"

"In June 1781, when the archbishop insulted me again, I could bear it no more, and I resigned out of pride, freeing myself completely from the court. Later I settled in Vienna and began to make a living from my own compositions, performances and teaching. I didn't earn much, but at least I could compose as I liked. On one hand, I studied the works of famous musicians; on the other, I spent a lot of time composing. I kept irregular hours, and I often felt sick. Moreover, I saw the dark shadow more often."

"You should have been careful, and stopped composing day in and day out."

"That would have meant I had even less income! Meanwhile, I needed to capture all the music inside my head. After I got married, I had little income, and my wife wasn't good with money. Life was very difficult for us. Sometimes we couldn't even afford to eat properly. One winter, it was extremely cold, and we couldn't afford proper clothes or even to keep a fire. I couldn't even lift my hand to write. My wife and I danced to stay warm. Symptoms of my sickness began to appear. I was powerless, and I kept seeing the dark shadow. I knew that death was close."

"Were you scared?"

"What would have been the point? Who can escape the fate the death? No matter how long one lives, the body will eventually rot. Death shows no mercy to anyone, no matter how afraid they are. I faced it calmly. I just needed to finish my calling, which was the completion of the music I was working on."

"Probably this is why there is no sadness in your music."

"Possibly. In the face of death, there is no use in running away, in begging, in trembling or crying. One should face it with a smile."

"And what was the name of that final piece of music?"

"*Requiem.*"

"I know of it. I've heard it before."

"It was a mass for a funeral. I remember it was a gloomy afternoon, and a man in black came to my house and asked me to write a requiem for him. I was stunned, but nodded in agreement. After the man had left, my wife said, 'But you're so sick now. You need to rest. Why did you agree?' I told her that I would write it both for him and for myself. The only thing I worried about was that my death would leave it incomplete."

"Yes, I believe it was only half-finished at the time of your death."

"Yes. Luckily my student completed it."

"When I listen to *Requiem*, there is no pain. Joy runs through your music."

"Death isn't the end of a human's journey. The soul will ascend into Heaven and start another life. Of course it should be joyful. When death greets us, we should welcome it as any other guest."

"Mr Mozart, you are only a few years older than me, but your mind is much broader than mine. I remember the first few lines from your *Requiem:*

Grant them eternal rest, O Lord, and may perpetual light shine on
    them.
Thou, O God, art praised in Sion,
and unto Thee shall the vow be performed in Jerusalem.
Hear my prayer, unto Thee shall all flesh come.
Grant them eternal rest, O Lord, and may perpetual light shine on
    them.

"Yes, well, we're here now, aren't we?"

"The *Requiem* reminds me of the chanting of an old lady I once knew:

Put down what you had,
Take back what you expect,
Forget your loss,
Toss away your sadness.
Remember your beloved family,
Appreciate your kind neighbours,

Bow to your friends,
Kowtow to your land.
Rest in peace, let go of attachment,
Rest in peace, let go of unfulfilled desires,
Rest in peace, let go of resentment,
Rest in peace, let go of worry.

30

S on, I am amazed by Mozart's perception of death. He really understood life and death. I heard *Requiem* once in the Tel Aviv Concert Hall, and it set me at peace. My mind was as calm and open as the starry sky at night. Captivated by the music, my soul was overcome with joy. That was the incantation of the spirit. I had no idea that Mozart wrote this music while impoverished, and literally on his death bed. It's extraordinary that he wrote it in such circumstances. When I come to the Fields of Joy, you must introduce me to him. I would very much like to pay my respects to him in person.

Son, I don't know how long all these interviews will take. But I hope you're not overworking yourself or giving yourself too punishing a schedule. I also want you to insulate yourself from all the sad stories and tragic experiences you hear during the interviews. Don't let them disturb your own life in the Fields of Joy...

Dad, don't worry, I know how to protect myself from all the sad stories in Heaven. Shortly after my interview with Mozart, Darya came to see me. I thought it was for another interview assignment, but it wasn't.

"Please get ready," she told me. "I will take you to the Holy Field tomorrow. God wishes to meet you."

I was stunned. "My goodness. Really?"

"No one tells lies here in the Fields of Joy," she replied.

"Why does He want to meet me?"

Darya shrugged her shoulders. "I don't know. Perhaps He has some more interview assignments for you, or maybe some other tasks."

"Does He often summon souls to the Holy Field?"

"He picks eleven people at random from the Fields of Joy as His guests every week."

"How do you mean, 'at random'?"

"He picks one soul from each district, regardless of gender, age or from which era on Earth."

"And why does He want to see souls from the Fields of Joy?"

"Mostly for suggestions about the management of life in Heaven. In most cases, He will just talk while roaming in the garden. Sometimes it's one-on-one."

"Will I be able to ask questions? Will He answer me?"

"Yes, of course."

"So, there will be ten other souls there besides me?"

"I don't know for sure. My job is just to escort you there."

"What do I need to prepare?"

"Review your recent interview cases, just in case He asks you about them."

"Yes, of course. Is there anything else I should know beforehand? Does He have a temper?"

"He is a kindly old man. You needn't worry."

"Are there any rules in the Holy Field?"

"They're the same as in the Fields of Joy, but it's more tranquil. You can only access the places you are allowed to."

"Why?"

"There are many secrets about Earth in the palaces there, like the Palace of Time."

"The Palace of Time?"

"Time is a form of life. The Palace of Time is about life. The books there mark the ending time of each person's life, and how their end will come to pass."

"Ah, but I know that many scientists are dedicated to researching how to prolong people's lives. The discovery of rapamycin was able to prolong a rat's lifespan by up to fourteen per cent. This research will be applied to people soon. How will the books in the Palace of Time remain accurate then?"

"Don't ask those questions. No one can answer you. Just stay away from those places."

"How long does it take to fly to the Holy Field from here?"

"Two to three hours. I'll pick you up after breakfast."

"Can I bring another soul with me?" I was thinking of Linlin. She would be so thrilled if I told her about this. But would her fiancé agree?

"No, all words from God are to be shared only with the invited souls."

The following morning, I woke up early and got myself ready. Shortly after breakfast, Darya came to my house.

We left together and flew to the Holy Field to meet God. *What will He look like?* I wondered. *Will He like me? What kind of place is the Holy Field? What will He talk to me about? What will my experiences there be like?*

Darya pointed ahead. "Do you see the golden light over there? That's the light from the Holy Field."

"Yes, it's so dazzling."

"We should enter the Holy Field from the South Gate before it disappears."

God, I am about to meet you. I have only one question for you, and I hope you can give me the answer: when will I be together with my parents again in Heaven?

NOTES

Preface

1. The annual National Day holiday takes place on 1 October every year. It commemorates the founding of the People's Republic of China on 1 October 1949, and marks the start of the Golden Week holiday across China.

Chapter 4

1. In Confucian, Chinese Buddhist and Taoist ethics, filial piety is the virtue of respect for one's parents, elders and ancestors. It includes taking care of one's parents; showing love, deference, courtesy and support; displaying sorrow for their sickness and death, and burying them and carrying out sacrifices after their death.
2. College Entrance Examination.

Chapter 5

1. The People's Liberation Army, the combined armed forces of the People's Republic of China.
2. Severe Acute Respiratory Syndrome, a viral respiratory disease caused by the SARS coronavirus. More than 8,000 cases were recorded during the SARS outbreak between late 2002 and mid-2003, resulting in 774 deaths in 37 countries. The majority of cases occurred in China and Hong Kong.

Chapter 13

1. Qigong is a holistic system of coordinated body posture and movement, breathing, and meditation used for the purposes of health, spirituality, and martial arts training. With roots in Chinese medicine, philosophy and martial arts, Qigong is traditionally viewed as a practice to cultivate and balance *qi*, or life energy.

Chapter 18

1. In Chinese and other Asian societies, a red envelope or red packet is a monetary gift given during holidays or special occasions such as weddings or the birth of a baby.

ABOUT THE AUTHOR

Born in Dengzhou, north-central China in 1952, Zhou Daxin is a novelist, short-story writer and essayist whose realist fiction mostly focuses on ordinary people in his home province of Henan. He made his literary debut in 1979 and has published nine novels, thirty-three novellas and more than seventy short stories, as well as numerous essays and plays. In 2016, People's Literature Publishing House published *Selected Works by Zhou Daxin*, a twenty-volume collection of novels, novellas, short stories, essays and a screenplay. Zhou has received numerous awards, including the National Outstanding Short Story Award, the Feng Mu Literature Prize, the People's Literature Award, the Mao Dun Literature Prize, and the Lao She Prose Essay Award. His works have been translated into a dozen languages including English, French, German, Japanese, Arabic, Spanish and Greek. He currently lives in Beijing.

ALSO BY ZHOU DAXIN

WHAT'S LEFT AFTER A LIFETIME OF SERVICE

IN THE CHINESE GOVERNMENT?

At the age of 66, Ouyang Wantong, the former governor of Qinghe province, was too young to die. He touched the lives of so many people during his time on Earth. Some of them loved him intimately, while many more held him in the highest esteem. But there were also those who hated him and wished him dead. And now the battle to find his rightful place in the history books has begun...

After the Finale is a fictional biography of an extraordinary man who grew up in poverty in China's Mao era and then rose through the ranks of government during the country's period of reform and opening up. It's a tale of love, leadership, betrayal, corruption, lust, greed and the nature of power amid the rise of the 21st century's new superpower.

AVAILABLE WHERE ALL GOOD BOOKS ARE SOLD